THE FIVE WARRIORS

THE FOUR WORLDS SERIES BOOK 1

ANGELA J. FORD

www.thefourworldsseries.com

ISBN: 1512163619

ISBN-13: 978-1512163612

ALSO BY ANGELA J. FORD

The Five Warriors
The Blended Ones
Eliesmore and the Green Stone
Eliesmore and the Jeweled Sword

Tales of the Four Worlds

Myran

Join the email list for new releases and more. Go to
TheFourWorldsSeries.com

DEDICATION

To my four hilarious sisters, Dorthea, Annie, Rebecca and Katrina, for being persistent enough to have an entire fantasy world created just for them.

CONTENTS

PROLOGUE

"Are there beings with the ability to shift forms?" he asked.

She reached out a hand to caress his serious face and laughed lightly. "Why would you ask me that?"

"Tell me, would I know if I saw one?"

"You are serious." She stood, letting the moonlight filter through the waves of her waist-length hair. "Changers are old beings from the beginning of time, the last scraps of the creator's spark which formed this World. You would be unlikely to meet one, for they are above us; too distinguished to flirt with the people groups, and too haughty to lower themselves to live with the immortals." Her long fingers rested on the balcony, gripping it tightly as she continued. "If you ever met one it would be unexplainable. They have two forms which makes them indestructible. One is physical and another is spirit."

"Would you know if you met a Changer?" he pressed. "Are they dangerous?"

She laughed again, her voice rippling gently through the air like the tinkling of silver bells on a crisp night. "Dangerous? There are no creatures in the World more powerful or dangerous."

"What if I met a Changer? What should I do?"

She turned back to him, bending to take his face in her hands. Her intense gaze met his questioning eyes. "Run as fast as you can, and never stop."

CHAPTER 1

THE ESCAPE

A shadow moved in the unceasing midnight blackness. Marklus tensed, then shifted on the grimy stone floor of his ghastly prison cell. Shivering from the bone wearing chill, he rubbed his hands over his thin shoulders and again recalled the hastily inked words that had started it all. The plan had never been to arrive at the northern side of the sea, lost and naïve, stumbling straight into a trap cleverly laid out for him. When the armed guards ambushed him in the decaying, hazy forest of Slutan and dragged him, lively and struggling, to prison, he'd known interrogation and torture were next. Stripped of his weapons and thrown into the blinding darkness of a deep cell, his screams and cries were left woefully unanswered. It seemed there was no reason for his imprisonment, waiting for fear and hunger to drive him mad. If they ever came for him, and even that seemed a bleak wish, he would be broken, ready to give in to their demands. Anything was better than the endless monotony of drifting time while the lack of light and warmth and the stench of death threatened to strip his sanity from him piece by lowly piece.

Marklus, a displaced warrior from the countries of Mizine in the south, had been invited to join a reckless band of rebels building a secret army. Motivated by the passion of his fearless leader—who also happened to be his best friend—Marklus made it his task to travel north for covert information on the enemy's plans. Unfortunately, his mission had gone awry, but the worst part of being trapped in prison was the knowledge that no one would come to his rescue. Since the band of rebels was not under official authorization by the various Rulers of the land, the repercussions for joining or further assisting the secret army were steep. The Western World was full of strife. The powers on both sides of the Dejewla Sea that separated the north and south were locked in a fierce struggle to rule the fate of the inhabitants of the Western World. The rebels of Mizine had grown suspicious when peculiar warriors began raiding their lands. Shouldering responsibility for the fate of the Western World, they took it upon themselves to discover what plans the north had for the south, and how to put an end to their reign of terror.

Now the year-old words from the parchment were naught but faded memory. Marklus remembered the nervous excitement of having a secret mission with his childhood friend. Their paths had gone separate ways after the disaster that struck Zikeland, Marklus' homeland. But it was the quest that brought them back together, reminding them how much stronger they were as a team.

Marklus sighed in frustration as he recalled the plans they'd made to sneak north into Slutan and travel to the enemy's base, an abyss called the Great Water Hole. In the far northwest corner, in a place long thought to have been abandoned, the still waters were rumored to move again. Legend told of the beauty of the Great Water Hole, a mysterious canyon with trails and springs leading to the source of its secrets if one were persistent enough. It was alleged that eventually the trail of water flowed into Oceantic on a current that led directly to the South World. Although those theories were as yet untested, there was something ominous about the enemy setting up base in the forsaken canyon.

The blackness of the merciless prison shifted as Marklus restlessly moved to the other side of his six-foot-long cell. Most days, if there were days anymore, a heavy-footed guard, annoyed with his mundane task, would deliver the daily rations, rudely slung under the bars. The door had not been opened since that day he had been thrown in, and as the hours shifted, his meal was delivered and he was forgotten again. If only he had listened to Crinte, who'd assured him he already had a scout willing to cross the sea. But the information Marklus sought was too valuable to leave to just anyone. He recalled that day vividly.

***

Crinte was absolutely sure of himself. He marched around the room, gesturing passionately and arguing forcefully with Ackhor. Marklus, sitting across the table from Ackhor, couldn't help but smirk privately to himself each time the

5

two fought. Crinte and Marklus has been long-time childhood friends, but when it came time to choose who would lead the camp of rebel warriors, Crinte had chosen Ackhor, a friend he had met when traveling the Western World with his father. It was true that Ackhor had much more strategic fighting experience. He had led expeditions to hunt mystical creatures in the Algrema Forests, coordinated peace treaties between the smaller countries of Mizine, and led troops to calm civil uprisings. However, Crinte and Marklus actually had a better mindset for working together.

"I'm telling you," Crinte announced incessantly, "there is more going on here than meets the eye. These raids, they are almost like distractions to keep our armies busy, keep them from seeing the truth."

"How many times do I have to tell you," interrupted Ackhor, as if he were trying to appease a child. "They are sending scouts over to test our strength. It's standard military strategy."

"That's what I'm saying!" Crinte insisted. "They come, they raid, they leave. There is no burning and pillaging. They aren't trying to destroy our resources, they are trying to keep us blind! There is more going on than meets the eye, Ackhor."

"Crinte." Ackhor's voice grew stern. "You have no proof, and I cannot authorize you to take a group of spies across the sea to discover what mysteries our enemy is hiding. That is suicide, and you only have a thought. What if you're wrong? We need our best warriors here, on the front lines, defending our lands."

***

6

Best warriors—Ackhor had chosen his words well. What he actually referred to were the fighting elite, not only warriors who were exceptionally skilled in fighting, but also controlled an element of power. As far as Marklus knew, there were only two—and he was one of them. That knowledge made his cage seem all the smaller, and his folly lay heavy on his mind.

A footfall hesitantly landed on the prison floor and Marklus' ears pricked up, his thin body rigid as the footsteps grew nearer. This was no ordinary prison guard. Normally, their footfalls were heavy and loud, laden down with the emasculating tasking of feeding the prisoners. These footsteps were barely perceptible and paused every few seconds. Marklus stood in his cell, forcing his eyes to look into the dim light, his heart thumping as he waited with bated breath. It was mere minutes before a shadow drifted close. Marklus could barely perceive two hands gripping the bars that separated them.

"Are you alive?" the shadow whispered.

Thrown by the unexpected question, Marklus attempted to gather saliva in his parched mouth to respond, but the shadow did not wait. "We are leaving. Wait for my signal."

"Who are you? What signal?" Marklus managed to croak out. But it was too late; the shadow was gone, as if it had never been there.

Lowering himself to the disgusting prison floor, Marklus began to wonder if he was losing his mind. Closing his eyes for a brief moment, he let his sensory input take over. He pricked his ears, listening hard, but the footfalls had vanished. Escape seemed a cruel joke, but he had to break free of his jail cell. Ever

7

since being captured a few months ago, his mind had been silently panicking because he was no closer to knowing the truth of what was happening on the northern side of the sea. To take his mind off the situation, he let his thoughts drift back into the past and what had led him to make such a daring trip.

***

"Maybe our best warriors shouldn't be hiding in the fighting camp training others," Crinte had retorted that day. *"Maybe our best warriors should be on the other side of the sea, finding out what really is happening. It is naive on our part to turn a blind eye to the truth. It's not mere battles that win a war. As warriors, we not only need skill with a blade, we have to outthink and outsmart our enemy. Playing it safe on this side of the sea does not cut it. If they can send troops over here to scout out our weaknesses, we can do the same. I'd rather invade their land than wait for them to bring ruin to this side of the sea. Turn a blind eye if you wish—I will not stand for it!"*

By the time Crinte finished speaking, his face was red and mere inches away from Ackhor's.

Ackhor stood firm, his arms crossed, glaring at Crinte as if daring him to speak further. "Do you think I don't know this?" he growled. "Wars are won by skill and cunning, and if you dare waltz across the sea into their hands, you will take all that with you. You asked me to come here to talk strategy, you asked me to help you plan to win a war, not just one battle. Is that what you still want?"

"We have to move faster than this!" Crinte exclaimed. "We have been at this for months, and where has it gotten us?"

"Recruits," Ackhor quipped. "We have recruits. We are training warriors, and the more the better—and don't you forget it."

Crinte turned around and shook his head. "Fine," he exhaled, as if giving up. "We will finish this another time. I am going to the training grounds." He looked to Marklus questioningly.

Later that afternoon at the shooting range, Marklus brought up the argument again. "What are you going to do? Ackhor is not going to change his mind."

"I know." Crinte pulled a white arrow tight in his bow and paused for a beat. As he released, the arrow zinged through the air but missed its mark. "We can't wait for him to take his time to decide; we have to find out what is going on across the sea now. I have a scout I can send, but one will not be enough. We need information. Over here we are sitting blind! This hiding and waiting will be the death of us."

Crinte lifted his bow once again. This time his arrow hit the mark, dead on.

That night, Marklus packed a bag of supplies. Before dawn, his trail through the Sea Forests of Mizine had grown cold.

***

Sometime later, a faint thud jerked Marklus from his insubstantial slumber. He opened his eyes, blinking rapidly to accustom them to the unsettling shades of blackness, but the shield of night hovered like a velvety blanket over the prison. Lifting his heavy head from the pillow of his crooked arm, he pricked his ears. This time, the sound drifted clearly, a combination of muffled footsteps and iron. Reaching for the rusted bars

9

of his cell, Marklus pulled himself to his feet as a clang echoed off the metalwork of the prison. His heart began to race in anticipation, thumping loudly in his chest as he strained to see something, anything, in that midnight hour. But just as quickly, the sounds of the night died away into an irksome silence. Marklus remained frozen, holding on to threads of delusional hope. There was a time when the darkness of the prison had stolen his optimism, and he'd dared not dream beyond his cell. It was true, he longed for freedom without fear of starvation in darkness and the chance to vindicate his homeland. Now, he held to the whispered words of the shadow, the desire for escape pounding so thickly through his veins he thought he would choke.

A sharp grating sliced through the silence, interrupting his thoughts, the scraping stinging his sensitive ears. Marklus loosened his hold on the bars of his cell as he felt them moving, lifting up and away, no longer holding him captive. Excitement turned to pain as he made a step towards freedom, only to find himself crouching in his cell, his tender ears crippled by the high-pitched screeching of the bars. The prison continued to groan and finally to shake with the weight of what was being asked of it, its wails droning on, mixed with the cries of what could be other prisoners, or even guards.

Finally, it stopped. The only reality now was the pain in Marklus' ears and a silence so loud he could hear it humming in the distance. He stood on shaky legs and reached for the bars, which were no longer there. A brief thrill shot through his body as he stepped out of his cell for the first time since being deposited there.

***

The shadow rose out of the darkness. Her scheme was now in motion, and it was up to the prisoners themselves to finish it. She had been strategizing a mass exodus for weeks, studying the guards, their habits, and ways in and out of the prison. She'd watched as they captured those astray in the woods and locked them up, one by one, until their wills were lost and strength forgotten. Free as she was, the prison was still a fortress, the routes unknown to her, the ins and outs patrolled much too carefully by too many sentinels. Escape had always been the plan; causing a riot was only a diversion.

She'd had to act sooner than intended. Unfortunate orders had arrived, and she knew it was time to flee before the web of delusion had been cast. Some of the prisoners were already too far gone to notice, no more than bags of bones in their cells, but many would run and die rather than lie down and give in. It was those hardy souls she was counting on.

Lifting her palms, she blew across the item held there. A wavering fog appeared for a moment before streaking off through the dark halls, lighting a path before her. The shadow ran through the path of light, calling.

***

Marklus paused in the hall, unsure of which way to turn. The blackness stretched unending before him, and at first there were no clues pointing him back to the land of the living. He pricked up his ears again to listen for the telltale signs he'd heard earlier. Sure enough, a stirring weaved through the air, but as he cocked his head to listen, he realized it wasn't the sound of footsteps or moaning prisoners. Someone was calling him.

A dim light began to illuminate the floor, streaking past him and guiding the way out. Marklus stared at it, unsure whether he was dreaming or not. Behind that light a stampede of escapees streamed towards him, seeking the light, dashing towards the dream before it ended. The leader was no more than a blur of shadow, gliding past him in order to catch the light. Those behind the leader were exhausted jail breakers, the stench of death surrounding them. Pale skin hung off thin bodies; bony feet slapped the hard stones, causing an eerie echo throughout the prison. Most of them wore dirty rags, the remnants of what used to be proper clothing. Their eyes were bloodshot from looking through darkness, and desperation was written all over their gaunt faces. These were the ones willing to escape, a force of prisoners sweeping through like a river, with the absolute but simplistic goal of overwhelming the guards by sheer numbers and reclaiming life itself. Marklus turned towards the light, joined their company, and ran.

The stream of light vanished as the courtyard drew near, but Marklus could see white moonlight shining in, a sight that hurt his eyes, causing them to tear up as he ran towards the opening. The sound of running almost drowned out the whistle of arrows, and just as the escapees reached fresh, unfiltered air, they were met with a volley of black tipped and feathered shafts. The front row went down immediately, and the beauty of the moon-light turned taunting and harsh as the air filled with the shrieks of those pierced, and the last death screams of those who would not rise again. Marklus threw himself to the ground and rolled towards the inside wall, hampered by the tangle of arms and legs above him. Desperation shifted to panic. Half of the prison-ers moved forward. The other half moved backwards, still clinging to precious life.

Knowing he would be trampled to death if he did not make a move, Marklus frantically looked around for cover or an alter-nate escape route. To come this far only to be killed or captured again would crush all hope. He could not go back to waiting in his cell for the end of days. He rolled to the side out of the crush and struggled upwards, only to bump into the shadow. For a moment, there was enough light for him to stare into her face in bewilderment. A vague feeling of déjà vu flitted across his mind. "I know you…" he started to say, although he could not place the memory.

"Shh," she snapped, quickly cutting him off.

She crouched there, blending into the darkness, yet Marklus thought he saw her cup her hands together. Her mouth moved down towards her fingers, and even though the shadows played tricks with his mind, he saw a flash of light. The ground he stood on was no longer firm; the stability of the prison began to dissolve. Now, the cries of pain were mixed with frightened shouts from the guards. Marklus moved forward as if in a dream, fighting to keep his balance as the gates around the courtyard began to fall.

The prisoners surged forward, hope renewed, escape a surety. Marklus among them fled through the moonlight into the surrounding forest as the stench of death faded. As he ran, he could still hear the whistles of arrows slamming into tree trunks, occasionally taking out a nearby fugitive. Only two things stood out in his mind: firstly, he had to find the shadow again, whoever she was, and secondly, he must answer his summons.

CHAPTER 2

A TRAIL OF LIGHT

Stamen was lost. And it was his own fault. He had wandered too far off the farmland in search of an apple tree, lost his sense of direction, and in a panic tried to return home. What troubled him was that he knew better. His people group, the Trazames, maintained an unspoken law; one always stayed at home and did not interfere with the world at large. There were those who protected it, and there were those who stayed at home and minded their own business. Particularly in the fragile state the Western World was in, it was imperative to only leave home long enough to tend to the fields and animals. Stamen sighed; he did not know what had gotten into him. It was highly unusual for him to wander this far, and normally his nose led him home. He had an uncanny gift—his sense of smell was useful in tracking anything down. Oftentimes, it led him straight and true, even though his people tended to make fun of him for his extraordinary talent. This time, he was growing confused. There had been an odd flash of light back there in the pasture, and while he could taste the sensation of dirt in his mouth, he knew he was not yet close enough to find his way home.

He balked when he heard the gentle lapping of waves nearby. It was a large body of water, stretching unendingly east and west, which meant it had to be the Dejewla Sea. Stamen's heart sank as he listened. Now, he would never get back home. Crossing the sea was not something one did. As a matter of fact, none of his kind had ever gone to even see the sea, since it took three to five days to travel to its banks. Nervously, he walked out from behind the tall trees, and the sparkling body of water appeared. Baby waves surged across the surface, gently playing with each other before slamming up against the muddy shoreline. He knew he should walk away, but something intriguing held him there. Lifting his face to the warm sunlight, he wondered how many days he had walked along the edge of the forest. What had pulled him in deeper? He sniffed the air. The scent of home had faded as if it were no longer an option. Replacing it was a bitter, menacing taste. There was something going on he did not want to be a part of.

Stamen spooked when he saw two people climb out of the sea. He moved back to hide behind a tree, peeking out to stare at the people. One was a male from the people group called Crons. Crons were the adventurous folk, overly curious, fond of the unknown and always ready to take action. They often found themselves in all sorts of trouble because of their inability to stay put and keep their nose out of others' doings. However, the Cron walking out of the sea looked defeated. His skin was a sickly pale, his curly, light brown hair long and unkempt while his body was gaunt and haggard. Stamen wanted to vomit. He'd only heard vague stories of those from the other side of the sea, and this could not have a happy ending for him.

The male's companion was of a people group Stamen could not quite place. Her eyes were intense, yet she was one of the most beautiful females Stamen had ever seen. Her skin was a nutmeg brown and her jet-black hair hung, dripping wet, to her muscular shoulders. She also looked unnaturally skinny, and there was a dark hollowness in both hers and the Cron's eyes. The male immediately lay down by the sea, his chest quickly rising and falling as he gasped for air. The female stood, surveying the area with suspicious eyes. She turned to her companion and said something. He nodded and stumbled to his feet, almost falling into a bush as he steadied himself.

Stamen wondered if they had been turned. Only transformed creatures came from the other side of the sea. He smelt the air once more, hoping for clarity of direction. Instead, he caught a faint whiff of the rotten smell of decay. Shuddering, he glanced back at the forest. He had to start moving to find his way home before he too ended up crawling out of the sea, looking like a lost soul from the world beyond. The two set off in the opposite direction from Stamen's hiding place, disappearing quickly into the woods. Stamen mentally felt relieved, but only for a moment. He heard the splashing of water and turned back to the shining sea. More of the haggard Crons were swimming his way, their faces pale, dirty hair long and wild. Some of them were scarred and wounded, their bloodstained clothes hanging in rags. There were even more behind them, heads bobbing in the waves, struggling to stay afloat. Without hesitation, Stamen turned and fled into the forest, almost tripping over his own feet in dreadful haste.

***

The newly resurrected were coming, swimming across the Dejewla Sea, bridging a gap between them and their former home. Prison. Some of them had been there over a year, others mere weeks or months. All of the escapees had something in common. They were all Crons with a spark of hope within, and they were feverishly following the light. Some of them were strong enough to swim the distance; others were weak and held onto floating tree branches or ill-made rafts to bridge the gap. The sea was quite narrow at that part, which helped their progress, but made the fear of being followed quite real.

The night before, they had streamed out of the prison, taking down every guard they possibly could. Stumbling over the broken rubble of the gate, they made for the forest, following the light which led them straight and true. To where? No one questioned, but it was the reason for their escape, and it was enough to believe. All of them were sure in their convictions, but none of them were innocent. At one point or another, they had gone too far and had been caught. Innocent only by their own standards, they had disobeyed the law of that land. And for that, they must pay.

***

Marklus collapsed on the ground, attempting to draw breath. His lungs felt as if they might burst. "Please," he whispered to his companion, the shadow. "Please."

"It grows dark." She stood above him, glancing warily around the forest. "We will be hidden by the cover of night. Although we have crossed the sea, they are still coming."

Marklus was silent, focusing on calming his heartbeat. He could taste the blood in his mouth from running too much. His throat was raw, his legs weak and painful. His companion could not have been in the prison long, or he underestimated her. Although too thin, she still looked as if she could continue on into the night. Only she wouldn't. The only words exchanged between them the night before had been a confirmation of who he was and where he was going. Questions rose on his tongue, but there had been no time to voice them in the midst of the prison escape. They had run without hesitation through the forest towards the sea. The shadow had pushed hard, forcing them to swim across before taking a break. It certainly had taken its toll on Marklus.

After a few minutes, she sat down, leaning against a tree trunk. The wary look never left her eyes. As the dusk deepened, Marklus turned his head towards her. "Who are you?" he whispered, unable to find his stronger voice yet.

She looked at him, even as she blended into the darkness. "What is your mission?"

"War," he replied. "I want my world back."

"We all do. But how do you plan to accomplish that?"

Marklus raised himself on one elbow and looked at the shadow. "If we band together, if we create a force that can take over instead of waiting for them to destroy us, we will have a much better chance. Now tell me; I know you. Who are you?"

"You must not know me very well if you have to ask," the shadow quipped. "I am Alaireia the Ezinck from Srinka in the Forests of the Ezinck."

Marklus looked warily at her again. The people group of Ezincks were rarely seen in the Western World, since they tended to live hidden in forests amongst their tribes. Most Ezincks had dark skin, allowing them to blend naturally into hidden places of the forest, and they were known for their un-matched strength, agility, and beauty. They shied away from mixing with the other people groups and interfering with the political matters of the world.

"I am Marklus the Cron of Zikeland," he told her. "But tell me, why do I know you? We have met before?"

Alaireia straightened. "Likely you had a piece of parchment in your hands, a message. Since it is easy for me to slip into se-cret places and hide myself from unwanted eyes, I became one of the messengers for the southern end of this land. Oft times I left the message in view where the intended would receive it. Sometimes I hid it on their own person. But with you, I actually delivered the message into your hands. I remember it was im-portant, and I had to look into your face and ask your name to verify it was indeed you. That was long ago. What happened to you?"

"What happens to us all? We fall into their hands, only to wrench ourselves free again. This must end, and I think I know where to start. Will you come with me? Will you stay?"

Alaireia cocked her head and looked at him. Twilight had gathered and he could no longer see her. His eyes were closing in exhaustion. "That all depends," she whispered, "on how good your plan is."

If he heard her, he gave no indication. Thus, nightfall overtook over the land, yet the trail of light glimmered faintly in the gloom, leading on those who followed.

***

The night was too much for Stamen. He fled until the darkness stopped him, once again, another night lost in the woods. He did not understand why everything he tried to do ultimately failed. His only desire was to go back home, but it was as if his home had become an island, and he was trying to find it on a ship with no compass. Exhausted, he crawled into a bramble and finally gave in to sleep, hoping in the morning he could start afresh.

Morning broke gently, aware of those struggling along the bank of the Dejewla Sea, fighting to follow the path. Stamen woke hungry and cognizant of a strange light in the forest. It threaded itself among the plants, moving south, a sure indication of the way out. He stood hastily, no question in his mind the path of light was sent to lead him home. If he hurried, he could arrive in time for the second meal.

21

***

Legone stood on the barren mountain peak in the thin air. Lazy clouds passed below his black shod feet as he gazed at the wrecked beauty of the world. All was still and quiet. Not even a loose twig snapped the silence of his world. He raised his heavy head to breathe in deeply, the chill mountain air stinging his nostrils. He closed his eyes for a moment before looking back down at the shattering drop off the gray cliff he stood on.

The greenery of the mountains was slowly fading, the glory of his terrain turning black and barren. A bleak pallor was spreading over the land, and he knew what he had to do. He knew where to go to stop it, yet part of him was still torn. It was his fault he was burdened with this knowledge.

Long ago, when he was young, he'd left the Afrd Mounts and crossed the sea because his wanderlust would not leave him be. Paying no heed to words of warning, he lost himself—and more—on the northern side of the sea. Curiosity drew him in until he understood why he never should have left. What was happening now was his fault. When he returned, he refused to speak of what had taken place across the sea. He refused to think of Her. He had tried to forget, as if by hiding it from his memory, the past could be erased.

He despised moments of clarity when he knew what to do. Why must he be burdened with this knowledge? Why should he know what to do best? His mind knew, his heart knew, and yet his body was unwilling to go, to say goodbye to life and the possibility of ever living peacefully in the Afrd Mounts. To say goodbye to ever coming home again, welcomed with open arms by his people. If he left, it would be the end, and he did not know if he would make it back to see the sun rise over the mountains and burn off the fog. To see the hints of a crystalclear rainbow spreading over the falls and the mountain peaks in all their majesty as the snow melted off them. He did not know if he would be back to feel the exhilaration of climbing up those peaks, the heady breeze at the top of those mounts and the feeling of being free. No one could hold him back up there. There were no laws, no destruction, no war, and if he could help it, there never would be.

He knew what he had to do; he just did not want to close the door on possibilities for himself, on possibilities of seeing Her again. He called it selfish, his desire to live his dear, precious life free in the mounts. This would be his sacrifice for his silence, this would be his redemption. He reached for his bow and aimed a white arrow at the highest snowcapped peak. He would never see it again.

***

Marklus traveled with Alaireia through the Sea Forests of Mizine. It was a damp rain forest and every hour or so, a brief shower would soak them through. Despite the miserable dampness, Marklus felt much better with the light meal Alaireia had foraged for them and knowing they had not been caught yet.

They were late setting out, but as they walked, Marklus could not help but glance behind as an eerie twinkle lit up his path. "What is following us?" he asked after a while.

"What do you mean?" Alaireia feigned ignorance.

"The light," Marklus explained. "I only just noticed it, yet it follows."

"Ah." Alaireia did not even give it a glance. "The others are following us; it would not be kind to leave them without a guide. After all, I did help them escape."

"How?" Marklus felt his suspicions growing.

"Marklus, you ask too much sometimes. The less you know, the better."

"I don't think that is necessarily true. Besides, I know you read my message. You read all of them. You already know enough. What powers do you hold? You caused the earthquake at the prison, and now a path of light I suspect only prisoners can see and follow. What else can you do?"

Alaireia had just opened her mouth to answer when she was bowled over by a male running through the woods. He uttered a shout and tried to leap away from her. Marklus stared as Alaireia and the stranger struggled on the forest floor. "What do you think you're doing?" she exclaimed.

"Please don't hurt me!" he cried.

"I'm not going to hurt you," Alaireia replied. "Next time, just watch where you are going."

But the stranger was already distressed. "It's gone!" he whimpered. "Where did it go?"

"Where did what go?" Alaireia held up her hands and backed away from him.

He looked distraught and turned around, gazing unhappily at the forest floor. "The light. It was leading me home."

Marklus turned to look at Alaireia with a pointed expression, curious to hear what she had to say for herself.

Alaireia just sighed and crossed her arms. "If you're lost in the forest, you shouldn't follow random lights. They don't lead home."

The male stopped and stared at them, as if seeing them for the first time. His eyes widened and he turned and ran off into the forest.

"What did you do to him?" asked Marklus.

"Nothing," Alaireia hissed. "Let's just keep going."

"Did you notice?" Marklus started moving forward again. "He was a Trazame." The people group called Trazames lived by an unspoken rule—home was the safest place, and curiosity only led to death. They were peace-loving homebodies who rarely moved beyond the boundaries of their land. Farming and feasting were their main reasons for living. Trazames tended to have tanned skin and sun-kissed hair; their lazy accents and muscular bodies sculpted by farm work gave them away immediately. "Strange things are happening if the Trazames are coming out."

Alaireia nodded distantly. "We have been in prison too many months. We need information."

***

Stamen watched shakily from the forest floor as the Cron and his odd companion moved on through the woods. After they

25

disappeared from view, he noted the trail of light was there once more. Confused, he tried to come up with a reason for the reappearance of the light. It had to be a kind of evil spell in the forest. He shouldn't follow it anymore. Yet he needed to get back home—or at least out of the forest and back into civilization where he could ask for directions. Weighing the pros and cons was not his strong point; there was little else to do besides follow the light. Nightmares from last night shook his memory. Those people crawling out of the sea…What if they were following the light as well?

CHAPTER 3

THE EKA FIGHTING CAMP

Dusk was gently falling as Marklus and Alaireia approached the massive building. It looked as if it had sprung unbidden from the forest, made of gray stone and covered in crawling dark ivy. The building was stoically silent, divulging no lights, no sounds, or guards, or anything at all that indicated life. Pinpricks of uncertainty began to grow inside Marklus' mind. Had he been gone too long? Had the Eka Fighting Camp been overrun and emptied out shortly after his imprisonment? He glanced apprehensively at Alaireia, but no emotion displayed on her watchful face. She turned to follow his lead as they reached the three wide, rough steps leading to the doorway. Marklus walked up them alone and paused to listen, but the stone sealed out all noise from even his keen ears. Two imposing double doors stood at least ten feet tall, glaring down unwelcomingly at the dirty intruders. A small iron knocker rested in the middle of the right-hand door, a weak link to the stone, looking as if any use would render it ineffective.

Too exhausted to try, Marklus looked to Alaireia. She nodded, reached up to grasp the handle, and knocked twice. A dull thud echoed from within, more for the benefit of those outside than those inside. There was a pause; then, a window in the door slid open and an inquisitive nose poked out, followed by a pair of sharp green eyes, and finally the full face of a male Cron. For an instant, his face registered surprise and brief recognition as he looked down at Marklus and Alaireia. In a hurry to cover his consternation, he barked out, "What brings you here?"

Alaireia stepped back, leaving Marklus in the spotlight of the demanding eyes. "I am Marklus the Cron and this is Alaireia the Ezinck. We have come to see Crinte the Wise."

The Cron abruptly withdrew his face and the window snapped shut and locked with a clang. The right-hand door gave a whining groan as it reluctantly began to open. Pools of flickering yellow light streamed out, briefly illuminating the forest. The Cron stood in the middle of the doorway, dressed in armor from head to toe with five curious guards peering over his shoulder. "Welcome to the Eka Fighting Camp," he announced grumpily, and ushered the two guests inside.

The entrance opened into a wide hall with torches casting light off each wall. Several passageways streamed off from the it, their openings guarded by more flickering torches. A host of armored Crons filled the entryway, weapons by their sides. Some sat on wooden stools, chewing bits of bread dipped in steaming bowls of gruel. Others paced the stone floor, their footfalls ringing across it as they talked quietly and heatedly to each other. The Crons glanced up curiously and eagerly at Marklus and Alaireia as they entered. The Cron who had bid them enter turned to the five guards behind him. "Please find Crinte and let him know he is requested at the mess hall." He turned back to Marklus and Alaireia. "Come, you look as if you could use a meal."

Surprised but relieved at the lack of questions and the promise of a warm meal, Marklus followed the Cron down a hallway. Alaireia treaded warily behind, wondering if she would need to escape before the night ended.

The mess hall was buzzing with conversation. Rows of tables covered the hall with Crons crammed around each one, boisterously eating and loudly discussing. A few Tiders were sprinkled in here and there, calmly assessing the situation. The Tiders were an introverted folk who enjoyed dwelling at high elevations. Many of them called the Afrd Mounts in Wiltieders home. Although they liked to explore the ranges of the land and did not mind interacting with the other people groups, because they were of few words, most people were unsure and confused about their mortality. Many theories were put forth regarding the Tiders, and although many a Cron had taken to the Mounts to investigate, none had returned with a satisfactory answer, if at all. The fact that there were Tiders at the Eka Fighting Camp was not a surprise; the fact that they were getting along well with the Crons was.

Strength regained after partaking of the last meal, Marklus and Alaireia had nothing left to do but wait for Crinte to appear. The Cron sat with them, unable to hold his tongue. "I am Elam the Gatekeeper," he said finally. "A Cron from Norc. Where are you coming from?"

Alaireia interrupted. "We should wait for Crinte. Besides, if you are the Gatekeeper, more will come."

Elam the Gatekeeper looked perplexed by her ambiguity. He gave her a cold, sour look before standing to meet the guards as they returned, escorting a tall, blond Cron. He appeared the epitome of strength and wisdom from his waves of blond hair dancing near his shoulders to his chiseled jaw. His strength was obvious from the muscles that stood out on his shoulders to the surety in his face as he marched towards the two. His expression changed as he approached. "Marklus!" he exclaimed and reached to grasp his friend's shoulder. "I thought…" he began, words failing him.

Marklus smiled for the first time, his weariness slipping away at last. "I was delayed, er, detained," he explained, "and Alaireia here helped me escape."

Crinte moved to Alaireia and welcomed her by clasping her shoulder as well. "There will be plenty of time to talk tomorrow. For now, both of you could use a wash and a good night's sleep." He turned back to the guards. "Please, provide them with our best and bring them to my chambers in the morning."

"She said more are coming," announced Elam the Gatekeeper in an accusing tone.

Crinte paused to glance at Alaireia for a moment. "I see," he said. "Take care of them. We shall question them in the morning."

Elam the Gatekeeper motioned to his guards. Curiosity unsatisfied, he brushed past the others to return to his post.

Meanwhile, the guards escorted Marklus and Alaireia to wash away the grime from their time spent in prison.

***

One by one, each of the lost souls knocked and were admitted into the stronghold of the Eka Fighting Camp. Each of them were lightly questioned, fed, bathed, and sent to sleep before the thorough investigation in the morning. Guards paced by their doors, conscious of their weakness, yet still aware of the need to protect their stronghold from the inside, if necessary. Of those who were admitted that night, most were Crons, but one stranger was a Trazame who finally got the courage to ask for help.

***

Marklus woke to light instead of darkness, on a soft warm bed, instead of a cold, grimy prison cell. He sat up slowly, drinking in the feeling of freedom as he stretched his aching muscles. A relieved smile covered his face as he quickly dressed in clean clothes, buttoning his green tunic and belting his brown pants. Refreshed, he opened the door to find two guards waiting. They straightened quickly and fell in on either side of him, escorting him to Crinte's chambers. He found it unnerving to have guards surrounding him again, and his initial reaction was

31

to lash out and flee. Already, he missed the Sea Forests of Mizine and the fresh scent of nature surrounding him. He was not meant to be cooped up indoors, and if he could have his way, would never be again. Even when he had joined the rebels, he had rarely set foot inside the stone fortress, and most parts of it were new to him.

As they walked through the stronghold, Marklus saw eerie inscriptions and drawings on the walls. Some depicted battle scenes with monstrous creatures, others displayed elaborate drawings of the southern side of the Western World, from the Afrd Mounts in the southwest to the Forests of the Ezinck in the southeastern end. The stronghold had been built long ago, in place much longer than many lives of Crons. It seemed odd to Marklus that such a stronghold had stood empty until it had been taken over and set up as a training camp for those about to go to war.

Finally, Marklus was ushered into a chamber. Filtered sunlight streamed in from a high, barred window, reminding him of prison once again. At a table in the middle of the room sat two Crons; one was Crinte, the other had a long scroll of dried paper and a jar of black ink. He twirled his elaborate quill while waiting for the interrogation to begin. Alaireia sat calmly at one end of the table, facing Crinte, watching everything out of her dark eyes. She ate the first meal slowly, chewing thoughtfully. Marklus sat down beside her while the guards took up residence on either side of the room. Invisible, yet there, watching in case of danger.

"Crinte," Marklus began.

"Please, sit down and eat," Crinte said apologetically. "I am trying to keep this as informal as possible, however there are certain laws I must follow here. You know the enemy is becoming too clever, and we cannot be too careful."

Markus stole a glance at Alaireia before reaching for the steaming bowl before him. As much as he wanted to get the interrogation over with and hear Alaireia's side of the story, the prospect of having more than one meal a day was entirely too tempting.

"Tell me," Crinte began evenly, "what happened? Start at the beginning and think it through. Carefully."

"It's quite simple." Alaireia shrugged, lifting her face to meet Crinte's questioning eyes. "We wandered too far into enemy territory, looking for answers, and were captured by the Slutans. A few days ago, there was a prison riot and we escaped."

Crinte sighed, slightly bemused and frustrated all at the same time by Alaireia's brief explanation. Lifting a hand, he ran his long fingers through his blond hair and turned his intense gaze on the guards. "That will be all."

There was an uncomfortable moment of hesitation before the guards reluctantly moved towards the door. The record keeper looked at Crinte for guidance, and at the barest nod, quickly gathered up his paper and ink and stalked from the room, muttering under his breath. The door slammed shut, leaving the three alone at last.

"Alaireia," Crinte complained, "you are going to get me into trouble."

"What was that about?" Marklus interrupted.

Pushing the first meal aside, Alaireia scooted her chair closer to Marklus and leaned over the table. "Crinte, you've said it yourself. We can't be too careful. What I have to say should stay between us here and Ackhor, since he first employed my services. You are raising a secret army, but we don't even know what we are fighting. Have you heard that the Great Water Hole is now the Slutans' base? They are concocting a transformation potion which empowers those who go through it to become better warriors. They are unstoppable, with less emotion. They are out for blood and won't quit anytime soon. I started the prison riot because the transformation formula has been perfected, and the Slutans were getting ready to send all the prisoners to the Great Water Hole. After you go through it, you become just a shell of a living being with one purpose only: to serve and obey. This is what we are up against. Is this what your army is training for? To go up against the most indestructible warriors? We have to take a stand, but you must have some other plan."

Eyes flashing, Alaireia shut her mouth and leaned back, giving her words time to sink in. Marklus recalled earlier discussions he'd had with Crinte before he left to cross the Dejewla Sea into Slutan. He had been aware of the Great Water Hole, but the words tumbling out of Alaireia's mouth had a new severity to them. The words on parchment had confirmed Crinte's plan to raise a secret army and take it into the very nest of the enemy to destroy them. Marklus knew the ultimate goal was to take a stand against the Slutans, but now with the information becoming common knowledge, Crinte's plan had to be much more complex.

If the news intimidated Crinte, he did not show it. Instead, he prompted Alaireia further. "What else did you learn while you were imprisoned?"

"We knew that out of the two countries across the Sea, Slutan was completely overrun. But now, Asspraineya has sworn allegiance with the Slutans and their land is turning into a stronghold. The Slutans and Assprainites combined means our forces are already at a disadvantage, even with Asspraineya being a desert land and having a smaller population. We have to keep in mind that when we do send our force across the sea, there will be no rest. We don't even have eyes over there, no spies, nothing. It was while I was trying to get a sense of the lay of the land and complete the other task you sent me on that I was captured. I should have started in Asspraineya, which is where I will go next time I get a chance. There is rumor of a route or invisible road they are building to help them travel quickly and in secrecy. We need to find that path and destroy it. It is leading towards us. They will be here at our very doorsteps before we know it."

Crinte shook his head, and although his face was impassive, Marklus could tell he was quickly thinking through scenarios. "They have already started testing that invisible road; groups of the transformed started appearing in Mizine some time ago. We send out troops of warriors to scour the land and keep our countries safe, but we never know where they will strike next."

Alaireia sat back and crossed her arms, a scowl of frustration on her face. "Tell Ackhor that if he wants me to continue as a messenger and spy I will, but I am taking more than just a dagger with me this time. I need a sword. And tell him if he does

35

not act soon, we will all perish here." She stood rather too quickly, sending her chair clattering to the floor.

"I thought you had a sword," Crinte said, perturbed and standing as well. "I will personally escort you to the armory and arrange your meeting with Ackhor. But please do not leave us yet."

"I have to practice," Alaireia retorted. "I have not used the sword in a while. Besides, you don't need me to catch up with Marklus. I will find you when it is time." With that last statement, Alaireia slipped from the room before another word could be uttered.

Crinte dropped his tense stance as he retook his seat. His tight shoulders began to relax and a genuine smile covered his handsome face at last. "Marklus."

"How do you know Alaireia?" Marklus jumped in curiously, his brain bursting with numerous questions for Crinte.

"Where do you want me to start?" Crinte began. "Long has it been since I last saw you, and the truth is, much has happened within that time. Some of it too quickly, which means we must be conniving and fast if we have any hope of crushing this new terror before it completely takes over the Western World. Alaireia came to us because she is strong and invisible. She also carries an ancient power we can leverage. I think she knows people could use it to their advantage, which is why she is quite tightlipped about her abilities. She is loyal, and while I'm not at liberty to share where she came from and why, if you get close enough to her and gain her trust, she may tell you herself."

"This wasn't a coincidence at all." Marklus paused with a furrow in his brow. "The prison break was something she did on purpose to save the prisoners from transformation. But it felt as if she were trying to save just me, to bring me back."

Crinte nodded. "That is entirely possible. Sometimes, I'm not sure of her motives, but she knew I needed you if our plan is going to work. To be honest, after you disappeared months ago, I asked her to see if she could find trace of you."

Marklus leaned forward towards Crinte. "Thank you for that. So, your plan must have changed. Was any of Alaireia's information new to you at all?"

"I wouldn't be second in command here if I didn't already know those things." Crinte's voice dropped and took on a new edge. "Yes, I do have a plan, but we should discuss later. Dark times fall upon us, and I need a force I can trust to follow me blindly into the night."

"Second in command? What happened after I left to seek answers?"

"Ah, that is part of the plan as well. Ackhor has to think he is in charge in order for my plan to fall into place, and now that you are back, we can get to work. But come, tell me how you stumbled into Slutan."

***

Alaireia became a shadow again, slipping into the lightless cold passageways of the Eka Fighting Development Camp. The further she drifted, the mustier the air grew, reminding her of the smell of the dead. Brushing those dank memories away and focusing on the plan, she followed the trail until it ended and she found them. The lost souls had drifted together into one square shaped room, cut off from the warriors in the Fighting Camp. Some walked, testing out their sore muscles from their flight. Others ate, hastily and greedily, as if unsure when their next meal would come. Another group sat dazed on mats, their eyes vacant and staring into nothing. Some slept, waking frequently from nightmares only to realize they were safe from prison. Alaireia walked into the room and those that were awake looked at her. The path of light ended at her feet and they recognized their savior from torment and death. She planted her feet, her hands on her hips. "I need you." Her voice rang clear. "Will you fight with me?" The thunder of voices shook the room. If they had not had strength and a voice before, they did now. Fists raised high, they shouted. There was only one who turned his face and refused to answer the summons.

CHAPTER 4

ZIKES

There was time before violence began to spread in the land, when the crackle of power was potent across the mountains. There was a time when the immortal "wild things" were not simply whispered tales of old, hushed into stories told to babes in their cradles. Tales that were once true stories, only to become forgotten and hidden in mystery. That was the time Legone thought of as he ran through the Algrema Forest, keeping to the southern curve of the wildwood. He was aware of the shift in the air; of the change in the way the plants grew, the way the people of the forest hid from him. Their eyes watched him even as he moved silently through their territory, unable to hide from them, yet a blur stained in their memories all the same. Legone did not know how he knew where to go; it seemed a hidden path was guiding his footfalls. A name stood out in his mind. One who had seen the world. One who had a formidable plan. One willing to risk it all for the safety and peace of future generations. This leader, Legone had met long before, in a time and place not shrouded in mist. He remembered the persuasive strength of him. He was from the Order of the Wise, one who could not fail. Legone doubted he would be remembered, but that was not the point. Leaping over obstacles, he continued as dusk fell. There would be no rest from here on out.

***

Back at the fortress, Crinte and Marklus talked until the afternoon shadows lengthened and began to fade into dusk. They were brothers in a way, having grown up close to the borders of Cromomany. Crinte hailed from Norc, but his family moved to Zikeland when he was young. Marklus hailed from Zikeland, a flat, prairie town, named for the people in the grass, Zikes. At that time, no one quite knew who or what the Zikes were, since they had not been seen in those parts for decades. No one knew they often appeared as stocky blades of grass stinging with poison if touched. Their incredible camouflage abilities kept them hidden for the most part, and Marklus, on the fateful day he met Crinte, had managed to trick one into revealing its true identity.

***

Seeking Zikes was a game for children. No one had ever seen one, therefore the thrill of finding one and boasting about it encouraged exploration. Such was the way Marklus felt as he stumbled through tall rings of lime green grass higher than his waist. He carried a thick brown stick in hand, using it to push back grass as he searched for trouble. Stealthily, he made his way through the grassy prairie and accidentally stumbled upon a barren path. Hidden in a grassy hollow was a green tunnel, funneling close to the ground but leading forward into the wild. That's when he knew he had come upon on a secret. Only ten at the time, and more than willing for an adventure, he immediately wiggled down and started crawling his way through the circle of grass into a world only filtered sunlight could reach.

It was not five minutes later that he felt the first prick. Hot, searing pain overwhelmed him, knocking the breath from his body, forcing him prostrate on the ground. Tears burst from his panicked blue eyes and rolled down his suntanned cheeks as he attempted to rise, but the sensations increased. Lying there as the blanket of grass held him against the ground, he cried out in pain, yet through his tears, saw it.

It would have been about his height, if he were standing tall, and wore a deep green cone on its head. The cone seemed to shift with the sunlight—either that, or there was something electric dancing inside it, keeping the cone pointed firmly at the sky. The Zike itself wore a sort of suit Marklus was unable to see clearly, but the eyes were what froze his tears. They were emerald green, round and wide, pulling him in, locking his gaze. He felt as if he were drowning as the pain and mesmerizing gaze paralyzed him on the ground. But the longer he stared, the more the menace in those eyes faded, changing to panic and fear.

That's when he heard it. A mirror of his own. Screams of pain in the distance. Marklus startled, and the slight movement was just enough to tear his eyes away from the false glare of the Zike. As he moved, he could feel warmth spreading through his body, devouring the pain, removing the paralysis. His hands, as they lay against the ground, levitated just a bit, and a blue light crackled between his fingertips and the dusty ground.

Distracted, Marklus glanced at his hands. When he looked back up, the Zike had vanished, but a faint whimper of agony continued. Finding himself in full control of his limbs again, Marklus cautiously continued forward, slithering through the tunnel of grass until he reached a small crossroads. One way led out back into the sunlit prairie, the other led him deeper into the secret entrance, where some creature was being tortured by the Zikes.

A few minutes later, Marklus found him. It was a boy about his age, slightly taller and fairer. His long blond hair was covered in grass and mud, his dirty face bright red with streaks of tears running through the grime. He lay on his back, his muscles tense as his body convulsed against the unforgiving ground. His cries grew quieter as he submitted to the pain; the fight was fading away from his empty round blue eyes, staring yet not seeing the curtain of green.

Marklus crawled forward anxiously. Had the Zikes done this? Were they truly evil creatures of the prairie who sought to harm and kill small children? There in the shadows of the grass, hidden from the world, Marklus sat down beside the strange child to keep him company while his life expired. "I'm sorry," he whispered. "I wish I could help."

The strange child said nothing; his body shuddered against the ground once more. Marklus reached out to comfort him, laying a hand on his shoulder. The blue light ignited again, flowing from his hand into the boy's chest. For a brief second, it seemed as if the world froze. The boy went still. His eyes closed. His whimpers faded, and he began to breathe.

Marklus snatched his hand away, staring first at the boy and then at his hand, but it appeared normal. When he glanced back at the strange boy, he was sitting up and looking at him in awe. "You saved me." His tongue stumbled across the words. "How did you save me?"

Marklus shook his head, his eyes wide. "I don't know…" His voice trailed away.

The strange child grinned, his teeth flashing white. He held out his hand as a token of thanks. "I am Crinte."

The sun was beginning to descend when they emerged from the Zike's tunnel of green back into the wide-open spaces of the prairie. A gentle breeze was blowing, ruffling the light hair of the two, welcoming them back to life. Marklus could feel the thrill of adventure leaving him as he relaxed into the seemingly sympathetic arms of the wind. Although it may have been childish fancy, he sometimes thought he could see something of substance in the breeze. It was only when Crinte grabbed his arm to still him that he realized they were not alone. Covering the meadow as far as the eye could see was an army of Zikes. They stood unabashedly in the sunlight, their cones pin pricks in the sky, hostile emerald eyes staring at the two children.

Marklus froze, his heart beat steadily increasing. He could hear Crinte's shallow breathing beside him and knew they were in deeper trouble than they'd ever intended.

The Zikes marched up to them, surrounding them in a wide circle that smelled of fresh cut grass. The wind died away as if it

43

knew the moment had come and the two Crons were left to fend for themselves.

The incredible silence was the last thing Marklus remembered before the voice took over. For a moment, it was inside him, and then he realized it was Crinte, his true voice, loud, powerful, and authoritative. "What do you want?" he demanded.

One of the Zikes stepped forward. It pointed a finger—if it could be called a finger—at Marklus. "We cannot harm you," it said in an earthly voice which Marklus envisioned embodying the freedom of running outside, playing in the mud, living wild and free close to the earth. "We pledge our allegiance. When you need us. We are here."

One moment the Zikes were bowing, their sharp cones pointing directly at Marklus and Crinte. The next, the meadow was empty with only stalks of tall grass waving at the boys. The wind stood behind Marklus and Crinte as if to calm them, while they wondered if what they had seen was real.

CHAPTER 5

AN UNEXPECTED DUEL

It was days before Marklus saw Alaireia again. During that time, he met with Ackhor, the fearless leader of the Fighting Camp, to account for his whereabouts the last few months. Ackhor listened but did not have much to say. In the end, he encouraged Marklus to take up training, lest he wander into enemy territory again, unprepared. Sensing the underhanded rebuke, Marklus once again took up the bow and arrow. Crinte refused to provide any more insight into exactly what was going on at the fortress, besides the obvious training of an army. He told Marklus they were leaving soon and he should recover his strength before their journey began.

One morning, as usual, Marklus selected a practice bow and sheath of arrows from the armory, and followed a group of archers to the training grounds. The training grounds were wide open spaces hacked into the forest floor that lay just behind the fortress. Here and there, low stone walls surrounded the terrain, with guards perched on top. They watched the forest for intruders and called out words of encouragement, or critiqued the technique of the warriors practicing. Each weapon had its own station with instructors standing by to teach beginners, assist intermediates, and coach the more advanced warriors. Marklus saw a troop led off into the forest on an endurance run, while others were wrestling in the mud. At a further distance, stout Crons were grappling with the mace, a large, unwieldy tool for those who possessed great strength. Maces typically had sharp spikes on the ball at the end of the chain, but the practice ones were blunt. Even beyond them, Crons and Tiders threw blades and spears against stationary and moving targets. Out of sight were the practice targets for archers, a safe distance from the blade and spear throwers just in case of an accident. As Marklus followed the trail through the training camp, he heard a clamor of excitement coming from the sword fighters. He left the path for a moment to glance downhill at the duelers.

Alaireia was surrounded by a ring of warriors ready to jump into action. They all held unsheathed swords whose blades glistened dangerously in the light. The Crons and Tiders, unable to refrain from vocal admiration, roared shouts of encouragement to the poor chap who was unfortunate enough to challenge Alaireia. She was in complete control of the duel; each warrior would step up to combat her and three strokes later had to stumble out of the ring, sword dragging and pride gone amidst the shouts of his fellow warriors. Curious to see her in action, Marklus drew nearer.

The warriors wore breastplates to ward off blows, yet the rules of the duel were unclear. Swordplay, tripping, physical fighting, and other unexpected methods to down the other duelist seemed to be included. Alaireia did not blink or hesitate for one moment; her strokes were sure, her blocks were clear, and when her opponent fell, he never saw it coming. As Marklus watched her, he began to wonder if he and Crinte truly were the best warriors in the land. Crinte had a knack for attracting power, and now, as Marklus watched Alaireia, it was clear to him her skills were not completely natural. He had not done much besides thank her for the role she played in releasing him from confinement, but if she held such power, he certainly wanted to earn her trust.

Marklus walked downhill, closer to the circle of warriors for an upfront view. As he moved forward, he saw someone he did not expect to see, and a vague recollection clouded his memory. The male was no Cron. He was no Tider, either. Yet he stood sword in hand, waiting for his chance to combat Alaireia. His face was pale and his hands were shaking. Fear. The cold sweat of it was written all over his body. Pausing, Marklus almost walked up to him, but it was too late. Alaireia's last opponent stumbled out of the ring and a lively Cron shoved the fearful male inside.

The male raised his sword in both hands, then dropped one and swung at Alaireia. She ducked and brought her sword up to parry his blow but she was too late. The male had already shifted positions to throw a foot under Alaireia's, and the two of them toppled to the ground. Alaireia quickly recovered from the surprise move and leaped up. Feet apart and sword lifted, she posed for the next attack. The male was a bit slower but seemed to understand the need to quickly gain higher ground. There was a momentary pause as he stood, straightened his shoulders, and calmly slid one foot in front of the other before launching into an aggressive attack. Alaireia, thrown off by his speed and surety, was unable to disarm him as quickly as she had the others. She met his sword, blow for blow, parrying and thrusting, but the onslaught continued.

The shouts from the warriors hushed to an awed silence. Some sheathed their swords, others leaned forward to examine the technique, or started chanting under their breaths. It was an old chant from the Miften language, a term not common among the people groups. It was a name for an expert, a champion of the land, the best of the best. Slowly, the chant grew as the duel continued, and Alaireia's calculations about the male's next move were proved wrong.

"Starman. Starman. Starman," they chanted over and over again.

Marklus could see hints of anger in Alaireia's movements; the sword slashed too quickly. She was getting sloppy, but his precision was perfect. Although his brow was wet with sweat and his face still pale, his hands no longer shook. He was sure in his movements. He was the superior with the sword. Marklus, standing apart, remembered the Trazame from the woods, the nervous aura he'd given off when he stumbled into Alaireia and fled as soon as he sensed outwardly power. Marklus hesitated. He wanted to watch the end of the duel but instead he turned around and ran.

***

"Crinte!" Marklus burst into Crinte's chambers, not even hesitating to knock in his excitement. "The best warriors in the land, that's what you're looking for!"

Crinte looked up from the maps he was studying. "At least shut the door," he complained.

"Come with me," said Marklus. "You have got to see this!"

Crinte opened his mouth but Marklus grabbed his arm and dragged him out the door. The two raced back to the training grounds, where the size of the crowd had doubled. Alaireia and the Trazame were still locked in a duel. Now, the Trazame was on the defense, backing away from Alaireia but still meeting her every blow. Marklus could not tell if he was determined to win the fight or too frightened to give up.

"The Trazame," Crinte said in awe beside him. "I did not know he could fight."

"I did not know he was here," Marklus added.

"He came with the rest of the escaped prisoners," Crinte explained. "But I have not spoken with him."

Marklus shook his head even though Crinte's eyes never left the duel. "No, he was not in prison with us. He was already in the woods on this side of the sea. I'm not sure how he ended up at the Fighting Camp, unless he followed us. Alaireia and I ran into him on our way here."

Now the Trazame was gaining ground, and the shouts of the spectators became louder. He was gaining on Alaireia and it was her turn to back away, seeking an error in the onslaught of his sure and steady blows. He slashed towards her waist, only to be cut off; the next blow dove for her heart but was struck away. He reached higher, aiming for her neck, but her sword met his again and again, blocking as she backed away.

"I have dueled Alaireia," Crinte said. "It is no easy feat. How this Trazame still has his sword is amazing." He paused for a beat, then placed his hand on Marklus' shoulder and said in a low voice, "We may need him."

"I know."

Crinte continued, his voice dropping lower as the cheers of the crowd grew louder. "Then you know my last conversation with Ackhor did not go well. He knows how to raise an army, but we need to be two steps ahead of the enemy. As I told you, I need scouts to go to the Great Water Hole with me, discover what their true plan is, and put a stop to it. But I need a great force to come behind us. I need the armies of the Mizine to rise and follow us, wiping out this unnecessary uprising before it can take over our lands. This time, you cannot go running straight into their hands again. You will need the best of the best with you, because it will not be easy. I want warriors who are not afraid to stare death in the face and keep going. I want warriors who can think on their feet, who are passionate about saving our lands, and who can rage in battle. If this Trazame can do so, we may require his services."

Marklus smiled, his blood boiling at the words Crinte spoke. "When do we leave, then?"

"Two weeks."

Feeling satisfied with their decision, the two turned one hundred percent of their focus back to the duel. Alaireia was backed into a corner. She had nothing left to do but surrender her weapon. There was a brief second of indecision before she threw down her sword in frustration. She was breathing hard, furious that a mere Trazame could best her strength and skill. Glaring at him with hostile eyes, she waited. He hesitated, glancing questioningly at her sword then back at her intense eyes. The noise from the onlookers hushed as they watched the conclusion of the most exciting duel they'd seen from the two most unique warriors at the Eka Fighting Camp.

Alaireia reached out her hand, signaling a draw. The Trazame paused for a beat, either unwilling to give up or unsure of Alaireia. He sheathed his sword slowly and took her outstretched hand. The spectators roared and raised their swords in the air, chanting for their hero. "Starman! Starman! Starman!"

Alaireia grasped the Trazame's hand. "I have never met anyone who could fight evenly with me. From now on, we train together."

Although Alaireia's words were serious and solemn as she refused to humble herself, the Trazame lost his shy look as the witnesses shouted. "You think so? I am glad of it. I haven't had much practice with the sword." He smiled a bit uneasily and despite herself, Alaireia felt her hardened heart lift just a tiny bit.

***

After the two escaped from the many admiring and congratulatory warriors, they found themselves awkwardly walking through the training grounds.

51

"We have met before," Alaireia said finally, gauging the Trazame's face for a reaction. He stiffened immediately. "Ah, so you do remember."

"What were you doing out there?" He could not look at her. "I saw you crawl out of the sea with the others. Are you one of the turned ones?"

"Turned?" Alaireia scoffed, but she noticed the Trazame was visibly shaking with fear, and he very much looked as if he would like to flee. "How do you know about the turned ones?"

"Everyone knows." He shrugged. "Ever since they started appearing on this side of the sea."

"No," Alaireia corrected. "When I left, only a few knew there were turned ones, and now, if everyone knows, we don't have much time left." She momentarily forgot about the mysterious Trazame as thoughts flew through her head. She had been gone much longer than expected, and now it seemed maybe Crinte's plan was the only hope. She had considered going off on her own again, but given what had happened on the other side of the sea in Slutan, strength seemed to be in numbers. She knew Crinte was going to take action, but he had not informed her of his strategy or his timeline. All she knew was that his plan would be more actionable than Ackhor's. Then again, she owed everything to Ackhor, and did not want to hurt his feelings. She felt a twinge of guilt as she realized she still had not been to greet him after her safe return from the other side. But part of her shied away from what she had to say to him.

"Are you one of them?" the Trazame pressed.

"No." She again noticed how afraid he was and sighed. "I would not be here if I were one of them. After all, this is the Eka

52

Fighting Camp; only potential warriors come here. Tell me, why are you here?"

"I was lost." He looked confused. "I walked too far from my fishing hole and lost the smell of home. Then, I followed the light in the forest, and it led me here. The others, down there in the fortress, they said a miracle had helped them escape a prison and they were forever indebted. They said if I want to leave here, I need to learn how to fight, so I can go home."

Alaireia raised her eyebrows. "You followed a light in the forest?" She shook her head at his tale. "Tell me, who are you?"

Finally, he stopped and looked at her. "I am Stamen the Trazame from Trazamy City."

"Yes, I could have guessed that," Alaireia interrupted impatiently. "But who are you? What led you to leave home in the first place? How do you know how to fight like that?"

"It is as I told you. I was walking the fields and I strayed too far into unknown lands. I did not mean to leave, but I lost the smell of home, and the light led me here. My mother used to tell my brothers and sisters tales of old, and we would act them out, especially the fighting scenes. It seemed that way again as I was dueling, practicing with you, as if I were the hero in those old tales."

"My name is Alaireia the Ezinck," she began, starting to walk slowly in circles around the Trazame, who now stood quite still. "They call me Lightfoot, but those are only names. My people are nearly extinct after the Wyvern attacked Srinka, my homeland. That makes me who I am. My strength sets me apart; no man or beast is able to best me. I am less than I seem, yet I am more than I am. To know who I am is to know danger and desire for more. You followed my light, yet it was not meant for you. I cannot believe your coming is a mistake. Who are you? One named Stamen yet they call you Starman. You are my equal with the sword yet you show such fear and know so little of this world."

The Trazame appeared troubled. He looked back at Alaireia pleadingly. "I don't know," he whispered. "I just want to go home."

CHAPTER 6

NEWS FROM THE OTHER SIDE

Crinte was troubled. He spent his days planning and strategizing, pouring over maps of the Western World, reading of unexplained oddities in the history of the World, and putting each piece of the puzzle together. It was all he could do to force himself to take breaks to practice his skills with the sword at the training grounds and spend time instructing new recruits. Thoughts solely focused on the war, he knew they had to act swiftly, in such a way it would not only bring Ackhor around, but all the numerous armies on the southern side of the sea. King Arden of the Country of Norc in the west had been kind enough to turn a blind eye, knowing full well what Ackhor and Crinte intended to do: build a well-trained army that was loyal to no king or country, strong enough to overthrow every deity in Mizine. It was a concerning political move, for, after all, a ruler must be conscious of those who seek to overthrow their kingdoms. Some Rulers of the Countries of Mizine had already issued harsh edicts and repercussions for those attempting to join the rogue army. For some, the threat of a loss of status was enough. For others, the removal of limbs, time spent in the stocks, or a flogging kept them in reserve. There were reasons Ackhor and Crinte kept quiet. All the same, Crinte knew it was those in authority he had to daringly visit and persuade of their dire situation. Yet, irritatingly enough, there was still something missing.

Rifling through disorganized papers, he momentarily lifted a thick piece of parchment depicting an aqua battle scene. A Cron stood on a shore, and in front of him rose a great and terrible monster. Eight unwieldy arms and legs, longer than an elephant's trunk, flailed in all directions, a few reaching for the Cron as if to crush him. It rose out of the water, three times as high as any castle, with large round eyes, black as ink, sucking out the brave Cron's soul.

Shuddering, Crinte dropped the drawing back into a pile. There were many known and unknown dangers throughout the world; those who followed had to be willing, as he was, to take the brunt of the risk upon themselves. Crinte remembered days past when he traveled the southern end of the Western World from coast to coast with his father. Adventures in a time of peace were appealing, but adventures in a time of war were another thing entirely.

Loose papers scattered as he stood and turned to the small barred window. Sunlight tentatively warmed his tan cheeks as he crossed his muscular arms and closed his strained eyes. Memories danced with visions of golden fountains and winged creatures playing the most delicate music he'd heard in his life. Thoughts flitted back to the intoxication of the Afrd Mounts, a crisp, cool air blowing on his face, and the freedom of standing on a mountain top, looking down at the world with everything he desired within his reach. He remembered the weightless feeling of flying on the back of one of the most fearsome creatures of the air, and seeing the kingdom in the sky from afar. He recalled the mysterious secrets of the Algrema Forests and the waterfalls creating a trail into the innermost sanctuary where the Ezincks dwelt and taught him how to live off the land. Reality came thudding back as the terrors of the prairie once again materialized before him. All was not beautiful. Now, if he let it go, his memories would be nothing more than an exquisite dream.

With a sigh, Crinte turned back to his maps and again studied the lands on the other side of the sea. They were his weakness. He knew the lands to the south by heart, but walking blindly into enemy territory in the north would lead to certain death. His attempt to send scouts ahead had failed miserably; Marklus had been captured, and Alaireia had become too distracted rescuing him. Again, he wished he had been able to send the two off together to combine their unique strengths. A heavy-handed pounding on the door dispersed his thoughts. Perturbed, Crinte quickly crossed the stone floor and flung open the door to reveal Elam the Gatekeeper. A disgruntled look was plastered across his face as he mumbled, "A Legone the Tider is here to see you."

Crinte turned the name over slowly on his tongue. "Legone the Tider?"

Elam the Gatekeeper nodded.

57

"Please, bring him here." Crinte paused and added, "Your guards will not be needed."

With a huff of impatience at Crinte deliberately undermining the rules, Elam the Gatekeeper marched down the hall to escort yet another unaccountable guest to Crinte's chambers. Crinte shut the door firmly as a chill shook his body. He attacked his disorderly papers again until he found it. He held it up to the light. An Xctas, a great winged bird with a sharp beak and far seeing eyes, stared back down at him.

***

Legone should have been exhausted. After all, his four-week journey from one side of the Western World to the other would have taken any normal person months. An Xctas, a great winged bird, had taken him from the deep mountain ranges to the prairie ground. From there, he had run as if the ground were crumbling beneath his feet. The journey was all it took to make up his mind. Now, standing inside the walled fortress, he was reminded of how much he missed the freedom of the mountains and forests. Already the walls were closing in; the ceiling felt like a weight pressing on his heart. Legone bowed his dark head as he waited for the One he searched for, ignoring the curious guards around him. Part of him felt relief that he no longer had to carry his secret alone. At least the burden would be passed to another. The sound of his name jerked him out of his thoughts. The procrastinating Gatekeeper waved his hand, motioning for Legone to follow him.

***

As Elam the Gatekeeper ushered the guest into Crinte's private room, recognition flooded Crinte's memory. The name on the Gatekeeper's tongue had sounded familiar, but the image of the Tider standing before him rang clear bells of warning in his mind. Legone the Tider was as tall as Crinte remembered, standing just over six and a half feet with piercing sky-blue eyes that mirrored the view from mountain peaks. His aura was just as stiff and frosty as the unrelenting walls of the mountain, rugged and craggy, warning of danger but promising life to those who survived. Long chestnut hair tumbled down his broad shoulders, almost to his waist. It was loose and tangled now from the Tider's journey, and in some places, leaves and twigs still clung like burs to his long strands. His muscles rippled under his forest green tunic, and on his back, a sheath of white-tipped arrows and an engraved wooden bow rested. He looked down at Crinte over his long, pointed nose and extended his hand. All the while, no trace of emotion softened his hard features.

Crinte looked past the Tider and nodded at Elam the Gatekeeper to dismiss him. "Thank you." Crinte knew he appeared calm and collected, but truth be told, the sight of the Tider fresh from the mountains troubled him. "Why have you come here?" he asked as soon as the door shut.

The last time he had seen the Tider was at the edge of the Dejewla Sea. Headstrong and young, a prince of the mountains, Legone the Tider had chosen to follow his restless heart and

59

cross the sea. Since he had begrudgingly guided Crinte and his father through the Afrd Mounts, they were happy to provide guidance to the sea. From that time, Crinte knew Legone was full of wanderlust and selfishness. He paid no heed to the rules of his people and instead chose to live free and lonesome. Yes, he was skilled with the bow and arrow, and friends with all the wild beasts of the land, yet the fact that Legone the Tider arrived at the Eka Fighting Camp at all was unsettling. It was strictly against his character to join any sort of cause unless he was to benefit from it.

"Can I not go where I please?" the Tider asked, his voice quiet. "Crinte the Wise, I know it has been long since we met, but I have news for you."

Crinte finally took his hand. "Legone, are you aware that Ackhor is the leader of the Fighting Camp and all knowledge must be shared with him?"

Legone sneered before brushing those words aside. "If I had wanted to speak to Ackhor, I would have asked for him, wouldn't I?" He purposefully took off his bow and arrows and lay them by the door as a sign of peace. "My words are for your ears, Crinte, because you are the only one who can do something about them. From what I know of you, there is no possibility that Ackhor is truly in charge here."

Crinte shook his head and offered the Tider a seat before taking one himself. "And from what I know of you, the fact that you are here does not mean anything good."

"That depends on how you look at it. Viewpoints are everything." With those words, he took an object from his tunic and laid it on the table. He looked at Crinte and calmly began to speak. "It was 10 years ago to the month when I left the mountains for the very first time. Some said it was a foolish choice. There is a reason we keep to the mountains, they said. We do not deal with those on the other side, they warned. But why not? I was curious. So I went. I can protect myself. So I went. There was no need for fear in that time. So I went. After we parted ways, I set loose my boat and took the most beautiful journey across the sea. My trip was calm and steady but I crossed at such a wide opening it took a fortnight before my vision was graced with the coast of Asspraineya. During that time I partook of dried meat, berries, and nuts to sustain myself, and drank the salt-less refreshing sea water, which tasted of the dreams sea creatures are made of. My Xctas flew above me by day and rested on the prow of my boat by night, watchful and cautious, unlike myself. When at last we arrived and climbed the sandy knoll, I pulled my boat up on the shore, yet a sneaking suspicion arrested me. Feeling like a trespasser, I pushed my boat back out to sea, cutting myself off from Mizine. My journey was not full of backup plans to return home. Forward was my only option.

"The land was surprisingly sandy, and further inland, that sand turned to dust and rock, quite different from the nourished countries to the south. I roamed aimlessly here and there, living off what nature provided. Every now and then I stumbled upon a small town or large city full of people much like you and I. They had adapted to the strange enviornment and did not seem to mind the long, hot days of intense sunlight, or the cool nights that were my favorites. The land stretched on, barren and bleak, yet at times I would lie outside at night, watching the multitude of stars and enjoying crisp, cool air. It was then I felt at peace with my decision and my nomadic lifestyle continued.

"I cannot say that I was lost; there was no road for me to follow, no end goal other than life itself. Yet one day I heard crashing waves, and climbing atop my Xctas, flew over the eastern end of Oceantic. Waves pounded against the shore, demanding obedience. Seagulls wheeled below me, calling, nay, shouting with joy to each other. My heart overflowed and I leaped from my Xctas, only to find the breath knocked out of me when I reached those icy waves, foaming over my head and calling me under. At first I thought it was the end, until a slick wet body lifted me, and up popped an otter to laugh at my folly. Who knows how many months I spent by Oceantic living the life of a sea creature myself. It was when my Xctas began to fly off for days at a time that I determined to follow it. Oceantic would always be there for me to return to. Again hiding my presence, I wandered through canyons and valleys, barren lands and sandstorms, terrible winds, and freezing snow until I reached the border between Asspraineya and Slutan, where a great green forest grew."

His words dropped away into silence and for the length of a few breaths, there was nothing. His eyes clouded over, no longer seeing Crinte across the table, as if he were being transported back into his deepest, darkest memories. He shook his head once as if trying to clear it, to determine what words were needed and what knowledge needed to stay hidden, for now.

"I have told no one of the time I spent on the other side. They know I left. They know I returned. And life continued as it always did. The sun rose, the sun set, and yet I always saw it through the eyes of another, and I wondered if I had made the greatest mistake of my life. Walking into the forest was like stepping into an ethereal world. It was as if time stopped and the years fell away like snowflakes in the sun. I cannot tell all that I learned there, only, I fell in love with the forest. I fell in love with its creatures. Yet all was not as it seemed.

"It has always been rumored there are immortals among us, if only we open our eyes. We have seen them and yet we haven't, but I have, and I am ruined. I cannot tell if I am one of them or not, but it seems likely they would have poisoned me with their soullessness. Some days, I believe I am immortal, and at times, I wonder if my body continues to age, or if all was halted by dwelling too long in their presence. The Green People are real, their stories are truth, and they awoke a great evil, deep in the forest, and allowed it to grow. No, that is not right. They encouraged it to thrive, and once it became too strong for them, instead of destroying it, they unleashed it. That darkness is what is coming for us; that darkness causes the transformation. How, you ask?

"There is a power known to the immortals, the power of life and death, and few immortals are born with that dominance. Those who have it live hidden because they know others will abuse those abilities. But the truth is, they remain hidden because they know there is a ritual that if performed will allow powers to be transferred from one immortal to the other. And there is one in need of those powers for his plans to come to fruition.

"You know of the Four Worlds; the North World, the South World, the Eastern World, and ours, the Western World. There are greater beings, born out of creation and dwelling in the South World. Among many desires, one of them is to merge the Four Worlds and rule them as one. The purpose is yet unknown, but to join all Four Worlds together into the middle of Oceantic would take great power, and the move itself would cost many lives. Unless, a hardier People Group could be born that would endure such a drastic transition. If the worlds were moved together, there is no knowing what ancient immortals might awaken from the deep, or what others would be attracted to such a feat of power. An act of such magnitude is a challenge and demands an answer, and should the beings succeed, they are asking for war, and will need a stronger People Group to go to war for them.

"Why, you ask, should the immortals play with us in such a way? How are we to withstand such power? We cannot. Which is why, in all my years, I have never come forward with this knowledge, because what is the point? But now that it has begun, I rue the day the immortals thought they could play with mortals. We should not make it so simple for greater beings to take over our world and wipe out life as we know it for a superior People Group. I refuse to live to see such days, which is why I come to you now. You know the Western World and have traveled it like I have, living off the land, satisfying your wanderlust with no other purpose. Were those not the happiest days of your life?"

His words drifted into a muted silence, settling heavily throughout the room. As Crinte took in the words of Legone the Swift, a dread sat heavy on his heart. With the news he had brought him, he doubted anyone would follow him if they knew the truth. He looked back up at the cool eyes of Legone. "Why now?" he puzzled. "Why come to me with these warnings now?"

Legone stood. "See, you already believe me, although you mistrust me. Years ago, my words would have been the ravings of the mad one."

Crinte pointed to the small object on the table as he rose. "And what of this?"

A shadow of pain passed over Legone's face, almost too quickly for Crinte to see. "Keep it." He backed away. "It is a token too strong for myself: the power of mind control. You of all people are wise enough to control it, but I warn you, it is your gamble now."

The object glittered at Crinte as he uneasily gazed at it. "How did you come by this?"

Legone picked up his quiver of arrows and gently fitted it on his back. His eyes focused on his bow as he mumbled in a low voice, "The creatures of the wood gave it to me, just in case."

Sensing the end of Legone's open confession, Crinte moved to open the door for him. "Thank you, Legone. You have risked much to come here, and I would prefer these words not pass lightly between any others."

"As you wish. But should you and I fall into their hands, there are others who should know the truth."

"I will ensure the truth does not stop with us. But let us speak of this no more."

Legone hastily exited the room and Crinte leaned heavily against the door. He would have to tell Marklus; he would even have to tell Ackhor. It was time to resort to their last defenses. If the Western World failed, it would not be because they did not try. Walking to his desk, he took a piece of parchment, wetted a quill, and began to write.

CHAPTER 7

RELATIONSHIPS OF THE PAST

Alaireia found herself reluctantly walking towards Ackhor's quarters before heading to the training grounds as usual one morning. Even though Ackhor let her enjoy her freedom and had avoided summoning her for debriefing, Alaireia was aware she should have made a point to meet with him the moment she entered the Eka Fighting Camp. Instead, she found herself hesitant, shying away from the one question he might ask. Her relationship with Ackhor went back years. He had appeared in the forests of Srinka shortly after the incident that took her family away. Instead of being put off by her frosty attitude, he'd provided the deadly weapon that led to her revenge. When the emptiness of loss set in, he distracted her from sorrow by showing her the glories and mysteries of the Western World.

Following directions from Elam the Gatekeeper, who knew everything about the fortress, she made her way to the meeting rooms Ackhor kept. Outside the frowning door, she halted and took a deep breath to still her jumpy nerves. Calmly, she reached for the doorknob, and before she could change her mind, burst into the room without knocking. Her eyes flew immediately to him and she saw, with relief, he was already preoccupied. Ackhor stood in the middle of the room, surrounded by three animated Crons talking intently. They glanced up in surprise at the intrusion, but much to Alaireia's disappointment, Ackhor motioned for her to shut the door and turned back to them. She took in the details of the room while she waited, noticing the way bright light poured in from an oblong window, highlighting the many books and papers stacked by the walls, on tables, against shelves, under chairs, and by the window. The walls were covered in detailed drawings and paintings depicting landscapes and peoples of the Western World. Often the shock of walking into Ackhor's rooms was enough to silence anyone until they became used to the idea of stepping from the neutral walls of the fortress into a bizarre land.

The Crons quietly finished their conversation, shook hands, and filtered out of the room, glancing curiously at Alaireia. Ignoring them, she turned to Ackhor, and despite herself felt the corners of her mouth lift in a smile. Ackhor strode to her. He was a tall, burly Cron with shoulder length, rich brown hair pulled back to clearly display his wide face. His catlike eyes were kind and understanding, and much like Crinte the Cron, he emitted an aura of authority. Alaireia reached out her hands to welcome him but he held out his brawny arms and wrapped her in warm embrace. "Alaireia." His voice was deep and melodic, sending calming vibrations through her body. "I know better than to worry about your comings and goings, but I wondered when I would see you again."

"Ackhor." Alaireia gave in to the warmth of his hug for a brief moment before pulling away. "The errand I went on took much longer than expected. But I am here now with news for your ears."

Ackhor chuckled affectionately. "Of course, Lightfoot, little sister. I would expect nothing less. Come, sit, and tell me all." With his arm protectively around her shoulder, he steered her towards the carved bench under the window where they sat, side by side.

Alaireia turned to him, her face earnest as she began to speak. "Ackhor, there is much going on in the world. Honestly, I left because Crinte asked me to. His friend, Marklus the Cron, went to scout out the other side of the sea. He, of course, got lost and captured in Slutan. He's essential, you know, to Crinte's plan." She paused and looked at Ackhor, waiting for his reaction.

"I do know," Ackhor confirmed, his expression cautious. "Crinte has a plan and he will tell me when he is ready."

"I thought you might," Alaireia affirmed. "I had to use the Clyear to break out of prison." She smiled up at him and her voice became hushed. "It worked flawlessly; thank you."

"Ah, I am glad to hear that." His words hung delicately in the air as if there were more to say. He paused before asking, "You say Marklus the Cron is essential. Do you know of his powers?"

"No." Alaireia's face turned thoughtful. "I only intended to return him here, safe and sound, before going my way. I never thought to ask…"

"Maybe you should," Ackhor prompted. "It would not hurt to know more of the warriors here. After all, this is the Fighting Camp. We are supposed to be useful to each other, not going our separate ways." He looked at her pointedly.

Alaireia bit her lip at the rebuke. "Yes, but large numbers are your expertise. I work much better solo. Besides, we should send more scouts to the other side to find out what is actually going on. I know you will say I sound like Crinte, but it is my plan to return there. The land is odd, and even those on this side know of the turned ones. What is even worse is that I heard that information from a mere Trazame."

"A Trazame? I heard one came here, that same night you and Marklus appeared. I think the Clyear may have worked much better than you had hoped, for a small army of prisoners came as well."

"No, that was intentional," Alaireia interrupted.

"Tell me more about this Trazame then, the one they call Starman. I hear he bested you with the sword," Ackhor teased.

"Argh!" Alaireia groaned in frustration and stood up, pacing back and forth. "He did not best me with the sword. He is my equal! A mere Trazame, and yet they praise him. There is no one better than I, and yet he will not tell me who he is. He swears he grew up in Trazame, the farmlands, but a farmer should not know how to wield a sword like that!"

Ackhor stood as well and began to speak, his voice calm but firm, packed with warning. "Keep him close. A time may come

70

when you need him. Alaireia, hear me out. I know Crinte is overly concerned with what is happening on the other side of the sea, and yes, it is to our advantage to discover their secrets. I believe it is our highest priority to build an army that will defend our homeland. We are only rebels, and if the Rulers of Mizine find out what we are doing, they will want to use our armies for their own needs. We need to present a united front and it is not my wish to go against Crinte's plan, but it is too dangerous to go across the sea into an unknown land looking for hidden motives. I don't like the thought of you willfully running into certain death with him, no matter what kind of fearsome and powerful warriors Crinte attracts. If you do decide to go, against my wishes, at least tell me before you disappear into the night. You are the most skilled warrior I know, but you are also like a sister to me. At least do me the honor of letting me say goodbye."

"Oh, Ackhor," Alaireia replied in frustration. "Of course I will weigh the cost with you before I leave, but now is not the time to play it safe. Remember when the Wyvern attacked Srinka and you told me attempting to kill it would risk my own death? That the risk would be worth it compared to living in anxiety and fear, waiting for its next deadly attack? This is the same situation, only on a grander scale. It's not my death that hangs in the balance; it is the death of our countries and life as we know it. If it is solely up to me, I will take that risk—again. Life lived in defense and fear is no life at all."

***

Tincire was a weapons maker. When he was young, he began working with his father, the town blacksmith, creating unique tools out of lumps of iron and steel. He was fascinated with heat, the way it melted and distorted the strongest metals, contouring them into new shapes and forms. The flames spoke to him, their warm voices whispering, revealing secrets of the craft, influencing the outcome of the tools and weapons he designed. At the Fighting Camp, he studied the warriors and watched them train, learning their strengths and weaknesses. Every now and then, an idea would come to him and he'd scurry back to the furnaces with new designs to coax from the flames. Then, he would assemble the warriors who awed him most and present them new weapons, custom made for their skills. He would explain why he made the weapon and what made it special for that particular warrior. It was a rite of passage, and warriors knew they had achieved the highest honor when approached by one of Tincire's messengers. Now, Tincire had his team working day and night to perfect weapons for a certain group of warriors. His gut told him time was of the essence, and his inklings were never wrong.

***

Try to fit in. Those were the words of Crinte the Cron after their lengthy conversation. Try to fit in. That was days ago. Legone shook back his long hair and raised his curved bow to his mouth; he took aim at a practice mark and hit it so hard it vibrated for minutes afterwards. He had never been good at fitting in; everyone wanted to fall into a similar routine, but he was always doing things differently. Chores were lost on him. Why chop wood when he could explore the forest and discover the secrets of the trees? Why save for winter when he could ask the beasts of the air and earth, and they would share with him? He pulled another white tipped arrow out of his sheath and calmly fit it between his fingers. There were other Crons and Tiders surrounding him on the practice ground. He could hear the thud of their arrows striking home, but he felt alone. He let the arrow fly, long and free like his heart, until it smashed through the mark, its point shattered from force. Try to fit in. Crinte had said they were leaving soon and asked if Legone would serve as a guide since he had been to the other side. Legone had not said it then, but there was a stop they would have to make along the way, and he could not tell Crinte without raising suspicion. Already at times he felt he had said too much, and exposed himself and them. Anger boiled up again as he pulled another arrow, and a voice beside him asked, "Are you Legone the Tider?"

He turned his head cautiously, but it was only a Cron he did not recognize. Curly brown hair danced over his forehead and he, too, carried a bow and arrow. "I'm sorry to interrupt your concentration," he said, "but Crinte said I might find you here." The Cron lifted his bow and arrow and aimed; it was a poor aim, Legone noted. "Tonight, after the last meal, come to Crinte's room."

The Cron let the arrow fly. He missed. Legone wanted to laugh. "Try to fit in," Legone told the Cron, and turned back to his target.

***

Marklus only stayed at the shooting grounds a few more moments after he had passed the message to Legone the Tider, who was just as fearsome and as cold as Crinte had described. But then, all the warriors Crinte selected were tough. Even his attempts to get past Alaireia's walls of silence proved futile. Now he had to find her. As of late, he noticed she had been keeping company with the solo Trazame, the one everyone called Starman, after his unbelievable duel with Alaireia. Even as Marklus stood still in the trees, he could hear the clang of steel on steel and the roar of warriors watching. He shook his head. At this rate, the turned ones would likely hear all the clamor and come racing to overtake the Fighting Camp before the warriors were truly trained. Marklus turned and pointed his feet towards the sound.

***

Crinte was torn. The object Legone the Tider had left with him was dangerous, unethical, and in Crinte's mind, wrong. It was a power that should remain hidden and unused, yet he found it hard to believe the creatures of the wood had entrusted

Legone with such a rare gift. Crinte knew it could be their salvation—it was the missing piece he was looking for, a way to bind the wills of all people groups to himself, a way to remove the choice that stayed their hands, a way to force a great army to overtake the northern side of the Western World. It was a power he was sure had a small aura of darkness around it. He wanted to destroy it yet he knew that would be impossible. But was their salvation worth it?

CHAPTER 8

THE FIVE COME TOGETHER

They came stealthily, hiding in the shadows of the fortress, as if they themselves were rebels within a rebel camp. Marklus was the first, slipping into Crinte's room before the last meal had even ended. Next was Legone the Tider, his cool presence quieting the air. Alaireia was last, and with her, she brought the Trazame.

"Thank you for coming this evening," Crinte began as they gathered around the table, waiting expectantly. "You may not all know each other but I find each of you essential to the future of this world. Marklus the Healer is my childhood friend; he saved my life a time ago. Alaireia the Lightfoot has recently escaped from the other side of the sea with Marklus. Legone the Swift has traveled from the Afrd Mounts with dire news from the other side; his knowledge is imperative to our mission. Stamen the Starman has lost his way, only to find it here with us and discover his talent with the sword."

Crinte looked at the four standing before him. "There is only one way to do this." His voice rang clear with clarity and dogged determinedness. "There is only one way to end this for good. If we want to give the people of Mizine a fighting chance, if we want the Western World to rise victorious and see glorious days ahead for our country, we have to put an end to this! The enemy is much stronger than us. They are conniving and moving into our territory. I will not see our people transformed; I will not see our country fall to its knees, worthless slaves unable to have a mind of our own. We must stop this before it goes too far! There's only one way to kill a beast—find its weak spot and destroy it from the inside out. We are going to do this, and I will lead this group. We have to be fast, we have to be strong, and we have to give this our all. We have to do the unexpected and outsmart our enemy. We have to have a plan and we have to attack. Our goal is to go to the Great Water Hole, and destroy this new power by exposing its weak spot so our army stands a fighting chance at defeating him. This is our mission. Who's with me?"

Silence claimed the room for a few moments as questions filtered through the heads of the warriors. It was finally Starman who spoke up. "Not to…er…disrupt your plans, but would you mind leaving me at home before you cross the sea? I'm not comfortable joining this army and my people aren't warriors. You don't need me for this."

Alaireia scowled at Starman but did not voice her opinion. It was Crinte who broke the awkward silence. "Starman, you have only been here a couple of weeks and yet you display a great courage we have seen in no other Trazame. Although you think light of your talents, there will come a day when your power will be essential to the fate of the land. Don't throw it away because you don't believe you are worthy enough."

Starman nodded, his face red. It looked as if he would have liked to argue further, but Crinte's compelling voice silenced all resistance.

"Crinte," Marklus objected. "You mentioned our enemy as being a 'him,' but this is the first I have heard of this information."

"Yes, we have Legone to thank for that. He has brought some revelations about what we are up against, which is why I have a plan." Crinte unrolled a large map of the Western World and spread it over the table. Despite themselves, the four eagerly leaned in. Crinte pointed to the Sea Forests of Mizine. "A scout has spotted a troop of turned ones crossing the sea. In retaliation, the Fighting Camp is sending a group of warriors to face them tomorrow morning. We will be a part of that group, but it is only a starting point. After the battle, we will push on east. Each of you have armies you can call to our aid; you will need to tell them to be ready when you call."

"Excuse me," Starman interrupted. "I don't have an army."

This time, Crinte, Marklus, Alaireia and Legone all glared at him. "Excepting Starman," Crinte added. "I must call in some favors, which means we must venture near the Mounts before crossing to the other side of the sea. From there, Legone will be our guide, as he has been there before. It will not be an easy journey. The turned ones have taken over the lands to the north, and we will be aliens in a foreign land. We must be cunning and fast, but I have chosen each of you because together we can be

78

an unstoppable force. I need you to be sure, because once we start, there is no turning back."

***

Crinte pulled Alaireia aside after dismissing the others. Picking up a thick scroll, he pressed it into her hands. "Give this to Ackhor. I want him to understand why we are doing this."

Alaireia was not used to questioning the messages Crinte gave her to pass along, but now she looked searchingly into his eyes. "What is this, Crinte? What have you withheld from us?"

"I thought it might be easier if you did not know all. Legone brought dark tales from the other side. I will let Ackhor decide how much the Fighting Camp should know. It is his responsibility now."

Alaireia nodded, turned, and faded into the night, unrolling the scroll as she went. She was only halfway through the parchment when someone called her name. "Alaireia," a voice said from the shadows, "where are you going?"

She could just make out Marklus' curious face in the dim halls. "To call my army. Come with me," she replied, quickly tucking the parchment into her tunic before he could see it.

Marklus fell in step beside her. "So you are coming with us then?"

She nodded. "I will do what I can, but tell me, did Crinte tell you the whole story?"

"What do you mean?" he asked, perturbed.

"Did he tell you what Legone the Tider told him?"

"I'm not sure what your question is. I believe we hold the same knowledge. Alaireia," he paused and put a hand on her shoulder, turning her to face him, "is there something else?"

"Marklus, you should know the truth before you run head-long into danger again. There is a dark power beyond what we can control that stirs in this world. All this could have been avoided if Legone the Tider had come forward sooner."

"You can't know that," a cold voice interrupted. Marklus and Alaireia turned, only to come face to face with Legone himself. "You don't know what it was like over there. Don't presume to judge me with your limitations."

"I was not judging," Alaireia protested. "Only, if you had come forward as soon as you had found out, things would be much different now. The south would never have allowed such an evil to grow."

"Wouldn't they?" Legone questioned as he glared at her. "The south has a way of turning its ears away from bad news. They never would have believed my tale. And the north, for all their powers, unleashed it. Since you know so much of the world, tell me, do you believe my tale? Would you have believed it unless the turned ones began to appear in your lands?"

Marklus, seeing the look in their eyes, quickly stepped between the two. "It does not matter now. We are all in this together and should not talk of what might have been. There is no going back. Legone, walk with us. We might as well learn how to get along."

Alaireia looked at the tall Tider. "There is only one thing that matters now." She stared up into his sky-blue eyes. "Are you with us?"

Legone defensively stared right back at her. "That is a question you should not even have to ask," he replied tightly as he turned and walked away.

"Alaireia," Marklus groaned, "you have insulted him."

Alaireia huffed. "There is something about him I cannot put my finger on. He is hiding something."

Marklus looked thoughtfully at her as they reached a flight of stairs, descending deeper into the fortress. "Crinte said the same thing to me," he whispered, "which is why we have to keep him close. He may be our guide, but if there is more to the story, he will need our trust, something I fear he has not known. Alaireia, there are secrets you have not told me, because I do not have your trust yet."

"I know. Since we are leaving together, it is time you knew."

As they stepped off the stairs, into gloomy, torch lit halls, Alaireia reached into her tunic and pulled out an object. She held it in the palm of her hands and lifted it up so that the flickering torchlight fell on it.

"It cannot be!" Marklus exclaimed, staring at it in wonder. "How did you come to find it?"

A genuine smile lit up Alaireia's face. "I know, isn't it beautiful?"

"Alaireia." Marklus stared at her, noticing again how lovely she looked as the yellow light spilled over her hands, highlighting her cheekbones and shades of dark hair. "Do you know what we can do with it?"

"I do." She never took her eyes off it. "How do you think we escaped prison?"

"Oh." All the pieces came together now. "Your army, the prisoners."

"Yes, you see now. They followed the trail we left them, which led here, all except for Starman. He should not have seen it."

Marklus shook his head in wonder. "We are stronger than I thought," he said finally.

Alaireia turned questioningly towards him as she put the object away. "What powers do you hold?"

"Nothing I can show you." Marklus shivered. "I stand between life and death; I am a healer."

Alaireia reached out and took his hand, then looked up at him in surprise. "You are not a healer; you are The Healer. I can feel it, even now."

"Have you met healers before?" Marklus asked in confusion.

"Yes, some of my kind, but their auras were not like yours."

"Then you think there is hope?" Marklus could not help but ask.

"Hope." Alaireia turned the words over on her tongue. "I don't know about that." Then, she turned abruptly and led him down to the depths, where her small army slept, waiting.

***

Crinte had barely closed his eyes when he heard the door to his chambers swing open. Sighing inwardly at the interruption, he reached for his sword, which never left his side, even in slumber. "It's just me, Marklus," a voice hissed out of the darkness.

Crinte sat up. "Oh, Marklus?" He fumbled around for a light. "What brings you here at this late hour?"

Marklus sat cross-legged on the cold, stone floor. His feet were bare and the dancing flame highlighted his curious eyes. "I was with Alaireia. You did not tell me she has the Clyear."

"It was not mine to share."

"Then, will you share with me what Legone the Tider told you? He trusts you and no other. Alaireia hinted at darker forebodings than I imagined."

Crinte's face grew still, watchful. "Marklus, he trusted me. There is an account of events I shared with Ackhor. I think it will be enough to persuade him, and his relationship with Alaireia? Well, he will not want to lose her if she comes with us. It will be easier to be more open once we have left this place. I don't want words repeated and echoing off stone walls."

Marklus nodded thoughtfully. "And what of the Trazame?"

Crinte shook his head. "We have to take him home. He cannot walk blindly into this, even if he can hold swords with Alaireia. I would not trick a Trazame into death. But don't tell Alaireia. She will be against it. I think she is growing rather fond of him."

Marklus laughed ironically as he stood. "She is fond of no one. The Tider is cold as ice, the Trazame is clueless, and you and I?"

"Marklus, this is no joke. I need you to call the Zikes."

Marklus froze, and his voice dropped away into the shadows of the night. "But what if they kill us all?"

Alaireia sat in the large square room in the dungeons with her army. It was a poor army; she had counted them twice and each time the number barely hit one hundred. They would not be much help at this point. Some of them had used their last strength getting to the Eka Fighting Camp. It was late and most of them were asleep, but Alaireia's eyes wouldn't close. She felt calm, yet the haunting tale of Legone the Tider bothered her. Something was not right. Even if he had endured horrors from the other side, there was something about him that made her feel reluctant. The problem was she did believe his tale, and wondered if she should.

She felt him approach before she saw him. "Alaireia," he said. She turned her face to him. He was about her height with sun-kissed brown hair, so short it tended to stick up from his head. His skin was darkened from time spent working in the sunlight, and his soulful eyes were deep brown. She could see mirrored in them the emotions they all felt deep down inside—uncertainty and fear. From the time she'd spent training with him, she found him the least knowledgeable person she had ever known; but then again, she had never met a Trazame. He sat down beside her, shoulders hunched apologetically. She wanted to reach out to him, to tell him he wasn't lost and alone anymore. But the words he spoke changed her mind. "I talked to Crinte." Alaireia looked sharply at him. "He said I could go home."

"Is that what you want?" she demanded, her voice coming out harsher than intended.

He shrugged. "I'm not meant for this war. You and Crinte and Marklus, and even Legone, are all warriors. If this is the end of the world, I want to be with my family, those I love most."

Alaireia's face grew still, as if she'd been slapped. "I see," she said.

Sensing her mood change, Stamen stood up. "I just wanted to tell you that."

Alaireia turned away from him. "I see." She looked out at her pathetic army. "Starman," she said as he walked away. "There's a reason you followed the light, and the light doesn't lead home." He did not reply, and despite herself she felt a pang of disappointment.

After he had gone, she stood and reached for the parchment Crinte had given her, words she did not desire to share, but as a messenger she would complete her assignment. She slipped out of the room and headed for the rooftop where she knew Ackhor would likely be brooding into the night. When she reached the balcony and stepped out in the cool night air, he looked up as if expecting her. "You have decided," he said as she glided forward, merely a shadow in the darkness.

"Crinte asked me to give you this," she said, pressing the thick scroll into his hands.

"I assume you are familiar with these words?" Ackhor asked gruffly, slowly taking the parchment from her hands.

"Yes," her words tumbled out in a rush, "and I am leaving with Crinte."

"I am disappointed." Disapproval dripped from his lips and he turned away from her briefly. "But I cannot stop you."

Alaireia stood beside him and looked out over the darkened land, attempting to explain herself. "I will regret it if I don't take this risk. You, of all people, should know about risks."

"Aye." Slowly, he turned back to face her. "I understand your desire to go, but you are making a mistake. At least, take care of yourself." Ackhor reached out and pulled her into a brotherly hug, his chin touching the top of her head. "Goodbye one last time, little sister."

Involuntarily, she stiffened at his touch before relaxing, reminding herself of all Ackhor had done for her in the past. She left him without a sound, sneaking back through the empty halls.

Ackhor returned to his chambers. He took the Clyear he had lifted from Alaireia, wrapped it in burlap, and placed it in a ceramic pot. Since Alaireia had chosen to be foolish, he must keep it safe. Better to use the Clyear at the Fighting Camp than for it to fall into enemy hands. Satisfied with his deception, he lit a candle and sat down at the table. Taking the scroll, he unrolled it, carefully holding down each end. Before him lay Crinte's handwriting, but the words told the story of another.

CHAPTER 9

WORDS ON PARCHMENT

I, Legone the Tider, swear these words to be true. It was ten years ago to the month when I left the mountains for the very first time and crossed the Dejewla Sea. I wandered through canyons and valleys, barren lands and sandstorms, terrible winds and freezing snow until I reached the border between the countries of Asspraineya and Slutan, and there a great green forest grew.

I could feel its age as I stepped beneath its boughs and the dryness of the desert faded away into green. It was as if I were back in my mountains, and as I breathed in the pure air, I realized I missed them more than I had known. I felt that I had come home. For long moments, I stood on that sacred ground, breathing in the air until my feet reminded me there was much to explore and I drew closer to its innermost sanctuary. It felt as if the forest was watching the first few weeks I dwelt there, but as I chose to live off the plants of the land and not the animals, it relaxed and began to accept me. I made myself wander through the forest until I was lost entirely, but I could tell something was keeping track of me, even if only in a curious way, and it bothered my mind.

One day, I heard the voice of a river and camped along its edges. I followed it for a short while until I reached the end of the forest and found myself staring up into dry cliffs. Unwilling to leave the forest behind for more desert lands, I turned to go back, and that was when I first saw one of them. She was standing beside a tree, her hand resting on its trunk, her large, pale eyes calmly, quietly watching me. Her skin was a pale green and she wore a long pale dress, the color of it ever shifting. Her ears were quite large, so they stuck out from her head; even her waist-length pale hair could not hide them. She saw me see her and met my eyes. We held the gaze but for a moment before she turned and slipped back into the woods. I made as if to follow her but could find no trace of her presence. Despite myself, a chill awoke my heart and I almost left for those dry mountains to warm myself again. Alas, that it was not to be.

She began to appear daily—when I was fishing, before I slept at night, when I scaled trees to find my Xctas who had taken to flying far from me. Finally, in frustration, I asked what she wanted of me, and it was then she invited me in. She beckoned and I followed, down hidden paths into the secret place of the forest where the creatures of the woods dwell. There were hundreds of them and she was only one, just as curious about the world as I. She listened to my stories and told me her own, of her people and from whence they had come, of their customs hidden away in the forest, of their knowledge of the world and their power. She was curious and impatient and nothing like anyone I had ever met. She introduced me to her world, her people, and despite myself, I gave up my lonesome ways and lived among the Green People.

One day, I was summoned by the King and Queen of the Green People. They cautiously welcomed me into their midst and from there I became a guest in their great green halls. Their land teemed with life; all that is good and green grew about them. Their halls were filled with the sound of music, the trickling of waterfalls and the rushing of the winds. I wandered too close to their portal, guarded by the King's own daughter, Lady of the Green People, who warned me of its power. After that, my eyes were awakened to see just how powerful the Green People are, and what they used their powers for. There was one they welcomed through their portal, a sickly shadow whose coming was intense enough to close the gateway to worlds beyond. This shadow they healed and nurtured, yet as it grew healthy, it also grew an impossible mind of its own. A rift formed between the Green People—there were those who sought to destroy it before it could become something unthinkable, and there were others who protected it like a child, believing in redemption, promising a better future with age.

But it did not get better.

At first, there were only accidents, those turned to incidents, and finally blatant terrors. At last the King and Lady of the Green People rose in full strength and banished the shadow from their land to the mountains. They conjured a great storm and wasted much of their people's powers, for by this time the shadow had grown strong, feeding off their energy. Instead of destroying it, they tossed it out into the wild to teach it a lesson. They closed their doors on it, and it became a him, and he drifted in fury and might and disappeared into the desert mountains of Slutan.

The Green People, cautious and broken, sealed their land, but before they closed their portal of powers, I made my presence scarce. I took the Horn of Shilmi and ran like never before. It felt like my feet never touched the ground, and I do not know if it was fear or traces of immortality, but ever since, my steps have been faster and surer. My path lay before me. I left the forest and entered the bleak desert of Asspraineya, and it was not until I broke free of those forests that I saw my Xctas once again. We ran as if the shadow was behind us until we reached the sea. I climbed upon my Xctas' back for one last flight. We flew until we could fly no more, then weary wings dropped and we crashed into the sea. Alone, I swam until I reached the southern shore, and alone I lay on the bank until breath entered my body naturally and I no longer tasted terror and darkness and corruption. I felt as if I had passed through the doors of death itself, and having lost everything, I wondered for a moment, but knowledge was my strength.

I walked back to the Afrd Mounts for my heart was too heavy for my feet to take flight. I kept the Horn hidden because it holds a deep power. There is a reason it has been in my possession for a time, and now I pass it to you. When the time comes, those you need will come to your aid and their minds will be aligned with yours, and all that you desire shall be accomplished. Use at your own peril. I wish no more than to do my part to end this power struggle. The next step is ours. If we do not act, the immortals are coming for us, and there will be mortals no longer.

CHAPTER 10

TRANSFORMATION

Fire ignited behind the orbs of his deep eyes as he concentrated. He ignored it, familiar with the senseless buzzing as his body complained from overuse. Creating potions of transformation was difficult, complex, and time consuming. Time was what he had the most of; he was blissfully aware of the eternity of time stretching endlessly into echoes of darkness. Time. Alone. He blinked and stood at last, stretching his tense, sore muscles. The body he'd assumed was weak and mortal, easily tired from the endless hours he spent perfecting his transformations and watching the clock of the Western World shift and muddle. His original form was what he desired, and to be united again. But not with his brother and sister who had unceremoniously kicked him out and chased him through the portal for not agreeing with their grand schemes. No, he wished to be above the World in paradise, a place where he belonged. And if he were to accomplish that, he had to call down the greater beings beyond the end of the Four Worlds to take him there.

Even now he could feel the undercurrent of potential power. The untapped resources that lay across the Western World, a shrine of his desires. There was only one thought that irked his mind—the thought of a mere mortal, a Tider, who would likely challenge him. He was close with those demented beings, green immortals. They thought highly of themselves, the most powerful beings in all of the Four Worlds. Born into the Western World, they thought themselves Keepers of Power until he had been thrown, flung into their midst. It had been all too easy to blindingly charm them with his prose and elegance. They saw him as they wished to see him until it became truth, and there was only one who saw his other form, what he really was. He remembered twisting out the Queen's red heart, chilly pleasure rippling through his spirit as the fleeting life escaped her heaving soul and the remnants of power clung to his own. It was an act of defiance. An act that, at last, incurred the fury and wrath of the green immortals. They cursed his life, making the exchange as he desired, forcing him to face the mountains and begin the work of a lifetime of study.

The reverberating crunch of iron on iron scattered his thoughts. A metal creature rose out of the searing heat, horns aglow from the intensity of the waters. Its eyes were hollow, staring and dead, its mouth a grim mask of slabbed iron. Fleshless arms creaked as it lifted them to salute Sarhorr the Ruler, looking down upon the work of his hands. He opened the portals of its mind and removed its screaming consciousness, tossing it back into transformative waters where thoughts were silenced. Sarhorr the Ruler lifted an object and peered into it until the wan face of his assistant appeared. Nervous eyes darted back at the him and the thin, high voice quavered as it whispered, "Nothing to report."

"Ah, but that is not why I called you. I have made something new. Look." Sarhorr the Ruler smiled as he turned the object like a mirror, looking down upon his new creation. "I call them Xeros, made from giants. They guard my lands, they guard the Tunnels, and let me tell you what they can do."

CHAPTER 11

THE FIRST OF MANY

The sun was still slumbering behind clouds when Crinte rose. He dressed rapidly in the darkness, tightening the belt on his pants, clamping on his battle breastplate, and yanking his green tunic over them. He pulled his black boots on and tucked daggers into the hidden folds. Finally, he fastened his sword at his waist and picked up the Horn of Shilmi. It was a small object, one he held securely in both hands. A band of gold surrounded the mouthpiece yet the horn itself was bronze and the opening was covered in silver. Its rounded edges shone with a light of their own, but even as he gazed on it, Crinte could tell it was whittled out of bone and molded in bronze, silver, and gold. His hands grew cold at the thought, and part of him wanted to return the horn to Legone and rid himself of the dark encumbrance. Yet, knowing better, he slipped it into a hidden, inside pocket of his tunic and left his dark chambers. No sooner had the door closed than he bumped into someone. "Crinte," she whispered frantically, grabbing his arm and not allowing him to move away. She leaned in to whisper in his ear. "It's gone. I woke up this morning and I can't find it anywhere. I've

94

searched and searched but it's nowhere to be found. We can't leave like this. Please."

Crinte pulled back to look at the distraught face of Alaireia. Her dark eyes were wide and she was breathing quickly. He took her face in his hands, calming her with his touch. "Where did you last have it?"

"I showed it to Marklus then put it away. I still had it when he left me."

"Who else did you see last night?"

"Legone. Marklus and I ran into him before, though. I don't know what powers he has but he could have followed us. You don't think…" Her words trailed off.

"Legone is nimble but no, he desires no obligation when it comes to power. Who else?"

"Ackhor, to hand over the message, and Starman." She looked searchingly into Crinte's eyes. "Crinte," she probed when he did not respond right away.

"You've said at times it flies off by itself?"

"Yes, but on this night? Right before we leave? Why would it forsake us?"

Crinte shook his head. "I know not, but I will keep my eyes open. Who else have you told?"

"Just you. I am not sure who to trust right now."

"Do not speak of it to anyone else."

Alaireia nodded, but she felt bereft. If someone had taken the Clyear of Power, they were lost. The abilities the Clyear granted were unnatural and gave the holder an advantage in any situation. Its gifts ranged from visions of the future to episodic increases of power. Typically the holder was faster, better, and

stronger than anyone they came up against. The Clyear of
Power did not conform to intent, darkness or light; it recognized
its handler only and followed their desires.

"We must go," he said, taking her hand from his shoulder.

"But Crinte, it is the Clyear; we can't just leave without it."

"Keep looking," Crinte said, "and find the others. This is an
opportunity we cannot pass up on."

Frustrated, Alaireia pulled back from him. "You told Starman
he could go home?" she accused.

Crinte raised an eyebrow at the change of subject. "Yes, I
know you trust him, and I agree, I would prefer him to come
with us. But the choice must be his. None of us are walking into
this without being one hundred percent committed, and I need
that commitment from him if he is to come with us. He will
travel with us as far as Trazamy City. From there, we will leave
him at his own doorstep. We have until then to persuade him to
believe in himself."

"Crinte, I am telling you, we need the Clyear and we need
Starman. We will not be successful without both."

Crinte looked her in the eye and touched her shoulder. "Persuade him." Then, he rushed off down the stone hall and left
Alaireia alone in her agitation.

***

The warriors gathered in the entryway of the fortress. A
group of fifty was being sent out to quash the troop of turned
ones who had been spotted in the Forests of Mizine. They were

armed from head to boot and carried a variety of weapons. All of them had swords, daggers, bows and arrows, some carried spears, others maces and axes. Helmets in hand, they stood a fearsome force, waiting for direction. Ackhor had arranged the force and instead of naming Crinte their leader, named his brother, Tincire, the weapons maker, the commander of their raid. Tincire looked like a brute himself, standing taller and bigger than Ackhor, his muscles hard from years spent in the forge. He planted himself in front of the warriors, rousing them with his gruff voice.

"Warriors, today we march out to face the turned ones. The enemy on the other side of the sea continues to test our strength. Let there be no survivors this day to return to the other side. We go to battle to show them who we are. We stand our ground, we defend our countries, and we are a force to reckon with. Arise, warriors, and fight with me. Let us show them our strength." He raised his arm and the warriors raised theirs as well with a shout.

Elam the Gatekeeper gave the word and the gates of the Eka Fighting Camp creaked open. The sun was just beginning to rise as the warriors disappeared into the forest. Quietness settled across the woods as the warriors marched through. Aside from the constant dripping and frequent downpours, life itself seemed to have forsaken the Sea Forests. Even the warriors only spoke in hushed tones, if at all, stealthily moving through the trees, not bothering to cover their tracks for the rain washed them out. Now they wore their helmets, covering their heads from the wetness, yet it was still a miserable march. The hours passed slowly. The second meal came and went but the warriors did not stop. They ate as they marched and continued on.

Tincire signaled for scouts to run ahead. Crinte, in charge of scouting, motioned for Alaireia and Legone to follow him, and they dashed ahead. "See if you can find a trail, figure out which way they are coming from. I'll look ahead." He reached for a leafy tree trunk and within minutes was scaling it.

Alaireia and Legone looked skeptically at each other for a minute. "Let's look east," Legone suggested. Alaireia gave a brisk nod before taking off through the trees.

Crinte looked down for a moment as he balanced his weight on the fragile branches close to the treetop. For a moment, his vision changed and he thought he saw a fierce Xctas flying above a gazelle as they bounded through the forest. He shook his head and looked again, but this time the broad leaves hid his view of those down below. He raised his face to the sky and looked east as raindrops tumbled down his cheeks. His eyes showed him the stretch of trees and beyond them he felt his gaze zoom in over the landscape. Keeping still, he continued to look, searching for signs of life, looking for movement in the grasslands. His vision showed him nothing.

At first, Alaireia and Legone ran in sync, moving quickly and silently through the damp forest. Alaireia found herself surprised at Legone's skill; he was just as surefooted as she was, but as they gained speed, leaping over small bramble and bushes in the way, he began to outpace her. As he pulled away, she could see his strides lengthening and his speed increased. She slowed as she watched him vanish into the forest. She stood still for a moment, letting her heartbeat slow, then she turned towards the sea and ran north.

It was an hour or so before Alaireia and Legone returned to report to Crinte. "I scouted north by the sea. Nothing to report," Alaireia announced in hushed tones as she returned.

"I scouted east. Nothing to report," Legone replied.

"Let's loop back to the warriors. I will let Tincire know. Be ready to scout again at dusk."

The two nodded and jogged back together. Crinte watched them for a moment before following, but the trick his eyes played on him earlier did not happen again.

Evening fell, eventless and silent, the forest giving away nothing even though Crinte, Alaireia, and Legone looked ahead one final time. When they returned, Tincire called for them to rest for the night. At last, the warriors halted to set up camp, rolled out their bedrolls, and pulled out their meal rations. Soon, a low hum of voices filtered through the forest. Even in the darkness, scouts stood watch, though it seemed they were alone in the woods.

***

Marklus heard it first, and jolted out of sleep as if from a nightmare. He sat up quickly, brushing sweat from his forehead. Turning his head from side to side, he pricked his ears to listen all the more intently. "Crinte!" he whispered forcefully into the air.

Crinte sat up immediately, as if he hadn't been sleeping. "What is it?"

"I hear them," Marklus announced. "They are coming."

Crinte was on his feet almost before Marklus finished speaking. He reached for the Cron closest to him. "Prepare for battle," he whispered urgently. "Pass it on."

Marklus scrambled up, securing his sword around his waist and reaching for the bow and arrows that lay beside him. He turned in the opposite direction of Crinte as he snatched up his helmet. "Prepare for battle," he called in hushed tones, shaking the Tider near him.

All at once, the camp became an unorganized buzz of activity. Crons and Tiders stumbled out of sleep, some scrambling to pull on their armor and find their weapons in the husky darkness. Tincire hissed out orders, ignored as warriors speedily stumbled over each other, attempting to file into an orderly rank for the attack.

Marklus found himself back with Crinte. "They are nearly here. They will reach us first."

Crinte turned to see who was on the other side of him. "Legone, how good is your sight in the dark?"

Legone drew nearer. "Not as good as yours," he replied.

"Can you take them down from above?"

Legone nodded and began to climb the closest tree.

"This forest is a terrible place for battle," Alaireia remarked as she walked up to the Crinte and Marklus. She had already drawn her sword but stood calmly as if the impending battle did not bother her. "With the darkness and the closeness, it will be a wonder if we don't slay each other."

"Alaireia." Marklus sighed disapprovingly, shaking his head.

"What should I do?" Starman cried, agitated as he ran up to them, his hands shaking.

"Duck!" shouted Alaireia. She whipped out her blade and slashed at the creature that lunged out of the woods. Her sword cut into its belly and ripped it open just as Legone's arrow struck its head. The creature fell away and five more leaped in its place.

"Archers at the ready!" Tincire ordered from a distance.

"With me," Crinte commanded as he swung his sword around, connecting with the odd weapon the creature held in its hand. The creature bellowed and instead of drawing back for another attack, leaped forward as if to smash Crinte where he stood. Crinte threw up his sword hand and fell backwards to avoid the killing blow. He rolled to the side and leaped up on his feet in time to drive his blade between the creature's shoulders. With a roar, it fell, and another beast toppled on top of it, three arrows in its side.

Crinte lodged himself against a tree trunk for a moment. He tilted his head backwards and rolled his eyes back in his head before opening them again. His eyes glowed briefly as they adjusted to his night vision. He could see the creatures clearly now. They looked as if they had been made from globs of mud and stood taller than any Cron or Tider he had seen. Their build was quite stout, to the point they looked as if they were sagging with the weight they carried. Round bellies poked out from their midsection, giving them an off kilter gait as they lumbered forward. Their deformed faces appeared to be slowly sliding downwards toward their long, flabby arms. They carried thick, rough clubs which looked as if they were created from the nearest tree branches and stripped of all bark. The creatures did not walk but rather lurched out of the trees, smashing everything in their wake. Crinte raised his sword and moved back into combat, sticking the nearest creature's belly. Its insides fell open and the creature collapsed to the ground, roaring in frustration and pain. Crinte turned to survey the warriors and found Alaireia was on his right and Starman on his left. "Aim for their bellies," he called to them. "They are weak there." Two arrows whizzed past him, taking out creatures on the other side of the trees. Crinte glanced up briefly and noted Legone shooting from one of the lower branches. Marklus had carved out a circle and stood within it, shooting in all directions as best he could. Crinte turned his gaze to the trees where he could see dark shapes move towards them. "More are coming!" he shouted. "Pass the word to Tincire!"

"How many?" a Cron shouted back.

"I can't tell," called Crinte. Scenarios ran through his brain. Quickly, he sheathed his sword and reached for his bow and arrows. "Alaireia, I'm going to pick off the ones coming in. Keep this area clear!"

"Got it!" she shouted as her sword made contact with the club of one creature. She shoved it away, knocked it over, and drove her sword into it. Three strokes then death was her signature move.

"They are coming from the sea," said Starman, his voice quavering.

Grasping at the information, Crinte lifted his bow and shot a creature in what he could only hope was its heart. "Marklus,"

Crinte shouted above the noise, "take my place." Marklus' sensitive ears picked up Crinte's voice as he threw a dagger before bounding over fallen creatures to where Crinte stood.

"We need to get to the sea," Crinte announced, shooting arrows with Marklus for a moment. "We can win if we have the moonlight and drive them back into the sea. I must find Tincire."

Marklus nodded and concentrated on his aim in the dark. Every now and then, a slice of moonlight would filter through the trees and make it easier for him to hit his target. He stilled his heartbeat, lifted his bow, and aimed. Death flew through his fingers as a creature leaped out of the woods, arms in the air, only to be thrown backwards when the arrow slammed through its eye socket. Marklus grabbed for another arrow and realized he was already running low.

Suddenly, Legone appeared beside him in a blur, daggers in each hand. "I'm out of arrows," he said, standing behind Marklus.

"Take mine!" shouted Alaireia. In one hand she swung her sword, while with the other, she slung the quiver of arrows off her back and tossed them at Legone. He caught them quickly and before Marklus could blink, his bow was loaded and an arrow zinged off into the darkness.

Marklus did not have time to be impressed with his speed. "I hear more," he said. "We need to send them back to the sea. Legone, Alaireia, Starman, ready?"

Starman shook his head; he had no words to say. His hands would not stop shaking and the only thing that kept him going was the certainty that every time he swung his sword, a creature went down. They had not touched him but that did not make them any less terrifying. "Starman." He heard Alaireia's voice penetrating his fog of fear. "It's okay, it will get worse for a moment but we will end this. Legone, you're fastest."

"Point me in the right direction," Legone said.

But it was Starman who lifted a hand and pointed. "That way."

Legone turned, raised his arms, and hooted out the strangest sound Starman had ever heard. Then he turned and dashed off towards the sea.

"Clear a path!" shouted Marklus.

The creatures roared and dashed after the sound Legone was making, clubs raised. Marklus lifted his bow as the stampede began and took down as many creatures as he could. Alaireia and Starman had already left him and were running with the creatures, driving them onwards.

It took a moment for the rest of the warriors to come around but they did with a shout, egging the creatures on towards the sea. There was only one Cron who stopped in puzzlement and watched the battle being taken out of his hands. He realized his brothers' suspicions were right; there was more afoot than expected. For months he had been tinkering between choices but now, as the battle was swept down into the sea, he realized his mind had already been made up.

AFTERMATH

Moonlight flooded over the sea, providing enough illumination to reveal the strange creatures as they rose out of the water, clubs in hand, and leapt up onto the shore. Shaking the wetness from their mud colored skin, they moved towards the trees, only to find a steady stream of arrows hindering their progress.

Legone found himself surprised at how easily Crinte's plan was working. As he ran, he found the scattered trees closer to the sea filtering in more moonlight, allowing full view of his prey. He scaled a tree as soon as he reached the sea, taking out the lumbering creatures with his arrows. He could tell they were having a harder time seeing in the moonlight but even so, it wasn't long before he heard the roar of the other creatures catching up.

Alaireia and Starman arrived shortly after Legone. It was only after they reached the sea that Alaireia realized what a foolish plan it was. The rest of the warriors had not caught up yet, and in the light, she could see creatures rushing out of the sea faster than Legone's arrows could pick them off. Even worse, a mass of club-wielding, disfigured creatures turned on her and Starman as soon as they ran into view.

Everything was a blur for Starman. He could hear Alaireia yelling out orders but all he could do was bring his sword up again and again to protect them. The sea sloshed ahead of him and he could hear an odd whooping sound each time the creatures climbed onto land. Now in the moonlight, he could tell there were too many of them and his arms were beginning to ache from constantly swinging his sword.

"Garrrrrrr," three creatures roared as they descended on him. Starman lifted his blade to stop the onslaught as a club swung down on his sword with a loud crack. At the same instance, Starman reached for a dagger and threw it, blade up, at the creature advancing on the other side of him. It simply batted the blade out of the way as if it were a mere toy. Starman kicked out at the last creature, which only managed to throw him off his feet. As he thudded to the ground, he could see the creatures descending on him, clubs raised over their huge jiggling bellies. A crash echoed through the underbrush. Distracted for a moment, the creatures paused while Starman took the opportunity to wiggle out of their reach. Breathing hard, he began to frantically retreat even though he could hear the rest of the warriors catching up at last. They eagerly entered the thick of the battle and confused creatures began to retreat into the sea. Starman grasped the freedom in front of him and dashed eastward through the trees. Home lay somewhere near, and as the smell of death began to leave his nostrils, he knew he was heading in the right direction.

A shadow leaped up behind him and threw him to the ground, sending his sword flying through the underbrush. Starman went down with a cry, kicking and punching until he realized it was Alaireia. "Where do you think you're going?" she demanded.

Starman threw his hands up. "Just let me go," he wheezed, attempting to catch his breath. "This is horror. I wish to be no part of it!"

"Starman, why?" Alaireia pleaded. "At least come back with me. Stand with the victors and know you have aided in winning this battle. The first one is always the worst."

Starman shook his head. "I would not go back there. I need to find my own way."

"But you'll only be lost again, adrift in the woods. More turned ones will continue to come over. Where will you stand without protection?" She stood and held out a hand to help him rise.

"I have my sword," Starman retorted, crawling over to hunt for it in the thicket.

"You will be alone," Alaireia prompted, watching him. "Crinte said we will take you home, didn't he? Wouldn't you feel better traveling with us versus alone, not knowing where you are going?"

Starman sighed as his retrieved his weapon and sheathed it. "I'd rather not face the garrr-crats again."

"The what?" Alaireia questioned, taken aback.

"Those creatures—you know, first they yell 'garr', and then their clubs go crack, and it's all over."

"Huh, the Garcrats," Alaireia puzzled. "Will you come back with me?"

Starman walked up to her as the gentle glow of moonlight filtered through the trees casting an oblivious halo over the death and destruction occurring near the sea. "Is the battle over?"

"Let's find out." Alaireia turned to head back to the scene of potential victory but Starman stood alone in the wood a moment longer. He could feel his heart rate slowing, his hands had stopped shaking, and the heaviness of sleep had drifted from his eyes. He could still smell death behind him, but for a moment the fear was gone, and he felt as if he could walk straight home without incident.

***

Marklus raised an unbroken arrow in the air, threw back his head, and roared the battle cry of the victors. Around him, each warrior lifted their weapons and followed his lead. As Marklus rejoiced, he wished their enemies could hear their response. The warriors of Mizine were not going down without a fight. Even as the warriors quieted down, Tincire was shouting out protocol for the battle aftermath. Slain bodies were tossed into the sea while Marklus walked through the battle scene, seeking out the wounded and restoring them to full health.

When he'd first discovered he carried the power of life and death, his abilities seemed limitless; he could cure anything and anyone. But after the incident with his mother, he was always more careful. Holding sway between life and death seemed less of a power and more of a burden. Crinte passed him before pulling close. "Have you seen Alaireia and Starman?"

Marklus paused, glancing over the battlefield. "No, why?"

"Alaireia, I have news for her."

"Did you see a vision?"

Crinte nodded. "It changes things slightly, but keep to the plan."

Crinte moved on, leaving Marklus to continue his healing duties.

***

Legone had not bothered to swing down from the tree after the battle ended. The loftiness was a reminder of the Afrd Mounts. His homesickness lessened as he relaxed on a branch, gazing up at the now calm night sky. Crinte's warriors from the Fighting Camp seemed to be less affronted by his coldness during the battle. He considered telling them more but wasn't sure if they would understand why critical details were withheld from them. Crinte alone he could trust, and to solidify that trust, the Horn of Shilmi had been exchanged. The thought of it made him shudder. The others, he wasn't sure how clear their alliance to Crinte was. He would start with Alaireia the Ezinck. She clearly mistrusted him but he could feel the aura of power surrounding her, and it was exactly what he needed.

***

Crinte, finally spotting Alaireia, maneuvered through the trees towards her. A heavy hand landed on his shoulder and yanked him back. Crinte turned to find himself face to face with Tincire. A stretch of silence passed between the two Crons as they eyed at each other, neither ready to admit their hand in the turn of events. Tincire crossed his arms gruffly. "You are leaving with your warriors," his low voice rumbled, more of a statement than a question.

"What makes you think that?" Crinte replied defensively, crossing his arms as well, not giving an inch.

"My brother suspects you. You mean to break in the morning, leaving me no choice but to report you, and your comrades, missing after the battle. All five of you."

"You don't mean to try and stop us?" Crinte challenged.

Tincire's rough voice grew even lower. "No, I think you should go, but before you leave, come back to the Fighting Camp with us. I know time is of the essence but you should not leave without the weapons I made for you and the other four."

Crinte paused, reading Tincire for a moment, then nodded. "I do not want Ackhor to know we returned or to trap us in the Camp. Can you make it so?"

"Aye, there is a way out through the forge. No one will be the wiser."

Crinte reached out his hand and Tincire shook it.

***

Alaireia cleaned her blades, keeping one eye on Starman and the other on the sharp edges of her daggers. She did not understand why he wanted to run off alone into the wide world. She was sure he would not survive, but he seemed determined to push her away. Maybe he could see she was simply using him for his skills with the sword, but it was more than that. Crinte walked up, shattering her muse. She could not read his face, but he leaned in and whispered, "Change of plans. I know where it is.

CHAPTER 13

THE GIFTS OF TINCIRE

A day later, the Eka Fighting Camp saw forty-four warriors return successfully from their mission. They were welcomed back into the Camp and celebrated with a large meal and a break from training and war preparation while they entertained with tales of the battle by the sea. Their fearless leader, nowhere to be found, was reported to have returned to his forge, requesting to be left alone.

Meanwhile, Tincire led the five warriors through the tree foliage alongside the training grounds. "I have an entrance in the back but we have to hurry," he told them. "Once Ackhor realizes I went to the forge instead of reporting to him, he will come find me. My workers will delay him momentarily, but we must move quickly."

"I would rather Ackhor did not know how much or how little of a lead we have on him. A civil disruption is the very last thing we need right now," Crinte said.

"Why are we acting like this?" Alaireia asked, annoyed with the sneaking about. "I told Ackhor I was leaving with you,

112

Crinte, and he did not object. What makes you think he will try to stop us? Aren't we all on the same side?"

Crinte looked back at her briefly. "I am relying on new information." His eyes turned gold for a moment, speaking a silent warning.

Alaireia fell uncomfortably silent.

"Why are we going back for weapons?" Starman complained. "We have weapons. I don't want another sword."

"An excusable question," Marklus answered excitedly. "You likely don't know, but weapons made by Tincire contain a sort of mythical element. I don't know how he does it but rumor has it he makes the best weapons in the land. A weapon handcrafted by Tincire is one of the highest honors a warrior could receive. We are lucky to have him on our side."

"But I am not a warrior," Starman protested.

"You'll see." Marklus winked good-naturedly.

Tincire paused at a clearing in the woods and reached behind a large oak tree for a hidden door. He pulled a rusted black key from inside his tunic, twisted it in the lock, and yanked the door open. "Inside, and quickly," he growled.

The five moved into what looked like a storage room which was immediately secured in darkness as Tincire shut and locked the door. He moved his hands over the floor by memory until he pulled open a trapdoor, leading down. "Follow me," he called.

The air grew chilly and musty as they descended into the earth, yet Marklus could already hear ironworkers at the end of the passage, and Starman could smell the sharp sting of fire searing onto metal. They could all feel the coolness melting away into blasting heat as they stepped out of the wide passageway into the forge. Flames leaped from one side of the room while a small flurry of Crons constantly hovered around it, keeping the fire burning bright, taking pieces of metal in and out in such a quick fashion it was a wonder they did not burn themselves. Even as the golden yellow flames licked up every inch of fuel, ironworkers hammered bright orange pieces of metal on anvils, causing a beautiful shower of sparks that winked across the workspace as they brought their hammers down again and again. Each of the Crons had a similar build to Tincire, broad shoulders, and thick arms with hair pulled back from their flushed faces. The Crons did not even glance up when Tincire entered with the five. They continued to work tirelessly, their huge muscles bulging.

Tincire led them across the room to a wide wall rising ten feet above the ground and covered in long swords, short swords, small, thick, and curved daggers, bows and quivers full of arrows, and other strange, fearsome weapons. The steel glinted deviously from the wall, as if each weapon had a spirit of its own, birthed from the flames. A light gleamed in Tincire's eyes as he stood in front of the wall, gazing at his handiwork.

"I have experimented long with these weapons, and now I know why." He looked back at the five briefly. "The perfect combination has come together and I do not believe it is a coincidence." He reached up and pulled a medium length sword from the wall. Its hilt shone silver in the light and as Tincire pulled it from its sheath, the blade appeared to leap and dance, as if begging for combat. Tincire held it dearly for a moment,

114

like a father reluctant to let go of a child, then placed it back in its sheath. He turned.

"Starman, this is your sword. You will find it will serve you well on the battlefield and if, at times, it seems to lead the way, follow. This sword knows how to slay its enemies."

Starman's protests died on his lips. Despite himself, he found his arms reaching for the sword, welcoming it home with his very actions. As his hands touched it, he felt an odd calming sensation, as if the sword were whispering words of promise to him. He felt a new hope surge within him, and not waiting to unfasten his old sword, he pulled the new one from its sheath and gazed on the blade as light danced within it. "Thank you," he said in an awed whisper, his eyes never leaving the shiny blade.

Tincire turned back to his intimidating wall, reached up, and took down a much longer sword. The hilt was simple but covered in silver like a jewel. As he pulled the naked blade from the sheath, a sharp gold line appeared, running vertically down the blade. Despite themselves, the five could not tear their eyes away from it. "Alaireia, your sword has a minor mesmerizing power if your enemies gaze too long at the gold light. It will also provide light in darkness. Soon, you will learn how to control it."

Alaireia stepped forward to receive her gift, speechless for a moment. "Tincire," she breathed, "this is incredible…" She faltered. "I will use it well." As she lay her hand on the silver hilt, the gold line on the sword flared for a moment but calmed as Alaireia slid the sword back into its sheath. She buckled it around her waist and stood tall, feeling she had earned a new power. Tincire's intense face softened for a moment as he smiled fondly at her before returning to the wall.

He pulled down a medium sized bow carved of a dark wood, and a quiver full of blue tipped arrows. "Marklus, these are for you. The bow is newly made of wood from the Algrema Forest and carved with old symbols of our country, Mizine. The shaft of each arrow is dipped in blue instead of white, which symbolizes Mizine. Let them be a warning to all you come into contact with. Mizine will not lie idle while plots are formed against us. You cannot miss with these arrows. They are light but will fly quickly and hit their mark strong and true every time."

"Many thanks." Marklus reached for his gift, gazing at the markings on the bow in admiration. As he placed the quiver of arrows on his back he thought he heard hushed voices. He pricked his ears for a moment but all was still within the quiver.

"Crinte, I give you the sword of a leader." Tincire pulled a sword of great beauty from the wall. Its hilt was gold, but as he revealed the blade, strange markings winked into view before disappearing again. Tincire handed the sword to Crinte. "You will find it will serve you well."

Crinte held up the sharp blade, testing the weight of the sword but it balanced perfectly in his hand. Even as he looked at the blade he saw images dash before his eyes in a blur.

"Thank you, Tincire, this gift is…" Words failed Crinte for the first time as he gazed at the blade.

Brushing Crinte's words away, Tincire turned back to the wall for the final time. "Legone the Swift, these are for you." He pulled down another set of bow and arrows. The bow was quite similar to Marklus', made of dark wood and engraved with

116

symbols of Mizine, although it, and the quiver, were slightly bigger. "The quiver was made to keep up with your swift and nimble way. It never runs out of arrows."

Legone stepped forward with a brief nod and fitted the quiver onto his back. An odd sensation passed through his fingers as he did so, bringing back the long-forgotten memory of a darker power.

"Now you are truly prepared for your quest. You must go quickly before you are discovered here. Crinte, I have mapped out your way through Cromomany. Stop by the home of Oman the Farmer and tell him I sent you. He will prepare horses to speed you on your journey."

"Tincire." Crinte reached out his hand. "We cannot thank you enough. I feel much more confident in our success, knowing you have prepared us for battle. We will send word as we continue on. A time will come when we will join forces again and wipe out the abomination which has taken hold across the sea."

Tincire shook Crinte's hand and nodded briskly and gruffly. "Go now, and farewell."

AN ANCIENT POWER

Legend told that in the beginning, gifts were bestowed upon the Four Worlds to remind its inhabitants they were not alone in the miraculous land they were given. These gifts hinted at a greater potential to those who found them and learned how to wield their powers. Seven such gifts were bestowed and they were called Clyears. Each one held a particular identity, which could be used in combination if one held the others. But there was one Clyear which superseded them all: the Great Clyear of Power. It was an ancient power source and only as powerful as its owner. Some said the Clyear of Power chose its holder; others claimed the holder chose it. Either way, it had been passed from generation to generation, fought over by kings and queens, divided brother and sister, brought together the most unlikely friends, and was used, misused, and abused, until it was finally lost for years. It had last been seen in the South World but now had appeared unexpectedly in the Western World. The hunt for the other six Clyears was only a story for curious children, the hope that there was still a quest for those who were not yet grown, that they might seek adventure throughout their years.

Those were not the tales Legone held in his mind as he walked stealthily through the halls of the Fighting Camp. Holding his new bow close to his lean, hard body, he brought up the vision Crinte had transferred to his memory. Again he saw the ceramic pot blending into its surroundings. He saw the hands that placed it on the shelf and moved several scrolls in front, hiding it from curious eyes. Legone stood still in the hall, shaking the vision from his eyes. All was quiet and he moved on. His eyes began to burn the closer he walked and he blinked them rapidly, not caring for the temporary power Crinte had lent him.

Early morning after battle, Crinte had pulled him aside. "Legone, I have a task for you. Will you accept it?"

Legone stood in the dewy darkness and nodded his bare head. "I will. What do you ask of me?"

"There is an object that lies back at the Fighting Camp. It was stolen from one of our own and I need you to retrieve it for us. I know where it rests, but risk drawing attention to myself. It would only cause another delay I wish to avoid."

Legone simply listened. At this point, he was not one to question Crinte's wishes, as long as his ultimate plan was coming to fruition.

"I can guide you with my mind," Crinte went on. "Will you let me share my sight with you?"

Legone sighed. "As long as you don't make this a habit."

Crinte smiled slightly. "Just this once. Close your eyes and focus. Tell me what you see."

"I am returning from the training grounds. They are empty but it is an hour when warriors should be training. I am entering the fortress. There is no one around. I am walking through passages and halls, climbing staircases, headed towards...Ackhor's room...humm...it

119

is empty. I see shelves and scrolls and behind those scrolls a ceramic pot. Now all goes black."

"Good," Crinte coached. "Now hold that vision in your mind and follow it. You will know when you have reached the end. Once we leave Tincire, head to the fortress. After you have stolen the ceramic pot, meet us back on the road that leads towards Cromomany. Give to Alaireia what you find."

"Alaireia?" Legone asked, dizzy for a moment as he recovered from the vision.

"Trust, Legone. If we don't trust each other, how will we fight and win together?"

Legone stood outside Ackhor's chambers. He felt every inch the intruder and hoped there would not be any unpleasant surprises waiting for him on the other side of that door. He turned the handle slowly but the door swung open without hindrance. Legone felt the gates to a different world had been opened to him. Strange and fantastical creatures danced on the wall, brought to life by the ink they were created by. Stacks of books and papers covered the room and light streamed in, highlighting the dust and dirt collecting in the corners. Legone shut the door gently behind him and turned in the great room, losing site of the vision for a moment as jagged memories flooded his mind. He remembered spending days sitting in sunlit halls reading books of old, opening age ridden scrolls to find what lay there, learning the language of the "wild things" and practicing it until it flowed as fluidly from his lips as the language of Mizine, called Miften. Legone reached out his hands and picked up a book. He flipped through its pages for a moment, watching the dust fly off it and dance in the sunlight before settling nearby on a pile of scrolls. Was he truly ready for the task laid before him? To lead the four warriors into a dark land, full of secrets, to discover its biggest one?

Frustrated, Legone closed his eyes, recalling the vision Crinte had given him. He walked forward, passing shelves until he reached one towards the back of the room. He opened his eyes and brushed aside a pile of scrolls. They scattered at his touch, rolling out of the way, some dropping into the floor like a gentle rebuke. Legone reached for the neutral, ceramic pot he found behind them. At first he was tempted to look inside, but realized if it was something Crinte wanted, he probably had no interest in it. Their desires did not often align. He held it for a moment, then reached around and slid it into his quiver. If anything did happen, it was likely the last place anyone would look. Quickly replacing the fallen scrolls, Legone decided it was time to return to freedom with the others. He was just replacing the last scroll when he heard voices on the other side of the door.

"How dare he return without coming to me first. Does he seek to undermine my authority in this place?"

"He asked to be left alone in his forge," a calmer male voice replied. "But we can interrupt his solitude if you prefer."

"I'm supposing Crinte and his band of rebels did not return?" Legone now realized the voice had to be Ackhor's, and the second one belonged to Elam the Gatekeeper. He glanced around for a place to hide.

"If they did, they are with Tincire."

There was a pause as the handle jiggled, then, "I will speak with Tincire first." The footsteps began to retreat. "Find me a locksmith. I want a lock put on my door immediately."

121

Legone remained frozen for a few moments longer before opening the door and peering out. A glance both ways told him the halls were deserted once again. He quickly closed the door behind him and fled. The front entrance of the fortress was heavily guarded. All that remained was for him to sneak out to the training grounds and loop back around to the road that led towards Cromomany. Even as he rushed through the Fighting Camp, he could tell the celebration had dispersed and the warriors were returning to their daily training routines. Acting as one of them, he stood tall and joined a group of warriors as they walked to the training grounds. From there, he left them and ran east, his feet barely touching the ground.

***

Ackhor stood firmly in front of his younger brother, his arms crossed and face set. "Explain yourself!" he demanded as Tincire looked up from the flames.

Tincire lightly tapped a piece of metal with a hammer and sat it down, ushering Ackhor out of earshot of his workers. "What is your beef with Crinte?" he asked gruffly.

Ackhor tapped his foot impatiently against the warm stones. "Crinte's actions are the problem. He has his mind set on crossing the sea to antagonize a monster. Does he not realize retaliation will be swift and strong, and destroy us all? We are only rebels; the armies of Mizine are not united. If war comes to the countries of Mizine, we will be thrown into irreversible chaos. Yet he turns a blind eye to this and persists with his own plans. If the leaders of the Fighting Camp cannot be united, what hope do we have to save Mizine?"

Tincire crossed his arms and stared into the fire, his brow furrowed. After a moment of thought, he looked back up at his brother. "Ackhor, you know I am always with you. But, what if Crinte and his small band of spies succeed in sneaking into Slutan, and provide valuable information on how to end this once and for all? Once we have that information, we can use it as leverage to unite the armies of Mizine and attack Slutan and Asspraineya before they have time to attack us."

Ackhor balled up his fists in frustration. "That is a risky plan we cannot put much faith in. Armies alone cannot stand before the transformed ones. Our army of rebels can only do so much to protect the countries of Mizine, and even in that we risk a death by treason. King Arden of Norc may be on our side, and he will join. But how will you convince King Dain of the Afrd Mounts? Who will go to Cromomany and risk a beheading to bring King Merek over to our side? The leaderless peoples of the Algrema Forest hide from us, and the Trazames of Trazamy City will never join our cause. We need to more than just unite all Rulers of Mizine. We need power..." His words trailed off as his thoughts began to take form.

"Then, you will not send a troop to return Crinte and his warriors?" Tincire questioned.

Ackhor shook his head impatiently. "No, let him choose his own death. Now tell me, what new weapons have you crafted of late?"

Tincire's face beamed as he led Ackhor to the wall and began to explain.

It was mid-afternoon when Legone finally saw the four ahead of him, and despite his cold heart, realized he was returning to where he belonged. He paused for a moment to lift the object out of his quiver, then settled for a walk, his long strides quickly bringing him alongside the others. Crinte, out in front, turned his head. "Welcome," he called. His eyes met Legone's for a moment and the two nodded knowingly.

Marklus, in step with Crinte, turned as well. "I was wondering where you got off to. It's not the same without you."

Legone fell in step with Alaireia and Starman. "Actually, we were talking about you," Starman began. He stood a little taller, and a determined light sparked in his eyes, his mopey demeanor all but disappeared. "I've decided to call Alaireia Lightfoot since I can never hear her approach, and she does that shadowy thing. I'm called Starman, for no fault of my own, and I'm going to call you Swift, because you're like a streak of lightning."

Legone grimaced for a moment. "They do call me Legone the Swift," he replied formally.

"Swift it is, and now for Crinte and Marklus…they are hard. Marklus, would it be strange to call you Healer?" Starman called.

"Yes," Marklus instantly replied, shaking his head in disapproval.

"Lightfoot," Legone murmured, passing her the ceramic pot.

Alaireia looked at him, confused. "What is this?"

124

"I don't know. Crinte asked me to retrieve it and give it to you."

Alaireia twisted off the top with some difficulty and looked inside. She gave a small cry of shock as she pulled out the object and dropped the pot on the ground, where it shattered into pieces. Crinte stopped and turned at her cry. The other three followed his lead, curiously surrounding Alaireia as she held up the object for them to see. "The Clyear," she breathed.

It looked like a winged horse carved out of the finest crystal, yet as the five stared at it, a radiant light began to stream from its wings. Catching the sunlight, it turned into a prism and shot out a rainbow of light from every angle, bathing their faces in color. Even as they breathed in, they could feel some unknown ability stirring and awakening within them. The crystal winged horse stretched its legs, tucked its wings behind its back, and bowed to them. Then, spreading its clear wings once more, it flew to Alaireia's shoulder and there it disappeared. Yet the light remained a few seconds longer as the five gazed upwards until at last the sharp reds, vibrant blues, electric greens and deep purples faded into their skin. There was an intense moment of silence as they attempted to process what had just happened.

"What was that?" Starman whispered, gazing wide-eyed from Crinte to Alaireia.

"The Clyear of Power," Alaireia replied. "I have never seen it do that before."

"I can still feel it," Crinte added, "almost as if it blessed us. Don't you feel the power surging within you?"

Starman still looked just as confused and lost. "What is a Clyear?" he asked.

"It is an ancient power," Legone began, his voice low. "There are six of them, and each possesses a trait the holder of it can use if they know how. There is also the Clyear of Power, the seventh, which holds all of the traits of the six. The one who wields its power must be strong and wise, lest it be the destruction of us all."

Alaireia felt the sting of Legone's last words as he cautiously warned her. "Where did you find it?" she asked him instead, steering the conversation away from the dangerous topic.

"In Ackhor's chambers," Legone replied, missing the look in Crinte's eye as he shook his head.

"Oh." Alaireia said flatly. "Are you sure?"

"Yes, I used Crinte's vision." Legone nodded.

"Oh." Alaireia's voice sounded tiny as she looked from Legone to Crinte, her face transforming from surprise into guilt. In one bold move, she lit off down the path.

CHAPTER 15

THE CLYEAR

Too stunned to react at first, Legone, Marklus, and Starman stared after her as she disappeared into the trees. Crinte, realizing something was indeed amiss, immediately leaped after her shouting, "Alaireia! Stop!"

"What just happened?" Starman asked in confusion, looking to Marklus and Legone for answers.

Marklus shrugged. "Let's find out." He moved forward off the road in the direction Crinte and Alaireia had gone.

When the bewildered trio finally caught up, Alaireia was standing in a clearing, looking defensive. Crinte stood in front of her, his arms crossed with a frown upon his normally calm face. "Alaireia, what's going on?"

"Crinte." Alaireia reached out a hand as if to appease him. "I never wanted to tell you this but…" She paused, looking for an out.

Crinte just stared at her, his face set.

"Okay, Crinte." Alaireia took a breath. "Technically, the Clyear belongs to Ackhor." She took a step away from him and waited.

"Alaireia." Crinte's voice rang with disapproval. "You mean I sent Legone to steal something which belonged to Ackhor the whole time?"

"I know you're upset," Alaireia said, "but I can explain."

Crinte ran his fingers through his blond hair in frustration. "You can explain? Alaireia, we need Ackhor on our side! I sent him a slightly threatening message with a clear indication of what kind of power we have the ability to use should he choose to ignore our needs, and now I steal the Clyear back from him? He likely needed it as insurance against us, and now he has nothing. What do you think will happen?"

Alaireia sighed and looked over at Marklus, Starman, and Legone, who all stood at the edge of the clearing, a distance from the two. She waved them over impatiently. "If you hear my tale, you will understand. But we should put as much distance as possible between the Fighting Camp and us. I will tell you all when we rest for the night."

Begrudgingly, Crinte walked past her, his face a mask of thoughts. "We should hurry, then," he said tersely.

An aura of silence surrounded the warriors and even the willowy trees seemed to frown down upon them as they continued deeper into the forest. The hum of impending rain and the buzz of hidden creatures captured their senses. It was not until the mysterious lightning bugs of the forest began winking in and out of view like a watch in the night that Crinte called for them to halt. The fading sunlight shot prisms through the broad green leaves of the wood, as Alaireia sat, cross-legged, on the grassy knoll.

***

Crinte was quiet as he sat down across from her, his silence bringing an air of oppression to the gathering. Marklus sat down beside him, but Starman placed himself a safe distance away. Legone stood to the side, watching the forest, his bow in hand.

Alaireia stared off into the trees. "I was born in Srinka in the Forests of the Ezinck, a country called Quaziner." She spoke quickly, barely letting one word drop away before she uttered the next. "My people dwelt in the southwestern corner of the forests within reach of Oceantic. For those of you who don't know," she glanced briefly at Starman, "Ezincks are people of the land, friends with the plants, beasts, and sacred grounds of the beautiful forests. The Healers lived in caves near sparkling waterfalls, and almost every day, I walked the botanical gardens to learn from them how best to cultivate and thank the land for the bounty it brought us. I learned to care for the weak and help them stand tall, and fight to defend my lands, although peace was, at that time, the one ruler of Quaziner. I learned to face my fears, to hunt the beasts of the air and of the land, and to build my home. I never expected to leave those woods. Even my father told me there is nothing good outside of the forest. The countries that belong to Crons and Tiders are always full of strife. The conquest of power and constant bickering between the free countries of Mizine is not a political war any should desire to be part of. I was content, nay, satisfied to live out my days chasing the beauty of the forests of Srinka.

"One fateful day, while hunting with my cousin, Alegore, we chanced to stay out much later than intended. I will never forget that night. The stars burned through the heavens as evening dropped and a chill descended on the forest. Fearing a storm, Alegore suggested we seek shelter in a nearby cave. When we entered, we saw a wondrous silver light pulsing from within the subterranean tunnels. Curious, we began to follow the path that led towards the light, marking a trail for our return. As we progressed, a sense of foreboding overcame us and we realized we treaded where we were not wanted. We looked at each other, asking the unspoken question: should we safely retreat, or continue into the malevolent domain? Heat began to rise as we drew further. While it was preferable to the chill outside, we could tell it was an unnatural heat. At one point, we stopped to draw our daggers and crept forward until the cave widened. The path came to a stop and dropped off, opening up to the great floor of a cavern which lay below us. Around the edges shone the silver light, but its source we could not determine, for a great beast lay slumbering in the belly of the cavern.

"The vision of that beast made me want to gaze on its strength and power yet run at the same time. There was something hypnotic about the way it slept in its own heat, curls of white smoke gently filtering out of its large nostrils. Such a creature could be nothing more than a demon of the dark world. It had two great legs, each one about ten feet long that curled around its immense body. At the end of those legs were wicked claws, outstretched as if ready to defend the creature, even in sleep. The silver light highlighted the tips of the creature's scaly back for it was covered in a tough hide that glimmered in the lighter shadows. Great wings lay folded on its back, and short horns grew out of its head and its long body stretched away into darkness. A moment was all it took for us to realize we looked on a Wyvern, a horror from tales of old, known to have disappeared from these lands. What brought it back, I do not know, but in its lair by Oceanic lay hidden the Clyear of Power." Alaireia looked at the expectant faces listening to her tale. Again, she felt the anguish of that time well up within her and threaten to choke her voice with pain. She lifted her chin and thought of the task at hand.

"By the time Alegore and I reached the end of the cave, the storm had started to rage. Rain pelted the underbrush of the forest as we ran to warn our people before the beast awoke. Only we were too slow and too late. We had barely run a mile when slices of lightning began electrifying the forest, and above our heads, we saw the winged beast glide by, aroused by the storm, keen to hunt. There has always been one detail I have been unable to decipher. How did the Wyvern appear in our midst unknown? Ezincks know the forest like a child knows their mother and father. It was as if the creature materialized out of nowhere and slept until the storm came. Everything that happened after that seemed intentional, as if a greater force was ordering events."

Legone, who had been watching the darkening forest while Alaireia told her story, now turned. His eyes bored into her as she spoke those last words. His expression, ever watchful, began to change as he took in the new information. He opened his mouth to speak, but thought better of it as she continued.

"That night, the storm and beast were one, ravaging the forest, searing the delicate leaves of plants, felling trees, destroying homes, and terrorizing the animals of that land. Even as Alegore and I fought through the tempest, the spirit of the forest broke and wilted before the onslaught. We could feel it limping and mourning for what was lost, and when at last the brutal night ended, the forest was not one we recognized. I cannot explain what it was like to come home to find it a smoking ruin. Many were crushed while they slept, and those who survived stood wailing in the destruction. We felt death take that land, and Alegore and I promised we would kill the beast.

"It took us a couple of days to find the resources we needed, but it was one morning as we watched that Ackhor and his Crons entered the forests of Srinka. Crinte, I have told you this before; they were searching for a treasure that brought them to the edge of the world. They were lost at that time, and I, worried they would obstruct our plan to kill the Wyvern, went down to warn them. Ackhor was surprisingly sympathetic; he had entered the forest the night of the storm, but did not know the damage that had been done. He agreed to join us in destroying the beast—partly, I believe, because he is a Cron, and Crons do not back down from a challenge, but also because he knew the Wyvern would interfere in his treasure hunt. He brought supplies and better weapons he shared with us, promising to help us rebuild as soon as our enemy was vanquished. I must say, Ackhor surprised me. He was the first Cron I'd met, but he actually kept his word, which made me begin to wonder, for the very first time, of venturing into the world outside the forests of Srinka.

"Wyverns fancy water holes and darkness. Using that knowledge to our advantage, we strategized a plan to end its domain in Quaziner. It was near nightfall when Alegore and I took to the coast, bows in hand. We lit fires up and down the shore in part so that we could see, and also to replicate the fires from the storm as much as possible. Ackhor and his Crons set up a perimeter around the Wyvern's lair to prevent it from coming back home and to provoke it to hunt by Oceantic.

"It was a clear night when we took our places and waited. I remember the quiet lapping of Oceantic as it rolled inland and back out. The fires danced as the cool air threatened to quash them, and finally, a dark shape shut out the starry night as it glided noiselessly over the water. For a moment, I thought it might fly off across Oceantic, never to be seen again, but it dived and turned, and that's when I stood and took aim. Alegore and I, standing on opposite sides of the shore, assaulted the beast from both angles, aiming for its tough wings. We shot in a flurry, using all our arrows, but most of them glanced off the beast. A few of them struck true, making the beast roar in fury until it flew away from Oceantic to heal its wounds. We waited for a while, but it never returned that night. At last, I went to find Ackhor and tell him of our failure.

"When I reached the cave, his Crons told me he was inside. Again, I walked the tunnels, and again, the silver light pulled me in deeper. This time when the path ended, instead of finding a beast in its belly, I saw Ackhor. He stood in the pit and the silver light filtered around his feet, clearing a path to what he desired. I could feel myself gravitating towards the light as well, and when I called out to Ackhor to tell him the creature was still alive, I was not surprised when he motioned for me to join him.

"Climbing down into the cave was like climbing down the face of a cliff, yet the unnatural heat was gone and the malevolent spirit had dispersed. When I reached the bottom, the silver light was much brighter and I could see they were actually silver horses, winking in and out of existence. For the first time, I forgot my anger and grief and stared in wonder as Ackhor took my hand and led me further in. We followed the horses until we reached a sub terrestrial kingdom, and there darkness was eliminated. As we watched, the silver lights gathered together until they formed a full sized winged horse, which stood at least fifteen feet tall. As we gazed on it, the light burst away and it became flesh and blood. It looked at both of us and spoke. "I have come at a time of great need. Use me well." Its throaty voice echoed around the cavern and when it stopped speaking, Ackhor held the Clyear of Power in his hands and the light was gone.

"It was daylight by the time we left the cave, and when we reached the outside again, Ackhor handed me the Clyear and told me I would need its power to slay the Wyvern. He told me my need was greater than his at that moment, but a time would come when he would require the Clyear. But as soon as he placed the Clyear into my hands, I knew it was mine and I knew exactly what to do. I took my sword and killed the Wyvern that same day, and the forest began to heal. I left my cousin, Alegore, in charge there, and took my leave with Ackhor and his Crons. We've been close ever since, bound by the finding of the Clyear and his selflessness in sharing his gift. There have been times when he has held it, and times when he lent it back to me. But my need is still greater than his. I cannot return it yet."

As her last words dropped away, Marklus was the first to stand. He walked over to her and placed a warm hand on her shoulder. As she looked up into his gentle eyes, she felt something surge through her, holding her pain and grief at what was lost, mending the broken places within her soul. For a moment, it felt as if someone were holding her tight, pulling her away from the edge of a cliff, but when they let go, she felt as though she would remain safe and secure for a time. Just as quickly, Marklus dropped his hand and Crinte stood.

Alaireia blinked rapidly as she turned to hear Crinte's words. He looked at her, his face unreadable. "I see," he said. "I can neither condemn nor affirm your actions. I had hoped your relationship with Ackhor would allow him to see our point of view, yet holding a token of power that should belong to him might alienate him further." He sighed. "Nevertheless, in the morning, we will continue with all speed. My goal is to travel to the mountains to meet with Srackt the Wise. He will know how to unite the armies here while we are on the other side of the sea. I must also meet with the Mermis, for we are in dire need of their assistance. But first, we go to Zikeland."

Marklus, who had been gazing off into the trees, turned back to the company. "Zikeland will be dangerous," he warned, and blue sparks momentarily sprung from his fingers.

CHAPTER 16

ZIKELAND

Days later, the scattered trees of the Sea Forests of Mizine
ended abruptly, leaving the five standing before rich, green
grasslands, stretching over unending rolling hills. Here and
there, golden stalks of wheat lifted their buds to the warm, yellow sunlight. Sun rays danced over Marklus' head as he took a
tentative step into the green meadow, cautiously stepping
through knee high grass.

Ten years earlier, he had turned back for one last glimpse of
Zikeland, taking in the ripples of carpeted green, relentlessly
holding tight to the dark secrets of the land. His vision had been
fuzzy and blurred with tears he'd hastily attempted to wipe
away, lest his mother and father see signs of his weakness.
Home was ingrained deeply within, his very soul united in the
roots of the tender soil, and leaving was ripping him apart. His
neighbors had left one by one after the Zikes awakened, scared
off by the incidents. First, stiff, frozen animals appeared nightly.
Then, people began vanishing, and finally, one day, the wind
ceased to blow across the prairie, soothing and cooling many a
weary traveler. Marklus could not forget the cold panic that rose

136

like bile in his mouth the day his older brother, Locklen, never returned home. He had sat on the doorstep past midnight, watching the silver light gradually fade into rays of a blood orange sunrise. His ears pricked, attentive, listening to the silent vibrations left by the absence of the wind and loss of a beloved brother. Inside, he could hear his mother pacing as she watched and worried.

He felt a pang of guilt each time he saw her in pain, knowing if he had not been so eager to use his gift of life, she would have passed from the world, never knowing another moment of sorrow. He wasn't sure how it had happened; maybe the Zikes had poisoned her with a slow death. Maybe it was an illness, but she declined, slowly and surely. Yet as she ailed in her sickness, Marklus was surprised at how much peace and calm she felt. "It is my time," she'd told him. "You have to let me go." As the land declined as the people groups of Zikeland faded, so did she. Until Marklus, unsure of the strength of his powers, pulled her from the doorstep of death, back into the land of the living. As soon as he did it, he saw his mistake. He saw the look on his mother's face when she awoke, and the hidden glimpse of disappointment when death forsook her. He did not understand it, how she had wanted to die, to pass from those lands. Her life had never been the same, though. She grew old and frail, and there was an unhappy pain behind her eyes. After that incident, everything that happened to his family took a turn for the worst. And every time he looked at her, he knew it was his fault, and cursed the power of life and death.

Thus, that night, Marklus had waited, alone, until he knew what he must do. Since his father had not yet returned from his last trading trip to Trazamy City, which lay to the northeast, it was up to him to take action.

Earlier that morning, when dawn snuck over the horizon, Locklen and Marklus had tumbled out of bed and torn out of the hut. With faces still smug with the telltale signs of a blissful night of sleep, they shoved each other playfully as they strode out, bows in hand, to check their traps. Locklen had been buoyant that day, his feet floating off the ground, unable to stay still. He was seventeen, three years Marklus' senior and a tall, strapping Cron. His bronze face crinkled when he smiled and his curls danced over his head charmingly. He was always excited and optimistic in a coy way, his warming persona causing everyone he met to instantly love him. Even the animals of the prairie could not stay away from him, and he had names for them all. Often, when Marklus returned from another adventure with Crinte, he could hear his brother playing his flute over the grassy knolls, and oft times he danced with the wind. Marklus and Locklen were children of the land, loved by it, raised by it. Giving up and letting go was not a reality Marklus could forgive himself or his parents for. He was sure the Zikes had a hand in Locklen's disappearance, even though they'd feigned innocence when confronted. It was only months after Locklen's disappearance that his parents cowered before the unforgiving land and moved to Cromomany. Marklus, in bitter frustration, had not returned since.

Now an eerie whisper of silence blanketed the land. Birds did not fly overhead, small woodland animals did not roam, gathering food for their young or storing up for the winter ahead. "Home," Marklus whispered, lifting his pale face to the light and drinking in the unfiltered air. Perking up his sensitive ears, he waited for the familiar voices of home to fill his senses, welcoming him back and begging him to stay. Disappointment was swift as a deep hum of undercurrent tension met his eardrums. Otherwise the land appeared empty and stale. Swallowing hard, he turned to the four standing behind him, unable to hide the keen pain creeping into his eyes. "Come on." His voice sounded dead as he beckoned them.

Alaireia fell alongside him, glancing anxiously at his face. "What happened here?"

"Do not ask me that." Marklus shook his head at the insignificant question. "Much has happened here in the last twenty that years words cannot explain. I have asked myself again and again; what powers allowed these Zikes to enter my land and turn it into a barren one?"

Starman crept nervously behind Marklus and Alaireia, his brown eyes wide as his gaze darted quickly across the still prairie. "What are Zikes?"

"Creatures of the grass," Marklus replied bitterly, cautiously placing one foot in front of the other. "They are often invisible, maintaining a green camouflage unless tricked into revealing their true form."

Starman shivered. "Why are we here?"

"This is the quickest route to Trazamy City," Crinte offered. "And we are in dire need of armies we can control. The Zikes offered their help if we should ever need it. We return to claim that offer."

Starman turned his frightened gaze on Crinte, a turmoil of questions rushing through his overtaxed brain. "But they are a menace!" he sputtered.

"That is true," Marklus agreed angrily as he spat his next words out. "They draw their fiendish ability from a deadly poison, but if we could persuade them to use it against our enemies, we can claim the upper hand."

"Poison?" The word fell from Legone's lips like a dagger, and he mechanically reached for an arrow. "Twenty years ago, you say? Alaireia, when did the Wyvern appear in Srinka?"

She glanced back at him, her eyebrow lifted in consternation. "Ten years ago. Why do you ask?"

"The portals…" Legone's sky colored eyes glazed over, staring into nothing as thoughts flittered through his brain. Distressing memories of forbidden words spoken in hushed corners of the forest rekindled the clarity he was seeking.

"Legone?" Crinte's voice called him out of the void, snapping him back to the present moment.

"It is nothing," Legone lied, shaking his head warningly at Crinte.

***

As the five walked through Zikeland, they saw the wrathful wildness the empty land had become. The blades of grass mirrored each other, bravely holding their faces to the sunlight in the windless prairie. Marklus guided them through the grasslands which sometimes stood as tall as their heads and stung their fingers when touched. But Marklus refused to let them cut the grass out of their way. Lost in their own thoughts and cowed by the intoxicating ambience of secrecy, their heavy words lay unspoken. It wasn't until sunset that Marklus finally halted and turned to the others. "I hear stirrings beneath our feet. They know we are here."

"I don't like this place," Starman said uneasily, looking at the ground and glancing over his shoulder.

"That is the very reason no one lives here anymore," Marklus told him.

Crinte turned his farseeing eyes over the land, walking slowly in a circle as he looked north, south, east, and west. "All is clear, as far as I can see," he announced. "We should camp here for the night, but keep watch."

Alaireia was the first to put down her pack and sit on the overgrown hillock. Hungrily, she pulled a bite to eat out of her pack while the others followed her lead. "Marklus, is there much game to hunt out here?" she asked, reaching for her bow.

Despite the unique weapons gifted by Tincire, the five continued to carry other daggers, blades, bows, arrows, and any other weapons they could tuck away without becoming too laden down.

Marklus shook his head. "There used to be. Herds of antelope hiding in the tall grass, foxes and cougars slinking through to chase them. We had the birds of the air and the animals of the land, larks, ravens, rabbits, badgers, snakes. They were all here, from the horned monsters dominating the grasslands, to the moles underground. But the animals have left as well. I do not

141

know what Zikes hunt, but when we began to find stiff, poisoned animals, it became clear what we ate was not safe anymore."

Starman lay his portion of the last meal down, his appetite suddenly gone. "We are next," he mumbled, dropping his hand to his sword hilt. A shock vibrated through his body as his fingers brushed the sword, as if it were begging to be used.

Alaireia sighed and looked over at him, suddenly curious at the strange Trazame. "Starman, did not you have to walk through Zikeland in order to reach the Sea Forests of Mizine? It would have taken you weeks to go around."

Starman wrinkled his face at her, confused. "What do you mean? I was in the fields of Trazame one moment, and the next I was lost in the forest."

Alaireia narrowed her eyes. "That's not possible."

"Everything is possible these days." Crinte's gentle voice wafted over the prairie.

Starman hung his head, miserable at his circumstances. "I wish I were home."

Alaireia, feeling bad for snarling at him, stood. "I'll take the first watch."

"I will take the second," Legone offered. "But it's doubtful we shall sleep in these lands."

"It's the silence," Crinte told them as he sat, chewing methodically and watching. "Back in the days I dwelt here, the wind was always whistling nearby. Sometimes I thought I could see it, brushing through the grass as if it were combing its hair."

"I remember." Marklus' voice spoke of longing. "I could hear it whispering, speaking a strange tongue to the growing plants and creatures."

"If the wind should return," Crinte added thoughtfully, "I think the others might begin to. Wind made this place home."

"If I could persuade the Zikes to leave, I would be the first to claim this land again," Marklus lamented.

Legone moved closer to Crinte and Marklus, his voice hushed. "You might not have to persuade the Zikes to leave. Crinte, you still have the Horn of Shilmi?"

Crinte's face contorted as if Legone repulsed him. "We should not use that here," he warned.

"You can use it to drive the Zikes out and send them where you wish."

"What is this you speak of?" Marklus looked curiously from Crinte to Legone. "Is there another ancient power source?"

"It is dangerous," Crinte objected. "We do not truly know how to use it, and there will be repercussions for abuse of power."

Unhappy with Crinte's answer, Marklus turned to Legone. "What is this Horn of Shilmi?"

Legone opened his mouth but realized Starman and Alaireia were now listening intently. "I discovered it during my time on the other side of the sea in Asspraineya."

"And what is its purpose?" Marklus demanded.

"If you use it, you may align the minds of those you think of, to help you achieve your purpose until you release them," Legone explained.

"It is mind control," Crinte interrupted disapprovingly. "It is no better than the transformed."

"But what of dark creatures, like the Zikes?" Marklus protested. "Is it wrong to use mind control on them?"

"It must be our last resort." Crinte's voice was distant.

"Crinte," Alaireia spoke earnestly. "Sometimes I feel as though I know what you know and we are of one mind with our quest. Times like these, you seem to know much more than you are revealing. Why?"

A full moon began to hover on the edges of the transitioning sky as Crinte spoke. "I want each of you to know what I know, but knowledge is daunting. Sometimes it is better to walk blindly for a time. As we continue, there is little I can do to shield you, but at least until Starman is home, let us continue. When we reach the house of Srackt the Wise, I will tell you all that I know."

***

Marklus woke on the hard ground, shivering in the cold. The moon hung pale and wan in the starless sky. His companions lay in an enchanted, deathlike sleep, and he felt his heart pounding as he rose in the darkness. Moonlight flooded the prairie, showing him quite clearly exactly what he expected to see. The Zikes surrounded him, their numbers blending into the shadows of the night. They stood patiently, just as he remembered them. Hundreds of round, emerald eyes stared at him from expressionless faces, if they had faces. Their four-foot-long bodies were hidden by blades of grass, but the green cones of their heads hummed in unison, binding them together. Marklus waited, fighting to calm his racing heartbeat.

"Why have you returned?" the Zikes demanded, their voices raised in unison. "These are our lands now."

The overwhelming smell of fresh cut grass began to infiltrate the air, and as the voices resounded, Marklus was reminded of the rich earth, allowed to grow freely without a multitude of Crons thwarting it. For a moment, he saw the land as the Zikes saw it, and he understood why. "I am Marklus the Healer, one you cannot harm. Twenty years ago, I awoke you from your slumber, and you took these lands as your own. Unasked. Unwelcome. Now, a new force has taken over the northern side of the Western World, and I need you to fight with me."

The Zikes laughed as Marklus spoke, a horrible, haunting laugh that rippled through the prairie, giving Marklus goosebumps as he stood, waiting. "What is in it for us?"

Marklus kept his voice stern. "You will leave these lands and never return. Otherwise, this new force will take over what you claim as home."

"Never." The Zikes continued to laugh. "We are invincible."

Marklus stepped forward, years of pent up rage overwhelming him at last. "You are not invincible," he declared, his voice becoming louder as he continued. "Your power belongs to me. You will not poison this land or the people who dwell here unless I say so. Your day has come. Your tricks have ended. The time of the Zikes is over, unless you fight with me!" When he ceased speaking, blue waves crackled on his fingertips. The laughter of the Zikes had died away and Marklus could feel their fury sparking in their green cones. He moved closer. "I am invincible." For the first time, he reached out and touched the green cone of the closest Zike.

A bang popped his eardrums and Marklus felt his body forcefully hurled backwards. He hit the ground with a jolt, the air knocked out of him. Spots of green light danced before his eyes as he opened them, unseeing for a moment. When he put a hand to his ears to stop the ringing, his fingers came away glistening wet with blood. Slowly, his vision began to clear and Marklus struggled to rise. The white moonlight shone across the grassland and Marklus saw the prairie had been flattened and the Zikes lay prostrate before him. Even before he opened his mouth, he could hear their voices in his head.

O Marklus the Great Healer, we will fight for you, you own these great lands and you are invincible. Your will is our command.

Marklus could feel the oppression of the Zikes lifting as he again stood before them. "Rise," he commanded. "Go to the Dejewla Sea and protect our borders. You shall harm no one except for the turned creatures that come from the other side. Slay them all. A troop of you shall follow me at all times. I am going to the Great Water Hole. When I call, you will come, and we will fight together. Then, and only then, you will return to your slumber underground, and never wake until you are needed once more."

O Marklus the Great, the Zikes murmured, we hear and we obey.

Slowly, they began to shrink back into their camouflage as blades of grass. As Marklus watched, he saw them scurrying through the grass, and even as they left he could hear their now high-pitched voices ringing in his ears. *Hurry. This way. To the sea.*

He turned back to look at his companions, who continued their enchanted sleep. Sitting cross-legged on the ground, he waited and watched as the moonlight faded and the sunrise began to spread over the horizon. At last, the heaviness on his heart began to lift.

***

Crinte sat up in confusion, his mind hazy, his tongue thick. He blinked his eyes slowly, forcing them to accustom to the morning light. He felt sore and stiff, as if his body had been forced against his will. He rose hastily, reaching for his pack and noting Legone, Alaireia, and Starman nearby, still sprawled out uncomfortably in a haphazard slumber. Marklus stood a few feet off on a hilltop, the sunrise bathing his silhouette in light. His shoulders were up and back, his head held high. He looked much stronger and taller. "Marklus, what happened?" Crinte slowly climbed to stand beside him. "I don't remember much from last night but the air feels…" He toyed with words for a moment before settling on one. "Different."

Marklus' face beamed with pride and satisfaction. "Crinte, the Zikes have surrendered. They are on our side now."

Relief flooded Crinte's face. "Well done, Marklus! I knew you had it in you."

"Indeed." Marklus crossed his arms. "I did not realize they needed a display of power to bring them under control. I should have known because it was healing you that made them take notice the first time."

Crinte placed an approving hand on his shoulder. "Marklus, when this is all over, if we survive this, your country will be waiting for you to make it home again. Not just how it once was, but a place where all the animals of the land will dwell in peace, and those who return will delight in the safe haven you create. For as long as you stand between life and death and hold control over the wellbeing of the beasts of the land and air, there will be peace in Zikeland."

Marklus felt thrills of power fluttering through him, but he could not help but feel those words were spoken twenty years too late.

Legone woke with a jerk, finding himself uncharacteristically sleeping when he should have been keeping watch. He noticed the vibe of the countryside as he rose, quietly calling Alaireia's name to wake her. She, in turn, reached over to shake Starman.

They stood slowly, gazing unsteadily about. The grass was flattened in every direction as far as the eye could see, as if still bowing from the events of midnight.

"We should make all haste," Crinte called, gathering his supplies. "Marklus has sent the Zikes to guard the sea."

Legone picked up his bow. "I'll scout ahead," he volunteered.

"As shall I," Alaireia replied, pulling her pack onto her shoulder.

Legone nodded at her and the two ran off, side by side.

Marklus, watching them, shook his head. "They went the wrong way."

Crinte looked in the direction they had gone. "They will come back around," he said. "Come, Starman, it is time for you to go home. If you still wish it."

Starman hastily gathered his things, "Good." He shuddered. "This land is strange. And you say you used to live here?" He shook his head, already dreaming of a warm homecoming.

***

They had not been running long when Legone dragged Alaireia to the ground. Breathless and surprised at his actions, she pushed him away from her. "Swift, what is it?" she asked, staying low and glancing at their whereabouts.

Legone squatted beside her. "I wanted to be out of earshot and eyesight from Crinte and Marklus. I have a favor to ask of you."

Alaireia, annoyed at his actions, glared at him. "Why don't you want the others to know?"

Legone held her gaze. "I want to be sure of myself and I don't want to answer to the one they call Starman."

Alaireia looked away from his piercing blue eyes. "Because he is leaving. I know."

"He is a coward," Legone muttered.

Alaireia punched his shoulder. "I am tempted to leave you without hearing this favor you ask. Crinte may trust you, but you've given me no cause to."

"The Clyear," Legone said. "You said you found it in the lair of the Wyvern. What else did you find there?"

"Why?"

"I seek the truth. When I dwelt in Asspraineya much was hidden from me, but I learned there are portals between worlds. The Green People managed to close one, but a portal leaves remnants in its wake. I'm starting to believe portals have been opening across the Western World, and when they do, dark creatures come through them to terrorize the land. Here in Zikeland a glimmer of a portal remains; maybe one does in Srinka as well."

"What does it matter if it is true?" Alaireia demanded. "There is nothing we can do about portals."

"There, you are wrong. If we know how many portals have been opened in the past twenty years, we have an idea of how many creatures have come through and what we might deal with as we pass into Asspraineya."

Alaireia looked into his cold face and, sensing she had the leverage, asked, "Swift, what actually happened on the other side that made you this way?"

Legone looked away.

"Lightfoot," he faltered, "I must borrow the vision of the Clyear to ensure we are on the right path, but I am afraid to look. When I left Asspraineya, I fled like a fugitive. You who have lost everything know what it feels like to stand on the edge and look down into the abyss. As long as I stayed in the mountains, I could forget. Now I must go back and right the wrong, but all the pieces have not come together yet. I need your help to make it so."

"Do you know what you must do?" Alaireia reached for the Clyear.

"I must go to the Green People and ask them how to break this dark force that now rises."

"Why must you break it? Do they not have power?"

Legone gazed on the Clyear. "When you have family, it is hard to destroy them. Family knows you better than anyone else. They know what your actions might be before you take them. They know when weakness will strike you. It is better the blow come from the outside."

Alaireia paused. "I know your secret. I read the words of the scroll Crinte gave to Ackhor. I know that he was one of them until they forced him out. Have you met him? What is he like?"

"Yes." Legone's voice was small and haunted. "There is nothing right about him, nothing redeeming. How could they think they could save him?"

Alaireia opened her palm and a mist blew over Legone's face. "Look, and see if your path is right."

He opened his eyes, and opened them again, and he looked, and he saw, and he knew. When he turned to Alaireia, there were tears in his blue eyes and she did not know what to do. "Swift?" But even as she said his name, behind him she saw a dark mass on the horizon, moving rapidly towards them.

***

"Legone and Alaireia are catching up," Marklus remarked as they plodded east.

Crinte glanced behind and for a moment again, he thought he saw an Xctas flying and a gazelle bounding their way. "They are running, fast. Something is wrong."

Starman nervously followed Crinte's eyes, but he saw nothing stirring in the grasslands. Marklus stopped walking. He lowered himself to the ground and pressed his ear to the earth. For a moment, he felt the awe and reverence of the soil as it stirred beneath him. Then, he heard the muted thud of a great many footsteps marching in sync across the ground. He leaped up, and searching his mind, called, *Zikes.*

Eager voices chimed back in his head. O Marklus the Great, we hear, we obey.

Slow them down.

There was a rustling as a small troop of Zikes scattered throughout the grasslands. It wasn't long after they were gone that Legone and Alaireia appeared. "They are coming!" Alaireia shouted. "We should run!"

"What have you seen?" Crinte asked.

"A dark mass speeding our way," Alaireia gasped. "More of those foul creatures in this land."

"The Zikes have gone to distract them," Marklus confirmed.

"There are no hiding places in this land," Crinte agreed. "Our best chance is speed. Come!" And he set off in a dead run across the plain.

STARMAN'S HOMECOMING

Days later, weary travelers crossed the border of Zikeland into Trazamy City, an ever-growing trade point, farmland, and home of the peaceful Trazames. Trazamy City hummed with life as the five warriors entered, coming to well-manicured lands full of color and vibrant energy. Starman, exhausted and dirty from trying to keep up with the others as they raced through Zikeland, smiled and relaxed. He turned his grimy face on the city and raised a hand. "Welcome to my home!" he exclaimed jubilantly.

In the distance, low lying buildings rose out of the ground. Waist high stone walls surrounded the structures and even gates had been constructed. It was not a rich city, and the poor attempts to make it look so made it seem even more a country town and less a magnificent city. As they walked towards it, a tanned shepherd led fluffy gray and white sheep out to pasture.

Goats grazed here and there, keeping the stretch of green before the gates trim and neat.

"I have never been here," Alaireia remarked curiously as she strode beside Starman.

"You are in for a treat," Starman boasted excitedly. "The city is bursting with endless varieties of food and flavors, and the meats are a special cut, thick and juicy. The wines and ales will make you heady and happy. Best of all are the celebrations of a great harvest. We celebrate for days and everyone travels to the city to feast."

"A life spent eating and drinking," Legone murmured under his breath.

Starman took no notice of his stinging words. "I must check my orchard first," he went on. "The goats will have missed me. I hope they haven't destroyed too much..."

"Starman," Crinte interrupted, "how long until we reach your home."

"A few days. My family lives in the farmlands on the outskirts of the city. It's peaceful out there; I feel like I can breathe."

"Well then." Crinte smiled at the others. "It won't hurt to stop at the nearest inn to rest and refresh."

"I know exactly where we should go," Starman announced, and led the way into Trazamy City.

Intricately designed leaves intertwined with fruit and vegetables covered the city gate. Someone had clearly taken great care to create an archway that welcomed visitors to the land of plenty, yet the gate was made of wood instead of iron, and the bolts that held it shut were wide open. The archway was decorated with carved grapes and goblets, depicting the drink

Trazames loved most, the fruit of their labor. The city opened to a wide, cobblestone road of green, with persistent weeds growing over the stones. Around the homes, built in a tight row, grass grew and danced around slabs of gray steps that led upwards. Here and there, gaps in the rows displayed even more stained brown buildings with thatched straw roofs and sky painted doors. Despite the unique conditions, each building had a smoking chimney out of which delicious aromas flowed, making mouths water in anticipation.

At last, there was life and sound again, mothers warning their little ones as they dashed through the street in bare feet and loose hair, eager to gather as much sunlight as possible. Children shouted and laughed as they played, ducking around the traders and animals that blocked their path. Goats and sheep bleated contentedly as they grazed from feeding troughs and pockets of green weeds. Chickens pecked here and there, left unattended to fend for themselves. One squawked angrily as a Trazame tripped over a nest of eggs it had laid in the middle of the road. The roar of Trazames and Crons bartering and trading filled the air, doors opened and slammed, and people yelled out sales, bargains and discounts from their booths. It was a beautiful, chaotic city, sizzling with energy.

"They are too close to the sea to be this unprepared," Crinte whispered urgently to Marklus. "If a raid swept this city, it would be gone in the blink of an eye."

"I am surprised Ackhor does not have troops stationed here," Marklus replied. "I thought that was his goal."

"It is, or it was. There are those who think little of the Trazames, but they deserve protection as well."

155

"I can have the Zikes send a message."

"Please do. Tell them to let Ackhor know the cities by the sea are unprotected and we sense more of the turned creatures."

Zikes. Marklus summoned them in his head and sent them off.

"Aha!" Starman gestured at the building they halted in front of. "We have arrived at the Ajke Inn, where the traders from near and far stay." Indeed, a large brown building rose out of the ground, almost leaning over onto the street with the weight of the tales it carried. Its door flapped uneasily on broken hinges and above it a crooked sign was nailed into the wooden door frame which read: Ajke Inn: Home of the Nutty Ale. "At last, good food, good drink, and a warm bed!" Starman opened the door and blissfully sailed through it.

Marklus, Legone, and Alaireia turned questioning eyes to Crinte. "As he said, good food and warm beds." He looked at them warningly. "And mind you avoid the heedless talkers."

The heavy smell of meat and garlic drifted past their noses and rough voices assaulted their ears. The entry hall opened into a wide, windowless room, dimly lit although lanterns hung from the four corners of the chamber. Low, round and square wooden tables were scattered in a haphazard way across the floor with chairs and benches pulled up to them. A tall white candle burned in the middle of each table, but it was hard to see, for the room was already crowded with mostly Trazames and a few Crons scattered here and there. A haze of smoke from a combination of steaming food and tobacco pipes hung over the air. The aroma of fresh bread tangled with roasted potatoes, the sharp tang of onions, sautéed squash, and cuts of lamb and mutton roasted to such perfection the meat merely slipped from the bone.

Starman had already climbed behind a table and was dipping his face into an enormous mug. He waved them over enthusiastically. "I already ordered a meal for us, the very best, and the innkeeper is preparing rooms. Come, sit and enjoy!"

The boisterous roar of voices and laughter dropped, and curious eyes turned on Crinte, Marklus, Alaireia, and Legone as they weaved between tables towards Starman. A low hum began across the room as Trazames and Crons alike gossiped, pointing at the five. Starman, noticing the change, shook it off. "They probably want to know what you have come to trade, and we haven't seen an Ezinck in these parts...well...ever."

"We should eat and leave. I don't like this place," Legone murmured.

"These are goodhearted people," Crinte rebuked him. "They mean us no harm."

"Have you been here before?" Starman asked.

Crinte nodded. "I have been most everywhere this side of the Western World. I feel a pull within my spirit and must follow where it leads."

A plump maid with sunflower braided hair and cheeks smudged with flour brought them piping hot bowls of soup, topped with a crusty round of bread. She smiled shyly at Crinte before rushing away beyond their sight. A moment later, she reappeared with tankards of nutty brown ale to refresh their palates. Starman almost slurped gravy out of his bowl in his

157

haste to enjoy the legendary food of Trazamy City. Even Legone's features brightened as he bit into the warm bread and felt its buttery crust melt in his mouth. Marklus' first taste reminded him of winter in Zikeland, when his mother would make a thick stew out of carrots, onions, potatoes, and the best cuts of meat from deer, rabbit, or lamb. Alaireia could almost name the flavors; a lick of salt, a sprig of parsley, a hint of lavender, and some other rare herbs. Crinte felt the warmth fill his body and he was thankful he could give his warriors a brief reprieve.

No sooner had they drained their bowls of the last delicious drop of stew than an unruly Cron at a nearby table leaned over, his unkempt wild hair spilling into his face. Stroking his dark beard conspiringly, he looked at Crinte. "You seem familiar," he said curiously. "An armed Cron, stomping in here like this with representatives from each of the people groups. Are you from Norc?"

"Why do you ask?" Crinte questioned, although his ears perked up at the thought of news from the country to the west he was born in.

Marklus, sitting across from Crinte, looked curiously at the sloppy Cron, a name on the tip of his tongue.

The Cron dropped his voice and leaned in closer to Crinte, his round eyes bright, lively. "On account of your clothes. You have no symbol of authority on your cloak, the sign of fealty to a Ruler. Everyone knows the King of Norc supports the Rebels."

Crinte looked at him evenly, offering no words, while Marklus turned his head sharply, his eyes peeling across the room. Alaireia and Starman conversed quietly while Legone sat at the end of the table, a grim look on his distrusting face. The

Trazames and Crons in the Inn had left off staring at the five and were caught up in their own business once again.

The Cron guffawed at Marklus' caution, slapping a hand over his bearded mouth as his eyes danced from Crinte to Marklus. "There are no soldiers here! Don't you know, Trazame is a free, unruled country? What do they care here for rebel armies and political gain?" He lifted his tankard of ale and raised a skeptical eyebrow.

"What do they call you?" Crinte asked in response. "One who speaks so boldly must have a name? And if you know so much, why haven't you joined the Rebels?"

The Cron's face widened and he stuck out a hand, causing long locks of hair to dance across his face. "They call me Simon the Brave."

"Simon?" Marklus chimed in, sticking his head around to get a good look at the Cron's face. "I know that name! You sold me a horse not long ago in Cromomany."

Simon the Brave gave a sly grin. "Oh, but it was long ago. How did that horse turn out?"

Marklus shook his head. "I would say I was swindled but you warned me well. Crinte, this fellow is harmless enough. Although, Simon, I am surprised you still have your head."

Simon stroked his neck lovingly, his lively eyes lifted to the ceiling in mock gratefulness. "Yes, I have been in many a tight spot. If only my tongue would stop a-flapping, I might be able to live a peaceful life."

Marklus shook his head, a boyish grin spreading across his face. "You and I both know that will never happen. Come, tell us what news you have of the world."

Simon pulled his tankard closer and leaned in towards Crinte and Marklus. "Ah, but if you are with the Rebels, you already know. We are doomed, scattered, leaderless, and those destructive creatures are coming to take over."

"Everyone knows that," Crinte interrupted. "The question is what are you going to do about it?"

"Well," Simon the Brave said as he leaned back, shaking his tunic until he found a pouch of tobacco. He plopped it carelessly on the table and reached for his pipe. "What am I going to do? Stay here in the happiest place in the world, with food, drink, and females." He winked at Marklus. "What else am I supposed to do? Join the Rebels?" He laughed. "That's what you would do!"

"Actually," Crinte lowered his voice, "joining an army would be too boring for you. Wouldn't it? No, for a Cron of your personality, you'll need more. You like to talk, wager, make rumors on the fly, and walk right into the lion's den, if you don't mind me saying so."

Simon smirked as he struck a match, concentrating on lighting his pipe for a moment. He puffed for a second before turning his dark eyes on Crinte's face, Marklus forgotten for the moment. "Normally, I would not let just any Cron talk to me the way you do. What do they call you? And what mission do you have for me? Because I just might be in the mood."

"I have no mission for you," Crinte countered. "No direction for a loyalty challenged Cron such as you. All I will say is that each of the ruled countries of Mizine has a Ruler with a harsh edict against joining the Rebels. Yet each Ruler has an army, but they force Mizine to remain, how did you say it? Leaderless.

Scattered." Crinte stood. "Only a fool would start a rumor. Only a fool could trick the Rulers into combining forces."

A band of fiddles and flute players struck up in a corner, drowning out conversation with their boisterous melodies. The lively crowd began clapping, some dancing, while Crinte and Marklus left the fool, Simon the Brave, to smoke thoughtfully into his mug of ale.

That night, the five warriors washed away the travel stains and slept with full bellies on beds of straw. Contented and happy, it seemed the darkness spreading from Slutan was all but a dream.

Trazamy City lay inland at the furthest point from the sea. Still, a journey to the Dejewla Sea from the city would take at least a week. The farmlands of Trazame were spread out, surrounding the city, some only as far away as a three-day walk. There were those who dwelt closer to the sea and others that lay closer to the east, towards Wiltieders and the Afrd Mounts. Starman and his family lived in the lowlands, a three-day journey from the sea. They had never ventured there and never expected to, but twice a year they made the trek to the city to feast and trade and celebrate.

"I see why you love it here." Alaireia fell in step with Starman the next morning after they had eaten and reluctantly left the Ajke Inn. "The city is part of the world, yet it seems untouched by the troubles of the world. You have strangers walk in and out of your midst, but their opinions do not hold sway here. I am impressed with the caring and generous attitude of your people. If I had known, I would have come here sooner."

Starman looked into her dark face. Her eyes shone with sincerity and for a moment he wanted to embrace her. "You mean that?" His face lit up in a smile. "You should come back here, when it's all over and the turned ones are no more."

"I would, Starman," she replied gently, "but where I am going there may not be a return."

Starman's face fell. "Do you think the enemy is truly stronger than us?"

"Only that he has the upper hand because he has been strategizing his takeover much longer, and he has created the turned ones. Now that is an unnatural power. Starman." She touched his shoulder, forcing him to stop and look at her. "He will not stop until he has vanquished all lands, even Trazamy City. Will you come with us and save your home from being destroyed?" Starman looked down but she went on. "I have seen my home claimed by the darkness and all I cared about wiped out. I would spare anyone from knowing what that grief feels like."

Starman gently laid his hand on hers, looking into her earnest face. "I have never traveled. And I don't know how or why my steps took me so far from home. But it is an adventure I do not regret. I have met you and learned much of this world. I have seen the sea and the forests and the prairie. I have trained at the Fighting Camp, fought Garcrats, and run from invisible armies. I have met Crinte and Marklus and Swift, all great warriors you travel with. But that is enough for me. I am home now."

At his words, Alaireia sighed, but she thought of the Clyear and the deception she could wrought using its power. The thought briefly slipped through her head and her eyes glazed over for a moment, heady with the knowledge. As her vision cleared, she shuddered and her eyes met Crinte's. He was a ways ahead of her and Starman, but for some reason he looked back, directly at her, and she felt as if his eyes perceived her thoughts and disdained them.

The humble city of Trazamy disappeared from view as they entered the peaceful farmlands of Trazame. Starman knew almost all the farmers, and the first night they slept in a barn and in the morning enjoyed a bountiful meal from the generous farmer and his wife. The second night, all was still and barren. The farmers had gone; even their animals were missing. A foreboding hung in the air, making the five talk little and travel quickly. Even Starman, sure of his way, woke early on the third day, marching forward with an anxious determination. It was not until mid-afternoon that he spoke. "I can't smell home," Starman whispered. Standing still, he lifted his face to the wind. "I smell..." His face grew pale and his words dropped away. A realization began to dawn, and with a cry, he began to run.

"Starman!" Alaireia cried, but Crinte held up his hand before she could run after him. He walked forward a few steps and turned his far-seeing gaze on the land before them. "Danger approaches. Marklus, what do you hear?"

Marklus pricked up his ears. Zikes. There was no response. "Nothing," Marklus said after a moment. He put his ear to the ground and continued to listen, worried the Zikes were not answering him.

"I was afraid of that." Crinte continued to look around. "Alaireia, go to him. We'll sweep the land, although it looks like the turned ones got here before us."

Starman ran, not ready to believe what his nose told him. His feet pounded over the ground but already he could see the ruin of his family's farmland. The farmhouse was flattened, the barn merely a pile of rubble. There was no one left. No people, no animals, nothing. "Nonononononon!" he howled, pounding down the dusty path to where his home used to be. All that remained was the wall surrounding the land. When the farmers first heard of the turned ones, they had begun to build walls around their lands—better to secure themselves inside and wait out the raiders rather than actually take up arms. Obviously, they had built too slowly. Walls had been mowed over, fire set to buildings, and the gray ash Starman ran his fingers through was still warm. Starman stood in the destruction, his black boots stained with the ash of ruins. He lifted a hand to wipe moisture from his face, leaving trails of soot on his cheeks. In disbelief, he gazed about, searching for any clue of life. Falling to his knees as the truth sunk in, he threw his face to the wind, clenched his fists, and screamed in rage.

It was a rending sound of heartbreak that ripped through the land, and Alaireia, walking hesitantly towards Starman, understood it all too well. She remembered years ago, when she had run, heart in her throat, back home, only to find the beast had beat her there. She recalled standing outside the charred ruins of the glade her family called home, knowing they hadn't even had time to escape. Cursing and screaming, she'd vowed revenge until her anger turned into panicked wailing and she had collapsed in grief. Now, she walked towards Starman. His face was red, his muscles contouring as the grief blindsided him. He looked at her and she saw the bloodlust behind his eyes. "Who-ever did this, I will kill them all. I will make them pay." His voice was a low growl.

"Starman?" Alaireia questioned hesitantly, reaching out a hand. But the look in his eyes frightened her.

A NEW FORCE

The morning Starman had strayed from home had been fair, just as beautiful as the day before. The generous sun blazed over the earth, warming the turned dirt with its light. Even before he opened his eyes he could smell fresh bread and bacon, and hear his younger brother and sister chasing each other round the kitchen. His mother was still scolding by the time he tumbled out of the loft, pulled on his tunic and pants, and found his way to the table. His two older brothers had already left for the fields as they always did at sunup, while his older sister fried more thick slices of sizzling bacon and affectionately refilled his plate. "Going fishing today?" she asked him. "I could use another huge catfish."

"So you shall have many!" Starman announced. He snatched one last mouthwatering bite, grabbed his fishing rod, and jaunted out into the sunlight. Intoxicated by the beauty of the day, he strode unhurriedly through the farmland as he made his way to the watering hole. It was tucked away, a calm, secluded pond the neighboring farms shared. Mayhap there was a magical hue to the waters, for fish from that pond averaged three feet long and provided one of the most heavenly meals in Trazame. Which was saying a lot, since the food and drink of Trazamy City was legendary. Starman planted his line deep in the muddy water and settled down, hidden by the tall bulrushes, to wait. Bug-eyed dragonflies hummed lullabies as they passed overhead, their silver wings almost invisible in the sunlight. Frogs hopped through the mud, freezing in camouflage for a moment, croaking out warnings as shadows flew overhead. Eventually, Starman woke from a nap and checked his line to find it, surprisingly, empty. Hungry, he got up to search for food, remembering he had passed an apple tree on his way. He meandered along, humming a tune to himself, and did not realize when a flash of light appeared. Oblivious, he tripped over the remnants of a portal and landed in the Sea Forests of Mizine. From there, his life had taken an unexpected turn and four weeks later, when he finally arrived home, he could not understand why he'd escaped their fate.

A sound made Alaireia turn to the north, where the road to the sea led. Indeed, a dark mass was coming, traveling quickly in a southeast direction. "Starman, we have to run."

His hands went to his sword and even as he closed his fingertips around the hilt, the blade sang. "No." He stepped forward, his voice quivering with emotion. "I will kill them all."

A distance away from Starman and Alaireia, Crinte and Legone watched while Marklus lay with his ear to the ground. "Something is wrong," he said. "Either I have lost control of the Zikes or…" His voice trailed off. "I hear something coming. It is a large group and they travel swiftly."

"I see them," Crinte replied. "Starman is angry and hurting and seeking revenge. He is going to fight them."

Marklus leaped up. "Not good," he began, but the voices of the Zikes interrupted him. Marklus the Great. Run! We cannot hold them all!

Legone drew a blue arrow from his quiver and fitted it into his bow. "I need higher ground. Marklus, are you coming?"

Surprised at the offer, Marklus nodded as adrenaline began to course through his veins. "Crinte, we are doing this?"

"Yes, we can only run for so long. If we don't fight, it will be the death of Starman. The broken walls may be the highest ground you can find, even though it is not ideal. I will go down to Alaireia and Starman. If we use the ruins as shelter, we may have a chance."

Crinte walked over to where Alaireia and Starman had been standing earlier, only now, Starman continued to walk towards the dark mass, sword in hand, his eyes black with anger. Alaireia followed closely behind him, drawing her sword and looking worriedly from Starman to the encroaching mass. She was not concerned about the actual battle, but she knew, firsthand, the false strength grief presented. The Starman she knew had run from the last battle, in fear of the turned ones. Now, there was no telling how long his bout of fury would last. When at last he came to his senses, would he run again? She thought about using the power of the Clyear to keep them safe, but the thought passed fleetingly as vibrations tingled through her fingers as they grasped her sword. The gifting words danced through her memory: *Your sword has a minor mesmerizing power if your enemies gaze too long at the gold light.*

Alaireia raised her sword above her head as the turned ones drew nearer and the sharp gold line blazed bright in the sunlight. Starman was running now, his mouth open in a cry of rage as he raced to meet the Garcrats who drove forward eagerly, roaring and waving their clubs. There was a brief pause as their eyes were involuntarily drawn to Alaireia's sword, slowing their momentum. Starman, taking advantage of the moment, ferociously drove into their midst, gritting his teeth and slashing his sword at the first Garcrat he reached. It raised its club slowly but he chopped off its arm, whirled around and sliced his sword through the guts of the creature behind him. Five lay dead behind him before Alaireia even came into contact with the first Garcrat.

Crinte broke into a run as soon as he saw Starman reach the creatures, reeling in astonishment as he saw him quickly gain the upper hand. Alaireia joined him, and as the hideous creatures fell before them, Crinte realized the true gift of Tincire's weapons that matched not only their combat style but synced with their wills. He drew his sword and visions danced before his eyes as he strode forward purposefully, but the creatures that ran towards him were not Garcrats.

Legone leaped up onto the crumbling wall which shuddered, almost unwilling to hold his weight. He paused, allowing his feet to regain balance before lifting his bow once more. Marklus joined him, dragging a blue tipped arrow out of his quiver. "Your aim is poor," Legone stated. "When you loose your arrow your bow comes up, forcing you to miss your mark. Line up your arrow with your mind's eye, and do not move until it flies."

"You have seen me shoot before," Marklus said, "but you have never said anything until now?"

Legone shrugged, keeping his eyes on his target. "Practice is over. I need your arrows to fly true and straight every time."

Marklus took aim and let his arrow fly. It whistled past Crinte and struck one of the creatures racing towards him in the head. It fell backwards with a cry and disappeared beneath the others. "Like that?" Marklus asked proudly.

Despite himself, Legone felt one of the corners of his mouth tug upwards in a slight smile. "Yes, like that."

As Marklus bent back his elbow to reach for another arrow, he heard what sounded like a cheer rush through the air. He was almost positive it came from his quiver. As his second arrow took down its mark, he heard it again. He glanced at Legone to see if he noticed, but Legone had a concentrated look on his face. "These are not the same creatures we slay by the sea."

Gangly creatures moved quickly, skillfully, towards them like a mass of ants descending on their fallen prey. Perhaps they had once been people; Tiders, Crons, Ezincks, or Trazames. Now, they were monsters, stripped of flesh and left with sickening bone, recovered with blistered and burned skin stretched taut over skeletal bodies. Each had an abnormally large head. Perhaps it was the lack of hair and flesh that made it appear large and misshapen. Maybe it was the unsettling, enormous black eyes that stared out of sunken skulls, dead and emotionless. Shirts of chainmail reached almost to their knees, keeping blows from reaching their chest and torso. Around their waists, a black, belt-like contraption held multiple weapons which included swords, knives, and axes. They were nimble and surprisingly strong as they hurled themselves across the battlefield.

Arrows sang as they whistled past Crinte's ears, serving one purpose only—Death. Alaireia and Starman were too far away, surrounded by Garcrats, and he could not warn them he saw more coming out of the east. With a cry, he raised his sword to meet the new force and struck a high blow to the head, knocking a creature to the ground. The next one swung at Crinte's neck but he ducked and sliced low at its legs. He heard snapping sounds as its legs collapsed. Arrows threw back two creatures who were about to advance. An axe landed in the ground beside him, seconds after he had moved his foot, and even as the speed of arrows from Marklus and Legone continued, Crinte knew he was grossly outnumbered.

Alaireia and Starman mowed through the Garcrats without hesitation. Alaireia was sure it was a combination of Starman's fury and her hypnotic sword. Turning her back to Starman, she proceeded to cut down the creatures attempting to sneak up behind them. As she whirled, her eyes scanned the farmland and she found herself shouting, "Starman! Fall back! Fall back to Crinte!" Not bothering to wait for Starman, who seemed to be able to hold his own, she kicked a Garcrat out of her way and ran towards Crinte, sword held high. A Garcrat roared and lunged for her. Alaireia pulled a dagger from her belt and hurled it at the creature. The dagger sunk into its neck and it collapsed with a gurgle, brown blood gushing out from the mortal wound. Another one of the strange creatures leaped into her path, throwing an axe towards her chest. Alaireia dove for the ground, rolled over, and leaped into the air inches from the creature's face. Bringing her sword around in an arc, she cleaved the head from its body. The creature's headless corpse wavered a few seconds before crashing to the ground. She bounded forward again, only to be blocked by two hideous creatures. One of them licked its skinless lips with a forked black tongue and turned hostile eyes on her. As it pulled a wavy knife to throw at Alaireia, its eyes caught the gold line of her sword. Alaireia turned her head but not fast enough; she felt the sharp metal cut across her cheek and the warm ebb of blood began to drip down her face. With a growl, she plunged her sword forward and it struck the creature's chainmail shirt. There was only a begrudging hesitation before the chainmail parted and Alaireia's sword went through the creature's chest and out the other side. Yanking its axe out of its belt, she threw it at the creature watching. The weapon sunk into its skull as she pulled her sword free and ran on.

Starman felt no fear. He heard Alaireia calling but her voice sounded far away. In his numb rage, all he could feel was the intoxicating power gained as each Garcrat dropped, roaring before him. They lifted their clubs in vain, fell begging at his feet, but Starman was too fast, too angry to engage in a duel. Death was his only goal as he stood on his farm, defending the ground that had raised him, fed him, and blessed his family with abundance. His sword sang with each swing, and at times it seemed to have a mind of its own, guiding his strokes and blows, slashing and killing. It was only when the stench of death entered his nostrils that he began to realize what he was doing.

Awareness began to return to his body. His arms ached for a break, his hair was plastered to his sweating head, and his heart was pumping at breakneck speed in his chest. The creatures continued to roar and Starman tripped over mangled bodies as he attempted to retreat. But the Garcrats pressed forward relentlessly, eager to send him to an early death. Clubs cracked around him as he stumbled, waving his sword halfheartedly as he backed away. He heard shouts behind him. At last, breaking loose from the Garcrats, he turned and ran to where Alaireia had joined Crinte in holding back the new force.

"More are coming," Crinte gasped. "We need to end this."

"Crinte, fall back to Marklus and Legone!" Alaireia ordered. "I've got this!"

It was only when Crinte turned that Starman saw his side, damp with blood as he stumbled away, and he knew it was his fault. He did not have long to contemplate his folly as Alaireia called, "Starman, with me!"

He raised his sword once more, feeling its desire for blood surge through him. With a cry, he plunged back into the fray, stabbing and slicing and swinging and slaying. Alaireia began to back away while Legone and Marklus' arrows continued unabated. Alaireia held her sword before her and began to speak in an ancient tongue. As she did, the gold light on her sword began to glow. The creatures slowed, unable to look away. A paralysis came over their feet and they shook where they stood, staring at the light. Starman brought his sword down and followed their eyes to Alaireia's sword. Her eyes were closed and her lips continued to move quickly. Silence quashed the sound of battle and the creatures dropped their weapons as they stared. The light continued to burn brighter, cleaving away from the sword until it burst into the air with a snap and fingers of light rushed out, reaching for creatures. Chaos ruled again. With a shout, the creatures tried to shield their eyes. Then, they turned and ran north, back towards the sea, back from whence they had come. As they fled, the fingers stretched larger and longer, reaching for them, chasing them down. Starman turned and saw Alaireia drop her sword in exhaustion. He saw Crinte, bent over, holding his sword, while Marklus leaped off the wall and ran towards him. He saw Legone standing alone, a force to reckon with, his bow still raised. He saw his farmland ruined with ash and smoke and the bodies of turned ones from the other side. He saw and he knew his home was truly gone.

CHAPTER 18

STARMAN'S CHOICE

Marklus reached Crinte just as he lowered himself to the ground. "They stabbed me deep," Crinte grunted, gritting his teeth as he moved his hand away from the wound.

"This might hurt," Marklus advised as he peeled back the tunic to take a look. Blue light surged from his fingers and he placed his hand against Crinte's skin. Crinte felt the pain intensify before his burning skin was soothed and the muscles and sinews began to pull together, quickly closing the wound. "Thank you," Crinte breathed as he felt the pain subside.

Alaireia lethargically limped up as Marklus gave Crinte a hand up. "That was amazing," Marklus praised her.

Alaireia spit blood into the mud as she bent over, breathing hard. "It took everything I had. I did not know it would require that much energy."

Crinte turned his farseeing gaze over the land. "They are still fleeing," he said.

Starman was last to join them, a hollowness in his chestnut eyes. "I am sorry," he mumbled. "I did not know there were so many."

Crinte moved forward. "Starman, there will always be many. But if you are to come with us, you must fight and retreat only when I command it." Starman bowed his head. "And Starman," Crinte placed a hand on his shoulder, "a homecoming such as this should never happen to anyone. You fought well. I would be grateful if you came with us to the Great Water Hole to end this once and for all."

Starman blinked hard. "There is nothing left for me here except death."

"Then you are one of us now." Legone's voice was surprisingly warm as he lowered his bow and arrow. Walking up to Starman, he placed a comforting hand on his shoulder.

"It grows late. We should put distance between us and this battle before sunset," Crinte announced.

Marklus pressed a hand to Alaireia's cheek. "It is merely a scratch," he said as the wound closed.

"Thank you." Alaireia straightened.

The five were solemn as they cleaned their weapons, gathered their supplies, and trudged forward. The comfort of Trazamy City was forgotten as they walked east towards Wiltieders. As night fell, they set up camp in an empty pasture and Crinte pulled out his maps to study their path. "From here, we go to the edge of the Afrd Mounts," he informed them, "to the hidden home near the slopes."

***

Starman passed out quickly that night, flinging himself to the ground and falling into a deep sleep with the potential of pleasant dreams of days past. Alaireia sat calmly beside him, cleaning her swords and daggers repetitively, her thoughts elsewhere. Occasionally, she glanced at Starman and watched his chest rise and fall, hating the world for stealing his innocence. Now, she understood why she liked him. He was unspoiled, untouched by the deep cares of the Western World. He was simple, but happy in his own way, caring for what was most important, a full life spent the way he wished it. Grand adventures were for others; earning recognition from Rulers and standing in favor of their power was not something he cared for. He was much different from most males she had met, Ackhor the Cron and Crinte the Wise included. She watched, afraid for him to wake and see the empty look in his eyes again.

Marklus lay back with his eyes closed, listening to the aura of the world around them. He could hear the nocturnal creatures whispering to each other as they woke and eased out of their lairs to hunt through the night. To his relief, the Zikes were speaking again in his mind. *Marklus the Great, they flee before us!* they called in glee.

Let none escape, he commanded them.

Legone paced uneasily around the camp while the stars of auld began to twinkle in the clear night sky above them. Crinte touched his side gingerly where the skeletal creature had stabbed him, but the rips in his flesh were nothing more than a painful memory. He watched his warriors as they lay silent in the darkness and wondered what pure evil he was leading them into. He shook back his head at the blue blackness of the moonless night, and when he surveyed the land again, his eyes shone gold. He could see single blades of grass waving in the light wind the night brought. A distance away towards the south, he saw the flicker of a flame from a campfire. So they were not alone in the farmlands after all. A shadow moved past him and he saw Legone continue to pace. Crinte closed his eyes again, turning off the night vision. "What distresses you, Legone?"

Legone did not pause his gait as words tumbled out of his mouth. "My visions of late. My family is dying. Time is running out. The portals are closed but their remnants remain. The turned ones are growing stronger. We need a power stronger than us all to turn the tide once and for all."

"What is it you seek?"

"An immortal being who holds sway to take notice and lead us into battle."

"You know that will not happen."

"No. It will not. We are on our own."

"But not alone. If the free peoples of Mizine will fight with us, if the Mermis will come down from their Kingdom in the clouds, if the Zikes of the field and the Xctas of the air join forces. If the captive ones are set free, we have a chance."

"Not if he knows we are coming. As sure as we set our feet across the sea, we shall be overwhelmed with his forces, and they will hunt us down and destroy us."

"I have already taken that into consideration with my strategy, only I must seek counsel with one who has lived much longer than I."

"Crinte, my faith in what must be done does not fade, but I fear what might become of us on the other side."

Crinte turned his golden gaze on Legone the Swift and gazed into his eyes for a long moment. "You have looked into the Clyear of Alaireia and your hope has been stolen. Tell me, what did you see?"

Legone paused and looked directly at Crinte, his voice hard. "My family is dying."

***

Starman jerked awake in the darkness, unsure of where he was for a moment. The familiar traces of home surrounded him but seconds later, the nightmarish day came crashing back into his memory. He clasped a hand over his mouth at the shocking horror and rocked gently back and forth on the ground. He swallowed hard, but the tears of rage and sorrow refused to come. All he could feel was bitter anger, seething within, blackening his soul. Cautiously he rose, glancing at the two Crons, the Tider and the Ezinck. Dawn was approaching, yet Crinte sat in the tall grass, his eyes golden, watching. Starman wasn't sure, but he thought he saw Crinte's head bob, as if confirming he could leave or perhaps he was scratching his chin. Unsure, Starman turned around and began walking hurriedly, away from the purpose bound warriors, away from certainty of death, back towards home.

The air was chilly as he walked, and when he breathed out, curls of musky air clouded his sight. He walked steadily, no destination in mind, no goal on the horizon. Life as a Trazame was assumed and set. No choices had to be made; life just unfolded as it should, simple as that. The land was farmed, the animals taken care of, and the land and animals, in exchange, provided bountiful food. Eventually, during one harvest celebration, he would dance with a female from a neighboring farm, and they would have children to toil the soil, graze the animals, fish from the pond, and celebrate the harvest with. It was the cycle of life, unchanging, unending. But now, homeless, family-less, his place in the ritual of life had been snatched from him. It was true, he could return to Trazamy City and find work at a trade post or at the inn, and re-join his brethren. They would feel sorry for him, for a time, and already he grew annoyed at the thought of anxious, nervous faces, farm wives reaching to pat his cheek while slipping food into his pockets. As if food could cure all. It was the one comfort in disappointment and sorrow, a belly full of food washed down with a stout ale. He had seen the drunkards before, laying down pint after pint until they were tossed out with the pigs, no decency left. It was his only option, yet a pinprick of doubt played on his mind. Suddenly cold, he rubbed his hands over his arms and shuddered. There was just one small problem. What would happen to Trazamy City if the turned ones returned?

It was hours later, when the shadows began to fade into fuzzy pink hues, that he found himself sitting in the dew damp grass, his eyes red and wet, his throat dry, his head buzzing. His breath came fast and panicked, and in all the wild, wide world, he realized he was truly alone. Family was most important. They had always been there for him, his best friends, playmates, and challengers. Everything. He remembered when his little sister was born. It had been a tough nine months. Mother had almost not pulled through, but when she did, and when a second little girl entered the household, they had shouted and celebrated, laughing and crying with hope and happiness. Now, it had all been for naught.

A wordless shadow glided near on the edges of the vision. Too miserable to acknowledge her, he remained frozen while Alaireia sat down, a few feet from him. She said nothing, did not even glance at him, but he could feel her caring aura reaching out for him. She would never patronize him, or stare at him with sorry eyes while passing him sweet, stuff pastries for comfort. She would never bore him with stories of how kind and gentle his parents were—he knew—or what potential his brothers and sisters had—he knew that, too. She would never tell stories at the great harvest of his family and what they meant to Trazamy City; nothing, but more food. She would do more for him than anyone in Trazamy City would. At that moment, the only action he could take to honor his family, the action they would want him to take—and if he had thought about it more, he would have realized he was wrong—was to avenge their deaths.

The sun was high in the sky when he stood at last, turning around to look at Alaireia, who stood up as well. She had braided her dark, black hair back, but it hung loose at the ends and brushed against her shoulders. She was almost his height, but slimmer, even though at times he could see her powerful muscles rippling beneath her dark skin. Her eyes were clear, shining with strength, gleaming with power. She looked at him, and her gaze was not one of pity, but of understanding. "Where to, Starman?"

Confused, he furrowed his brow. "What do you mean? Don't you have to catch up with Crinte and the others?"

At the sound of his dry voice, she passed him a water skin, moving closer. His hands brushed hers as, relieved, he took the water skin and drank greedily. He wiped his mouth clumsily and held out the water skin, looking at her expectantly.

"Starman," she said earnestly, "I can catch up with them later. You're the one who is important right now. So I'm here. What do you need? Where do you need to go?"

He stared at her in surprise. "Why?"

She bit her lower lip, looking down for a moment. "I guess I know what it is like to be alone in this world. And you, Starman, are surprising and more courageous than you know. I like what I see in you, and so, I want to help you. Not for any greater purpose. Just you."

"Oh." He looked at her for a long moment before holding out his grubby hand. "I'm coming with you then. Where you go, I go."

She closed her hand around his and held on, tight.

CHAPTER 19

WILTIEDERS

Elam the Gatekeeper could not stop quaking in his boots at the earthly thing that stood before him. He could have been imagining it, but the thing appeared to be impatiently tapping its foot, although it had no feet that he could see. Its hypnotic emerald eyes stared, bored, at him, and Elam felt it would consume him. He wished Ackhor the Cron would hurry up. The thing on the doorstop of the Fighting Camp refused to explain anything until Ackhor appeared. What was more unsettling was that five what he assumed were bodyguards stood a few paces from the impatient leader, green points crackling on their heads. Although, he wasn't sure he was looking at a head at all. This was why Crinte had deserted, with the best warriors of course. At least, that was the story circulating around the Fighting Camp. But everyone knew better. Everyone knew Crinte and his warriors were going to do what everyone wished they were brave enough to do—go to the source and destroy it. They were proud, nay, jealous of Crinte's wisdom and commitment to righting a great wrong. But Crinte had made it clear that Ackhor was in charge at the Fighting Camp, and they were to obey him.

Now, Elam wasn't sure whether the creature on the stairs was one of the transformed or not, and he shuddered to think what message it carried from the other side.

Ackhor took his time, not pleased with the demanding intrusion. Yet the gate was heavily armed with archers and sword fighters, so he made his way down to confront the demon from the other side. Elam the Gatekeeper made way for Ackhor as he marched up to the gates, which were thrown open with curious Crons peering from every side. When he saw the thing, his heart grew cold. Just like in his adventures, something unexpected was always turning up, but the four-foot green thing with terrible eyes, he could not place.

"Are you Ackhor the Cron?" it demanded in a dead, gravelly voice.

"Yes," he said with a nod, attempting to retain his firm voice of authority.

The thing bowed, hauntingly and mockingly. "My Master, Marklus the Great, sends his greetings."

"Marklus?" Ackhor could not hide his surprise.

The thing twitched disdainfully at the interruption. "My Master, Marklus the Great, sends his greetings." It repeated mechanically. "He requests troops for Trazamy City which is being raided by creatures from the other side. My kind have been sent to guard the sea, but we cannot hold them all." The thing turned around, as if to walk away.

"That's all?" Ackhor called. "He does not want a response?"

The thing gave what appeared to be a noncommittal shrug. "I only serve those who stand between life and death." Then, slowly, it and its guards faded from view.

Astonished into silence, Elam the Gatekeeper was the first to recover. "Marklus the Great, eh?" He shook his blond head. "I have many questions for him the next time I see him."

"As will we all," Ackhor confirmed. In one swift motion, he turned back to the Crons, regaining his leadership. "I need volunteers to go to Trazamy City!"

***

The air turned crisp as the five warriors, reunited, continued their journey. The manicured fields and pastures of Trazame faded away into the wild meadows of Wiltieders. The greenery changed and wild flowers of purple, blue, and yellow hues sprang out of the grass, shooting their colorful petals into the wind only to turn to seed and grow again once returned to earth. Large orange fruit on stubby bushes were scattered across the countryside, and at the encouragement of Crinte, the warriors collected and ate them, sticky juice dripping from their chins. Rabbits occasionally hopped out of burrows, noses twitching, to curiously watch the intruders in their terrain. Tan cats as tall as a Cron's waist chased butterflies through the flowers and pounced each time they almost caught a rabbit, hedgehog, or squirrel. When they drifted too close to the five, they could see razor sharp teeth glinting behind their padded mouths. Mammoth oak trees sprung up here and there but at a distance from each other, as if cautious of intruding on each other's spheres of influence. Great roots rippled across the glade, providing shelter to the flightless creatures. Their trunks

185

were so thick, three people could stand on one side and not be seen from the other. Their branches were mighty and the birds of the air built nests and dwelt within their sanctuary. The ravens inhabited one treetop, calling rudely to each other and fighting needlessly over each nook and hollow. Golden hummingbirds flittered by, feasting on sweet nectar from the flowers with the flying petals. When they whizzed past, the five could see miniature golden crowns sparkling upon their heads.

A river sneaked its way through the land, creating a trail to the Dejewla Sea. Snow white and midnight black swans floated on the mirror of water as the river widened, their young trailing impatiently but obediently behind. At night when they slept, they could hear the lullaby of the river, gently soothing the young and hushing the beasts of the night. In daylight, when they continued, the river blocked their path, but offered passage across on slippery, moss covered gray stones. Silver streaks shot past them and they could hear laughter and shouting on the playful breeze. A clump of birch trees by the water's edge hid shy deer who peeked out at the strangers in their lands, their white tails standing straight up. Further ahead, a herd of wild white horses startled, pranced for a minute in acknowledgement, then galloped off into the distance, kicking up a cloud of dust as they passed. When at last the cloud cleared, a great black badger with a brilliant white stripe across its back glared angrily after the white horses, annoyed at being woken at such an early hour. On a hill, a huge yellow lion looked down at the land, then trudged back down the other side, ignoring everything in its wake. The five gasped and stared, but the beasts of Wiltieders feared nothing at all.

Starman walked in awe, gazing at the vibrant lights and sounds and intoxicating colors of Wiltieders. "I did not know such a land as this existed," he whispered.

"This is nothing," Legone spoke kindly, "compared to mountains."

Indeed, as the days passed, the shadow of the Afrd Mounts in the distance grew visible, and each morning as the fog drifted away, the reality of where they were headed grew more tangible. At night, when the sun reluctantly set, forcing its beams to remain in the air for as long as possible, the lights of the mountains would shine.

"Are those fireflies?" Starman asked, watching the golden lights twinkle into view once darkness took over the land.

"Nay," Legone explained, "they are the Iaens of the Mounts that glow in the dark. There is one for each home and they shine upon the doorstep. Travelers carry them instead of lanterns, for their light is eternal. Most of them produce golden or white light. The white light carriers are rare, but mayhap you will see them where we are going."

The warriors relaxed around Legone as they prepared for a night's rest. Crinte, despite the enchantment of the land, continued to watch their surroundings. Marklus lay back, the flowers behind his head flinging themselves out of the way before he could crush them. Alaireia twisted petals into a crown and held it to the wind until it carried it on its waves into the twilight. Starman lay facing the mountains, watching the mysterious lights twinkle.

"Swift, where do you live?"

"Ranges beyond ranges," Legone replied. "We are only in the shallows. It would take a great many days to reach the high peaks where I dwelt."

"We will stay in the shallows," Crinte confirmed. "The house of Srackt the Wise is not far from us now."

"How come we haven't seen anyone?" Marklus questioned. "With beauties such as this land possesses, how can any stay away?"

"Oh, but the land is full of inhabitants," Legone explained. "They mostly keep to themselves and live in the great oak trees we cross now and then. Most prefer the mountains to the shallows, though."

"I have seen travelers such as us." Crinte surveyed the land. "To the north, a small group camps. I thought it best to avoid them. One may see Crons and Tiders travel across Mizine together, but questions will arise when all four people groups are seen together."

They were silent again beneath the shadow of the great gray mountains.

The next day, ever so gently, the ground began to slope upwards. Now, slabs of rock jutted out of the grass and the wild flowers grew over them. Eventually, they had to use their hands to steady themselves as they continued upwards, and the balmy wind became even more pleasant as they wiped sweat from their faces. Around mid-afternoon, Crinte paused and turned. "Look." He pointed from whence they had come.

Far below, they could see the bewitching meadows they had just journeyed through, which seemed tiny and insignificant in comparison to the colossal might of the Afrd Mounts. Marklus, as he looked down, could hear the spirit of the wind and trees far below and the voices of the beasts of Wiltieders. He almost opened his mouth to tell the others what they said, but thought better of it as their voices faded.

Crinte led them on, and as they rounded a large boulder, he remarked, "Ah, the road at last."

Starman stretched his nose to the air and inhaled deeply. "What is that smell?"

Marklus pricked his ears. "And what is that sound?"

"Welcome," said Legone, "to the Afrd Mounts."

CHAPTER 20

THE AFRD MOUNTS

As the five climbed into the arms of the mountainside, they could see peaks towering far above them, reaching towards the heavens. In the distance, round stone huts perched precariously on high ledges, adorning the mountain peaks. Occasionally, Tiders and Crons appeared far off, winding their way through the crests. Rams bounded past them on their way to the heights, and a pool of water trickled by on its way to waterfall back to the shallows.

"I don't understand," Alaireia told Legone as she climbed beside him, "why you would leave a place such as this for the other side of the sea."

"No, you wouldn't understand," Legone answered. "But if you had lived here all your life and were curious for more, you might."

The mountain path led steeply uphill and sharply curved in places, as if it could not make up its mind which way to go.

"How far away are we now?" Starman called as he trailed behind, turning round and round so that his eyes could capture every glimpse of the behemoth mountain he walked upon.

"Nightfall should bring us to our destination," Crinte answered from ahead. He glanced behind, noticing the others were quite a distance behind him. "Or morning, at this pace."

"I hear voices singing," Marklus remarked. "Sometimes near, sometimes just out of earshot. They are rich and ethereal, not like the way we sing, loud and boisterous."

"There are many wild creatures that haunt the mountains. You have unique ears and can hear them better than us." Legone looked at Marklus admiringly.

"They have gone higher." Marklus looked up into the clouds. "I hear only echoes now." Finding his heart beating in anticipation, he continued to gaze upwards, unaware of the path his feet trod until his foot struck a loose rock and he tripped. A rattle of stones jiggled under his feet, and for a moment, his toes struggled to grip a solid piece of ground. In vain, he fell on the path, his arms swinging widely. Everyone paused and looked at Marklus as he sheepishly picked himself off the ground, brushing dirt and loose gravel from his clothes and hands. Alaireia clasped her hands over her mouth but was unable to stop the ripple of laughter that burst out. Her shoulders shook in merriment as she pointed at Marklus. "You might want to watch where you're going next time!" she choked out. "The voices of the mountains will take you away with them!"

Starman began to laugh as well, stopping to hold his side as he found himself winded from the climb up the mountain. Legone crossed his arms but even a smile of amusement appeared on his lips.

"Oh Marklus…" Crinte began, but a movement in the air above them caught his eyes. He looked up at the mountain ledge and two purple eyes stared questioningly, almost angrily, back into his.

"What is it?" Marklus asked as Crinte paused, happy to deflect attention from his mishap.

Crinte searched the mountainside again, but the eyes had disappeared into the shadows. "They know we are here," he said, reminders of his one weakness throbbing. "Let's keep moving." He walked forward again, down the curving path and away to the right. Marklus followed, his eyes watching his footfalls closely. Legone ran a hand over his blue tipped arrows but he did not draw one. Alaireia, laughing no more, looked back at Starman. He grinned at her, and for a moment she hoped he could forget his sorrows.

Night fell quickly in the mountains, the great rocks hiding the last rays of sunlight. Even as the sun disappeared, the song of the crickets chirped in the valleys of the mountainside. The lights of the Afrd Mounts began to shine, and one round white orb drifted near Crinte, hovering in front of his face. "Who are you seeking, stranger of the Afrd Mounts?" it hummed.

Crinte studied the white creature, its wings slowly beating as if it did not need to hold itself up. Light shone out of its naked body, blinding those who dared stare too long at its glory. "We go to the house of Srackt."

"Come, I will guide you." The orb floated down the path. "You are not far from whom you seek."

As night deepened, the five could tell they were certainly not alone. Yellow and white orbs drifted past them, guiding sometimes unseen travelers to journey's end. Carnivores slinked past them, on their way to find amusing nocturnal activities. It was not until the wolves started howling that the mountains seemed unfriendly, and the five sensed how pleasant a stone hut on a ledge would be. Their pace quickened as much as possible in the darkness, but the light led them straight and true. Despite the light, Crinte turned his night vision back on to watch the heights above them. Every now and then, he spotted the purple eyes. Heart in his throat, he continued to move forward as his memories reminded him of the last time he had walked the Mounts. They were just as terrifying as they were intoxicatingly beautiful. He preferred a nemesis he could see and fight, rather than the shadows of creatures that felt they owned the land.

At last they walked upon broad steps that led upwards to a round hut, perched on a ledge, and as they climbed the winding staircase, a sweet rain began to fall, clearing all hostility from the night air. Lights danced around the hut, which looked as if it were carved into the mountain. Its sides were curved to buffet the wind, forcing it to go around instead of becoming hooked on sharp corners. A door without a latch hid within the rounded turrets of the hut, and when the five landed on the doorstep, the orb bowed. "Here is the house of Srackt." It flitted away before Crinte had time to thank it.

He turned instead in the light rain and lifted his fist to knock at the solid sandstone door. It cracked open before his hand could touch it, and warm yellow light streamed out, clearly highlighting his face to the tall Cron beyond the door. A bearded face peered out at them and a deep voice chuckled. "Crinte, I was wondering when you would appear. Come in, come in."

The door opened wider to reveal the beaming face of a much older Cron. His thick head of hair and beard were speckled with silver and gray. There were crinkles and wrinkles around the lines of his nut-brown eyes and rosy round cheeks. His figure was stout and he wore a deep brown jerkin and sandals on his feet. He laughed as the five trailed out the rain, and the deep, throaty sound of it made them feel at home. In a rounded corner of the room, a fire burned merrily in the hearth while a kettle sang over it, white steam pouring from the spout. A round table with six chairs around it sat near the fire, but a great cushioned chair was closer. On the other side of the room, fruits and vegetables hung from the rafters along with smoked meats and an odd collection of furs. Here and there was space for invisible doors, and in one place, a ladder led upwards, disappearing into the sky.

"Welcome to my home in the Mounts," the Cron was saying.

It was Legone the Swift who narrowed his eyes. "Srackt the Wise," he said coolly. "Is this what you call yourself these days?"

The Cron's receptive face did not change. "Legone the Swift, is this how you would greet an old friend? Ah, but no time for words tonight. You all must be tired from your climb." He shut the latch-less door, which blended back into the wall, and walked over to the fire. Pulling the kettle from the heat, he poured its contents into five mugs sitting on the table. "Take these," he gave one to each of the warriors, "and rest." He waved his large hand and a door slid open. He ushered the five inside and the door slid shut once more.

194

The bedroom was white with curtains hiding each bed. As the five began to remove their weapons and sip the warm liquid, they felt the tiredness and ache of the journey lift from their bones. They fell into feather soft beds, and right before their eyelids closed, they heard the music of the night. Voices lifted in song tumbled through the chimney and permeated the house, filling every nook and cranny. They sang in a language of old, songs of celebration, songs of sorrow, songs of beauty and of nature, songs of war, songs of peace.

When at last their songs became mixed with dreams, the sweet rain ceased falling and the five slept. Starman had never dreamed before. When he slept, his mind slept as well. Now, the vivid colors were both exciting and terrifying. He felt his pulse quicken at times, then slow again as he found himself traveling and exploring, two things he never associated with himself. But as he went, he found himself enjoying the strange and exciting events until at last he found his family, safe from harm and well in spirit. With that thought, he began to hope.

Marklus rested, but even in his dreams he could hear the voices singing, lulling him to a deeper slumber. Yet when he opened his dream eyes, he found himself looking at what seemed to be a black tower, rising out of the ground. Around it, fog or smoke drifted, hiding its watching eyes from him, and him from it. He wondered, as he stared at it, if he should be afraid to face what was inside. But it seemed much had already happened, and his soul was too tired to fear anymore.

Alaireia tossed uneasily, flipping over to hug another pillow in her sleep. Dreams were omens, symbols of things yet to come, and what she saw did not make her very happy. She was standing on a ledge, and around her there was a terrible heat. The air was thick and foul, causing her eyes to water. In spite of that, she did not appear to be leaving at all. In fact, she pulled out her Clyear and held it to the light. She whispered to it gently and then, in the most unexpected gesture, she turned and handed it to the person standing beside her. She could hear herself giving it away, telling the person to take it, and the thought of ever giving the Clyear away made her feel cold.

In his dream, Legone did not think he had anything left to lose; he assumed the quest to the Great Water Hole would take his life. But as he lay on the ground, hiding from his oppressors, a thought struck him and he realized there was a way for him to win. He lifted the object he held in his hand and blew hard, and he saw the smoking canyon open and swallow him whole.

Happiest of all was Crinte as he slept in the house of Srackt the Wise. The following purple eyes had faded from his mind and left him adrift, closing his mind to what could be. He dreamt he stood at the edge of a pool. Behind him, a green forest lay thick and hazy. Before him, he could see cliffs, and a stream pooled into a river leading upwards into them. As he looked, he realized it laid out his path for him, so he followed it to a winding passageway, guiding his way into the bluffs.

CHAPTER 21

SRACKT THE WISE

A beautiful sunrise graced the mountainside and dew shone like crystals everywhere it lay. As the sun reached out to capture the dew, it shone like mirrors in its brilliance, and all those who saw it counted themselves lucky. A rainbow dared to glimmer for a moment, offering its colors to the sunlight before dissolving from whence it had come.

The five awoke to the flavors of fresh herbed bread and the sizzle of pork wafting through the walls. Refreshed, they dressed eagerly and found their way back to the main room. Sunlight streamed in from high windows and a thin male crouched by the fire, slowly turning the meat. He did not bother to acknowledge the five as they filed into the room. Crinte felt a vague cloud pass over his eyes as he glanced at the unknown figure, but it faded as soon as his gaze drifted away. The front door stood open and the tall Cron who had bade them enter stood in the doorframe as he did every day, basking in the glory of the mountain sunrise. He turned as they filed into the room. "Ah." He closed the door.

Crinte moved to his side. "Srackt, please let me introduce my companions. You know of Legone the Swift." Legone crossed his arms. "This is Marklus the Healer from Zikeland. I have told you much about him." The Cron reached out his large hand and shook Marklus' firmly. "Alaireia the Lightfoot from Srinka in the Forests of the Ezincks, and Stamen the Trazame, called Star-man, from Trazamy City." The Cron shook hands with each of them and his dark eyes dared to twinkle.

"Welcome, friends of Crinte the Wise. I am called Srackt the Wise. You must have dark stories for my ear. Come, we will eat and discuss."

"You are the name changer," Legone remarked coldly. "And none other than Crinte's father."

Srackt looked questioningly at Legone as he pulled out a long pipe. "True. I am sorry the words I last spoke offended you, but I am not sorry I spoke them. I am curious to hear about your time across the sea. I fear my words have come true after all."

Legone scowled but did not speak another word.

"Now," Srackt said when at last they were seated around the table and enjoying a warm meal, served by the strange, thin male. "Tell me why you have come."

Crinte looked questioningly from Srackt to the man sitting beside him, eating ravenously but avoiding eye contact with everyone.

Srackt, following Crinte's gaze, waved his hand noncha-lantly, brushing Crinte's concerns away.

"As you know," Crinte started, "the turned ones from the other side began invading our lands some time ago, stirring up fear and forcing us to take up arms. But they don't appear to be concerned about destroying our lands. They aren't raiding and pillaging. They come. They kill. They leave. I believe they are scouts, exploring the layout of our land, seeking out our weak spots, and seeing how much resistance they meet. Once they have gathered enough information, they will all come to conquer us, a war we are unprepared for. Legone, who has been to the northern side of the sea, knows there is a darker power leading this onslaught. The only way for us to stop this war, once and for all, is to take out their leader. I propose to go to the Great Water Hole, their base, and accomplish this feat. I take with me the best warriors in Mizine. Legone will serve as our guide; he has been to the other side before. Marklus will serve as our Healer. I cannot pretend we will not have close calls, especially in their territory. Alaireia carries the Clyear of Power, which is handy for getting out of a tight spot, and Starman wields the sword with a skill no one else can boast of. I know the journey will not be easy, but as we go we call armies to our sides and take the war to the Great Water Hole. My hope had been for Ackhor the Cron to unite the armies of Mizine and lead them across the sea to fight with us. As you know, he once served under King Arden of Norc in the land of Cromomany. As a gift, King Arden granted him the fortress and the lands beyond it where we based the Eka Fighting Camp, to recruit and train warriors to fight with us. Through our secretive efforts, with Alaireia serving as messenger, we inspired Crons and Tiders across Mizine to join us. Ackhor believes the army we raise must stay behind to defend Mizine. I say we attack before our enemy becomes too strong. Srackt, I ask for your help in uniting the armies of Mizine and bringing them across the sea to fight with us as we take our stand at the Great Water Hole."

Srackt the Wise nodded thoughtfully as he lit his pipe. "You are asking me to leave the Afrd Mounts. But tell me, what do you know of the other side?" He looked pointedly at Legone.

"I have been through the land of Asspraineya, and the great green forest that borders the land of Slutan and Asspraineya," Legone confirmed.

"Have you been to the Great Water Hole?" Srackt asked.

Legone shook his head.

Srackt nodded and took his pipe from his mouth. He laid a hand on the shoulder of the thin male sitting beside him. "This is Devine the Cron, or Sorn, as they call themselves in Asspraineya. He has been to the Great Water Hole."

Devine shivered and lifted his wide eyes to look at the five. His face was gaunt and weathered. His eyes had lost their light and stared vacantly. His long brown hair lay in limp, stringy strands to his shoulders, and the top of his head was balding. "We had no warning when they took over Asspraineya." His voice was high and halting, his speech in broken fragments. "One day, we were mining rock in Sornarky. The next, those fearsome beasts came sweeping in. Snatching us one by one. Forcing us to march to the Great Water Hole. Some they kept in prisons erected across the two countries. Seizing those found lost in the woods. Invading homes. Slaying those who resisted. Asspraineya is not a war country. The Rulers of our lands quickly struck a deal, promising cooperation and allowing the strange troops to invade our lands. At first they were Crons and Tiders in shiny armor. They were quickly replaced with the fleshy brown creatures that roar. We call them Garcrats because of the sound they make."

"I do, too!" Starman exclaimed.

The Sorn ignored him and went on. "Next came the skeletal creatures. A stronger army called the Gaslinks because of the way they sneak up at night. They are real warriors, faster, and difficult to kill. Third came the Gims. A spirit that wafts through the wind and appears suddenly. It is tied to what is called a Boleck. They may be immortal but some evil is controlling their actions. Gims are rare and the few that do live terrorize Asspraineya. Finally, there are the guards, Xeros. They are not made of flesh and blood. Their eyes are everywhere. To cross above land is to welcome ambush and death. If you would dare to journey to the Great Water Hole, you must take the Slutan Tunnels. They do venture there sometimes, but no one lives there. It is an empty route. There are dead ends and branches off the tunnels. But the main path will lead you straight and true to the Great Water Hole. When you climb out, you will be standing in his presence." He shuddered. "There is a tower where he dwells. And the smoking canyon is where the transformation takes place. Prisoners are tossed into those waters, washed downstream, and come out as one of the turned creatures. When they threw me in, I caught onto a ledge, crawled out, and escaped by the tunnels. It is only by luck I made it here. If you feel you must go, then go and lie low, and whatever you do, do not touch the water."

Crinte felt a twinge of doubt at the Sorn's unlikely tale. He nodded. "This is knowledge indeed. Would you mark the way for us on a map?"

The Sorn stared, fear shining bright out of his weathered eyes. "Srackt did warn me. It does not matter what I say; you will go nonetheless. But what is your plan once you arrive there? He is more powerful than any in the world."

"Who is this 'he' you speak of?" asked Marklus.

"Sarhorr." Devine spoke nervously. "That is what they call him. No one knows what he is, certainly not one of the people groups of the Four Worlds."

Legone's face was grim. "I know what he is. I have seen his face and I know who let him go. They will know what powers must be used to take him down."

All eyes turned to Legone. "Will you tell us what you have seen?" Srackt the Wise asked.

"When I left you on the edge of the Dejewla Sea," Legone's eyes were dark, "you had told me crossing the sea would be my undoing. I did not believe you then, for at first those were the happiest years of my life. But as I dwelt with the creatures of the wood, I realized all was not well. They had opened portals across the Western World in their desire for light and beauty and power. Dark creatures came through from other worlds, the Wyverns in Srinka, the Zikes in Zikeland, Sarhorr in Asspraineya, and perhaps more. A poison began to spread across the lands, and fear began to run amok even among the 'wild things.' He was a beautiful creature at first, or so they say, but he came through torn and weak, using his last strength to close the portal lest what had chased him here would follow. And now, I wonder what indeed was seeking to take his life and why we did not let it.

"He came full of promise and power, transforming the green forest into even more of a paradise than it already was with his illusions. He needed us to love him, desire him. But when I looked at him, I saw him with true eyes, and his dementedness would not let me rest. At last came the day death entered the forest. Through deceit, he slew the Queen of the Green People, the King's wife, and in a dark initiation transferred her power to himself. When we found him he feasted, intoxicated. There was dissension among the people, and at last a council was called and they made their ruling. The sentence was light, casting him from the forest, forcing him to become homeless and never return again, shutting him out of the power they held. He ranted and wailed but it may have been his plan all along. Weakly acclimated to his new power, he could not use it against the wild things, so he left and the civil struggle began. I spoke out in anger, telling them that under no circumstances should he have been allowed to live, and to this day I am not sure whether they were under his spell or not. I was forced to run, helped to escape, and since then I have sought to forget. But now he grows at large, and they know exactly how to stop him. As with all power, it ebbs and flows, and if it is stolen, the person will be no more than a broken shell. We must steal his power."

Devine the Sorn stared into the fire, his eyes glazed over and hazy. At last, he spoke in a lazy voice. "Power is intangible; you cannot steal what you cannot see."

Srackt the Wise turned over Legone's words slowly in his mind. A long moment of silence passed with only the sound of flames eagerly licking up the oxygen in the air around them. He looked at Legone as if trying to read him. "The words you say are true, yet I feel there is something you have not told us. Whether it is key to your quest or not, it is hard to tell. There are shadows around you. It is hard to know your true intentions."

"You have always thought ill of me," Legone accused coldly.

Srackt shook his head. "Only of your intentions. This time though, you have come in a time of peril, and for that, we are grateful. I will speak to the armies and Rulers on this side of the sea, and we will go forth on your heels to the Great Water Hole. Mizine will send out armies of their own, and it will be a swift and brutal retaliation. Although you have come to seek my counsel, it is clear you do not need my blessing to proceed. Take with you the knowledge imparted here and keep close the dreams the night brings. There is much truth in what you see as you lie sleeping. Now, relax from your woes. There comes a time when you must keep watch always, but for now, rest in the Mounts and enjoy the time you do have."

CHAPTER 22

A REPORT

Later that evening, after the entire house was asleep, Devine woke in his loft. He sat up slowly, pulling a crystal in the shape of a winged horse from underneath his bed. He remembered when he had crossed the sea, worn and exhausted from his mission, on the brink of giving up his duty. He had been ordered to seek out a Tider of the Afrd Mounts, and only a name was given. Now, he lifted the Clyear of Revelation, closed his eyes, and breathed upon it. When he opened them, he followed as his eyes were taken past the dark tower, before the face of the very one he deeply despised. "Report," the deep voice intoned boredly.

"The Five Warriors have come. Just like you said. And he is among them. They are coming to steal your power. They will take the route through the Slutan Tunnels."

"Steal my power?" The voice gave an ironic laugh, but there was a hint of devilish anticipation in it. "We will be waiting for them in the tunnels. What else?"

"They plan to travel to the border forest of Asspraineya. And meet with the wild things to discover how."

"It is too late for that." The voice appeared thoughtful. "What else?"

"My host is planning on uniting the armies of Mizine. Leaving them exposed."

"This shall be easy." The voice sounded pleased. "What else?"

"One of them carries the Clyear of Power."

This time, the voice did not speak again readily. "Now that is interesting," it said finally. "Devine." There was another pause. "Your work is done."

"Thank you, Lord Sarhorr."

"You have satisfied me. I have no further use for you." Devine choked as he felt the invisible shield of protection removed from him. "The Order of the Wise has failed," the voice laughed. "My plan remains in motion." Devine attempted to breathe in deeply but realized no air was coming through. For a moment, he struggled, and even as he did, the Clyear of Revelation slipped from his fingers and he collapsed into a fatal sleep.

CHAPTER 23

PURPLE EYES

When dawn broke, Crinte was standing on the rooftop of his father's home. They had talked late into the night but despite the early hour, the others were preparing to leave. Crinte watched the Mount as light began to gently touch its peak, encouraging life to shine forth. He found himself surprisingly frustrated when in reality he'd thought speaking with the wisest Cron he knew—who also happened to be his father—would confirm his plan was right. Mystified at the unsettling feelings, he hoped it was only anxiety regarding the task at hand. Besides, the Mounts were odd and secretive; their eyes were always watching. To the east, the sky was blazing with life, and suddenly, the air filled with the chatter and beating of wings as a thousand birds flew over his head. Crinte watched them calmly but his heartbeat was already quickening. So it was beginning.

"Crinte!" Marklus' voice rang up from below. "Are you ready?"

The warriors were filing out the front door, their packs laden again with food for the lengthy journey. Srackt the Wise was the last to appear, his face more serious than the night before. "Are you sure you won't stay just one more day?" he asked.

Crinte declined, saying, "We have already delayed too long. We must be away." He followed the winding staircase that led off the roof, back inside, and finally out the front door to his companions. There was no sign of Devine the Sorn, but his knowledge of the lands to the north, and the map he had marked for them, was all they needed.

The five said their goodbyes and walked down the trailing road. The birds of the air chattered eagerly above them, but the tongues of the warriors seemed to have left them.

It was mid-morning when Marklus finally heard the voices of the Zikes again. "Some good news!" he announced to the others.

Starman trailed slowly behind. "News; I am tired of news," he lamented. "The world is dark and everything is gone. How can news save us now?"

"Oh." Marklus had no words to cheer him up. "Well, at least Ackhor has deployed the army to the guard the sea, and the Zikes will meet us on the other side."

"That is good news indeed," Crinte agreed, "but something is wrong and I can't quite put my finger on it."

"I hear it," Legone said. "I must go to a higher mount and ask the Xctas to come fight with us." He turned off the road with feet as fleet as a mountain goat, and began to make his way to the heights.

"We will wait for you in Wiltieders," Crinte called after him.

"Is Srackt the Wise really your father?" Alaireia asked after Legone disappeared.

"Yes," Crinte replied offhandedly. "He is my father by blood and a nomad by heart. I inherit his skills and would have inherited his longevity as well."

"His magical home seems almost prison-like," Alaireia went on. "Latch-less doors and rounded walls."

"He has his ways," Crinte remarked, but his voice was quiet, ending the conversation.

"There's that smell again." Starman twitched his nose. "It's like a sweet syrup. Almost perfume like, but not quite."

"The voices have returned as well," Marklus observed. "They come and go at times."

Crinte began to walk faster. "Let's head north. We'll meet Legone at the glade."

***

Legone threw back his head, opened his mouth, and called. His voice echoed off rocks, slinking into the hidden crevices of the Mounts where creatures held their ears and asked him to stop. *Quiet, Legone,* they hushed. *We will not listen. We will not comply.*

Not you, he told the ravens and the hawks. *I know where your allegiance lies. To the sky only. Flee while you can. This world is doomed.*

Quiet, Legone. We are only doomed if they find us.

He called, the wind carrying his hoarse scream across the peaks. A lone coyote answered, howling from its interrupted sleep.

Come, the voice he sought out answered at last.

Heady elation consumed him as it did each time he felt wings sprout from his back. Sharp, curved talons grew in place of feet, and with a leap, he rose in the air, spreading his wings to soar above the peaks, free again. He could count on one hand the times the Xctas had allowed him to transform, for they controlled that innate ability. His sharp, beady eyes could see the birds of the air below him, crossly flying in opposite directions. The heart of the mountain beat feebly as he could see, beyond the grass and rock, deep below where the light did not shine, a poison seeping towards the core. Beating his powerful wings against the resistant air, he zigzagged higher towards the lonely peak hidden in mist that none could dare reach except by flight. A nest perched precariously on the utmost point, and when Legone dived into it, he found himself tumbling, rolling among brambles and sticks, a full sized Tider again. A talon snatched him up and before he could take a breath, he found himself hanging upside down over the precipice.

Why have you come? The voice was fierce, demanding.

Legone tilted his head in order to catch the eye of the giant Xctas holding him aloft. *War is coming. The very being who destroyed Lye, your brother of the air, is coming for all of us.*

The world spun again as he was tossed into the nest. Scrambling to his feet, he stood beside five fierce Xctas who perched on the edge, looking at him. They were his height, with long talons, curved beaks, and unforgiving eyes. Their features took on a rusted golden hue, and the very tips of their wings were pure white, blending with the mist of the air, rendering them invisible until they were on top of their prey. Legone stood calmly before them, as he had many times before. *I have told many stories with portions of the truth intertwined within my words. But you deserve to know what is really happening. After you have heard, I ask of you a choice. Will you flee with the others, or will you come fight with me?*

Proceed, an Xctas replied, moving its intimidating talons a hair closer to Legone. *And be quick.*

Calmly, Legone told his tale of his journey to the other side, ending with his flight back to the Afrd Mounts. *Before I fled, I made a deal with Sarhorr the Ruler. In fact, we all made deals with him. He asked me to bring him the most powerful warriors in all of Mizine. You see, if he drains the power from the People Groups and wild things, there will be none to stand before him, no resistance left. I agreed, in exchange for the lives of the Green People. But Sarhorr the Ruler may not make promises that he keeps. If he is lying, I must have some kind of insurance that could save the world. The Green People gave me the Horn of Shilmi, carved from the bones of their Queen. I travel with Crinte the Wise and his powerful warriors, each who have an army to call. I ask for your help, to provide distraction in order to give me enough time to turn the tides of this war.*

The Xctas closed around him, and Legone could feel their superior anger. *What will you give us in exchange?*

And for a moment, he almost could not answer them.

***

Evening brought them closer to the shallows of Wiltieders and Crinte led them to a grassy glade to camp for the night.

211

Dark clouds were rolling in even as they perched cautiously on gray rocks and slowly ate. Crinte still felt uneasy as he paced the glade, rubbing his blond head as moisture filled the air. His night vision was strong as he surveyed his surroundings for a hint of the purple eyes. He had seen them before, years ago, when first traversing the Mounts. At first, they had been appealing, pulling him inward, intoxicating him under its spell, but now his thoughts were interrupted. A shadow appeared at the edge of his vision, and he turned his head to see it fully. He saw a streak of red and a flash of purple. Without hesitation, he moved towards it, out of the glade, sneaking between the trees that blinded his view. He could feel anticipation clouding his judgment. They had come at last; now was the time.

"What is it?" Marklus' voice was no more than a whisper behind him.

Crinte glanced back with a finger on his lips, and then motioned with his hand for Marklus to follow. The two crept forward, and as they did, the song of the Mounts grew louder, and now they could almost taste the sweet perfume that wafted through the air. Marklus could feel the curls on his head tighten, and his breath became shallow as they drew closer. "What strange spell is this?" he whispered to Crinte, who continued to intently move forward.

"Look," Crinte replied, pulling Marklus to an opening between the trees.

Marklus saw the strangest yet most attractive creatures he had ever seen. All of them were female. Some had long black hair, sleek and shiny, that trailed down their backs. Others had hair the color of wheat that bounced around their shoulders.

And still yet others had hair the color of fire at sunset, tongues of red orange lapping at the air. Their skin varied, tanned by the sunlight or cooled by the deep night. They sang as one as they followed an invisible trail through the night. Milk white moonlight shone down on their bare heads and naked feet. With pointed toes, they seemed to glide through the wood, the light, sometimes catching the flutter of delicate butterfly wings that grew out of their ankles. Each of them brazenly showed off their long legs through the short tunics or dresses they wore, made of bits of cloud twined with feathers and mist, held together by braids of silver horsehair. Everywhere they floated they left their laughter behind, and a perfume of enchantment drifted through the air, calling those who breathed it in to follow.

Crinte, holding back no longer, moved forward, following the creatures as they roamed. Even in the moonlight, their beauty was so breathtaking it almost hurt. At times, it seemed as if there was something off, something too strong and too odd in their features, the way they held their necks, the curve of their noses, the strength of their cheekbones. He could not quite grasp what it was, but a hint of wrongness stood out. They opened their mouths and sang words of another tongue, and when the leader turned, she looked directly at Crinte and held his gaze with her purple eyes. Without pausing, the others turned one by one, and seeing Crinte and Marklus, danced their way back towards them. The perfume grew stronger as they drew nearer, along with a powerful sensation that made Marklus' skin crawl. But he could see their faces clearly. They stood at Crinte's eye level, and their large eyes were brilliant, bold colors of greens, blues, and oranges. Long lashes swept down towards their cheeks and they held out their slender arms as if welcoming the two. When they reached Crinte and Marklus, they continued to dance excitedly around them, singing for a moment, except for their purple eyed leader. She had a short, curved knife strapped to her waist, and her long black hair seemed to blend into the shadows, but as she drew near to Crinte, he saw it was actually as blue as the night sky. She came to a standstill in front of him, so close their feet almost touched. Her face was unreadable as she looked at him. The voices died away and Marklus wondered if he should prepare to fight or flee.

"You have returned." The female spoke bluntly. She reached out a delicate hand as if to touch Crinte, but changed her mind and dropped it to her side.

"Will you take us to your king? I desire to speak with him about the war quickly coming to the Western World," Crinte replied evenly.

"Why are you so keen on this war?" She seemed annoyed. "You would come here and infiltrate our sacred Kingdom with your woes."

Crinte's eyes blazed gold as he looked at her, silently warning her of things to come. "Your Kingdom will be sacred no more if these woes do come to pass. You know this. You know why I have come."

She ripped her eyes from his face and turned to address the female creatures standing behind her, who were eagerly gazing from Crinte to Marklus as if they would very much like to eat them. "Call the Silver Herd." She looked at Crinte, her voice low. "You know our king cannot help you." She turned after the other females and leaped into the air. They flew upwards, calling out in their language.

Crinte and Marklus stood alone, watching the vibrant colors disappear above them. "Mermis." Crinte turned to Marklus. "They are creatures of the clouds above us, yet they call the Afrd Mounts home in a way. They can be...unpredictable."

"Now what happens?" Marklus asked curiously, watching the colors twinkle out of view.

"We wait for them to return with our transport."

***

Alaireia and Starman sat side by side in the glade, watching the moonlight. "Where did they go?" Starman asked.

Alaireia glanced over at him. His shoulders dropped as he slouched against the gray boulder, and his fingers anxiously touched the hilt of his sword for comfort. "Chasing the voices of the Mounts, I'm sure." She shrugged, but something about Starman's troubled face made her keep going. "Starman, you still don't have to come with us. You could stay here where it's safe, away from the violence we are about to walk into."

Starman turned to her, his eyes sad and weary. "I know, but what's the point anymore? How can I stay here when I know what you are willing to do for the Western World? It was you who begged me to come, and you who told me you needed my skills. Now, at least, I am willing to join you. This is all my heart has left to give."

Starman's words struck like stones, and Alaireia felt his grief washing over her. Spontaneously, she reached out for him, wrapping her arms around his shoulders and pulling until he fell into her embrace, holding on as if he were drowning. "I am sorry, Starman," she whispered.

He laid his head against her shoulder, his arms tight around her waist. "It is not your fault," he sighed. "I understand the urgency now. I only wish I'd known sooner."

The voices of the Mounts faded away and silence consumed the glade. Alaireia loosened her hold to look into his face. "If I could change the past and bring your family back to you, I would."

"Thank you," he whispered, and in the most unexpected motion, cupped Alaireia's sincere face in his hands and gently kissed her lips.

Alaireia pulled back in surprise. "Starman!"

He leaned back, suddenly realizing how close they were and what he had done. "I'm sorry, I just..." His voice trailed off as his face heated up.

"No, I'm confused." Alaireia peered at him, troubled. "I was just comforting you. I'm sorry for what happened, but I think you're confusing your grief with something else."

"No, Lightfoot...Alaireia..." Starman stammered as she stood up. "I'm not confused." His eyes looked hurt.

She took a step away from him, calmly explaining. "Starman, I think I need to give you some space to clear your mind."

"No, Alaireia." Starman stood up and began walking slowly towards her. "It is true, I feel lost and misplaced. The world is not what I thought it was. Everyone I care about is gone now because of a terrible being and his turned creatures. Every portal that has opened has taken something away from you and something away from me. But now we have a chance together to defeat this, although I don't know how much of a chance there is. When I said I would go where you go, I meant what I said. And if this is grief, I can see clearly now, maybe I was saved for this, but I need you, want you, by my side." He had reached her now and took both her hands in his. "Don't leave me behind."

"Starman," Alaireia said doubtfully. "Everyone I care about dies."

"Well," Starman gave her a lopsided grin, "I'm not dead yet."

Despite herself, Alaireia smiled. "No, not yet."

She leaned forward, as if to kiss him again, but the moment was broken as Legone ran into the glade. He glared at them sourly for a moment as they quickly broke hands and stepped away. "Where are Crinte and Marklus?" he demanded.

"Chasing sounds in the night," Alaireia replied, shrugging unapologetically.

Legone crossed his arms.

"We're back!" called Marklus as he jogged into the glade with Crinte at his heels.

Crinte's face was flushed with excitement, and his eyes were alight. "Prepare yourselves," he announced. "We are going to visit the Mermis."

CHAPTER 24

MERMIS

As they waited, Legone sat down, positioning himself delicately between Alaireia and Starman. He looked at them, calculating for a moment, then stared straight ahead. "Take my advice." His voice was hard. "Don't fall in love. Trust me."

Before they could reply, the sound of beating wings filled the air. Silver horses sailed into the glade, their wings creating a mini cyclone of dust and leaves. They alighted delicately and folded their wings, revealing four colorful Mermis upon their backs. The lead Mermi dismounted in one fluid motion, her black-blue hair swaying behind her lithe body. She walked up to Crinte, locking her indignant purple eyes on him. "We have come to escort you to an audience with King Vincsir."

"Thank you," Crinte responded calmly, ignoring the hidden threat in her voice. "These are my companions who will be joining us."

"I thought as much." The Mermi tilted her head scornfully and snapped her fingers. The three Mermis behind her alighted and led five silver horses forward. "I am Malaseya," she added matter-of-factly. "We will be your guides. This is my sister

218

Melair." She gestured impatiently towards a redhead Mermi with green eyes. "And my cousins Ima and Ena." She pointed respectively to a Mermi with orange hair and orange eyes, an odd combination, and another Mermi with hair like wheat and eyes like sapphires. They, unlike Malaseya, smiled sensually at the five and beckoned them forward.

The giant silver horses bent their knees, allowing the five to easily climb onto their bare backs. With a command from Malaseya, they leapt into the air, their silver white tails streaming out behind them. They rose quickly, leaving the mountainside behind. The friendly lights of the Mounts winked behind them, gathering as if waving, then dispersing to lead on their followers. At first, the beating of the large silver wings of the horses brought on a chill, but as the five grew used to it, they could see, as if for the first time, the beauty of the night. A layer of dark clouds lay between them and the mountains, blinding the world from view only momentarily until they burst through and could see, at last, the true coloration of the night. The sky was composed of darker hues of blues, purples and reds, mirroring the shades of the Mermis' hair. White light streaked across it as the stars twinkled into view, a thousand dazzling lights breaking up the quilt of night and designing peculiar constellations across the universe. Creatures of auld and words of prophecy stood out in diagrams, appearing and disappearing as soon as the viewer began to grasp what mysteries were being revealed. Higher they climbed, into another wave of mist, and even as they flew through the clouds, mountain peaks appeared before them and the winged horses barely grazed their tops. The moon rose before them like a crisp, round wafer, as if they could reach out, touch its crust, and eat it. It lit their way, highlighting a path through the clouds and casting its glory on the sharp turrets of a castle far in the distance.

The air changed as they flew. Instead of becoming increasingly conscious of the shift in altitude, the perfume of the air made it easier to breathe, relaxing them as the horses climbed higher. Finally, they stopped ascending, and the invisible path through the air flattened out. The silver horses folded their wings and instead of flying, began to race across the sky, an odd, soundless gallop which brought splashes of mist spraying into their faces. As they moved forward, bizarre creatures smaller than an eyeball whizzed past them, shouting amicably in a language they did not understand. Laughter echoed off what might be mountain peaks, but whose voices the laughter belonged to was unclear. The stars gleamed brighter in glee as the castle in the distance grew larger and realer and sharper.

Finally, in the most disturbing way, the air became full of something. Although the light from the moon and stars lit up the invisible path they followed, Starman jumped when the first thing bumped against his bare skin. He yanked his hand away with a squeal, and a gentle pop made him look around. It became clear in an instant. Peach, round bubbles of all sizes drifted past them. Some popped on contact and others simply floated away in the windless night. The five gawked in confusion but the silver horses moved forward as if the bubbles were not even there. Looming before them, a castle hung suspended in the sky, surrounded by a multitude of Mermis, both male and female, dancing around the clouds it rested upon. Their hopeful, melodic voices filled the air as they tossed bubbles to each other in a strange ritual. When they saw the five approaching with the four Mermis, they dived away, hiding among the clouds, taking their wordless song with them. The silver horses slowed to a trot and finally halted in front of the broad staircase that led into the castle constructed of mirrors. Massive round turrets shot further into the night sky, their spiked tops shining warningly like a freshly sharpened blade. The wide golden doors to the castle sat atop a curved staircase with likely a hundred stairs leading up into its mysterious glory. Twenty Mermis could have stood side by side on the first stair and still left room to pass between them. No guards stood at those doors, nor any on the staircase. The castle stood free, providing open access.

Malaseya alighted on the staircase and waved her winged companion away. She stood in front of the others and opened her hands, palm up. "Welcome to Spherical, the Kingdom of the Mermis. Please take a deep breath and dismount."

"Dismount?" Starman blurted out, staring at her, baffled. "And fall out of the sky to our deaths?"

Marklus, who had trustingly started to dismount, paused to wait for Malaseya's answer.

She sighed as if explaining for the third time to a small child the way things are. "You have breathed enough of the air of our Kingdom to float. While you cannot fly, you will, at least, not fall."

Starman, unsure of what to say, looked over at Crinte for guidance. But it was Legone the Swift who lightly climbed off the silver horse and gently placed his weight onto the air. He let go slowly and glided forward. "It feels like nothing at all," he said curiously. Slowly, the others followed his lead, and indeed found themselves uneasily standing in the air.

Malaseya's face twitched in amusement. Twirling around, she turned her back to them and called, "Follow me," as she began to float up the stairs.

Melair, Ima, and Ena dismounted and followed behind while the horses spread their massive wings and flew off towards the white moon sitting behind the castle.

"No one from the lands below has ever come to our Kingdom before," Malaseya said matter-of-factly. "You should count yourselves honored. If it hadn't been for Srackt the Wise, you would not be granted this audience."

"Ah, so you do know him," Crinte said at last.

Malaseya paused to look at him, a private glance not meant for the others to see. She turned back to the staircase just as quickly. "Yes, he is the one who helped us create an antidote for the poison."

"Poison?" Crinte could not keep the blindsided surprise from creeping into his voice.

"Yes," Malaseya quipped. "We are cursed. He did not tell you?"

"No." Crinte's voice was quiet in acceptance. "When did it begin?"

"One year ago. When we set foot on the land below, we became gravely ill. It was only a matter of days before death started to consume us. We are immortals; death was not a fear we knew. Until now." She looked back at Crinte, gauging his reaction. "Don't look at me like that. You know this to be true. The bubbles are the antidote. As long as we smell them, we live."

222

Crinte stopped walking. "We should leave. Malaseya, clearly you are trapped here. There is no way your armies can fight with us."

Malaseya peeked back at him over her bare shoulder. "No. You asked for an audience with the King, and an audience you shall have. Tomorrow, I think. When the sky shifts to what you call day. I much prefer the night."

Marklus stepped up beside Crinte, his fists clenched. "No, you heard him. We leave now. We cannot waste time here when your assistance is futile."

Legone stood behind Marklus and raised his bow threateningly. Immediately, Alaireia and Starman dropped their hands to the hilts of their swords.

Noticing their defensive positions, Malaseya turned around to stare at them, but no fear shone out of her purple eyes. Instead, she laughed scornfully. "You dare bring your weapons against us? You people of the land who cannot fly? What do you think will happen? You will slay us and run away? To where?"

"We have not come to fight," Crinte objected, motioning for his warriors to stand down. "But your news has blindsided us. Had we known about the curse, we never would have requested an audience. The night is still young. You can return us to land and we will go our separate ways."

Malaseya tilted her head and the other three Mermis flew to stand behind her, their faces neutral. "The night is not young," she countered. "And you will not leave here until you see the King. After your audience, we will return you to your precious quest." She threw the last words in their faces, then turned and quickly walked up the rest of the stairs.

The five warriors did not move, even as the Mermis continued forward. "Crinte?" Marklus questioned.

"There is nothing for it," Crinte replied. His face tightened as
he stared after the carefree Mermis. "It is only one day, and I
would rather not alienate them, even if they cannot help us."

The air felt cold as they continued upwards, and Alaireia
strayed closer to Starman. "Stay close to me," she whispered.
"This is a peculiar place."

The Mermis stood waiting at the top of the stairs. When the
five reached the top, the golden doors swung open and moonlight streamed out of the castle, leaving them no choice but to
step inside.

CHAPTER 25

MIST AND FEATHERS

White mist covered the castle floor, hiding it from the five as they reluctantly followed the Mermis through the wide halls of the castle. At least they could feel something solid under their feet, so they did not utter a complaint. Psychedelic Mermis floated past, taking no heed of the late hour. They ignored the visitors from below, but Marklus could hear the hush of their voices and chanting song drifting through the castle.

At last, Malaseya threw open a heavy door to reveal a circular lounge. Rich throws and cushions covered the low-lying divans, while mist curled dreamily across the floor, giving the furniture the illusion of floating on clouds. A table in the middle sat low to the floor, covered with delicate fruits, silver goblets, and a carafe of blushing red liquid. Archways opened into even smaller chambers with beds made of mist and feathers. "Rest here for what remains of the night," she told the five as they filed into the room. Crinte was last to enter, and she caught his shoulder. "Do not fret." Her purple eyes bored into his. "And do not think little of the hospitality of the Mermis." Before he could reply, she grabbed the door latch and pulled. It slammed shut, rustling the mist near its edges. A second later, the five heard a distinct click as the door locked.

Crinte turned to his warriors, who looked more than a little alarmed at the rapid turn of events. "I am sorry," he began. "I did not know the Mermis would treat us like this."

"Are we their prisoners?" Starman said on the edge of panic.

"No." Crinte impatiently raked a hand through his blond hair. "But I feel a fool. We went to Srackt the Wise for information and he failed to tell us of the curse of the Mermis. We are wasting a day in this, I must admit, beautiful Kingdom. We don't have time for games like these."

"We could look into the Clyear," Alaireia offered.

Crinte shook his head. "There is no point. We should have looked before."

Legone perched lightly on a deep blue cushion near the table of food and drink. But, seeing as he did not fall through the mist, settled down more comfortably and picked a bunch of red grapes. "Crinte, how are you surprised? You have been here before." He carelessly popped grapes into his mouth, looking at Crinte pointedly.

Crinte shook his head as he walked over to pour a glass of the sweet liquid. "No, I have never been to this Kingdom. Yes, I have been with the Mermis before but..." He trailed off. His previous conversations with Mermis had led him to believe they actually cared about something other than themselves. But now the seeping, deadly poison seemed to have changed their frightful minds.

"What do we do now?" Marklus asked, taking the goblet Crinte offered him.

226

Crinte continued to pour drinks. "Rest here for the night and don't worry. We will escape from this mess tomorrow."

"I wonder though," Legone muttered in disbelief.

Starman threw himself down on one of the divans. "No one at home would believe this. We're in a Kingdom in the sky and we're still alive. And to think a short time ago I did not know Mermis even existed!"

"Aren't you glad you came with us?" Marklus remarked sarcastically as he picked up a piece of fruit. But Starman was already lost in the intoxicating liquid that flowed from the goblets.

"This tastes like flowers." Alaireia sipped the liquid hesitantly as she settled down.

"I think they intentionally meant to trap us here," Legone wondered aloud as he lay down his bow and took off his quiver. "With the perfumed air and this sweet drink and these delicious fruits. They mean for us to stay here. Forever. Away from the poisoned land. Think about it. A year ago, wasn't that when the turned creatures first started appearing?"

Crinte nodded. "This is no coincidence. If we are to meet the King of the Mermis, I have questions of my own for him."

Pensive and thoughtful, the five ate and drank. Words dropped away and as the night deepened, their eyes closed where they lay. If any Mermi had dared enter the room, they would have found the five warriors no more than sleeping forms wrapped in brightly colored blankets.

Starman was first to wake in the morning. At first, he could not recall the night before, but as he yawned, stretched, and tumbled off the chaise lounge, it all came rolling back. He stood slowly, glancing around the room. Marklus snored gently on the floor, mist tangling the curls of his brown hair. Crinte slept half sitting, half leaning back, a goblet still in his hands while his head nodded into his chest. Legone lay on his stomach, stretched across a divan with blankets scattered on the floor. His bow he held in one hand, while his quiver rested on the floor beside his other hand, arrows spilling into the mist. Alaireia had curled tightly into the corner of one sofa, her dark hair spread out on the cushion holding up her head. One hand held her sword, clasped tightly to her chest. Starman swallowed hard as he watched their peaceful faces, briefly wishing they could stay safely in the kingdom of the clouds. Taking his sword, he walked into one of the adjoining rooms. One wall of the room was pure glass, a picturesque window, offering a preferred view of the glorious sky. In front of it, a welcoming white bed was piled high with feather pillows and blankets, looking as if one would melt inside it. A basin of water had been placed by the door, and Starman took a moment to freshen up before walking to the window.

Outside, a sea of blue and white waves traversed the sky. The castle sat fixated atop of blanket of clouds. Everywhere Starman's eyes fell, peach colored bubbles as big as his head drifted. Male and female Mermis flew or floated, some riding the bubbles, others flying in herds as if they had a priority destination. They all appeared to be the same age and there were no children to speak of. Yet they seemed happy, singing and shouting and dancing through the mist. Occasionally, giant silver horses rushed by with a pair of vibrant Mermis on their backs. They galloped and dived, heading back to the lands below. Starman blinked as he watched them, the loss of his family potent again.

"Starman?" a voice asked behind him.

He turned, quickly blinking away tears as Alaireia walked up. "Look." He pointed to the window.

"Oh." Alaireia's voice became awed and she walked up to the window. "It is beautiful!"

Starman shook his head, thinking of the tall tales he would have told his younger brother and sister. His two older brothers would have laughed and teased him, claiming he had a runaway imagination. His older sister would have listened eagerly, asking lots of questions, but in the end, they all would have shuddered with their arms around each other, thankful they were at home and safe from the strange wonders of the Western World.

"I'd heard there was a Kingdom in the sky," Alaireia said with reverence. "But I did not dream it would be like this."

"Would that we could stay here," Starman wished. "It seems this Kingdom should be immune to the woes below."

"Maybe." Alaireia searched Starman's face worriedly. "But you heard the Mermis; the change in the land affected even them. I'm not sure they, nor anyone, could live off air forever."

A knock on the chamber door interrupted their conversation. The lock turned and Marklus rose hastily, shaking wisps of mist that clung to his curls. Ima and Ena entered, carrying platters high above their heads. Their long manes of orange and wheat hair were braided back demurely but their dresses had not changed. They smiled wordlessly at Marklus as they swept into the room, gathering the feast from the night before and whisking out again. Before Ima disappeared down the hall, she pushed the door open and whispered, "You are free to roam, but come back before noon. You meet with the King at midday."

Crinte stood as soon as she disappeared. "I'll be back," he called to Marklus who was sitting down to sample hot foods steaming on the table.

"Crinte?" Marklus started to say, then changed his mind.

Crinte cautiously stepped out of the room and found himself standing in a great white hall. His heartbeat quickened in anticipation as he gazed about the splendor of the Kingdom of Spherical. At first, he had thought the castle was an actual building, but now, as he looked, he wasn't quite sure. Yes, his foot stood on solid matter, but it wasn't stone nor iron nor wood. Above him, the ceiling rose and curved away with light streaming in from every direction. He walked down the hall, feeling the itching vibration in his feet, calling him to explore and wander and lose himself. He wanted the knowledge the Mermis held, he wanted to know how they came to be and why they built such a castle, and more importantly, how the antidote was created. For brief moments, the night before, he had questioned the truth of the so called curse Malaseya claimed. Why would his father hold such pertinent details from him? He remembered a decade before, when he and his father had walked through Wiltieders only to come out of it into the visionary beauty of the Mounts. Those days, he had seen the same purple eyes, watching and following him. It unnerved him that the creatures of the air had a greater ability than him, eyes to see above and eyes to see below with a wider range of the world.

Crinte continued down the hall until he reached the end and the castle opened before him. It was a clearly a structure meant for those with wings. He was standing on a high balcony, and looking down, he saw levels below him, staircases and ledges, as Mermis flew back and forth, carrying round objects. What they were doing he could not tell, but they all seemed to be preparing for something. He turned when he felt eyes watching him, and Malaseya floated down beside him. Her aura was friendlier than the night before, yet he could tell something weighed on her. His breath caught for a moment when her deep round eyes met his. "Crinte, I was hoping we'd meet again under different circumstances." She placed her hands on the railing around the balcony and looked out over the Kingdom. "I did not mean to be hostile, but you will understand once you talk with King Vincsir. There is a reason you are here, but what you desire to do is near impossible. You should be more careful whom you trust with your concerns."

Crinte listened calmly, remembering years ago when it had begun. A plan much bigger than him was in motion. He remembered the moment he was swept away in the enchanting song of the Mermis for the first time. It never failed to thrill his heart and he snuck after them, watching, listening, until she caught him at last, her purple eyes just as hostile them. "You," she had hissed. "I have seen you in visions. The last of the Order of the Wise."

"How?" he had asked half-heartedly, distracted by the perfume of her body and the close proximity she kept as she whispered secrets into his ear.

"They say a spark, a change infiltrates our World, dwelling in the west where none dare go. An ever-shifting evil growing in form and shadow, fed by power, destroyed by love. The last One will rise and go forth, calling all to his side and receding evil until the end of time." Her voice was sing song, attempting to rhyme the rhythm-less words.

He had stammered in confusion, "You think I am the last one?"

"The One," she had stressed.

Since then, every time he returned to the Mounts, he felt her eyes watching, tracking him. When the turned ones began appearing, he knew exactly what to do. At first, he thought he was in charge, but now he began to realize he was only a pawn. As he listened to Malaseya, he began to wonder if the idea to go to the Great Water Hole was even his own, or if it had been implanted by a series of incidents. He felt it for the first time, what others around him felt: uncertainty and doubt.

"Malaseya," he said quickly, to distract himself. "If I have learned one thing in my life, it is this. As soon as you let hope fade, the darkness will take over. As soon as you give up, you have lost the battle. Never give in to the desperation taking over, even if you are secluded from the World up here."

"Do you know what death is like? Have you felt its dark, cold arms reaching out for you? The antidote is only a temporary solution. Soon, all the Western World, even this Kingdom, will fall." Her voice broke as she turned, moving her fierce face closer to his. "Do you know what it is like to stand by, knowing you are powerless to do anything? I would go with you and fight beside you, but my death would only hinder you."

Crinte's voice dropped as he replied, "Do you know who I travel with? I have a Healer who can put a stop to all this madness."

Malaseya shook her dark head, placing a finger on his lips. "No. This is a malicious poison; the power of a Healer will only be a short-lived antidote at best. If you succeed in destroying the creator of this evil, you and your Healer must return to restore us to the way we once were."

"I see." Crinte pulled away from her with a question in his eyes.

"Remember the days when you first walked the Mounts?" she asked him. "We were young, and all was well. Yes, those down below squabbled and fought, but we let something slip past our sight, and it has come to this. The people of the Western World can never again be left to their own."

"There will never be one Ruler for the entire Western World." Crinte's voice was quiet in rebuke. "The people groups run free and wild. That is how it has always been. That is how it should be."

"Maybe, but even so, if you do succeed, there are those who should watch over this World. This should never have happened."

"Do you still believe the prophecy? That the One will come to destroy the evil in the west? Do you still believe I am the last One?"

She moved closer to him, cocking her head as she remembered. "The Order of the Wise has fallen. You are the last. But the last One? I know not. Visions of the future are dark and unpredictable. There are no guarantees of loss or victory."

233

Crinte, noticing how lovely she smelled, turned to leave. "I know. I carry this burden too," he reminded her.

"Yes," she agreed as the strength of her voice faded away. "Crinte, please save us."

He turned back, sensing how tiny and insignificant she felt at her failure to help. Now he understood the wrongness that stood out in each Mermi, the imperfection of poison and the pallor of indubitable death. Her purple eyes swam before his, and resistance dropped away. Giving in to impulse, he gently placed a hand on her cheek while brushing the other past her feathered garb. Placing a hand on her hip, he pulled her into his arms and looked down at her.

"Malaseya, I promise to do everything in my power to free the Western World."

"Everything?" she dared him.

"Yes," he swore, holding her securely. "And when I succeed, I will return with The Healer to free you and your people from this prison in the sky."

She squeezed his arms as she held onto him. "Sixty days. That is all the time you have left."

He looked searchingly into her eyes for more. "You tell me this now? After you delay us here?"

She smirked at him then, lighting the air. "For one of the Order of the Wise, you do not know all."

"No," he gazed at her, "but I do know what to do with the time I have now." At last giving in to temptation, he bent his mouth to hers and tasted her for the first time.

AN AUDIENCE WITH A KING

At midday the Mermis, Malaseya, Melair, Ima and Ena came to lead the five to the hall of the King. They appeared at the door dressed in pure white gowns, beckoning the five to bring everything and follow them. It seemed they walked in a dream as they glided through the wide halls of the castle. Clear bubbles floated above them, rising towards the highest towers. As the five followed the Mermis, the tune to their song changed and voices rose throughout the castle in a wailing song of honor and respect.

Looking behind, Marklus could see a multitude of Mermis falling in line behind them. The females wore long, flowing white gowns with their hair braided back, tied together with silver horse hair. The males also wore white with silver diadems on their heads, leaving their bright hair long and free. In both hands, each Mermi carried a small, solid, circular object, composed of a palpitating liquid. Their sweet harmonies blended like a spell as they filed into the heart of the castle. The floor, if it could be called that, was clear with clouds drifting below it. Elegant white columns that shot up to the open air far above them held up the room. Mermis cascaded into the heart, looking east towards a dais where their King stood.

King Vincsir was an ageless Mermi whose very presence commanded respect. He stood over six feet tall and carried a golden scepter with a globe undulating on top of it. On his head, he wore a golden circlet, simple like the ones the other male Mermis wore. His sleek black hair fell to his shoulders and one could tell his solemn face had seen many joys and unspeakable woes. His slim but muscular body was covered in a gold tunic made of feathers, and he wore a long, flowing, purple robe. He stood unmoving as the five warriors entered his shrine of light. As if performing a ritual, each Mermi walked to their places while Malaseya led the five to stand in front of King Vincsir. Malaseya took her place on the right-hand side of the King's dais, with Melair beside her. Ima and Ena moved to the left-hand side, facing the five warriors.

When the last Mermi had filed into place, they closed their mouths and the music faded. Above their heads, bubbles continued to rise into the sky, and the sweet perfume they produced grew even stronger. The five could hear the audible intake of breath before the Mermis began chanting. "All hail King Vincsir of Spherical!"

King Vincsir raised a hand to silence them. Then, he turned his gaze on Crinte, and Crinte found himself surprised to find the King's golden eyes mirrored his. "Welcome, Crinte the Wise, to Spherical. We have long awaited your presence here, and

236

have prepared a gift for you and your companions." Without waiting for Crinte to answer, he turned his gaze on the multitude of Mermis standing before him. "Prepare the serum," he commanded.

He lifted his scepter and all the Mermis lifted their spheres above their heads and released them. As if pulled by a magnetic force, the round objects drifted towards the King's scepter, emitting a low, humming vibration. In a strange fashion, the spheres began interlocking, forming a sort of canopy over their heads. The vibration intensified as the canopy grew, and for a moment it seemed as if a portal would burst open and hurl them into another World.

Crinte had the strangest feeling as he stood there, apprehensive about the gift the Mermis were imparting. He wanted to pause the ceremony and ask the King questions, but decorum forbade it, and he sensed the power of the Mermis was much stronger than he'd assumed. Marklus could hear the elements within those solid balls speaking to him, and yet they were voiceless. It was unlike anything he had encountered before, and while he was sure it would not harm them, he was sure it would change them.

Alaireia remembered the first time she had used the Clyear, the rush of power, the headiness when she realized she was in over her head. The giddy sensation returned and she could almost feel herself spiraling out of control, grasping for power that eluded her fingertips.

Starman's eyes were wide; he did not know what was happening, but the others appeared to be okay with it. He wanted to walk away somewhere safe, where he could predict what would happen next, but there was no escape from the kingdom in the sky.

Legone stood frozen in horror. He had seen grand displays of power before, and at first he'd thought them beautiful. Now, he wanted to run away as fast as he could, but it felt like his feet were glued to the floor. He blinked rapidly, trying to stop the dark nightmares from returning, but they came anyway, realistic and horrific.

King Vincsir pointed his scepter at the sphere of elements and the pulsing increased. "Warriors of the Western World." He turned his golden gaze on the five warriors. "I give you the gift of invincibility! For sixty days, your power will be unmatched across the Western World, and you shall complete the quest you have placed upon yourselves. Take the blessing of the Mermis, and if you should find life at the end of your journey, return to us. This exchange we grant you in honor of Srackt the Wise, and count his deeds as payment for this gift."

A beam of light shot forth from the King's scepter and pierced the sphere. It violently convulsed and finally exploded, bursting into light that flooded over the five warriors. As it fell, they felt themselves lifted up, weightless, and the strength of a thousand Mermis pulsed through their bodies. A terrible sound filled their ears and in the midst of the unexpected gift, they found themselves reaching for each other, holding tightly as the gift of the Mermis overwhelmed them.

***

It may have only been an hour later when they found themselves standing before King Vincsir. The heart of the castle had emptied and only Malaseya, Melair, Ima, and Ena remained. King Vincsir looked at them, and his eyes were no longer golden. The light in the castle seemed to have dimmed, and the perfume from the bubbles had lessened. Crinte was the first to regain his senses. In one motion, he stepped forward and bent one knee, kneeling before the King with his eyes cast downwards. Just as quickly, Marklus followed his lead, then Starman, Alaireia, and finally, Legone reluctantly knelt as well.

"We thank you for this great honor." Crinte spoke a bit breathlessly. "We accept the fair exchange you offer, and we will restore this land."

King Vincsir motioned for them to rise as he walked down the steps to stand in front of them. "We hope this gift will not be in vain. Crinte, the Order of the Wise is failing. You may be the last to truly understand what feats the people groups can accomplish. You seek to bind together mortals and immortals, and if I could, I would send such an army to fight with you. Understand that although we of the Kingdom of Spherical may be doomed to a slow death, it is a fight we have been unwilling to give up. The immortals are dying; soon, it will only be up to you to ensure the survival of the land. We may be creatures of the air, but the land sustains us all. My kin will take you to the Three Clouds Pass and my Silver Herd will leave you at the Dejewla Sea."

Crinte knew words would not be enough to express gratitude for what the Mermis had sacrificed. He now understood Malaseya's words from earlier, and that his father had only bargained the antidote in exchange for a blessing from the Mermis. He could see the path laid before him, tunnels curling away in the mountains.

"Again," he bowed his head, "our gratitude is with you. Your gift will not be in vain."

The King looked at each of them in turn, solemnly regarding them. Then he lifted his hands. "Hope goes with you into the darkness, a beacon alight in your hearts. As you journey through weary lands, remember who you are and do not let your hearts grow dark."

He turned and walked back up to his dais, dismissing them with his actions. Questions lay unasked on Crinte's tongue, but all he could do was follow Malaseya as she led them out. Crinte glanced back at his warriors and saw Marklus lay a hand on Legone's trembling shoulder. Starman appeared rather frightened, and Alaireia looked as if she had drunk from an eternal fountain. As Crinte looked at them, a sneaking suspicion grew, and he found himself worried they would not be able to withstand the powerful gift of the Mermis.

PART TWO

THE DEJEWLA SEA

Starman strolled with Alaireia through the scattered, overhanging trees at the edge of the sea. The last five days had been
less eventful from the air, but at least the Silver Herd had set
them down by land's edge. The five were more than grateful to
stretch their legs and walk upon firm ground again. Thanks to
the extra speed provided by air travel, Crinte agreed to camp on
the Mizine side of the sea for the rest of the day. They had
reached a narrow part of the sea, and with all hopes it would
take less than a day to reach other side. Alaireia and Starman
had walked off to scout ahead, leaving Crinte, Marklus, and Legone to construct a makeshift raft to take them across.

Starman stood at the shore of the great Dejewla Sea and
stared at the enormity of the swaying body of liquid. The water
shone like sapphires, beckoning him to crawl into its watery
graves and swim and dive as if he were a child of aqua. Waves
rippled across the surface but any animals that used to dwell
near the sea had long since disappeared. He could smell the

richness of the soil as the plants close to the water stretched their roots deep, bloating themselves on salt less seawater.

Alaireia, on the other hand, had already dropped her pack of supplies and was loosening the black belt that carried her long sword. "It's good we're camping here for a time," she was saying, sitting on a fallen log to unstrap her black boots as Starman continued to be captivated by the sea. "I, for one, would like one last swim before we enter the desert. Swift claims it is a dry, barren place."

"It smells like dead fish," Starman said, wrinkling his nose.

"Starman?" Alaireia asked, standing barefoot on the shore. "Are you coming for a swim?"

"Oh." Starman's face turned red. "I...I...uh..."

Alaireia laughed as she waded into the water to see how it felt. "The water is fine!"

"Uh..." Starman turned to go, almost tripping over his feet. "I'll go downstream with the others," he stammered.

"Wait, Starman," Alaireia called. He turned around, still blushing, but she stood knee high in the water, staring into it. "What did you say it smelt like?"

Starman opened his mouth to reply when something leaped out of the water, snatching Alaireia and dragging her under. "Fish! Crinte!" Starman shouted all at once. "Help! The fish have Alaireia!" He drew his sword and ran to the waterside, but all was still again. Eyes like saucers, he ran back to the trees. "Crinte! Marklus! Swift! Hurry!" he yelled.

He ran back to the sea, only to shout and leap back in surprise as a monster surged out of the water, its long, brown-spotted tentacles waving in every direction. Along the length of

243

each tentacle, suction holes moved in and out as if the creature were breathing in air and water at the same time. Its round head had barely emerged but it was the center of the tentacles with two horrifyingly large, ink black eyes. Starman could see a mirror black image of himself drowning in the sticky elixir of those eyes, and immediately leaned over to vomit in a bush. As he wiped his mouth on the back on his hand he saw Alaireia, wrapped in one of the sucking tentacles. It was one of the most beautiful and terrifying sights he had ever seen as she rose with the creature, streaming with now muddied water. Her black hair hung long and her shoulders were bare as she gripped the tentacle in both arms, her face a mass of concentrated fury as she struggled for release.

"Alaireia!" Starman yelled, dashing into the water with his sword raised. A tentacle reached out for him and he slashed at it, ripping it open and causing black blood to leak out. Starman almost gagged as the stench of decaying fish overwhelmed him in the water. Despite it, he moved closer to the great creature. It towered above him, lifting Alaireia higher into the air. Starman slashed at the next tentacle that tried to capture him, but ultimately failed as one wrapped its slimy length around him and hugged his body uncomfortably close. Still waving his sword, he proceeded to chop at the thick length that held him, but the creature was unforgiving. It reared its head even further out of the water, displaying a wide, gaping mouth. It opened it and roared.

Starman was unprepared for the massive stench. Slime, goo, water, and leftovers from the sea monster's breakfast slapped into his olfactory senses, offending them to the max. He felt himself heaving again, with nothing left to throw up into the churning waters. The sea foamed beneath him and for a moment, he forgot about his sword and realized the real danger he and Alaireia were in of being eaten for lunch. A second later, he found himself plunged underwater while tentacles waved through the air, creating bigger waves above his head. In the instant before his lungs burst, he saw the sunlight, warm, beautiful and caring; a moment later, he was back above the water, swinging high in the air. Coughing and spewing and gasping for breath, Starman felt the fight leaving him as the creature dunked him under again. When he was brought back to the surface, spitting up even more water, he could hear Alaireia shouting. "Starman! Don't give up!"

He looked up just as there was a sickening crack and Alaireia broke loose of the tentacle that was holding her. She fell towards the water but another tentacle shot out, locking around her foot and dragging her back, upside down, towards the creature's wide mouth. Starman lifted his sword. His arms felt heavy as another tentacle smacked into his chest, splashing slimy water into his face. Yet as he lifted his sword, he could feel it begin to zing, and almost before he could control it, it leaped out and slashed at an incoming tentacle before it could slap him in the face. That's when he felt it. Not the rage he felt in Trazame on his family's farmland, not the fear he felt at the battle in the Sea Forests of Mizine. He felt certain and calm. His eyes focused. He wiped water from his face as best he could. Taking his sword in both hands, he brought it down hard. A wall of water rose up around him as the creature let go; nevertheless, he swam forward into the fray of tentacles, hacking away with his sword as he went. Pieces of the creature flew through the air, splashing back into the waves to float on the surface, shriveling as if they'd been burned.

A yell of rage sounded from behind him, and Starman, swinging his sword in one hand, glanced back for a moment to see Crinte running towards him. His mouth was open, his sword was out, and his blond hair blew straight back in the breeze as he splashed into the sea. His first blow sent the creature reeling, but gathering its strength, it moved forward to take on the Cron and Trazame that dared challenge it. Alaireia was tossed aside, dropped into the swirling waters and caught beneath the creature's body. "Starman, watch out for the arrows!" Crinte shouted.

The creature's head reared above Starman, and as he looked up to take on the menace, two blue tipped arrows whistled past him. One of them pierced the creature's inky eye and continued on into its skull. A high-pitched scream echoed through the water, and the creature began to thrash in pain, slapping the water with its long tentacles, violently throwing Crinte and Starman out of the sea onto the shore.

"Stay back!" Marklus commanded as he stood with Legone on the shore. But Starman could not have risen if he wanted to. He had landed oddly on the shore with the wind knocked out of him. Marklus let loose his arrow and it flew through the walls of water, past the flying tentacles and into the creature's other eye. The scream it was emitting became even higher, causing the blood in Marklus' ears to boil. With one last cry, the creature descended, dashing underwater, leaving foamy waves behind.

The quiet sobbing of the waves remained, with streaks of black blood floating on its surface. Starman groaned as he slowly picked himself up, looking over at Crinte, Marklus, and Legone, and then he cried, "Where's Lightfoot!"

"I'm here," Alaireia called, deflated, as she dragged herself out of the water. She rolled on the shore in shock.

Starman hurried over to her. "Are you okay?"

She nodded, cracking a wry smile for him. "It takes more than a sea monster to take me down. Are you?"

"I don't know," Starman exclaimed in frustration. "Tell me, Crinte, we are not crossing the sea now. Not after that! What was it?"

"That was an Actimic." Crinte's voice was quiet and grave. "A sea monster of Oceantic. What it is doing in these parts we can only guess."

"Did we kill it?" Starman asked, concerned.

Crinte shook his head. "No, monsters rejuvenate in the waters of the deep. It will likely hibernate until it is healed and rise again in some other waters. We will not see it again."

"Are you sure?" asked Legone, his voice hushed, his bow still lifted.

Crinte looked at him, noting his stiff demeanor and still voice. "Change of plans," Crinte announced. "We cross now, before some other monstrosity appears."

"The rafts are not yet ready," Legone remarked.

"Dry off and finish them then. Be on your guard," he warned them. "The time of rest has ended. We cannot be soft on the other side of the sea. There will be sleepless nights and relentless days. But none of that matters, because we all have heart, and

247

we know exactly what we are fighting for. And if for a moment you think this war has not affected you, and that you don't have anything to lose, remember we have lost it all already. Now we are going to take back what was lost. We are the five warriors and we are invincible. Believe it and protect each other. We are all we have on the other side."

CHAPTER 28

THE FALL OF THE ORDER OF THE WISE

Night had fallen by the time the five warriors pushed their rafts ashore. They had stood, balancing precariously, and paddled across the sea, which shimmered and rippled as if it were no longer hiding monsters in its depths. The nightmares of earlier faded into cold anticipation for what would meet them on the northern side of the sea. But as the shore came into view and the white sands of Asspraineya stretched forward, there was nothing at all waiting for them. Cautiously stepping ashore, they waited a moment, testing the silence for hostility. After a beat, Crinte motioned for them to push the rafts out to sea and they did so, cutting off their path to the south.

"Now what?" whispered Starman, daring to speak into the cool night air.

"We walk." Legone stepped forward, taking the lead, sand caking his wet boots. "The night winds will blow eventually, hiding our footprints. But night will be our only security. There are no hiding places in these lands."

Alaireia stood calmly, feeling the white sands shift beneath her feet. "We can't know for sure what is hiding in the shadows." In one motion, she lifted up the Clyear, holding it high above her head with both hands. "Borrow the vision of the Clyear. It will tell us all." The crystal winged horse spread its wings, and even as the five watched, it sprung from Alaireia's fingers across the white sands. As it flew, the five saw their vision change and align with the Clyear's, displaying white sands below and relentless darkness head. It soared higher, showing them endless desert in every direction except the sea. It moved forward until, dizzy and heady, the five at last looked away. Instantly, the Clyear was back in Alaireia's hands, as if it had never flown away, and she tucked it safely away, turning questioning eyes towards Crinte. "There was nothing."

Crinte looked puzzled as well. He could feel a tingling sensation in his brain and he wondered why forces would not be guarding the sea. Would not the transformed be curious to know who would dare venture into their territory? After all, it was how Marklus was caught the first time. Now Asspraineya opened its lands before them, welcoming them inside. Crinte swallowed as he felt a hint of uncertainty and blind fear. What was he leading his warriors into? "We should rest here then," he said at last. "You all must be weary and will need your strength for what is ahead. I will keep watch." His eyes blazed gold as he looked across the lands.

The five settled apprehensively some ways from the shore, but the quiet lapping of the waves was calming, and soon Starman passed out, snoring gently on the sand. Legone paced, anxious and restless. Sleep was not something he wished, for of late his nightmares had increased. What was ahead he knew not; he only hoped there was still life.

Alaireia sat beside Starman's sleeping form, watching what she could see of the waves. The night sky was dark, as if the moon dared not shine on such a land. The air was chill but the cold spread deeper than that. She felt herself closing up and in, neutral about what was ahead but well aware of what she left behind. She glanced at Starman every now and then, wondering how he could sleep so peacefully with all the horrors from behind and those unknown ahead. She shivered as she remembered the sea monster snatching and yanking her underwater. How her strength had returned, enabling her to rip the tentacles away. She wondered if the power was her own or a side effect from the gift of the Mermis.

"Are we going to talk about what happened?" Marklus asked Crinte. He lay on the sand, staring at the dull stars with his hands tucked behind his head. His ears were pricked, listening, but nothing unusual stood out. He had called the Zikes earlier and they had replied; all was well and quiet on the northern side of the sea.

"No." Crinte shook his head, his voice hushed. "Not unless you have anything to say. What we experienced was not something mortals should dwell on."

Legone shuddered as he paced but said nothing.

"Their act was selfless but all the same we are bound by it," Crinte concluded.

"They were beautiful and hauntingly sad," Marklus remembered. "If I could, I would return to their halls of light and mist."

"Yes," Crinte agreed. "But speak no more of it." His thoughts flew back to the day they had left, and his troubled mind still turned over reasons why Srackt the Wise had not revealed all to him. It stood to reason there was a time when Srackt the Wise had met the Mermis, and used their precarious situation to make a deal. A deal which might, indeed, turn the fate of the world. The question was how he could have known.

Crinte and his father were descendants from what used to be called the Order of the Wise. Superior in thought, the Order provided counsel to rulers of kingdoms, offering insight into what was to come and how to prepare. The Order often studied histories of the world and oddities that arose to better prepare for future events. Yet the Order had never been able to predict the future, and an antidote in exchange for an invincibility power would be abnormal even among the wisest. The more Crinte thought, the more he realized his father had been shaping his actions, even down to meeting the warriors he now called his own. After all, when he was young it had been his father's idea to travel to the borders of Zikeland and stay for a while until the land fell into silence. It was his father who had introduced him at long last to Ackhor the Cron, who was held in high regard by the rulers of the land. He was a Cron unafraid of adventure and strife, able to look into the face of death and laugh. His adventures were legendary and it was through him that Alaireia had come to Crinte's acquaintance. It had been his father who had taken him to the Afrd Mounts and inquired of a guide, a Tider from the mountain heights, to show them hidden paths. And it was his father who taught him that all people groups are unique and have something to contribute to the world, even those given to farming and creating a comfortable life, like the Trazames. He could see it clearly now, every step of the way laid out, and he had involuntarily followed it like a trail of breadcrumbs. Suddenly he did not feel as wise as he should, and his head began to swim. To distract himself, he thought again of the day they had left the Mermis.

***

The last day they spent flying over an endless sea of clouds until finally it was time to say farewell. "We are coming to The Three Clouds Pass," Malaseya shouted from ahead. "And the Rainbow Bridge."

Indeed, three monstrous clouds cut off the road before them, and just when Crinte thought they were going to attempt to fly above them, the horses entered into the wet mist, fighting their way through. A blanket of white covered their eyes and it seemed as if they moved into nowhere and nothing. Minutes crawled by as slow as the darkest night while the horses flew forward from memory. Eventually, Crinte saw flashes of bright colors lighting up the clouds below him. At first, he thought they were Mermis with their colorful hair flying long and free, but as they grew closer the clouds bowed, parting before them. Ahead of them rose a massive rainbow arching up into the air and curving back down again. Its bright colors lit up the air, almost blinding them with its radiance. The sound of falling water could be heard somewhere ahead, and the bubbles had all but disappeared, yet a hint of their presence remained. The horses alighted gently on the bridge, sending puffs of incandescent color flickering through the mists. The Mermis dismounted, floating gingerly above the bridge, and motioned for the five to do the same. "This is where we leave you," Malaseya said. "The horses will take you as far as the Dejewla Sea."

Ena was the first to move forward. She placed her hands on Crinte's shoulders and looked him squarely in the eye. "The blessings of Mizine be with you."

She moved to Marklus, placed her hands on his shoulders, and repeated the same words, while Ima stepped to Crinte in her place. When Malaseya's turn came, instead of grasping Crinte's shoulders she folded him into her arms and held tight for a moment while his arms lay lank and useless at his side. "The powers of Mizine are on your side," she told him. More reserved, she let go and moved on to bid farewell to the others.

The Mermis were the first to mount up again as their silver horses turned back in the direction of the castle, the tomb in the sky. As they waved, golden creatures twinkled into view no bigger than Crinte's hand. They carried miniature harps and had tiny golden wings on their backs. They circled around the five and began to play a farewell song. The Mermis flew back into the mist, as if they were no longer beings of the Western World. And Crinte felt the end had come.

***

Legone stood in the white sands as the sun rose. Days they had walked through endless desert, and now it was as he

254

feared. He was not sure he could find the forest of the creatures of the wood again, even with the vision of the Clyear.

"What bothers you?" Crinte stood a pace off, surveying the land.

Legone glanced at Crinte as he watched. "The land, it has changed."

"It is ever shifting. Was it not this way before?"

"I do not remember." Legone shook his head, his long braid of dark hair swinging anxiously behind him.

"This endless sand is miserable," Marklus said as he ran up, out of breath. "Crinte, something is coming. I hear deep thuds around us. The sand rises and falls. It is not chasing us, yet it comes."

"What say the Zikes?" Crinte asked.

Marklus shook his head, causing sand to fall out of his curls. "The dryness is killing them. I sent them west along the shoreline."

"Let's move!" Crinte shouted behind to Alaireia and Starman, who were a distance away. "Marklus, there are foul things afoot in this land. Keep your ears open." His voice turned low, shielding his next words from Legone, who continued to walk ahead of them. "There is a wisp of smoke in the air, watching us. Be on guard."

Marklus nodded as he pulled out his dagger. "Crinte, I know we are going to the tunnels, but with the heat of the sun and the weight of our packs, we will be exhausted by the time we arrive."

"I understand." Crinte nodded. He reached inside his tunic for the map Devine the Sorn had marked, showing their route.

"The Natrogo Woods should be close. From there, we can follow the Eya River to the Slutan Tunnels."

He unfolded the paper slowly, already feeling the hot sun beating down mercilessly on his head. For a moment, he blinked as he opened the brown pages while the sunlight filtered through. He turned it over, but both sides were the same. Black ink had faded and now the map was blank. His vision swam and his ears rang as he looked at nothing. Quickly, before Marklus could notice, he folded the map up again, placing it back in his tunic. Taking a deep breath, he looked up at the sky, noting the direction the sun had risen in. He turned northwest and closed his eyes. He had studied the map many times and could almost pull traces of it from his memory. The land of Asspraineya covered half of the northern side of the sea. Along the eastern coast was the land of Barlen. Further north was Sera Land and Freedex, where Legone claimed he had gone to swim in the glory of Oceantic. The country they had crossed the Dejewla Sea into was called Sornarky, which Crinte assumed was named for the Crons who called themselves Sorns. The Natrogo Woods were in the midwest of the country, and from there, a river led directly to the Esife Peaks, where the entrance to the Slutan Tunnels lay. At least, according to Devine the Sorn. Speculation began to build in Crinte's head, but he had to be the leader, had to present a strong front to his warriors. He pointed his feet northwest and walked through the shifting sand dunes, attempting to use his far-seeing vision, but the sun blocked his view. Not knowing what was ahead or behind, he walked on.

"Crinte! Crinte!" Alaireia's adamant voice rang out behind him. He felt her grab his shoulder. "Crinte, what's wrong?" He opened his eyes. Her concerned face was close and she reached out to touch his forehead. "It's the sun, Crinte. The sun in this land is too strong. It's affecting us all. Sometimes it feels like we're walking in circles." She moved in front of him, forcing him to stop walking. "Something is not right."

"Alaireia, I know." Crinte looked at her with tired eyes, and he wished he felt more in control. "We need to reach the forest. We need to start traveling at night. We need shelter. We need…" His voice trailed off as he felt the ground shake.

"Crinte!" Alaireia was calling his name and her voice sounded like it was in a tunnel. He could feel the vortex sucking him in. He turned his face and he could see Alaireia screaming, reaching out for him as the curved walls took him away. At first there was light. Then, everything faded away, and he was lost.

CHAPTER 29

THE OTHER SIDE

Alaireia could not stop screaming in shock and terror as she felt Crinte ripped away from her. The winds captured him, opening up a hole in the air and whisking him away, leaving her behind. The worst part was he didn't seem to notice; he only stared at her with glazed, empty eyes as he disappeared. She felt her hands shaking as she reached out, grasping at nothing. "Crinte!" she screamed in a panic. Immediately, the fear rushed in, just like it had when the Wyvern attacked Srinka and life as she knew it burned. A chill gripped her heart, squeezing it until she gasped for air as the pain and shock of the sudden loss increased. Her legs gave way and she sank into the sand, shaking. Marklus was there in an instant, sinking down beside her. With blue tipped fingers, he reached out, grabbing her shoulders securely. At his touch, she felt the pain in her chest lessen, allowing her to breathe again, her breaths coming short and fast. "He's gone," she stammered. "Something took him; he's gone!"

Starman came running up, his eyes wide. "What happened?" he begged, looking to Marklus for answers.

But it was Legone whose shadow cast over them. His voice was dry and emotionless. "He must have tripped over the remnants of a portal. Seek with the vision of the Clyear. There is no telling where it has taken him."

Marklus, attempting to remain calm, demanded, "Tell me what you know about portals!" .

"They were eight to begin with—four on this side of the sea, and four on the other. They are all closed," Legone said. "At least, I believe they are. But, when a portal opens in this world, it leaves remnants. If you trip over them, it could throw you to another city or, in some cases, another world entirely."

Alaireia, Marklus and Starman looked at each other in horror. They were all thinking the same thing but no one wanted to say it.

"Alaireia." Marklus turned back to her. "The Clyear."

She reached inside her tunic and pulled out the crystal horse, which danced in the sunlight. She whispered brokenly to it and the horse spread its wings and lifted up into the sky. The ground below them bounced and flipped, and a rain of sand shot up into the air and came crashing down again, throwing the warriors off their feet and flattening them against the ground. Crouching and spitting gritty sand from his mouth, Marklus struggled upwards again, reaching out to help pull Legone to his feet. "There is no time." Legone's eyes were fixated on what was behind them.

Marklus turned, only to find the sun blocked out by shapes moving in the sand behind them. "Run," he croaked to the others, swallowing hard against the dryness in his throat. "Run!"

Racing through the sand was impossible. With each step, their footprints were swallowed into pools of sand, and when they pulled them out again to run on, they found themselves exhausted and out of breath. The hot sun beat down relentlessly, as if attempting to cook them within the shortest amount of time. But what distracted them most was not the difficulty of the ground beneath them, nor the fact that their leader had mysteriously vanished, or even the hotness of the sun. Behind them were huge monsters that shook the ground with every move they made, and they were coming for the warriors.

"There is no way we can out run them," Alaireia panted.

"Marklus," Legone called. "Do we stand and fight?"

In that awful moment, as he struggled forward, Marklus realized he had automatically inherited leadership. Legone looked to him, his face streaked with sand, his blue eyes clear. Alaireia's face had changed from distraught panic to a calm mask, but he knew she was frightened on the inside. Plus, the Clyear had not returned yet, and they were blinded without it. Starman was scared, plain and simple, and at that moment Marklus was not sure what to tell them. He glanced behind again and saw clearly. The monsters were actually giants, three times as tall as him with lanky arms and legs. Their smooth, round faces were interrupted with the abnormal size of their large noses and flared nostrils. When they saw Marklus looking back at them, they opened their mouths and let loose a deafening roar. Marklus clasped his hands to his sensitive ears as another jolt threw him off his feet, but before he fell forward, he saw there were only three giants, slowly marching after him. "This must be what ants feel like," he muttered bitterly to himself as he attempted to spit gritty sand from his mouth.

Legone was ahead, standing on the top of a sand dune, his original question forgotten. "Marklus!" he called, pointing. "We have a problem."

Marklus forced himself to stand. Scrambling ahead, he caught up to where Legone was standing with Alaireia and Starman. They had reached the crest of a hill, and looking down, Marklus was relieved to see the sand turned into solid, barren ground with tuffs of brown grass and scattered green cacti. Further ahead, he could see a dark line of trees he assumed were the Natrogo Woods, but even closer, a mass of troops marched towards them. They were Gaslinks, and there could not have been more than fifty of them, yet still they marched directly towards the four, towards the sea, towards Mizine.

"Marklus?" Starman's voice was trembling.

"Get down," Marklus hissed, flattening himself on the sand dune.

"There is nowhere to hide," Legone told him matter-of-factly.

"Wait." Marklus slithered to the other side of the sand dune where the Gaslinks were coming. "The giants can't see us on this side, and the Gaslinks haven't seen us yet because the sun is against them. But, when the giants move the sand moves, we need to hide under the shifting sand."

Legone opened his mouth to argue, but as a wave of sand washed over them, he immediately hunkered down, hoping to blend into the white sands. Alaireia and Starman followed Marklus' lead, creating shallow graves in the sand and lying still within them.

261

"Don't move," Marklus whispered. "And don't you dare look. If it comes to a fight, wait for my lead." He felt they were all going to die, ambushed by giants and Gaslinks. All the same, he lay still and pricked his ears.

The marching of the Gaslinks could not be heard in the sand, but the giants came on, creating waves as they moved forward. After a few minutes, all grew still and quiet, and despite himself, Marklus turned his head to look, shaking sand off his face. He had slid down the hill a bit and could see the Gaslinks marching. They were headed southeast and would cross a way from his hiding place. The giants had paused when they caught sight of the Gaslinks. Now, they roared and slugged forward, making their way downhill towards them. As the giants walked, Marklus could feel the sand continuing to shift. Inch by inch, he was sliding downwards and assumed Legone, Alaireia, and Starman were as well. He wrapped his fingers more tightly around his bow, ready to fight should they be discovered.

The Gaslinks emitted a hissing battle cry and increased their speed when they saw the giants. Their skeletal faces were covered in black hoods that protected their bony structure from the sunlight. They also wore long cloaks and footwear that appeared to glide above the sand. Lifting their axes, they moved forward, ready to take on the giants.

Marklus felt his muscles tense in apprehension. He knew he should stop watching, he knew he should put his head back in the sand, but he could not tear his eyes away. Out of the corner of his eye, he saw Legone twitch above him, and knew he was watching as well. It seemed the battle of the Gaslinks and giants would provide them the opportune moment to slink away in the sand, slipping down onto the road that led towards the wood. Before he could turn to whisper to the others he saw a wavering shape in the air. Initially, it was a black streak covered in gray, but it grew quickly until it was ten feet tall. It materialized in front of the Gaslinks, the mediator between them and the three giants. It was dressed in an inky black, loosely flowing garment with a hood hiding its face. Gray smoke emitted from its shoulders and faded, as if the creature were recovering from its transformation. A sharp, pungent odor inundated the air, coming from the weapon the creature held in one hand. It was a long, black pitchfork with fierce yellow orange flames leaping from the handle. However, the creature's hands did not appear to be burning. It stood tall, and the giants paused, waiting. The Gaslinks ceased marching and waited as well, in something like anticipation mixed with fear. The creature took its free hand and reached into its garment. It unsheathed a wide blade that momentarily blinded the onlookers as it glinted in the sunlight. In one move, it lifted the blade, and in a grand, sweeping motion, cut off all three of the giants' heads. When the last head rolled down and smacked into the sand, the creature froze, sword still raised, surveying its work. Slowly, its arm came back down and the creature rippled and faded from view, as if it had never been there. The Gaslinks did not utter a sound as they put away their battle axes and marched forward, unhindered. When Marklus came to, he found he was sitting straight up, staring in horror at what the mysterious creature had done.

CHAPTER 30

ENEMY TERRITORY

"Let's move!" Marklus commanded, even though part of him wanted to turn and run back across the sand dunes, to the Dejewla Sea, back to the land of the Mizine where horrific creatures did not appear out of thin air to terrorize the land. It was clear they were in over their heads, but at best, he had to get the warriors to safety before they could rethink their strategy. "Don't talk," he told them. "Don't think, let's just find cover."

Fear gave their feet wings. They dashed out the sand dunes, down through the barren land of Sornarky, towards the woods. As they ran, the Clyear appeared, flying before them. Their eyes were drawn upwards as it flew over brown barren land, across boulders and stunted trees, until they saw a great foreboding tower, rising higher than the tallest trees. High up in the tower stood Crinte, looking lost and confused.

The vision faded as they stumbled into the wood, stopping to catch their breath behind a twenty-foot-high cactus. Its thick stem was covered in sharp spines, reaching out to snag and trap anyone who ventured too near.

"He is five days from here," Alaireia said. "In the northeastern corner of Asspraineya, far from where we need to be. He was fully armed. I don't think they have realized the portal left him there."

"We must move with all speed." Marklus nodded. "Starting now, we travel at night; the sunlight wearies us in this desert land. We need to find the Eya River and refresh ourselves. It will be a long journey but we must go quickly. From here on out, we run."

They were all thinking it, but no one said anything about the creature with the pitchfork. Instead, they threaded their way through the dehydrated cacti, which puffed out their spikes even further to ward thieves off their inner water supply. A hardened brown road covered in cracks took them northeast through the desert forest. Legone ran ahead, suddenly sure of his way as they passed. Wild underbrush grew in selfish circles around the base of the cacti, unwilling to expand beyond the poor shade they could gather. Each plant was a flowerless, neutral shade, imitating the ones behind it, causing the scenery to fall flat and dull against one's eyes. Tense apprehension hung heavy in the air, as if life itself were waiting for a calamity to fall upon them, that they might pick up what remained of themselves and wait, again, for the next disaster.

"We should stop to rest," Marklus announced after a time, pausing as the endless heat continued to paw at him.

Alaireia stopped beside him, a hand on her sword hilt as she glanced warily at their surroundings. "What's the point?" she asked openly. "Whether we walk or sleep, we are losing time.

Besides, even if we do stop, I don't think I could sleep a wink in this heat."

Legone took a few steps towards Marklus and Alaireia, nodding in agreement. "Lightfoot is right—we should keep moving, at least while the lands are quiet and we can."

Marklus turned to Starman, who was lagging behind. "I, for one, would like to put as much distance between us and that thing that appeared back there," he said with a shudder.

"Alright then, onwards it is," Marklus said as he pointed.

"Besides," Starman went on, trudging behind Marklus, "who would live in a place as hot and hopeless as this?"

"It wasn't like this before," Legone remarked emotionlessly from ahead. The dry air let their voices easily slide to each other's ears. "It used to be beautiful, a desert, yes, but…" His voice drifted away as memories overcame him. He moved faster instead, leaving Marklus, Alaireia and Starman to plod slowly along in his wake.

Night fell swiftly in the desert. One moment the intense sunlight glared down upon them like a grumpy, disappointed parent, the next it had been snuffed out of the sky like an extinguished flame. Slowly, an icy chill began to creep out of the ground, curling around their feet and raising goosebumps on their once sweaty arms. The eerie silence of the evening unsettled them. Even Legone turned back to huddle near the others. "I can scout ahead, Marklus," he offered.

Marklus shook his head, motioning for them to rest in the middle of the path. "No, let's pause here to eat, then move on. Together. Once the moon rises, we should have the light we need."

Alaireia crossed her legs as she chewed, forcing dried bread down her throat. "The desert may come alive then. We should look out for water as well."

A mere fifteen minutes later, they heard the first sounds of scuffling in the underbrush. Marklus rose quickly and stretched his tired muscles just as the first beams of moonlight began to highlight the eerie shadows of the night. "Time waits for no one," he said, his voice hushed as his ears listened to the desert awakening. "We should run."

Marklus dragged them on through light and shadow, though no one uttered a word against him. Legone and Alaireia dashed on ahead, scouting, watching, and avoiding. Small creatures scurried by them in the shadows, chased by larger ones, too distracted by the hunt to pay heed to the intruders in their land. It was not until the first hints of dawn began to streak through the sky that Marklus bade them find shade to rest in.

***

Starman did not wake again until it was past midday and the waves of heat from the intense sun could almost be seen riffling the air. He sat up slowly, taking care to stay within the shade, and searched for a water skin. But when he lifted it, naught but dust poured out. With a sigh of discomfort, he turned to his companions. Marklus and Alaireia breathed deeply and slowly, lying on their sides on the hard ground. "Lightfoot took first watch." Legone's voice drifted to him. Starman turned, eyeing the solemn Tider. "If you'll take this watch, I'll scout ahead for water."

267

Starman nodded. "How did you bear the intense heat before?"

Legone stood, unfolding his long limbs and reaching for an arrow. "It is as Marklus said: travel at night, sleep by day; it is the only way." He left the bramble of dried bushes, exiting the gentle shade. "Keep an eye out," he called to Starman, before disappearing into the heat.

Starman sat quietly, wakeful, listening and watching through the screen of twigs. The land looked just as it had the day before, as if they had not transversed miles into the northeast. The hushed silence hanging over the land was final and disturbing. Again, he recalled the sounds of home. His siblings constantly shouting in the distance, the bleating of sheep and goats, the lowing of the cows as they grazed contentedly. The intoxicating smell of his mother's and older sister's cooking would have drifted over the lush pastures dotted with plentiful watering holes. The memories waved and faded as the heat and his thirst sliced through fond thoughts of home. He shifted his position on the unforgiving ground and blinked to stay awake. Time continued to drift by, and Legone had not yet returned. His eyes grew heavy as he waited and watched. His fingers, having nothing to do, stroked his sword's hilt in a calming motion. He was just about to nod off again when he smelled it.

The tasteful, refreshing sensation of water; it was in the air, somewhere near. His dried tongue was begging for it, and for a brief moment, he was tempted to wake up Marklus and sneak off the find the source. But he was a stranger in enemy territory. Moments turned into an eternity, and Starman was just waking from an unintentional nap when Legone stealthily slid back into their shady hiding spot.

His eyes were alight from his adventure, and he passed a full water skin to Starman. "The Eya River is only a few miles ahead. From there, the forest grows thicker and denser. We should be out of the desert by nightfall."

Starman nodded uninterestedly as he continued to guzzle water, his dehydrated body thanking him by buzzing with hunger.

"Starman," Legone added as he settled down to watch and wait. "Better have that sword ready. There are Gaslinks all around the land."

Starman choked mid gulp and coughed as he looked at Legone. "How close are they?" he asked, his words coming out surprisingly calm and hard.

"A few miles. They travel by day for some reason."

Starman glanced at the hard Tider and closed his mouth, unsure of what to say next, unwilling to break through the barrier Legone held in place. They could fight together, but friendship was not something the Tider offered.

***

They came with the darkness, sneaking through the filter between shadow and light, camouflaged in their dark robes. Marklus walked through the chill with Alaireia, Legone and Starman, watching their steps, waiting for the lights of the night to guard their way. Instead, the shadows moved forward and

269

Alaireia drew her sword. "The creatures of the night may be able to see us, but we cannot see them. Let's even the playing field."

"I would rather move in stealth," Marklus began, but his voice trailed off as he heard the movement in the darkness. The muffled sound of footsteps, a sound not meant for ears to hear. "Arm yourselves," he said instead. "We have company."

Alaireia's sword lit up the barren land around them. The cacti were scattered across the desert floor, growing fewer as they moved on. The smell of water hung like a tempting prize in the air as the four continued to walk forward, hardened and determined, no fear of what was coming next. There was a pause and then, like the night, the Gaslinks were upon them.

Alaireia narrowed her eyes and lifted her sword, the beacon of light blasting forth, illuminating the black, pointed hoods the Gaslinks wore. Bony arms raised, they threw the sun sheltering hoods back and twirled wicked battle axes as they silently, unnervingly, moved to attack. Alaireia was on the defense as she surged forward, stemming the tide of the rushing Gaslinks. With a grunt, she stabbed into one's midsection and sliced her sword out, whirling to chop off another arm and throwing back an elbow to knock a third Gaslink off kilter. The light pouring from her deadly sword appeared to fizzle and dance, much like a second sword as the sharped blade dug into the bony neck of another creature and dislocated it from its body.

Legone was not used to fighting in the dark, yet the light from Alaireia's sword guided his arrows and the bony flashes of white from the Gaslinks' overstretched skin clued him in to their locations. They moved much faster than the troops they'd fought in Trazame. These were the elite, the real killers; the army that was marching towards Mizine to overtake it. Legone lifted two arrows to his bow, pulling his bow string taut until the back of his hand brushed his mouth. Pursing his lips, Legone let go. The arrows surged forward, gathering wind to assist their flight, and plunged their stone edges deep into the eye sockets of one Gaslink. The next arrow had already left Legone's hands, spinning its way into what one could only hope was the heart of a second Gaslink.

There weren't many Gaslinks, but Starman could see they had surrounded the four. Alaireia and Legone were quickly sticking down the creatures on one side, so Starman turned to the other, striking low with his sword. Even as he moved forward, he felt the strength of his sword flow through him. Fighting felt different without the rage and anger, leaving nothing but cold determination. Starman punched a Gaslink in the gut and sliced off a skeletal wrist. His sword whined and sang as he gave it free rein, each stroke sure and fatal. Nightmares faded as he hit hard, his sword clanging loudly against a battle-axe, yet he swung it around and drove it into the Gaslink's neck. A curved blade flew towards his exposed chest, but Starman dived out of the way, breaking the legs of another creature as he went down.

Arrows slid past Marklus, each one he pulled whispering secrets as it took down its target. He could feel the strength of his companions and their raw determination as they drove back the Gaslinks. The cold fear of the other side had been quelled, and returning their lost leader was their focus, no matter what stood in their way. Marklus pulled another arrow from his quiver and sent it through the bare head of a Gaslink. Just as quickly, the darkness melted into moonlight, and bodies lay around the four as they slowly brought down their weapons, breathing hard. Marklus pricked his ears, but he only heard the creatures of night at their games again. He looked at Alaireia, her sword still gleaming a warning in her hands. He glanced at Legone, who still had an arrow ready to fly; he moved slowly in a circle, searching for one last enemy to take down. Starman returned his look. "Shall we?" he asked a bit breathlessly.

"Yes," Marklus agreed, finding himself unexpectedly surprised at the strength of the company. "Let's go."

CHAPTER 31

ORDERS

A wisp of smoke drifted through the air, materializing on the cliff where Sarhorr stood. The creature towered above Sarhorr, its hidden face bowed below the curve of its hood. It held a burning pitchfork unflinchingly, waiting, saying nothing.

"I suppose you want orders." Sarhorr spoke with mirth, considering his creation. Or rather, transformation. It had never sat well with him, the fact he was unable to create. He cocked his head to the side, turning his back to overlook the beauty of the canyon stretching before him. Sometimes, he stood endlessly from his side of paradise, up where the screams of the transformed were muffled and the stars drew nearer to revel in his superiority. Creation was not possible, but transformation was only phase one. He rubbed his hands together in glee as he thought of the endless ingenuity of his plan. Mizine was only a distraction. It did not matter whether the people of that country lived or died, there would always be more people groups to transform. What concerned him were the immortals.

"The Tider—I assume he has crossed the sea?" Sarhorr asked, turning back to the silent figure.

The creature moved its head up and down.

"Good. Kill their leader." He then waved his hand dismissively.

The creature vanished and the wisp of smoke drifted away.

CHAPTER 32

THE TOWER

The dark forest of Freedex lay in the northeastern corner of Asspraineya. Since it flourished on the waters of Oceanic, the plants were more abundant. Marklus, Legone, Alaireia, and Starman stood in the tall trees under the cover of night. A cold wind blew briskly as they stood on slippery pine needles, looking up at the fierce black tower where Crinte was trapped. Its spiked turrets rose higher than any of the tall pine trees of the forest, and its black edges glinted fiendishly, even in the darkness.

Starman shivered as he looked at it. The past week should have broken the spirit of any Trazame. They had spent long nights running through the land of Asspraineya, and days hiding from the sun, sleeping, and searching for food. Already, their supplies were running low. They were all thinner and a hungry, an almost desperate look shone in their eyes. But most of all, they were determined, and Starman could feel it welling up within him. "What is the plan?" he asked.

Earlier, they had seen troops of Garcrats and Gaslinks enter the tower, and assumed it was some kind of stronghold for them.

"We have to climb the outside of the tower," Alaireia suggested. "Going inside will be too risky, unless I go alone. There is bound to be an open window or a balcony where we can enter from the outside. They won't be expecting an infiltration and will certainly not be keeping watch."

"Good," Marklus agreed. "Can you tell where he is?"

Alaireia pointed up to the side of the tower closest to them. "The Clyear has led us straight and true. He is up there. Somewhere."

Marklus nodded. "Let's go."

He moved forward but Alaireia caught his arm. "Wait, let Swift and I go. Stay here in case anything happens. We may need you on the outside."

Marklus stepped back, remembering how Alaireia had broken him out of prison. He took an arrow out of his quiver. "Go safely and quickly, then."

Alaireia beckoned to Legone and they left the wood, glancing uneasily at their surroundings as they moved forward. The watching eyes of the tower were turned inward, and even though the doorway was closed and sealed, no guards paced before them. Alaireia led Legone to the bushes clustered near the walls, and using her hands, searched for a foothold. Sure enough, there were places where the stones were uneven and holds had been left to allow builders to easily navigate up and down the sides of the tower. It was typical for huge structures to include footholds for the builders as they rose above the ground.

However, they were supposed to be destroyed or filled in once the building was complete. For some reason, it had not happened with this tower.

Alaireia placed her fingers on the cold roughness of the unforgiving stone, and pulled herself up. She reached one arm above her head, searching for the next foothold. Dirt and pine needles fell away from where they had lain untouched for many months. As soon as her fingers closed around stone, she pulled herself upward. The climb went quickly but the wind felt stronger the higher she went, and her fingers grew numb from repeatedly clinging to the cold stone. Every now and then, she scraped her knees against the sharp rock, but dared not stop or look down. She knew she was close when the wind began to buffet around her and she had to hold as tightly as she could to keep from being blown away. She leaned into the tower, hugging it close until her fingers met rails. Looking up, she was relieved to find a balcony. She pulled herself up, rubbing her tingling fingers together. Staying in the shadows, her eyes quickly darted across the balcony as Legone climbed up and lightly landed beside her. They both took out daggers and moved towards the balcony doors slowly, nodding at each other in sync.

The doors swung open readily enough, welcoming them into a small room. But instead of seeing Crinte, they found hard eyes glittering at them behind a mail hood. The creature rose and moved forward, lifting a long sword. As it drew nearer, Alaireia and Legone could see it was a Gaslink wearing a garment of mail tightly around its boney body. It swung its sword quickly, forcing the two to back away towards the balcony. Alaireia twirled her dagger, aimed it at the Gaslink's head, and let it fly. It slammed into the Gaslink's head and bounced off its mail armor, spinning away to lie undamaged on the castle floor. Legone, unable to draw an arrow in time, dropped his bow and pulled another short dagger from his belt. He moved forward aggressively as Alaireia backed away towards the balcony railing. She drew her sword slowly, feeling its power like putty in her hands. The gold line glimmered as she held her sword high with one hand. The Gaslink turned, its glittering eyes drawn by the hypnotic light of the sword. Alaireia held her blade out over the balcony edge as the creature moved towards it. When it reached the verge Alaireia pulled her sword towards herself, the Gaslink whirled but Alaireia was faster. She swung her weapon into the Gaslink's shoulders, forcing it backward over the edge of the balcony. It teetered on top for a brief second, then fell over the edge with a whoosh, too surprised to cry out. Legone nodded at her admiringly, sheathing his daggers and reaching for his bow. The two moved into the darkness of the castle.

"He's not here," Alaireia whispered as they stood in the room, looking around.

"Let's move inward," Legone suggested. "What does the Clyear say?"

Alaireia reached for it but a rustle stayed her hand.

"It is only the wind," Legone confirmed, but an arrow was ready in his bow.

Alaireia led the way to the door, sheathing her sword when she reached it. She tried the handle but it was locked. She motioned for Legone to stay back as she forced the lock and cracked open the door. Peeking her head out, she scanned the dark hall for signs of life. Even as she looked, she realized they were too low. Crinte was trapped at least two floors above them. She turned to tell Legone but a tiny movement caught her eyes in the shadows. Reaching for her dagger, she moved forward. A shadow leaped to the other side of the hall but she could not see glittering eyes; nor was its body grotesquely large like the Garcrats. She inched forward, holding tight to the wall as the shadow moved towards her. A shaft of light from the open door lit up the hall for a moment as Legone exited the room, his arrow pointed at the darkness.

Alaireia halted, waiting, barely daring to breathe as she stood, momentarily blinded. Legone, paces away from her, froze as well. A voice spoke out of the blackness in hushed tones. "Alaireia?" it whispered skeptically. "Is that you?"

"Yes?" she answered, hoping it was whom she thought it was. "It is I."

The shadow drew nearer and she saw it was indeed Crinte, looking as if nothing had happened. His naked blade was held firmly in his hands, and from what she could see of his eyes, they were dark and determined. "What are you doing here?"

"Coming for you, and Legone is here with me."

Crinte moved closer to the two, relief suddenly flooding over his face. "Of course you would be here." He shook his head in wonder. "But come now, we must be away. I had to slay ten Gaslinks floors above us on my way out. As soon as they find out, well, it will be difficult to leave."

"It's back out the window then." Legone turned back to the room.

Alaireia moved to Crinte until she was close enough to grasp his shoulder. "Never disappear on us like that again."

Crinte just looked calmly at her. "I think this had to happen, Alaireia. I have news."

***

Marklus and Starman stood beneath the reaching branches of a tall pine tree. Its body was decaying, leaves of evergreen did not grow on its boughs, and every now and then, branches snapped off into the forest. Starman jumped each time the pine needles shifted and sticks crackled underfoot. He turned to Marklus in frustration. "How long does it take?" Starman fretted. "Should we go after them?"

"No." Marklus shook his head. "They will return. Just wait. If I hear anything odd, we will go."

"I wish I had the vision of the Clyear," Starman complained as the wind picked up, howling eerily through the barren treetops. "Waiting here is the worst part."

"I hear something." Marklus pricked his ears and moved forward. There was a whooshing sound and something struck the bushes below.

Marklus and Starman looked at each other and edged forward hesitantly, glancing up at the wickedly tall tower from time to time. The wind continued to shriek above them like a dark monster awakening, chasing its prey.

"It's only a Gaslink," Marklus said when they reached the place where the shadow had fallen. The creature lay face up in the bushes, its legs bent awkwardly from the fall. Its lifeless eyes still glittered hideously.

Starman shivered, moving away from it. "They must have climbed up this way." He drew his sword, more for comfort than for anything else, and strained his neck looking up, concerned about what was happening in the silent tower.

Marklus followed his gaze. "Do you hear that?" he whispered. Within the walls a chant had started with corresponding feet pounding on the stone floors. Grwahoo! Grwahoo! Grwahoo! Drums began sounding in beat to the chanting and pounding feet.

Starman stood still to listen. "Yes." He turned questioning eyes to Marklus.

Marklus yanked Starman down behind the bushes by the tower walls not a moment too soon. A horn blasted from far above them, and the great black doors of the tower were thrown open. The chanting grew louder as an army of Gaslinks poured out of the tower. There were no traces of the ungainly Garcrats they had fought in the Sea Forests of Mizine, or even the kind of Gaslinks they had fought in Trazame. These Gaslinks were expertly advanced and covered from head to toe in thick mail. On their heads they wore dark, rounded helmets, and in their hands carried long black spears.

"It's the army," Marklus whispered as he and Starman peered through the bushes. "The army Ackhor was worried about. They must be heading to invade Mizine."

They watched, helpless, as the black sea of Gaslinks marched forth, an unending snake slithering down the roads that led south.

"We need to stop them," Starman whispered urgently.

"Them?" Marklus pointed as the marching continued, "Yes, that is why we are here in this land. To stop them once and for all."

"No," Starman said as he shook his head. "I mean right now. At the rate they are marching, they will reach Mizine long before we reach the Great Water Hole. Look!"

"How?" Marklus looked at him, confused.

"I don't know," Starman replied, at a loss for words. "But...but...there has to be a way!"

"I will tell the Zikes to warn the people of Mizine. We have armies; we can destroy them," Marklus said confidently, but he doubted it as he closed his eyes and called. *Zikes*!

Starman shook his head, frustrated. "Mizine will be swallowed by them and here we sit, unable to obliterate them. This does not feel like war, it feels like a slaughter."

"It is," Marklus agreed. "That's why we're here and why we need Crinte. We are going to stop them."

Starman said nothing, feeling helpless and miserable. At last, he understood the drive and urgency the others felt, the fate of the world weighing on their shoulders. The longer he spent with them, the more his eyes were opened. Selfishness had faded and even as he hid, he knew he would do whatever it took to protect them. They depended on him and the strength of his sword, and in exchange he cared about them as if they were family. He felt the anticipation, daring to hope that Crinte was still alive and would be joining them shortly. His sorrow mirrored Legone's when he realized he might never see his homeland again. Marklus, he had yet to understand. At times, the Cron seemed impulsive and excitable, other times calm and serious. He was like Crinte, a leader in a way, yet one who had seen much joy and sorrow. Most of all, every time Starman looked at Alaireia, he felt something he had never felt before. He was in awe of her skill. She was unlike any female from his country, wild, independent, and taking control. She allured him, pulling him in, forcing the comfortable but humdrum expectancies of life to fade.

"As soon as the army disappears, we need to go up and find them," Marklus was saying, pulling Starman's thoughts back to the creepiness of the night.

"Look, Marklus, look!" he whispered, pointing upwards.

Marklus lifted his head to the tower wall. High above him he could see three figures, quickly moving down the walls. "Oh." He grasped Starman's shoulder harder than he intended as he breathed a sigh of relief. "They are coming."

It was only a few minutes later that Alaireia hopped to the ground, almost tripping over Marklus and Starman, who leaped out of the way, motioning for her to stay quiet as the stream of troops continued down the road. Crinte was next to jump to the ground. His face lit up as he greeted Starman and Marklus, reaching out to embrace them. Once Legone was safely on solid ground again, Crinte turned to them, his eyes gold with iron determination. "There is news I have for your ears, but unfortunately my trip through the portal has delayed us. We must hasten with all speed to the Esife Peaks. You have done well without me. I know it has been hard, and there may be harder times ahead of us. But remember, we will endure." He looked them in the eye, each of them in turn, reminding them of

why they were there. "I have faith in each of you. Well done."
Finally, he glanced back at the army marching towards the
south. "Let us be away from this foul tower."

He ran off, leading the way into the woods towards the
west.

***

A beautiful morning graced the land when they stopped at
last. The pine trees had thinned into a brown road covered with
overhanging boulders and rocks, winding away towards the
southwest. Crinte, spotting a shallow cave, led them there to
hide for the day. Pressing themselves against the cool rock out
of the beaming sunlight, they crossed their legs and ate the first
meal, all the while looking at Crinte expectantly.

"I understand now how the remnants of portals work," he
began. "When it first happened, I don't think I realized it until I
was standing in a room, alone. It was then I knew, and my first
thoughts were with you all. But I realized you will always know
your way, and it was up to me to find my way back to you. It
took some time though. The portal had thrown me into a space
between rooms, but eventually the light helped me crawl
through space until I discovered a way out. In the meantime, I
listened. At first, I thought, against all hope, I had reached the
Great Water Hole. But soon I learned I was in the Srineye Tower
in Freedex, their base in Asspraineya. Gaslinks were intending
to leave shortly for Mizine, the vast army you saw marching
out. They have built a bridge over the Dejewla Sea and intend to

surprise the armies of Mizine with it. Marklus, you must send the Zikes to warn them. If that bridge can be destroyed before the army of Gaslinks gets the chance to use it, they will have to slow down while it is rebuilt. That will give us time on our end to reach the Great Water Hole. Now." Crinte's voice grew low. "I discovered the wisps of smoke that follow us through the air are Gims."

"We saw one," Marklus interrupted. "Right after you fell through the portal it materialized before us and killed three giants in one stroke." He shuddered.

Crinte narrowed his eyes. "The good news is, if we destroy its Boleck, the object that keeps the spirit in this realm, the Gim will be trapped within it, no longer able to transform or harm us. Now, get some rest, we'll move again tonight."

"Wait." Marklus peered out of the shallow cave. "I hear marching headed our way." He hurled himself out of the way as an arrow struck the ground where his nose had been seconds ago. "They have seen us!"

CHAPTER 33

AMBUSHED

Legone and Marklus stood, grabbing their carved bows as Crinte quickly called out orders. Legone squinted his blue eyes against the bright sunlight as he peered out of the cave, attempting to locate the archer. He pulled an arrow taut in his bowstring, his strong fingers holding it sure and steady before letting it fly. The dark shoulder of a creature disappeared from view as Legone's arrow flew wide.

"Aim for the boulders on the high ground to the west. Keep to the rocks. They will provide shelter as we outrun this army," Crinte called. "Alaireia and Swift, go first. We will cover you. Stay low and move fast. We need to throw them off our trail as quickly as possible. Head west, and whatever you do, keep going."

Alaireia swung around to Legone. "Daggers." She pulled twin blades out of her black belt.

One side of Legone's serious face turned up in what could almost be called a smile as he nodded knowingly at her. He carefully secured his bow onto his back and moved towards the entrance of the cave. "Marklus, you have my back?"

Marklus lifted his bow, a blue arrow nocked and ready to fly. "You know it. My aim is much improved."

Without hesitation, Legone shot out of the low hanging cave into brilliant, blinding sunlight. Brown dust gave way under his pounding feet, and loose gravel slid downhill as he made his way uphill towards the overhanging boulder Crinte had pointed out. He heard a zing behind his ears, and out of the corner of his eye saw a thick black arrow whizz past him, too close for comfort. Not even bothering to slow his speed, he lifted an arm and threw his dagger as hard as he could at one of the archers. It sailed through the air, flipping twice before landing squarely in the Gaslink's forehead. It collapsed face down on the ground; the bow snapped roughly in half as the Gaslink landed atop it. Legone gained the hill, barely slowing down as he leaped up the crest. An arrow smashed into the ground at his feet. He twirled his dagger dangerously in the air as he located his mark, then hurled it in answer. It glinted off a rock and slammed through a creature's head. A few feet behind him, Alaireia dashed up the hill. A Gaslink sprung off a high rock, boney arms outstretched as it aimed to land on her. Alaireia threw her knees into the dirt, lifted her daggers, and slashed its exposed throat as it collapsed on her. She pulled herself free before she could become too deeply entangled, and kicked the quivering body away from her. By the time she made it up the hill, Legone was crouched under the rock.

"Right." He nodded at her in approval. "I am going up to the top for a better vantage point. Cover down here until the others arrive."

287

Alaireia drew her long sword, feeling a thrill of excitement as the golden line began to gleam in the sunlight. "Go," she said. She swung her sword, listening to it whistle a warning through the warm air. "We can take them." She felt her eyes grow dark and the bloodlust roar through her veins. A few arrows skidded to a halt by her feet, and she lifted her blade.

Legone scrambled ten feet up in the air to the top of a misshapen rock. Its peak was flat and burned his bare fingertips when he touched its surface. He felt a twitch of distress and lay low for a moment, gathering his bearings, making out where the other archers were. Sure enough, there were two behind him perched on top of higher rocks, aiming at the shallow cave the five had thought they could take refuge in. Several feet in front of him, nearer the cave where Crinte, Marklus and Starman were biding their time, were two more. A fifth was to the side of him, taking aim at Alaireia. Legone stealthily pulled a blue tipped arrow from his quiver. He felt the pointed shaft slip through his fingers as he placed it in his bow. Slowly, he moved into a crouch, his fingers covering the markings on his weapon. He loosed the arrow, hearing it zing off through the still air. Before it even hit his mark, he had another and took aim at one of the two archers behind him. The first arrow had only just met its mark by the time he loosened a third arrow, hearing the cry as it pierced home. By the time his fifth arrow had flown, Crinte, Marklus and Starman were halfway to the rock. Legone lay flat again, examining the landscape, his chin burning as he pressed it against the rock. To the south, he could make out a road, and far ahead, marching down it, was the black army heading towards Mizine. Towards the west, great boulders shot up here and there, providing plenty of hiding places not only for them but also for the Gaslinks. Not waiting for the others, Legone turned and swung down the rock, moving westward towards another.

Alaireia paused as she saw Legone move forward. Three Gaslinks darted out of their hiding places towards him, but his arrows were faster. Realizing she should be with him, Alaireia moved forward just before Crinte, Marklus and Starman caught up with her. As she ran across the loose ground, she could see more Gaslinks leaving their hiding places, running towards her. Part of her wanted to stand still and fight them, but she knew Crinte would want them to keep moving, out of the madness. Two Gaslinks ran out in front of her, their stretched faces washed out and oddly pale in the sunlight. They spun battle axes, barely the length of hand to elbow as they barreled down on her. Alaireia gauged her odds. Killing Gaslinks was not about stabbing vital organs, it meant breaking bone to the point the creature could not survive, which was much harder. Recalling the buoyancy of the invincibility spell, she swung her sword with all her strength. It sliced through the air with a wild scream, shrieking through mail and bone and flesh. Two heads rolled to the ground, empty eyes staring at her before they grew cloudy with nothingness. If her display was at all intimidating, it did not show in the demeanor of the other Gaslinks. They streamed on towards her, sure to overwhelm her by sheer numbers. Ahead of her, Legone leaped from rock to rock with a steady stream of blue floating behind him. Although the heights were perilous, there were few Gaslinks with bows. If there were more, they must have kept marching with the army. As Alaireia

289

reached the shadow of a rock, a Gaslink immediately leaped out at her, swinging a battle axe. She grabbed its arm and slammed it into the rock, forcing it to drop its heavy weapon and reach for a dagger. Just as quickly, Alaireia snatched up the heavy axe and drove it in the Gaslink's shoulder, pinning it against the rock. She sheathed her sword and, using the Gaslink as a stair step, swung her way to the top of the boulder.

Ahead of him, Crinte could see Legone and Alaireia dancing through the air, from time to time their feet touching the rocks for traction before they moved westward. On the ground, the swarm of Gaslinks increased, a black mass seeking to obliterate them. "Follow their lead!" Crinte shouted to Marklus and Starman. "Whatever you do, keep moving forward!"

Crinte hung back for a moment, watching his warriors leap ahead, strong and resilient. It was unfortunate, but already he could feel a vision clouding his eyesight, forcing itself in front of him. He saw his warriors running and himself far behind, attempting to catch up. They dashed from the shelter of boulders to fields of dry grass, and at last, a dark line ahead, which he could only hope was the boundary forest Legone had spoken of. A whooshing sound drowned all noise from his ears, and as he turned, a balloon of pressure rushed towards him. Right before he could reach out, it exploded, throwing him and his warriors into…

The vision faded before he could tell. He awoke, heart racing, as if out of a dream, and lifted his sword, the strange markings fading in and out of view, tantalizing him. A guttural sound behind him compelled him to turn, finding himself staring into the yellow eyes of what appeared to be a giant lizard.

Its long, scaly body curved away, mirroring the dusty ground. A pink forked tongue flicked in and out of its mouth as it summed up Crinte, determining whether it should eat him or not. Four stubby legs lay close to the ground, and Crinte was sure if the creature were vertical it would stand taller than him. The lizard lunged and Crinte jumped, landing squarely on its scaly back. He teetered for a moment as the lizard whirled around, attempting to shake him off. Crinte crouched low as the lizard moved forward in a surprisingly speedy fashion, shooting past Gaslinks who were thrown off guard for a brief moment before they ran towards him. Crinte raised his sword and roared as the lizard stopped short and threw him into the midst of the battle. Weariness left him as he slashed and kicked and slew and roared. He was, again, Crinte the Warrior, no longer Crinte the Wise, and he felt the confinements strip away as he let loose his anger at the unfairness of the World.

Starman ran ahead of Marklus, determined to catch up with Legone and Alaireia, but as the creatures streamed towards him from every corner, he wondered if they would make it at all. Adjusting his grip on the silver hilt of his blade, he prepared to combat the Gaslinks eagerly racing towards him. Behind him, an arrow flew, taking out the Gaslink in front of him. Quickly, he tripped one to his left and stabbed the one to his right in the face. Their deathly eyes glittered in the sunlight and he gritted his teeth, refusing to let their heinous faces deter him. He could feel a pulse of energy each time he swung his blade and it shattered bone. *This is for my family,* he kept telling himself. Deep in his heart, he knew his family would no longer recognize the Trazame who swung a blade better than any known Cron.

"Scale the rocks!" Marklus shouted to him from behind.

Although he wasn't as nimble or as quick as Legone and Alaireia, Starman reached a boulder and bounded his way up. The top of the next one was only a leap away, yet he hesitated with the sun in his eyes. Standing high above the world, he could see the endless swarm of Gaslinks and realized there in the desert they would make their last stand. He shook his head, sheathed his sword, and ran. His feet pounded across the rock and lifted off, airborne. With a shuddering crash, he reached the next boulder, stumbled, and rolled across it almost to the end. Catching his footing at the last minute he pulled himself up, feeling a heady rush from the experience.

"Watch out!" Marklus' voice rang out again as a blue tipped arrow shot past him, taking out the Gaslink climbing up the rock below.

Starman ran forward again, but as he leaped, he saw a Gaslink waiting for him on the next rock. Midair, he drew his sword and landed, slashing out urgently, forcing the Gaslink to back away until Starman violently kicked it from the rock. It landed with a crunch on a dozen Gaslinks below. They looked up, the bright sunlight glinting off mail, and yelled, scrambling up the rock for him like beetles escaping the hot sun. Heeding Crinte's words, he leaped forward again, only to hear a sickening crash.

The ground shook under Marklus' feet as he paused, trying to take down three Gaslinks who had snuck up on him. He knew he should seek higher ground but Crinte was trailing behind, and with the Gaslinks about to overtake them, he knew they needed something to happen quickly. Each arrow buried its head exactly where he imagined it would, yet it was not enough. Until he saw what caused the ground to shake. A great gray boulder, which should have been impossible to move, lay on its side covered with brown dust from the impact, the bones of a dozen Gaslinks splintered below it. Marklus could just make out Alaireia sprinting away from the boulder and running to another. She was circling back towards him and Crinte, ensuring they all escaped together. She yelled as another boulder crashed into the ground while Gaslinks shrieked and dispersed, some running away from her but others running towards her in confusion. Marklus raised his bow in the air and roared in encouragement, but it was short-lived. More of the Gaslinks made their presence known, and archers appeared again. Marklus felt an arrow graze the curls of his head. He quickly ducked to the side of a boulder, peeking out while shooting back. A moment's lull gave him the chance to climb up the side of a rock, his fingers slipping against the stone as he attempted to haul himself up. He gained the top, out of breath and sweating. Pulling an arrow from his quiver, he noticed he was getting low. Legone was too far out of earshot to call. Measuredly, he took aim while Crinte rode a lizard towards him. Already, he knew it was too much; they had been fighting too long, yet it appeared the Gaslinks' numbers had increased. It was then he saw the wisp of smoke in the air and dread clogged his throat. A blackness so deep his eyes sank in it appeared, and blood orange flames licked the air tauntingly. It materialized in front of Crinte, standing at least four feet taller than him. The hooded shadow pointed its pitchfork at Crinte, and the world exploded.

CHAPTER 34

THE TIME
CONTINUUM

Legone sat up quickly, reaching for his ribs as they cried out against his movement. Holding his side, he stretched out stiff fingers for his bow and arrows as his vision cleared. Goosebumps rose on his arms from the chill, and the pain in his stomach reminded him he was hungry. He felt for his pack, only to discover his bow and quiver of spilled arrows was all that remained. Staying low, he looked around as he pulled debris from his long hair. He sat in a brown thicket with low lying cacti pointing their thick, sharp spindles at him. They provided the perfect cover as he peered around, but there was no sign of the Gaslinks or Crinte, Marklus, Starman, and Alaireia. He rose gingerly, holding onto his ribs as he breathed deeply. Bone stabbed his soft insides, confirming that his ribs were indeed broken. He tested his weight against one foot but it did not complain. Slowly, he dragged his other foot forward, finding it stinging with pain when he stood on it. He wiggled his toes inside his boot. They felt larger than usual but no bone cracked under his weight. He would manage. He hobbled forward as stealthily as possible, keeping his ear pricked for enemies in the thicket. Yet as he moved to a clearing, he saw a sight that made him draw a sharp, painful breath.

***

Coughing violently, Starman rolled over onto his back. A sticky substance trickled down his face and he brushed at it impatiently with his free hand. He opened his eyes to find himself staring into a blue sky with dark clouds threatening to hide it. Still coughing, he sat up, turning his head quickly to determine where he was. A pack full of torn bread lay at his feet, but even as he lifted it he saw everything was spoiled and moldy. His tunic clung to his sweaty back and his head came to life, roaring at him as if it were splitting in two. Starman fell flat again, and the agony subsided to a dullness pounding on his skull. He touched the substance dripping from his head and held his dirty hand in front of his eyes. Maroon blood stained his fingertips. Starman sat up again but more slowly this time, waiting for the numbing panic to take over. He was alone, in a brown field stretching onward. Beside him lay his trusty sword, and as he picked it up, he realized he knew exactly what to do. Since his head would not let him stand, yet he tucked his sword into his belt and crawled forward, towards the shade.

***

An audible ripple brought him back to consciousness and Marklus lay frozen, listening for a moment. He had landed awkwardly on his quiver and his back ached as it bit into him. Yet he couldn't move as he listened to the ripple. He heard the sound of iron and metal striking each other. A cold fear struck Marklus, and fighting his paralysis he forced himself to roll over and push his weight off the barren ground. Dust covered his fingers, and even as he brushed the grime off, it smudged his cheeks and turned his hair a darker color. He reached for an arrow, only to meet air. His quiver was empty. Frantically, he searched the ground, but there were none. It was as if he had been knocked clear out of memory into…he wasn't quite sure. The sound continued to jar his eardrums. He pulled a dagger from his belt and ran forward.

***

Her whole body trembled as she knelt on the ground. Her hands, holding her up, would not stay still. Her insides felt as if she had been ripped apart and put back together. There was a whooshing sound in her ears which would not cease ringing. Each breath hurt like a blade stabbing her insides. Tears blurred her vision. A pure whiteness gazed at her, the Clyear in the form of flesh and blood. It lay on the ground, its long white legs curled under its giant body. Large soft eyes looked at her and for a moment, it spread its long white wings before folding them onto its giant back. Alaireia determinedly lifted her chin and gazed at it, blinking rapidly while her vision cleared. "What," she asked between gulps of air, "happened?" Her voice was pleading, broken, and the trembling would not stop. She remembered lifting the Clyear as the wisp of smoke began to transform. A fiery pitchfork reached out to consume her and she had shouted a command. Now, her body felt as if it would give way if she tried to use it. Her sword lay beside her, useless in the dusty brown grass. The golden line had faded, no longer glowing. The Clyear gave no indication it had heard her question. It arched its long neck and leaned its nose towards her. Its form became translucent, fading away until it was nothing more than a small crystal horse which could fit in her hand, lying on the ground in front of her. Her resolve shattered and she could hear a cold voice in her head repeating over and over. *The one who wields its power must be strong and wise lest it be the destruction of us all. The one who wields its power must be strong and wise lest it be the destruction of us all.* Weakened by her question, she reached out a hand to take the Clyear, but found herself folding up on the ground, sobs shaking her body despite her intentions. She had awakened a power and she did not know how to handle it.

***

Crinte saw it happening in slow motion; a dark pressure rushed towards him and the world exploded, whirling him into a cyclone. He could see his warriors ahead of him, tossed screaming into the void, forward across the miles of dusty land, across the time continuum. His sword hand hung limp as he was swept along, and he felt everything being torn away. The horde of Gaslinks faded, shrieking as the pressure pushed them backwards. At one moment, it felt as if the extreme pressure would break every bone, but he could not tell if he were shouting at all from the pain. He saw the sun, orange and low in the sky, and the moon, wan and faded. A dozen rushed sunrises and sunsets blurred through his vision and he saw a tree sprout, grow, and die in a matter of seconds. A wave of wind rushed past him, sweeping his breath away and threatening to drown him. Before it disappeared, it turned, and he saw a female standing in the wind. Her eyes were green as the grass in Zikeland and her hair the color of sunlit straw. It faded into the wind and with a swirl she was gone. A moment later, a herd of white horses galloped past him, their coats so white it hurt his eyes, but he could not close them. A giant white horse led them and when he counted, he saw the herd was only six. They spread their wings and leaped into a crystal sea. A moonless night rose out of a pink sky, hard and inky black. Shadows drifted through it, unseen yet recognizable. He was turned round and round until at last the world was still, and he was dropped, unceremoniously, onto the ground before a great green forest. His body cursed him as he tried to rise, for he saw the wisp of smoke that had been with him throughout. Already, the flamed pitchfork was in front of him, and he dared not look up into the face of the Gim.

***

A long, agonized cry echoed throughout the grassland. Alaireia found herself on her feet running, sword in hand. Each footfall burned as she ran, but it wasn't weakness. She felt the invincibility potion struggling within her, the surge of raw power. It hurt as it grew, and she felt a rage as she arrived. A black, ten foot tall hooded figure stood over Crinte, who lay prone on the ground, his chest ripped open, a sea of crimson flowing endlessly. Alaireia paused mid step as if she'd been slapped in the face. "No!" The words fell from her lips in a whisper and she felt the trembling begin. "Face me!" she shouted at the monster, who turned, its wide blade dripping with blood. In one hand it held a sword; the other, a burning pitchfork. It began to walk towards Alaireia, its face hidden within the dark hood.

Alaireia took a deep breath, her insides boiling as the thrill of power filled her. She reached for her sword, sliding it slowly out of its sheath, the golden line already glimmering as she took her stance. She lifted her blade in front of her, eyes narrowed as the creature glided towards her. The blackness of its cloak cut out the light, and every time she looked at it, the cold feeling of being lost on a bleak, dark night bit at her bones. She shuddered but refused to look at its face. It raised its sword and held the pitchfork out towards her. Alaireia sidestepped the pitchfork, pivoting herself to escape the flames and swinging towards the bloody sword. The Gim raised it to meet hers, the clash of blade resounding through the emptied pasture. Quick as a flash, the Gim moved its pitchfork towards her again and arched its blade in a beautiful curve towards her neck, causing spots of blood to splatter through the air. Alaireia threw up her sword to meet it, pushing the Gim's blade back up, away from her neck as it struggled to hold it down, inching closer to her bare skin. With a cry of rage Alaireia finally flung the sword away but the Gim advanced on her, bringing its pitchfork. The flames shot higher in the air as Alaireia navigated away. But the Gim was relentless, driving its sword towards her side in a killing blow. Alaireia knocked it away, chopping the Gim's cloaked hand. It moved it out of her reach and pointed the pitchfork at her as it swung towards her head. Alaireia ducked and swung her sword, slamming it into the pitchfork. Yellow sparks flew into her face as the gong of the pitchfork drove her backwards.

Inch by inch, the Gim gained ground as they continued their duel around Crinte's prone body. Alaireia could feel the fear impregnating the air, the force of the Gim seeking to pull her across the barrier between life and death, and as her sword blocked its again and again, she saw what it really was. A collection of spirits pulled from the edges of death, restless, trapped, tortured, yet completely mastered by the one controlling them. Alaireia struck, and struck again, each blow as ineffective as the last, a game of power against power. The Gim brandished its pitchfork at her again, throwing her off her feet, knocking her to the ground. Alaireia rolled to her side and struggled to her feet, panting.

The Gim waited while Alaireia regained her footing. She looked up into its faceless cloak for the first time. "You will not defeat me!" she shouted at it. She stepped forward, feeling the power flow through her body. The light on her sword began to expand, leaping out at the Gim, and she let her powers funnel through it. In a cry of rage, she ran forward, feet pounding the ground, prepared for what would happen next. The Gim pointed its pitchfork at her but she batted it aside with her sword and came on. The wide sword moved down, ready to cleave her in two, but she dodged it and leapt into the air. In one last effort, she swung hard at the Gim's cloak. There was a crack as her sword connected with the Gim's anchor, its Boleck. Her momentum carried her sword through its swing until she found herself thrown violently into the grass. The Gim's death cry pierced the air with a mixture of agony and relief, forcing all living things that heard it to cower. The last thing Alaireia saw before her eyes closed was the Gim fading away into nothing.

CHAPTER 35

INTO THE FOREST

Marklus ran up with wide eyes in time to see the Gim shrinking into its Boleck with a puff of gray smoke. Alaireia lay headlong on the ground, but it was Crinte that made Marklus drop his dagger, his bow, and throw his quiver. His chest had been torn open and a river of blood streamed out. His eyes had already glazed over, and his mouth was awry in surprise and pain. "No!" Marklus screamed as he flung himself to the ground beside him. "No, no, no, no! Crinte, stay with me, you've got to stay with me!" The blue light did not ignite from his fingertips quickly, and even as he touched Crinte's cold face, he could feel his power had been zapped. He bowed his head and placed his hands on either side of Crinte's face. He closed his eyes and breathed deeply, calling his flagging powers out of the deepest places within him. He lifted up his voice and called in the old tongue of Mizine, knowing he had not recovered from the explosion, unsure whether he would be able to bring Crinte back. He could hear the vessels of Crinte's body crying out; they still carried life and yet they needed something more. Marklus could hear his own body straining against his mind, begging for relief, a break, a rest. But Marklus did not have time to rest. He opened his eyes, desperately looking for a solution, and his gaze fell on Alaireia's prone body.

***

"Starman?" a hushed voice whispered.

Starman turned in the shadows of the forest, his heartbeat quickening. Legone limped slowly out of the shadows, his long hair a tangled mess and his clothing covered in dust. His quiver still clung to his back but his bow hung down as if his arms were too tired to carry it. "I am glad to see you at least," he went on. "Never thought I would hear myself say those words. Have you seen the others?"

Starman shook his head. "No. I was hoping I might find them here. Do you know where we are?"

Legone gingerly lowered himself to the ground. "This is the boundary forest, where the creatures of the wood live." His voice faltered. "Or at least they used to." He rested his head against the mossy trunk of a tree. "Starman, your head is bleeding."

"I know." Starman reached a grimy hand up to touch his wound again. "What happened back there?"

Legone shook his head, his blue eyes lost. "I wonder that myself. Something powerful must have brought us here. We are at least two weeks away."

Starman looked at him, alarmed. "But..." he stuttered, putting two and two together. "That's not possible!"

"I, for one, am too weary to argue. We must find the others."

Starman's hand tightened around his sword. "I don't know where to start. Should we wait here?"

Legone put a finger to his lips and sat up, cocking his head. "What is that?" he whispered.

Starman paused to listen but the cry was already fading away. Legone scrambled up, making a wry face as his ribs pierced his insides again. "Let's find out." He hobbled forward with Starman beside him.

They had barely entered the woods, only passing through the first few lines of trees to find shade from the heat and hide themselves from potential enemies. Now, as they walked through the thin line of sapling trees, they could see the mud colored grassland stretching before them, long and hot. In the distance, someone was kneeling and Starman began to run, leaving Legone to lurch forward as best he could.

Marklus looked up as Starman jogged up, his face frightened and bloody. "Marklus!" His voice was shaking. "What happened?"

The lump in Marklus' throat would not let him speak, and he thought tears would crack his voice when he let it come at last. "We will live," he whispered to Starman, nodding his head, as if by saying the words they would come true. "We will all live," he stressed.

Starman, seeing Alaireia passed out on her side, ran to her, kneeling to lift her into his arms. He looked over her dark head at Crinte as he lay on his back. His chest was bare and there was dried blood where his tunic had been ripped away, but no wounds appeared on him.

Legone, stumbling up in misery, calmly assessed the situation. Marklus acknowledged him but had no words to share.

"Whatever has happened wrecked us," Legone said at last. "We need to take shelter in the forest before anything else happens."

Marklus stood on shaking feet, holding the object in his hand out to Legone. "Hold this a moment while I lift him."

Legone reached out to take it but when he saw what it was, recoiled his hand. "No," he said. "I would not touch that!"

Marklus turned to Starman. "Take this, please."

Starman gently laid Alaireia on the ground and walked over. Marklus handed him the Clyear. At the question in Starman's eye, he sighed. "I was too weak to heal him."

He lifted Crinte, grimacing slightly under his weight. Legone reached out to help while Starman placed the Clyear in Alaireia's arms. He took her blood-stained sword from the ground and cleaned it. Sliding it into her sheath, he lifted her up, following slowly after Marklus and Legone.

The grassland was quiet as they moved forward, a slow journey of 500 paces. The forest stood strong and mysterious, fair, slim trunks growing up here and there in front of the older, darker trees. Their thick trunks reached up to the heavens with leaves as dark as ivy evergreen. Silence inhabited the wood as well. Either the woodland creatures were hiding, or they had already left. When at last they slid under the shady boughs, Legone could feel the energy of the forest as he once had. It was darker now, quiet, a faint pulse, a cry for help as it was being swallowed, cut off. Weary from the explosion, Legone could feel the hope dying away, and he feared to even think whether or not they would still be alive.

They collapsed at last by the roots of a great tree, sticking out far enough from the ground to hide them in its cove. "It would be foolish not to keep watch," Marklus said as they lay Crinte on the ground. "But honestly, we are all too tired. We should hide ourselves well and attempt to regain our strength. Later, we should hunt for food and refill our supplies." He flung his empty quiver from his back and suddenly wanted nothing more to do than lay his head on the emerald green moss.

Starman had already tucked Alaireia into a corner by a hollow in a tree, and lay down beside her with his sheathed sword in hand. Legone reached the ground with a grunt, settling his back against the wide trunk and resting his head against it. He breathed shallowly for a moment, then propped his quiver on the soft earth and rested his bow beside it. Closing his eyes, he remembered when the forest was full of life and light, and for a time, he'd thought he would dwell there until the end of his days.

Marklus opened his eyes. Thin light streamed into the forest but he lay on the soft carpet of moss and listened for a beat. Crickets hummed softly in the night, and cicadas called worriedly to each other. A twig snapped and a flutter of wings disturbed the leaves. He could hear the relaxed breathing of his companions, in and out, slowly and gently. They were alive. Marklus stretched, feeling his body regaining its strength. He stretched his fingers one by one, listening to them, but the healing power had not returned. He had heard of those who used all their power performing one act, and he wondered if saving

Crinte was the end of his. He'd needed the Clyear to assist him, but at first he thought even it would not be enough. He could still see the lights from it dancing lovingly as they mended Crinte's chest, and the panic that had sat heavy on his heart lifting when all the wounds were closed. As his eyes adjusted to the dimness, he could see each of his companions and almost hear their broken spirits, calling out to him for help. He closed his hands into fists. He needed more rest.

CHAPTER 36

DREAMS OF THE FUTURE

Alaireia opened her eyes slowly, allowing them to adjust to the dim light. It could be midday or evening with the way the giant tree rose above her, spreading its broad leaves of protection. She looked up at the thick dark trunk covered in gray green moss. Where the moss did not grow, its bark was peeling back, displaying the pale insides of the tree. Above her, its mighty branches continued until they were hidden by dark green leaves, individually growing twice as large as her head. Even in the forest of the Ezincks she had not seen anything like it. She turned her head. Back on the ground, she could see the old roots of the tree rising above the ground like arms, surrounding her. Starman lay on his side near her. His rhythmic breathing told her he was sound asleep. She sat up, checking to ensure her sword and dagger were in place. Somewhere back there she had lost everything else except for one thing. She looked back down and beside her sat the Clyear, unprotected. She hesitated before picking it up. The crystal was lifeless. She placed it securely in her tunic and stood, noting her body felt whole again. No more did the panicked trembles threaten to shake her sanity. Nor did the burning sensations from overwhelming power sting her insides. Relieved, she noticed Marklus and Crinte slumbered nearby, almost hidden in the roots of the tree. Legone opened his eyes as her glance fell over him, propped against the heart of the tree. He gazed back with a question in his eyes. She turned to the forest, beckoning him to come with her.

Legone followed Alaireia to the other side of the tree where she stood, taking in their surroundings. "Is this where you lived?"

He nodded. "What happened back there?"

"What do you mean?"

Legone sighed. "You know what I mean."

"We need to hunt before the others wake." Alaireia brushed his words aside. "You look rough. Will you lend me your bow?"

Legone looked at her a long moment, reluctant to let go of his custom-made weapon. "Don't stray far, and hurry back," he said at last.

"Of course." Alaireia nodded quickly. Even as she took the bow in her hands, it felt wrong. It wasn't made for her. She quickly looped his quiver over her back. "Keep watch. I'll be back."

In truth, she wanted to be alone for a moment to compose her thoughts before answering the questions she knew the others would have for her. She may have whisked them out of a tight spot, but it was all wrong. Had it not been for the Mermis' invincibility potion, they might not have made it at all. Stealthily, she made her way through the underbrush of the forest, listening, watching, and blending into the shadows. The apparent peacefulness of the forest made her feel jittery, and she swallowed hard when a black bird cawed as it flew through the leaves above her head.

***

They were all awake by the time she returned to camp with a few quails. "There's not much else," she said as she walked back into the cove. Laying her game on the ground, she lifted Legone's quiver from her shoulders and handed it to him with his bow. "All the animals have left or died out. Even the plants are fading." She passed around round balls of tough fruit. "Eat these before they spoil. You'll have to poke a hole in the side and suck out the sweetness inside."

Crinte sat cross-legged, his light blond hair unruly from sleep, but his face shone with an inner light, as if nothing had happened to him after all. "Any signs of the transformed creatures out there?" he asked as he sawed open the fruit with his knife.

"None, unless they are invisible." Alaireia shrugged and sat down beside Starman, completing the circle.

Marklus kept peeking at his fingers as he ate slowly. "What happened?" he asked curiously, peering from Crinte to Alaireia.

Starman eagerly looked up from where he was digging a shallow hole in the ground in order to cook the meat Alaireia had brought.

Legone, sitting on the other side of Alaireia, paused as he rubbed two sticks together. "Was it a portal?"

Crinte shook his head. "That was no portal. Portals are instant and don't zap your strength. Whatever that was should have killed us. It transported us through time in a matter of minutes. I saw it...the sun rising and setting, the world shifting below."

Alaireia lifted her chin before meeting Crinte's gaze. "It was my fault. I wanted the Clyear to take us away from the Gaslinks. There were too many of them, you saw." Her voice was quiet, apologetic. "I did not know it would throw us quite so far."

A flame ignited from Legone's sticks and he blew gently on it, coaxing the fire into life before dropping them into the shallow pit Starman had finished. "It would have taken us at least a fortnight to walk here."

Marklus lifted his head, his eyes dark and sad. "It seems my healing power has gone dormant."

Crinte reached out and laid a hand on his shoulder. "I am sorry."

Marklus shook his head. "Maybe I used it all up. Either way, I needed the Clyear to help me."

"Oh, Marklus," Alaireia said guiltily. "If only that Gim had not been there."

"Speak no more of it." Crinte shivered, recalling the searing heat of those flames. "We move forward from here. Think about it this way. We lost time when I walked through the remnants of a portal, and gained time when we were teleported here. Time is on our side again. Marklus, what say the Zikes?"

Marklus closed his eyes, weary again. "I cannot hear them." Everything had been a blur when Crinte made the announcement about the bridge. Unfortunately, Marklus could not remember if he had passed instructions to the Zikes before Gaslinks ambushed them. He attempted to establish the connection between himself and the Zikes, but, like his healing powers, there was nothing but frayed, dead ends.

"Look," Crinte went on, "let's eat and rest here. Tomorrow we can push on into the forest. I am hesitant to stay in one place for too long, but we can afford to take it slower. I need you at your best when we enter the Slutan Tunnels."

"What if..." Starman speculated as he tucked the skinned birds into the pit and covered them with leaves. "What if we actually make it to the Great Water Hole, and we win. What then?"

Legone's face registered surprise at Starman's question, as if he had never considered the possibility. "Life." He turned the word over slowly in his mouth. "Life after the Great Water Hole? I would not know what that would look like. My life has been lonely for the most part, and my happiest years have been snatched away. I do not know what I would do."

"Rebuild." Alaireia spoke without hesitation. "I did not stay to see life return to the Forests of Srinka and my people flourish again. Much that I have seen of the Western World is countries divided, focused on their internal struggles. I would see harmony passed from country to country, just as the people groups freely travel between them."

Marklus relaxed, propped up against a tree root. His face became gentle again. "Zikeland needs me. It has been freed at last

312

from the Zikes. I must restore life to it, that it may flourish as the land it once was before the Zikes inspired fear. The people of Zikeland must return and then, when I have a chance, I will ask the wind what happened to my brother."

"I saw her," Crinte remarked, glancing over at Marklus. "The wind. She is alive."

Legone smiled privately to himself.

"Crinte, what will you do?" Marklus asked. "You're always on some great adventure. I can't imagine it would end."

Crinte shook his head. "It seems I am bound to return to the Kingdom of Spherical to set things right, once and for all. From there? Well, I have some questions of my own of the mysteries of this world. There is much to learn."

Alaireia turned to Starman. "What about you?"

Starman gazed off into the forest. "I dreamed," he spoke at last, "when we were in the house of Srackt the Wise. My family was alive and well. If that is the case, I must find them."

Alaireia reached out and took his hand. "I would like to help you," she told him.

He squeezed her hand. "I would like that."

Crinte sat up straighter. "You dreamed at the house of Srackt." He turned the words over in his head. "Dreams there are true dreams; not dreams at all, but visions of reality. We all must have seen something that night. Something that is true or something that will happen. Do each of you remember?"

"A tower," Marklus recalled. "Not the Srineye Tower you were trapped in, Crinte, a different one, but I can't quite explain it. All I know is that it was shrouded in mist and the eyes were watching."

"Were you alone?" Crinte questioned.

Marklus shook his head. "That was not clear."

"I saw our path," Crinte told them, tracing it with his fingers. "Dark pools and a winding passage into the mountains with the forest behind us. I can see it now, quite clearly. From here, I know where to go."

Crinte and Marklus turned expectant eyes on Alaireia.

"Do you believe everything you see is true?" Alaireia asked, an edge of disbelief creeping into her voice. "Because I stood in a foul place and I did something I would never do."

"Never?" Crinte looked at her calmly, his eyes beginning to change colors. "Not even given the right circumstances?" He continued to speak, not intending for her to answer. "Visions are not given lightly, because seeing the future is hard enough. Most times it is not like we intend until we arrive. If Starman were told, a year ago, that he would join our company, he would have thought the teller a fool. Who you are today can be entirely different from the person you were in the past or the person you will be in the future. One comfort I have found from seeing is to take it as it comes, neither attempting to hinder nor hasten events."

Legone's face had grown cold and distant as Crinte spoke. He looked back at him as if they were strangers. "I also saw the impossible," he claimed. "I do not believe it."

CHAPTER 37

A MISTAKE

"What did you see?" Starman asked Alaireia later, after they had eaten, sharpened their weapons, and began to drift off to sleep again.

Alaireia sat facing him, her knees tucked up to her chest and her arms wrapped around them. "Honestly, I don't want to talk about it." She sighed and looked at his hurt face. "It's not like that, it's just…" She trailed off, shaking her head.

"It's okay," Starman offered. "We don't have to talk about it."

"Starman," Alaireia said. "I'm glad you came. I know it seemed I only wanted you to come because of your skills with the sword, but now, I enjoy your company as well."

"I know," Starman admitted. "When you came after me in Trazame, that's when I knew. I've never met anyone like you. At first you frightened me, but now you intrigue me."

Alaireia smiled at him, a genuine smile that lit up her tired eyes. "I'm supposed to frighten everyone," she teased. "If I'm not, I must be losing my touch."

"Hardly." Starman grinned shyly. "I think you just don't want anyone finding out who you truly are."

The lighthearted teasing drifted from Alaireia's face. "Starman, you're right. It's easier after losing everything to keep everyone at a frightful distance. It's harder to love when you know that person will be snatched away and it will hurt all the more."

"Yes," Starman agreed, his eyes beginning to cloud over in sorrow. "But it will only hurt as long as you're alive. If time is short, why not love, and love hard?"

Alaireia looked into his serious face for a moment, his light hair sticking up straight and his brown eyes deep with feeling. "Starman," she whispered, as if hesitant to break a spell. "Come, sit beside me and tell me tales of Trazame."

He scooted over until their shoulders touched, tilting his head charmingly towards her. "Only if you tell me of the mysteries of the Forests of the Ezinck."

"Of course," she told him, and smiled again into his shoulder.

***

Legone brooded against the tree trunk. He sat with his bow in hand, staring up at the treetops. He had finally allowed Marklus to bind his ribs and sprained ankle, and although Marklus claimed his powers were gone, Legone felt better. At least, physically he felt better, but mentally he wondered if the others could sense it. Part of him wanted to tear into the forest himself, searching for clues of life. The other part of him, the part that had fled those many years ago, wanted to flee again. The others did not know what darkness they were walking into, which was why he did not believe his dream. There was no hope left, no possible way for him to gain what he truly wanted.

As the days passed, the five drifted further into the woods, moving at a slow pace. The thick underbrush held them up in places, and Legone insisted on looking for the Eya River. Food was scarce, and when they did find game it was scrawny and tasted tough. "We are going to starve in these parts if we don't find food," Marklus complained.

"We need something with substance," Alaireia added.

"I have a thought," Legone offered. He turned off the thin brown trail they had been following and plunged into the woods.

"Wait!" Marklus cried after him. "I hear water!"

"I smell it, this way," Starman announced, taking the lead.

Legone turned back reluctantly. "Good, water is exactly what we need."

They picked up the pace a bit as they made their way through the wood. It warmed up the further they progressed. Now the sunlight cast a lighted haze over the woods and the large leaves it filtered through. The trees became more densely mapped together, their trunks slimmer, their leaves broader, and rotten fruit fell from their branches. The scent of fresh water and overripe fruit filled their nostrils. Soon, they all could hear running water and the cooing of birds of the air, swooping down to drink their fill.

"It's beautiful here!" Marklus breathed from ahead. He held onto a tree trunk as he looked down. Below him, a hill dipped away, sliding gently into the river below which trickled merrily over mossy rocks and brown stone, flowing westward. It widened as it curved around a bend, out of view. Small brown trees and yellow-green bushes shot up from the bank, offering shelter to any who might choose to make their home there.

Legone limped up to join Marklus on the overlook. "It was much more glorious back then," he remarked. "Follow me." He moved into the trees with a sense of purpose.

Marklus glanced back at Crinte, who nodded. "He knows this place."

As they followed Legone through the tangled bramble of woods, they could hear an eerie calling through the air. It sounded like an excited scream, echoing throughout the woods, higher and further away.

"What is that?" Starman asked.

"Stay quiet," Legone's voice returned from ahead.

They wandered deeper in, tripping over roots and snagging their clothes in brambles. The river followed, chirping away as its banks skirted in and out of view. The humidity in the air increased, growing thick and syrupy. A sweetness danced heavy on their eyelids. Legone pulled his long braid of dark hair over his shoulder as they reached a clearing. He looked around warily before stepping out into what appeared to be a garden. Black and white bugs the size of their fingers flew, buzzing around their heads. Dark ivy and vines grew close to the trees surrounding them, but out in full sunlight, lapping the waters from the river, grew stalks of tall light green plants. They rose five

318

feet into the air and had blossomed, opening their round white faces into the sunlight. Broad leaves an inch thick sprouted from their stems, reaching out to allow sunlight to filter through them.

"It's still here," Legone said in awed wonder. "The garden, just as it once was."

Crinte stepped out, joining him. "What are these plants?"

"They are called mocholeach," Legone replied. He stepped forward into the intense sunlight, reaching out a hand to touch the plant. He broke a piece off a leaf to taste it. "The creatures of the wood farmed this plant. It keeps for a long time yet it is filling and sustaining. We should take as much as we can carry."

Marklus walked forward, carrying the makeshift packs they had made out of leaves, passing one to each of them. They moved into the rows of plants, pulling the broad leaves and tasting them as they went.

"Leave the blossoms," Legone called. "They are inedible."

"This is strangely delicious," Starman remarked, slowly chewing a leaf. "I can't say what it tastes like though."

"Sunlight," Alaireia replied. "It tastes like the sun, warm and energizing."

Crinte froze where he stood, suddenly feeling cold. Something was watching them. Slowly, he withdrew his hand from the leaf he was holding and crouched low. The others were on different rows, chatting away about nothing of importance. He looked back the way they had come but the leaves overhung the forest, blocking his view. Yet he could sense the malicious presence. Dropping his makeshift pack, he reached for his sword and whispered, "Marklus!"

Marklus' keen ears picked up Crinte's voice straightway, but even as he blocked out Starman and Alaireia's voices, he heard something else.

"Thieves," a voice hissed, shaking the leaves. "Thieves."

He could sense the anger and frustration filling the air. Turning, he hustled over to Crinte, pulling an arrow from the quiver Legone had refilled for him. "I hear it," he whispered.

"They are watching," Crinte spoke, "but not attacking yet."

Marklus moved between rows. "Alaireia, Starman!"

"What is it?" Alaireia replied from ahead.

"Keep it down. Something is out there," Marklus instructed.

Crinte hurried to join them. "We should move on westward. Where is Swift?"

Legone stood at the end of the garden, facing his companions, waiting. His hands trembled as he held his bow; his heart beat quickened and he knew his face was pale. Briefly, he wondered if the others would curse him if they knew this had been his mission all along. He watched as they came, creeping out of the woods, holding long, pointed spears in their hands. They stood well over six feet tall, his height, as their long limbs strode through the garden. A pool of green light shimmered behind them, gleaming on their translucent pale green skin. Their long, solemn faces were taut, giving away nothing, even as they hissed behind their teeth. Pale hair fell in waves past their shoulders, taking on the color of the light that streamed behind them but ever changing within the shadows. Abnormally large ears stuck up from their heads, and long limbs moved forward, lightly and easily through the rows of plants, until they were brought to a halt by Crinte's sword.

"How dare you!" one of the tall beings spat, glaring down at Crinte. "Infiltrate our forests and steal our bounty. You must return what was lost or pay tenfold!"

Crinte lowered his sword as the being seemed to be willing to talk through transgressions rather than fight first and explain later. "We apologize. We did not realize these plants belonged to you."

The being crossed him arms, staring down his nose at Crinte.

"We only ask to take a few leaves with us, for survival, and would be happy to provide payment."

The being snorted. "You? Payment? You who have desecrated our hallowed ground? What could you possibility have that we would want?"

"Me." A voice spoke from behind Crinte as Legone limped up, his bow hanging by his side. "I have returned."

SHILMI

The beings looked, and even though they attempted to hide their surprise, Crinte could see their minds reeling as they stared at Legone. Quiet echoed throughout the garden. Even the buzz of the black and yellow bugs had stilled. Legone moved to stand in front of Crinte, eye to eye with the being who had spoken first. Spears were lowered and the malicious tint of the air turned wary.

"Come with us," the being said, his voice even. He swept his hand out towards the light.

The other beings parted like a river, allowing him to lead the way. Legone followed without hesitation, Crinte behind him as he sensed the change in the air. A brief nod to Marklus, Alaireia, and Starman told them to follow as well.

They walked as if under a spell into the pool of light that shifted and whirled, pointing their steps in a new direction. The forest rotated and it seemed they walked out of the trees. It was mere minutes before the blinding light faded and they found themselves standing in a green land. The sloping ground was a carpet of dark green moss that sank underneath their feet. Before them, lights of pale green lit up the gloom, for a darkness hung heavy over the land. Great trees sprung here and there, with pale white bark and bare branches pointing downwards. Gray, ivy-embedded stone structures dotted the countryside. A dry foundation lay to the left of them, an overrun courtyard a few paces ahead. The beings led the five to a ruined castle which rose high above them with great columns and ceilings but few walls. They walked down a flight of stairs alongside a dry riverbed, and through a covered passageway where remains of a garden lay crackled, dried, and brown. Up a winding staircase they continued, and around a corner, there was a lookout over the green land. Hills rolled into green glades where life flowed no more.

"What has happened here?" Legone said in a broken voice, thick with emotion.

The being in the lead said nothing but kept walking, his gait light and easy, strolling through the ruined castle.

Crinte watched Legone as they walked. His cold demeanor was fading, his head tilted, his eyes darted here and there. He was searching. His eyes blinked rapidly, his nostrils flared as he took in the apparent death and decay of the castle. Legone walked like one of them. Although he limped, his strides were long and silent. His dark hair caught in the shadows like one of them, taking on new hues as they passed through patches of silvery light.

Marklus could hear the wind rustling the dry leaves that lay fallen in gloomy shadows of the open passageways they walked through. Although their footsteps were silent, he could hear voices of days past filter through the wind. Ghosts of laughter and tears whisked past him. He looked to Crinte questioningly, wondering why they had detoured to such an odd place.

Alaireia and Starman walked behind Marklus, exchanging worried glances. They rounded a corner, and gray columns opened into a courtyard. Green light streamed in at odd angles, highlighting a circle of thrones which had been carved out of gray stone. There were a total of twelve; two sat on a raised dais and the other ten spread out equally on each side. Each throne had a bizarre headstone carved into the top. One looked like a slice of moonlight holding an emerald stone, another a triangle of sharp points, like a cactus, but holding a ruby crown. However, the two thrones on the dais depicted a sphere with a star within, and within the star a golden crown, and within the crown a green stone. The jewels within the stones appeared muted like the figures that sat below them. At first, they appeared to be engraved into the stone, but awoke as the group approached. A male and female sat on the two raised thrones, their pale gowns flowing to rest on the rough stones below. The male had thin, silvery white hair that fell to his shoulders, hiding within the folds of his clothing. His face was shrunken and pale, his nose a thin beak, his eyes a sharp pale blue. He stared at the five in a thoughtful manner as they approached; otherwise, he did not move. The female had round, large blue eyes and long white lashes. Her hair fell in waves past her shoulders, dancing in the wind. Pointed ears stuck up above her head and her skin shone pale green. She drew a sharp breath and a green light shimmered around her as the five approached. She almost lifted her slender form from her throne, but the male lifted his finger and she froze again.

The being who had led them there swept his hand towards the thrones, motioning for them to sit on the ones furthest from the male and female. Crinte nodded soothingly at his warriors as they tentatively sat on the cold stone seats. The being moved to the middle of the circle of thrones and bowed. "King Isilder. Lady Paleidir."

King Isilder nodded in acknowledgement.

"They," the being swept his arm towards the five warriors, "were found in our gardens, stealing mocholeach. They offered payment in exchange. We have brought them here for your judgment since one is familiar to us." The being looked at Legone for a moment with an unreadable expression.

"We see." King Isilder nodded slowly.

The being withdrew, stepping backwards politely to keep from turning his back to the King. The other beings surrounded the circle of thrones but stood outside of them, holding their spears, waiting, guarding.

A hush settled over the sphere as King Isilder stood slowly, as if daring to trust his bones to hold him. He stood well over six feet and looked down at the warriors, his piercing eyes coming to rest on Crinte. "Tell me, who are you and why do you find yourselves in these parts?" At his last words, he looked at Legone the Swift.

Crinte stood respectfully, holding his own despite the fact his stature was much shorter than the King's. "We have traveled far but our business is our own. We were under the assumption that plants in the forest were free for the taking; however, we admit our mistake and would be willing to conduct a fair exchange."

The King looked at him for a long, thoughtful moment while Crinte stared back evenly, his eyes beginning to gleam gold.

"We mean you no harm," the Lady said suddenly, causing a ripple of warmth to generate through the sphere. She did not stand, only looked at each of them with her round eyes. "I am Paleidir, Lady of the Green People. You have reached our home in Shilmi, a home poisoned with death. You must understand, mocholeach is our only source of energy left. We need as much as we can, and your theft hinders our survival. Yet, it seems you may need it, at least for a time. For you, the next thirty days will be crucial. I sense there is a greater purpose here you are reluctant to explain. That you shield knowledge from us is understandable, but you are not all strangers here." She turned her blue gaze on Legone.

Crinte sat back down, glancing at Legone. Waiting.

Legone's eyes were shiny and wet as he looked back at Lady Paleidir. "I have returned for one reason. My companions and I go to the Great Water Hole to stop Sarhorr the Ruler. We need your help."

Dry gasps echoed through the circle of thrones as the Green People failed to hide their surprise. King Isilder sat down heavily, his face paler than it had been. Lady Paleidir put a hand to her forehead as if her head had become too heavy to hold up.

"Do not speak that name here," King Isilder said faintly.

"A name which rose from here?" Legone challenged the King. "We must make things right, and you know how."

"Tell us," King Isilder demanded, "who are you to storm into our midst and ask of us like this?"

Crinte's eyes flashed briefly as he rose again, announcing himself. "I am Crinte the Wise, from Norc of Mizine. I lead these warriors forth and no one shall stand against us."

Marklus stood as well, more than ready to back up Crinte. "I am Marklus the Healer, from Zikeland of Mizine."

Starman stood awkwardly. "Starman the Trazame, from Trazamy City of Mizine."

Alaireia had a hand on her sword hilt as she rose confidently. "Alaireia the Ezinck, from Srinka in the Forests of the Ezinck in Mizine."

"You know who I am." Legone stood last. "Legone the Swift, from the Afrd Mounts in Wiltieders of Mizine."

"We will help you," Lady Paleidir said decisively. She raised her head and stood tall. She looked to the King, who nodded. "You may keep the mocholeach, and we will provide knowledge. In return, you must not fail." She looked at Legone. "I am sorry it has come to this." She began to walk, barefoot, padding across the stones. "Ilictor," she turned to the being who had led the five there, "have rooms prepared. They will join us for the last meal." She turned to the five who stood expectant. "Follow me. You look weary of heart. Today, you shall rest and heal. Tomorrow, at sunrise, you may return to your journey."

She walked past them, and slowly they followed. Questions died on Crinte's lips as the Green People watched them with downcast eyes, unsettled whispers filtering through their midst. As they walked, voices began to hum, breaking the vibrations of silence. A deep voice joined in, humming the bass lines. A tenor

327

followed, adding harmony to the song. A soprano wailed in the distance and an alto joined, adding waves to the song. The Green People followed Lady Paleidir as she led them through the dark, winding castle. Up they ascended, and below, the song wailed away and King Isilder sat alone on his throne with his head in his hands.

***

A time later, the five warriors found themselves sitting in a banquet hall with round tables scattered across it. The Green People had left them for a moment and they sat hushed, staring at the high stone ceilings where dusty cobwebs dwelt. Legone hung his head, feeling his fears fading inward. At first, he'd thought they might all be dead, but knowing they were alive was barely a relief. He looked at the others, seeing the questions in their eyes. "We were meant to come here," he said. "I need their knowledge to destroy the Ruler."

"We need their knowledge," Crinte added. "Tell us, Legone, is this where you spent your years on the other side with the Green People? Can we trust them, knowing they were the ones who banished the Ruler in the first place instead of destroying him?"

Legone shook his head. "They did not know what he is, what he would become. We can trust Paleidir, Lady of the Green People. Her father, King Isilder, is torn, broken. I fear his mind is deceived. Paleidir has a pure heart; she will know what to do."

"You have known her long?" Crinte remarked.

"Yes." Legone nodded, lifting his head. "She is my wife."

Crinte's eyes flashed. "Your wife!"

Marklus leaned forward curiously. "Was she the one who introduced you to the Green People?"

"No. That was another. She is dead now." Legone bowed his head.

"Swift," Alaireia put in, puzzled. "You said you were forced from here. If she is your wife, why didn't she flee with you, at least? Something made you run back to Mizine. Why would we return here now?"

"Can't you see?" Legone cried. "Their land is poisoned, they are suffering! All the immortals will die if they stay here. The Green People, the Mermis, they all will be no more!"

"How do you know this?" Alaireia asked.

Legone lifted his head. "I looked through the Clyear and I saw the end. Eight portals opened and poison seeped into our land. The Green People are my family, and they are leaving. Soon, it will be just like it was for you, Alaireia, when the Wyvern attached Srinka. Remember, Marklus, how it felt to leave Zikeland when the Zikes awakened? Starman, it is too near, too close, but you know the pain when your family has been taken from you. And Crinte." His eyes blazed as he turned to Crinte. "What have you possibly lost in all of this? You, our leader, who cannot relate to anything we have been through? What makes you so keen to save the world?"

Crinte's eyes shone gold in light of Legone accusation. "Ask yourself," he said sternly, "why you came down from the mountains to seek my help. Ask yourself why you sought out the last One of the Order of the Wise. Ask yourself, you who speak to animals of the air, who know the words of the old, old song. You saw the worlds align and the stars change, and the portals open and the poison begin. You know more than you have told us. A secret lies heavy on your heart and it is time, now that you are home. It is time to hear the truth."

Legone turned his furious eyes on Crinte, but before he could utter a retort, the Green People filed into the hall.

CHAPTER 39

WHERE THE WIND BLOWS

After the last meal, a silent affair, the Green People led them to their rooms. Legone stood outside his door, knowing she would come, dreaming she would walk by. At first, he did not hear her approach, but he could sense her presence and his heart began to pound. He turned his head away from her as if he could keep his strength.

"You left me." Her words fell to his ears like jeweled droplets falling into a pool of light.

"You know I had to." His voice was low. There was no resistance left. Out of the corner of his eye, he saw her slender green figure. Her pale shimmer had faded, yet she still looked unearthly, standing in her long gown, gazing out the archway at the starless sky. Her aura was wan and sad, and again he recalled her wailing song. "I did not warn them," he continued after a moment. "And now it has come to this."

She straightened and turned to him, and he quickly averted his face. "That is not true, but I did not come to argue."

"Why have you come then, Paleidir? The world is ending. You have sung your last song. It's over."

Suddenly, she was in front of him, standing as tall as him as she still gazed up into his face. "Legone, listen to me." Her delicate voice sent chills through his body. "There is hope. Now that you are here, I will give you all of my power. The time has come for my people to leave this world, but I would wait for you to return. I would fight with you if I could, but since I cannot, everything I have is yours..."

Before she could continue, he captured her mouth with his and wrapped his arms tightly around her. She leaned into him and responded as if their passion had never thawed through long years of separation.

When they finally let go both of them were breathing hard. She laid her hands on his chest and looked up at him, her eyes full and questioning. "If I could, I would build a world for just you and I..." Her voice trailed off.

"No, it is not to be. I will give my life to end this, and you must go seek a better one."

"Not without you. I have waited for this day when we would be together again, even just for this moment."

He sighed but gently kissed her this time. "Tell me what your people have done and what powers you have to undo it. If this world is destroyed because of what happened here, I cannot forgive myself."

"Tomorrow, bring your warriors to where the wind blows, and I will tell you all. Tonight, hold me like you once did when you loved me."

"I still love you," he replied softly.

She looked at him as if seeing clearly. "I am sorry." Her voice was no more than a whisper, and she began to shimmer green. He could feel the hum of her power as her hand pressed against his chest. He could feel her remorse seeping into his soul. "I am sorry we did not do right by you. I am sorry for the corruption of my people. I am sorry you saw the dark side of us. But hear this, we have lost everything, and I would not lose you. When this is all over, we will stand side by side and create a new life. You will live through this, and you shall return to me. So I say. So shall it be."

He looked down at her in wonder and remembered when they were young and when they first met. He had fallen in love with her strength and beauty. He had not seen the dark side of the Green People, or his eyes were blinded to it. When he realized he had been deceived, he was hurt and disgusted. He vowed to leave and never return, but they had begged him to stay, or at least keep their secret. They had threatened him, and afraid of their great power, he made plans to flee. Before he left, they told him they did not count him as one of their enemies, and if he returned, he would be welcome. It seemed the tables had turned. On his return, he held all the power, and they were ruined.

"So shall it be," she repeated, as if daring the silence to rebuke her words.

She remembered when he had come, and how happy she had been. He smelled of life and wild mountains, and for someone so much different from her people, she could not get enough. She remembered when they had gone to where the wind blows and confessed their love to each other, and she knew she could keep secrets from him no more. Now, as he held her tightly, she bound her words around them and sealed them. This would not be goodbye; that, she would hold onto. Even as she gave her powers away to save his world, she would not exchange his life for her mistake.

"As you say, so shall it be," he confirmed. Then, gently, he caressed her cheek and touched his lips to hers again. She responded hungrily, and as they kissed, the years of solitude melted away, and the winds of change began to blow.

***

Dawn broke, dark and surely over Shilmi. Marklus woke in the stillness, feeling a twinge on his fingertips. He raised them, touching them gently, but the blue power did not spark. He closed his eyes for a moment and called. *Zikes.*

Oh Marklus the Great, we hear, we obey.

Marklus bolted upright, surprised to finally hear the voices of the Zikes again. He asked the next question in dread and anticipation. *Has the bridge been destroyed?*

Yes, the creatures are furious at the delay.

Marklus breathed a sigh of relief. *Meet me at the Great Water Hole.*

He dressed quickly in the clothes the Green People had given him the evening before. The illusive Green People seemed generous and stingy all at the same time; nevertheless, it was gratifying to pull on clothes which were not bloodstained and travel worn. Marklus fastened his quiver securely on his back and walked to where Crinte had slept. Crinte was already dressed and sat on the edge of the bed, fastening his boots. "I sense you have good news," Crinte said as Marklus dashed in.

Marklus nodded vigorously, his brown curls flopping on his forehead. "The Zikes have destroyed the bridge. The enemy has been delayed for now."

Crinte stood, laying a hand on Marklus' shoulder. "That is good news indeed. Time is on our side."

Marklus lowered his voice. "What do you think of the Green People?"

"It is hard to tell." Crinte patted his sword, thankful the Green People had not seen fit to take their weapons away. "They are powerful immortals, but with Swift on our side, I hope they will refrain from doing anything malicious to hold up our progress. If, indeed, Sarhorr the Ruler did spring from here, there must be some left who are still on his side. Swift's relationship with them is odd. He is still hiding truth from us."

"He is angry about what happened here. I don't think he ever forgave them," Marklus agreed.

"There is some guilt." Crinte opened the door and stuck his head out into the quiet hall. Filters of green light pooled around the archways; otherwise, the darkness persisted.

"I don't like it here." Starman shuddered as he joined Crinte and Marklus. "Are we leaving now?"

"I believe so," Crinte replied reassuringly.

Alaireia walked out of the shadows. Her dark hair hung loose and long behind her. She stood tall and her eyes narrowed. "Where is Swift?"

Starman went to stand beside her. "We are waiting for him."

335

Alaireia turned to Crinte. "We have learned nothing here..."

"Yet," Crinte interrupted. "We have learned nothing here yet."

A moment later, Lady Paleidir glided up to them, one hand holding tight to Legone the Swift. "Come with me," she said. "Before my father and his counselors awake." Holding a finger to her lips, she turned her beautiful head and led them through passages, away from the ruined castle.

They walked across the moss carpeted ground into a wood of naked trees, stripped of their leaves with peeling bark. It looked as if someone had taken a knife and attempted to skin them. In the middle of the wood, a hill cut sharply into the landscape. Paleidir led them towards it and a heaviness filled the air as they began to ascend. Dry vines surrounded the base, and when at last they reached the top, it flattened out. The side they had come up remained mossy and green, while on the other side, a black trail led westwards, snaking away into darkness. At the top, Paleidir let go of Legone's hand and walked to the center. Facing the five, she lifted up her long arms and a green aura began to shimmer. "I see you!" she exclaimed in her musical voice. "You are The Five Warriors. Now, let go of the fears that stay your hands and the sorrows that weigh you down. Go into the west and vanquish all who stand before you."

As she spoke, a rustling in the forest began, and it seemed the voices of the innocent dead rushed around her, causing the wind to whip up. At first, it was only a soft breeze, but quickly it increased, turning to a full blown storm. The five closed their eyes and lifted their faces to the wind as it blew. There was something healing in its winds, and even as Legone's hair whipped around his face, he could feel his ribs pop back into place, and his foot no longer stung when he placed weight on it. The pounding in Starman's head receded, and when he lifted his hand to touch the scab from his head wound, smooth skin had already covered it. Alaireia felt the fear of the power of the Clyear fade, and although she was forgiven for what she had done, she knew she would never control the Clyear in the same way again. Marklus had felt it when he first woke, but now he felt it again with a surety: the burden of carrying the power of life and death was no longer his. But it was Crinte who moved past the wind storm and stood in front of Paleidir. She was slightly taller than him and looked down, her large eyes sorrowful.

"Crinte, last One of the Order of the Wise," she said curiously. "You have taken it upon yourself to be the leader because of the immortals and the words of an old prophecy. You seek to fulfill a purpose that is not your own. You know the paths, you can see your way clearly, but you do not have my trust, and that unsettles you. Ask of me."

"How?" he asked. "How must we stop Sarhorr the Ruler?"

Paleidir's eyes grew dark and the winds blew even stronger. "How indeed. There was once a Cron who searched for knowledge and looked too deeply into the creation of the world, and the immortals of the air sequestered him away. It is he you should have searched for, and he you should have asked all things. Alas, for you were tricked with a gift, a gift of invincibility and blindness, which is why you are the last. I tell you this: All beings have two forms, a physical and spiritual form. If you force the Ruler into his spiritual form and trap it, you can then destroy him. I have heard he transforms people groups into warrior creatures. It is through those transformative waters he can be destroyed."

"How do we force him into his spiritual form?"

Paleidir looked at him. "Sarhorr the Ruler was my brother. He took spiritual form coming through the portal and stealing power from our mother. We had nothing to trap him with then, but the pursuit of power is his one—and only—weakness. He is drawn to it, and what your warriors carry are a sure beacon, alerting him of your coming."

For a moment, Crinte could see with her eyes, and their visions were aligned. He saw the outrage and fear, the strife the dark creature, Sarhorr, awoke. He saw the disputes that broke out regarding his transgressions. Most of all, he saw how the most powerful immortals remained powerless in their own moment of need. "I see," he replied.

Paleidir placed her hands on his shoulders and looked him in the eye. "Crinte the Wise, you are the leader. You hold something powerful that will help you, though you are reluctant to use it. You already know what to do." She turned him towards the black path and gently pushed him away before he could ask another question. As she did so, Crinte felt she had passed him a token of her power. He walked down the hill without a backward glance, his footsteps sure and steady.

Paleidir locked her gaze on Marklus, who walked forward as the winds threatened to blow him over. "Marklus the Healer," she greeted him. She placed her hands on his head. "All has not been well with you in the past, but that has changed."

Marklus wanted to say something, to explain, but he felt intimidated by the voices of power he could hear around him.

She turned him towards the path Crinte had taken. "All is well with you." She pushed him away and a burst of energy snapped between them.

The winds turned on Starman and Alaireia, pulling them together into the center of the hilltop. Paleidir gently wrapped her arms around their shoulders. She looked first at Alaireia. "I never thought it would come to this, but my world has been destroyed. I will never see either of you again. Remember, although you may be tested as you descend into the evil of the Great Water Hole, your hearts are strong, and you will know when to make the right choices."

"What do you mean, 'tested'?" Starman asked, alarmed.

Paleidir turned to him. "All quests take a toll on the people who seek to set things right. Unfair as it is, sometimes life is demanded to pay the debt. I do not know all that will happen, but you were willing to give all before you joined this quest, and all may be required of you."

She pushed them away from her. "But sometimes," she called as they walked down the black path, "all is not so bad after all."

Starman reached for Alaireia's hand and did not let go as they descended into the darkness.

Paleidir turned towards Legone, her arms wide open. He walked to her and she spoke to him in the language of the Green People, and he replied, holding her tightly. She pulled away as the winds grew stronger. "Do you understand what you must do?" she asked.

He nodded, reluctant to leave. "I am glad, at least, I got to see you, before the beginning of the end." He let go of her hand as her face fell. "We cannot always win," he told her, stepping backwards. "We should pay for what we have done."

"Legone," she whispered.

"Goodbye," he replied.

She moved forward, her eyes wet with tears. "Come back to me." She reached out a hand, but the wind blew her back. As Legone disappeared down the black road, she lifted her arms to the wind and let loose a chilling wail.

THE ESIFE PEAKS

Pools of dark water glistened in the dim light. Shady colors swam back and forth, rippling the surface every now and then. Coal back stones crunched under their feet as the five walked out of the dead forest, three days later. Before them lay a stretch of black, lifeless land, leading to mountains. Crinte pointed. "At last, the Esife Peaks."

Sharp cliffs reached up for the sky, and a thin river ran between the pools of dark water, leading upwards into the mountains.

"What is that smell?" Starman frowned, pinching his nose shut.

"It could be the stagnant water," Marklus suggested.

"Watch your footing," Crinte warned them as he led the way forward. He peered into the first deep pool he reached. The stench of foul water reached his nostrils and he wrinkled his nose. Shadows stirred underneath the waters and he saw a scaly back pass close to the surface. "There are strange reptiles in the water," Crinte added. "Let's hope our passage does not disturb them."

It was impossible not to walk close to the pools of water as they dotted the open ground before the cliffs, almost as if warning travelers to turn back.

Crinte was reminded of his vision, and when he looked east, he saw one side of the forest was black and dead. The other was a green haze, but soon to be swept into blackness.

"Whatever those creatures are in the water, they are moving faster now," Marklus cautioned as he listened.

Starman drew his sword immediately as he discreetly walked behind Marklus. Legone pulled an arrow from his quiver and fitted it loosely into his bow, ready for action.

Crinte paused midway through the pools of water as a long snout poked out from one of the pools ahead of him. A creature made its way onto shore, pulling its scaly, muddy green body out of the dark water and turning towards Crinte. "Crocodiles!" Crinte called as he drew his sword.

Even as the words left his mouth, olive snouts peeked up from each pool and the crocodiles began to move forward, circling the five and cutting off their route to the mountains.

"Crocodiles are only fast in marshy areas. Once we reach the mountains, they will be unable to follow up," Alaireia called.

"That doesn't help us right now!" Starman groaned.

"Right," Crinte replied as he strode forward confidently.

The crocodile in front of him turned and snapped its jaws warningly. When Crinte did not stop, it charged, moving with uncanny speed over the black ground. Its long snout hung open, displaying gleaming rows of sharp, white teeth. At the last moment, it turned, swinging its long tail and knocking Crinte off his feet. Crinte slammed into the ground, surprised, the wind knocked out of him. But the crocodile was already advancing, its mouth open as it clawed its way up his legs. An arrow bounced off its scaly back but Crinte had the presence of mind to bring his sword up. Right before the creature's snout contacted his face, Crinte stabbed his blade into the crocodile's open mouth. There was a harsh, grinding sound as teeth screeched across the blade. The creature hissed and backed away in pain, allowing Crinte to stumble to his feet. Sensing defeat, the crocodile slithered back into the pool to nurse its injuries, but two more lay waiting in Crinte's path. "Watch out for their tails," Crinte shouted back to the others, slightly embarrassed at his lack of footing.

Marklus, who had no previous experience with crocodiles, continued to aim at the scaly backs of the two in front of Crinte. One of his arrows bounced off the back of one creature, while the other sank into the stubby leg of another.

"Their backs are too tough," Crinte called. "Aim for their legs, mouths, or underbellies."

"I wish we had brought spears," Legone complained as he kept pace with Marklus. He shot an arrow, aiming for a crocodile's leg. The creature reared up to catch the arrow, snapping it in half with its teeth.

"Yes," Starman said tentatively as he snuck around the dark pools. "I don't want to get close to them."

Crocodiles continued to pour out of the pools, stumbling over each other in their haste to taste the warriors. Their bodies effectively created a barrier, cutting off the route to the foot of the mountains.

Alaireia moved ahead of Crinte to confront them, leaping from the back of one creature to the other. One crocodile thrashed below her, but balancing carefully, she drove her sword into its skull.

"Watch out!" Starman called.

Alaireia nodded in acknowledgement as she leaped to the next crocodile, repeating her movements. Legone drew another arrow and began to follow her lead, dancing across the creatures, clearing a path towards the mountains.

"Hurry!" Crinte called to Starman, who was lagging behind.

Apprehensive about coming into contact with the vicious reptiles, Starman moved forward, just as he heard a roar of thunder. He sniffed, and even past the foul stench of water, he could taste fresh rain in the air.

Marklus whirled, sinking an arrow into the underbelly of a crocodile about to climb out of a dark pool. "A storm is coming!" he shouted.

Crinte felt the first droplets of rain caress his face. He paused and inhaled, unknowingly tasting the last drops of freedom. Legone moved past him in a blur and the crocodiles hesitated before turning back to their pools, unwilling to fight when they could enjoy the cleansing water. A sharp blast of lightning struck the mountaintop, and a rumble of thunder echoed in return, shaking the ground. Starman tripped on black rock, crashing on the ground and almost rolling into a pool of water. A nearby crocodile reached out, snapping at his shoulder as he scrambled out of the way. Crinte was by his side instantly, slashing at the crocodile while pulling Starman upward and pushing him ahead.

Alaireia and Legone were in the lead now, jogging towards the mountainside as light rain came pouring down on them. Abnormally dark clouds rolled across the sky, shutting out what remained of the light. The stretch of rock ended abruptly in the face of the Esife Peaks. "We have to climb," Legone said as Crinte and Starman jogged up.

"The rock will soon be too slick to climb in this rain," Crinte urged them.

Marklus opened his pack. "It's a good thing I have rope." He smiled, tossing it to Legone.

Legone looked admiringly at him as he took the rope. "You do well planning ahead."

"I mean, we are headed to a canyon," Marklus offered.

Legone grasped a shelf of rock and pulled himself upward, moving quickly up the face of the mountains. He climbed diligently, attempting to beat the rain as it drummed down harder and faster. Marklus stood below with his arrow pointed upwards, aware surprise attacks could be awaiting them around the corner.

Crinte stood guard between Starman and Alaireia, watching the dark pools ominously ripple in the rain. As the downpour increased, he lifted his head and rolled back his eyes until he could see clearly through the drops.

"Crinte," Marklus called. "Will you do the honors?" He pointed towards the rope Legone had secured at the top.

Crinte sheathed his sword and grasped a length of rope. Even as the rain attempted to soak through it, the strings remained rough, giving him the right amount of traction as he began to climb. His foot slipped as he pressed it against the rock. He tried again, shoving his booted foot firmly against the sleek face of the mountain. Focusing on using his upper body strength, he began to climb, hand over hand. Legone gave him a hand at the top, then secured an arrow in his bow, turning to guard the peaks while Crinte held the rope for Starman. Alaireia was next, but by the time Marklus joined them at the top, the pouring rain had turned into a full white out.

"Tie yourselves to the rope," Crinte called. "That way we won't lose each other in this storm."

Rain poured down in thick white sheets as Crinte took the lead, one hand holding the rough rope tied securely around his waist, and the other to his eyes, shielding them from the rain so that he could see ahead. The crumbling rocks gave way to foliage guiding the route into the heart of the mountains. Stout, leafless bushes stood five feet tall and created a curved path around the foothills. The surface flattened and Crinte drew his sword, prepared for the unexpected as they rounded the corner. The path continued on, but to the left, the mountain hunched over, like a giant sheltering itself from the storm. A gaping hole of blackness opened up, promising safety from the storm. Crinte stared at it, recalling his vision, but an ominous sense of foreboding filled his heart as he realized how far they had come and how close they were to completing their mission. His eyes had already begun to glow, ready to meet the shadows. As he moved forward, he felt the mountain shudder. The movement came from behind, and the rope around his waist was tugged forward sharply as Starman, Alaireia, Marklus, and Legone began to sprint.

"What is that?" Starman cried in terror.

"Run!" shouted Marklus frantically.

Crinte turned and found himself staring up into the blazing eyes of a ten-foot-tall monster made of iron.

CHAPTER 41

THE SLUTAN TUNNELS

The monster did not make a sound. Instead, it moved one enormous foot forward, jarring the mountainside as it sat it down. Blue rusted armor covered it from head to toe; even its face was simply a mask with dead eyes staring out of it. Two short horns stuck out from either side of its head as it slowly, heavily, gained ground. In an upraised hand, it held a curved blade, which it brought down suddenly on a barren bush in its path. The bush split in half effortlessly and the monster moved forward, its unarmed hand out, reaching for the warriors.

Crinte was swept along in the panic as his warriors dashed headlong for the looming entrance of the cave. Yet he could not look away from the monster. In the blinding rain, it pointed its shining blade at him, waving him on, daring him to come back. It was Alaireia who reached out and grabbed his arm, pulling him out of the rain into the musty tunnel. It smelled like stale water and leaves as he pressed against the solid wall of stone.

"What is that?" Starman's voice was trembling.

Crinte peered through the wall of rain once more. "That has to be an Xero," he whispered.

The monster bent down to peer at them in the tunnels. The five shrank back, even though it was too large to fit through the opening. After a moment, it appeared to give up. There was an audible sigh of relief as the monster turned its back on them and took a step towards the mountains from whence it came. Instead, its dark shape cast a shadow over the entrance to the Slutan Tunnels. It squatted before collapsing with a jarring thud on the ground, effectively trapping the five warriors in utter darkness.

The sound of rain hitting metal echoed eerily throughout the tunnels. Alaireia held her sword up and the light from it began to shine, displaying a narrow tunnel. "I suppose we should move forward now."

Legone reached up and touched the ceiling of the tunnel. "Let's hope we have reached the narrowest point of these tunnels."

Alaireia turned to the yawning darkness around them, briefly lit up by the light of her sword. There was only space for them to walk single file as the path curved around, sloping gently downwards towards the heart of the mountain. Legone walked behind her, loosening the rope that bound them together, letting his end trail away until he was free again. Marklus followed suit, collecting the rope as everyone freed their ends. "I hear something," he said into the silence, barely allowing his voice to hover over a whisper. He stretched his ears as he listened to echoes, layers beneath his feet. "It sounds like chipping. Someone is striking rock repeatedly."

"I see nothing but darkness ahead," Crinte chimed in. "Where is it coming from?"

"I can't tell." Marklus turned his head towards the sound. "There are more of them, echoing off the rock. It throws their location, though. I cannot pinpoint it."

"They must be miners," Legone told them. "The Sorns are known to spend their time digging for treasure."

"Makes sense." Marklus looked around wide-eyed. "But what kind of treasure could be found here? And at this point, who is left to mine?"

"It's better not to speculate," Crinte put in. "We just need to ensure they do not know we are here."

After a time, the rounded walls of the tunnel widened until the five were able to walk three in a row. Alaireia and Crinte moved to the front, while Starman walked between Marklus and Legone. He could feel the hair on his neck curling up as they walked. The clammy blackness behind him was unnerving. He almost expected to see the transformed walking out of the shadows. Reaching for the hilt of his sword, he felt the warmth of its energy vibrate from his fingertips through his body. Taking a deep breath, he let the feeling of calm pass through him before he was back in the darkness, creeping through the halls with his closest friends in the world.

"Lights ahead," Crinte warned sometime later.

"Should I put my sword up?" Alaireia whispered.

"They haven't seen us yet," Crinte replied.

Marklus could hear the creatures breathing in unison as they marched forward, boot clad feet sure and steady, unaware of the unwanted visitors.

"I thought this wasn't a well-used road." Starman's voice quavered with concern.

"We all did," Legone said dryly. He moved to the right side of the road, drawing an arrow from his bow. "Might as well be prepared."

Marklus glanced over at Legone before reaching for an arrow from his quiver. He moved to the left side of the tunnel, stopping when he was directly across from Legone.

"Starman, up here with me," Crinte ordered. "Alaireia, stand behind us and mesmerize them."

Glittering eyes floated into view, attached to darkly robed bodies. There was a surprised snort as a group of thirty Gaslinks caught sight of the warriors. Eyes narrowed as they moved forward quickly and silently, weapons drawn.

"Aim for their eyes!" Crinte ordered. "We hold this side of the tunnels; don't let any of them get past you."

"Marklus?" Legone questioned.

"Three. Two. One," Marklus counted down. "Fire!"

They loosened their shafts in a twin arch. Blue tipped arrows soared through the darkness, shafts fluttering before burying their heads in heartless yellow eyes. Two Gaslinks shrieked in pain and fell backward, desperately attempting to claw the arrows out of their eyes.

"Again!" Legone cried.

Marklus lifted his bow and they aimed together, reaching for another arrow as soon as the second ones left their bows.

"Ready, Starman?" Crinte asked as the Gaslinks continued their rapid approach.

"Let's break some bones," Starman agreed. His sword in both hands, he felt his strength and determination return. He struck before Crinte, shattering the wrist of the first Gaslink who raised

351

its battle-axe at him. Starman shouted as he drove his sword into the Gaslink's body, yanking it out in time to meet the sword of a second Gaslink. His strokes were sure, his slashes fatal as he cut down enemy after enemy. Crinte was on the right-hand side, his movements slower, yet he still drove his sword forward in a fury.

Alaireia stood between Legone and Marklus, letting the golden light stream out from her sword, brightening as it flowed. The Gaslinks moved as if in slow motion under the spell of the light. Alaireia could feel her power soaring through her fingertips into her sword. As she lifted it higher to finish off the creatures with a blast of light, a club slammed into her back, sending a jolt of searing pain through her. With a cry of surprise, Alaireia, knocked off balance, fell to the ground, the light of her glowing sword going out as it left her hands and clattered to the floor. Legone spun around, sending an arrow flying into the darkness, striking whatever beast was behind them. He drew another, tense, watching the dimness for movement. Alaireia recovered quickly. She snatched up her sword and with another cry of pain, dragged herself off the ground. Her sword began to illuminate her attacker as she lifted it, her face grim, her eyes dark. A Garcrat stood heavy and large before her. Brown skin hung limp over its rolls of fat, and one abnormally long arm held a club that dragged on the ground. Coarse hairs stuck out from its flared nostrils, and small beady eyes sat sunken in its oversized head. A stench of rottenness emitted from its body. It looked down at Alaireia, and its ugly face stretched into a grin. Crinte and Starman finished dismantling the last Gaslink and turned. Legone and Marklus both had their arrows trained on the Garcrat's body, yet something made them wait. A rough gurgle of laughter rumbled deep in the Garcrat's throat. It choked, cleared it, then spoke in a deep, painful voice. "I have a message for you," it rasped. "From the Ruler." Its voice started fading. "Welcome." It laughed, choked, then coughed again. "Welcome to the trap."

"Welcome to death!" Alaireia retorted as she drove her sword into its belly.

Two arrows joined her sword and the Garcrat crashed to the ground in a slosh of bile fluid. Alaireia pulled her sword free and turned to look at Crinte. "What did it mean?"

Crinte looked from the Gaslinks lying dead at their feet back to Alaireia. "I think someone wanted us here."

"Crinte." Marklus spoke up. "What do you know?"

Crinte picked up the torches the Gaslinks had dropped, re-lighting them as he handed one to each of his companions. "They are going to try to end us here. Something alerted him to our presence; hints of power yes, but more likely someone." He looked at each of them in turn as it dawned on him. "Someone who knew we were strangers in the land and wanted us here. Nevertheless, it doesn't matter. Their goal is to break our spirits and separate us. I must give you my vision so you can see your way forward, no matter what happens." Crinte turned to Starman. "Quickly now, we need to move with all speed." He placed his hands on Starman's head, imparting a vision of the Slutan Tunnels. He moved to Legone and Marklus next, before finally placing his hands on Alaireia's head. "Listen to me now.

It does not matter what happens here in these Tunnels. No matter how dark or unending it seems, I need each of you to stand with me at the end. Hold to that. No matter what happens."

They nodded in the dim light, their faces pales and serious. "Now, Warriors of Mizine, run with me. Fight with me."

Crinte set off in a jog down the dark halls, while the others took a moment to shake his vision into place before following him into the curving darkness.

CHAPTER 42

INTO THE DEEP

"We should sleep," Crinte announced, hours later.

"Here?" Starman asked, aghast, "in the middle of the tunnels?"

Crinte raised his torch. "I'm looking for other options. Keep your eyes open."

"Keeping my eyes open is not the issue," Legone murmured under his breath, for he was unable to see more than a few paces ahead in the darkness.

Marklus ran his hand along the tunnel walls, his finger touching, exploring grooves. Pausing, he pressed his ear to the wall and listened before moving forward again.

"What are you doing?" Alaireia whispered to him as she followed behind, trailing her fingers along the solid walls. She held a torch up, examining the curving stone, but nothing stood out to her.

"Miners," Marklus explained. "I still hear echoes of their pickaxes, chipping away in the deep. If miners carved these tunnels out of rock and mud, surely they would have created alcoves to sleep in, out of the way of the main path. Here, one cannot tell when the sun rises or sets. I assume they sleep in shifts, some always working."

Alaireia smiled in the darkness, her white teeth glinting oddly against the torchlight. "That's smart, Marklus. I like the way you think."

Turning his curly head, he looked back at her, catching her dark eyes in approval. "You surprise me. Sometimes, you seem to know everything."

"Maybe in the world of light," Alaireia replied gently, blending back into the shadows. "But in the darkness…" She trailed off, shivering.

"Ah," Marklus' voice sighed in success a few seconds later. "Here is a hollow in the stone. Crinte, your help with this?"

Crinte handed his unnecessary torch to Starman. Using his night vision, he leaned against the stone to help Marklus find a depression in the grooves. There was an audible click as they pushed together. Legone backed away as the stone shuddered away from the wall, an arrow in his bow in anticipation of any nasty surprises.

A jagged crack in the tunnel wall opened up as Crinte and Marklus pushed against the stone. As soon as it was loose it slid back smoothly, revealing a long, narrow inner chamber.

"Think we will all fit?" Starman asked, raising his torch skeptically.

Crinte pulled back sharply with a finger to his lips. "This spot is already taken."

Starman jerked his torch away, his hand flying to his sword hilt.

Marklus reached for the curve of the stone door to push it back. "Did they see you?" he whispered.

"I don't think so," he answered, helping Marklus close the stone door. "Hurry, let's go."

Alaireia led the way, running down the path opening before her light, Starman and Legone at her heels. A moment later, Crinte and Marklus fled after them, but it was too late; they heard light footsteps chasing them.

"Aye!" a high voice shouted from behind, as if unaware there were transformed creatures roaming the tunnels. "Who goes there! It's not time for the shift change yet!"

Crinte slowed, turning his golden gaze on two scrappy Sorns. Their faces were dirty and smudged while their clothes hung in tatters. Unwashed, they stood arrogantly in the middle of the path, their eyes wide from staring into darkness.

"Aye!" a Sorn called again, but he couldn't see far enough in the darkness.

Crinte watched them calmly as he slowly backed away. The shouting Sorn slapped the other one in the chest, pointing down the road and uttering words, just out of Crinte's earshot. Marklus moved up behind Crinte, touching his shoulder. "We should go."

"What are they saying?" Crinte asked. "They don't seem as concerned or fearful as I would expect."

Marklus gestured to the two Sorns. "He asked if they are here yet. I'm not sure what he means, but it doesn't sound like he means any of the other Sorns."

Marklus and Crinte looked at each other for a moment, knowing they were both thinking the same thing. "We knew what we were getting into," Marklus said at last. "This is the worst part. We are so close to the end."

Crinte nodded, squaring his shoulders. "I have no doubt, but I have a sneaking suspicion we are still missing something. Even the Green People did not give us the answers I expected." Crinte raised a finger. "I need to think."

Marklus pushed Crinte ahead of him, away from the vague shapes of the two talking Sorns. As they moved to catch up with Alaireia, Starman and Legone, they found them standing at the top of a steep, downward incline. Alaireia turned as they walked up, her eyes questioning. "Crinte, can you see what lies at the bottom?"

Crinte leaned over, his golden eyes straining. The incline was black and slick, seemingly impossible to walk down. It stretched beyond what Crinte could see, turning sharply into more blackness. "No," he replied. "But this is the way."

"Well." Alaireia turned calculatingly back to the dark slide. "Together?" Without waiting for another word to be uttered, she placed her hands on her shoulders, crossing them on opposite sides, and stepped off the edge. Instantly, she was sucked away into the darkness, vanishing from their sight.

Starman leaned forward in surprise. "Wait, no," he blurted out, turning questioning eyes to Crinte. "Is there no other way?"

Crinte shook his head, but Legone had already moved forward. He stepped off the edge in one elegant move, his toes pointed as he shot away.

Starman shrugged unhappily as he moved forward. He stood uncertainly on the edge, attempting to calm his quickening heartbeat. "Here goes." With one last sigh, he gave himself over and tentatively stepped onto the incline. With a whoosh, the road sucked him in, forcing him flat on his back as he shot downwards. He squeezed his eyes shut and gritted his teeth as the slippery slope curved around his body. It held onto him like a giant hand, guiding him down as if he were on a sleigh. A sharp bend threw him in the air, and for a second, he almost cried out when he found himself spinning effortlessly through the air. Yet the road rose before him, gathering him into the funnel of its arms. Starman opened his eyes then, and wished he hadn't. The absence of light was thick and intense; he could almost feel inky dark fingers reaching out for him, cold and unfeeling. The aura in the air had changed from the lighthearted gloom of the upper tunnels to the innermost chambers of fear and obscurity. Invisible fingers of horror and death stretched around him, while his mind screamed for vision. He snapped his eyes shut again, swallowing hard against the awareness. Something evil stirred in the deep and he couldn't shake the feeling he was plunging into the very heart of it.

***

Alaireia felt herself hurled out of the air, free floating. She pulled herself into a ball, minimizing the impact as she rolled onto the stone floor, tumbling aimlessly as she flung out her arms, attempting to stop. The momentum left her as quickly as it had come. Alaireia untucked herself and stood up slowly. The air hung thick and musty over her, stale from sitting, unbreathed in its prison. She drew her sword, watching the golden light flicker into being, illuminating the sweeping hall she stood in. Uncarved square columns rose above her, as if the architecture had been crudely hacked into place. Open space stretched further than her light could illuminate, and she turned as Legone came flying out of space, landing a few feet away from her. He sprung to his feet, as quick as a cat and pulled an arrow into his bow, glancing around in the stream of light from Alaireia's sword. Seconds later, Starman rolled to a stop with a grunt, lying prone on the floor, catching his breath for a few seconds.

"Are you okay?" Alaireia asked him. She turned in circles as her light shone brighter.

Starman rose to his knees, shaking his head. "That was terrible." His voice faded into the mustiness as he coughed.

"Do you hear that?" Legone asked in hushed tones as Marklus joined them.

"You hear it now?" Marklus noted as he stood gingerly, brushing himself off.

Alaireia held up a hand for silence as she listened. "I hear it too," she agreed.

Crinte landed with an audible thump, the air knocked out of him. He grimaced as he stood and joined the circle.

"Where are we?" Starman asked.

Crinte looked up at the wide expansion they stood in. "Deep within the Esife Peaks. Come, let's rest and discover these mysteries another time."

Their footsteps were muffled as they walked forward, and now all of them could hear the sounds in the distance. Reminding them they were not alone.

VOICES OF THE NIGHT

Marklus jerked awake and sat up, blinking as his eyes adjusted to the dimness. Days they had been sneaking through the tunnels, and his eyes were becoming used to the lack of light. His tunic was stuck to his back from where he had sweated uncomfortably in now forgotten nightmares. He pricked his ears, still hearing the endless chipping of pickaxes against stone, the sound they could all hear now, surrounding them in the wide halls. As luck would have it, they found alcoves and shallow rooms to rest in when their bodies grew weary of being dragged through the night. And the restless, adventurous, determined spirits of the warriors were beginning to wane. Marklus dared not think of how much time remained, long, endless, miserable blackness with hints of panic darting through his mind. There was no telling what was around each corner. Even though Crinte hid them from groups of Sorns marching towards their shifts, they all felt the apprehension, knowing something else was watching for them in the shadows.

Marklus stood and crept to the opening of the alcove where Legone the Swift stood, still as stone, staring into nothingness.

"Listen," Marklus whispered as he joined Legone in the doorway.

"What is it?" Legone lifted his bow in preparation.

Marklus listened, the sounds drifting to him through the shadows, and he realized they were voices of the night. They spoke to each other, long, dark moans of seething anger and vengeance. A message was exchanged, one to another, and as it was passed more voices joined the howling, intensifying the moans. The hair on Marklus' arms began to rise, standing up straight as he listened to the raw emotions thunder into his eardrums. He stepped back as if pushed aside by the storm of feelings. "It sounds like wolves," he told Legone, almost disbelieving the words coming from his mouth. "Wolves with voices. They have been told to hunt, to seek, and kill. We should go." He turned urgently. "Crinte!"

But Crinte was already awake and moved to wake Alaireia and Starman.

"Time for my watch?" Starman yawned and stretched as he stood.

"No," Crinte replied. "Marklus hears wolves. We should put some distance between them and us."

"Wolves?" Alaireia questioned in surprise. She snatched up her pack and moved to the doorway.

"Turned wolves?" Starman asked. "Is that possible?"

"Anything is possible down here," Crinte replied, his voice sure yet questioning.

"We should run." Marklus' voice was edgy.

Crinte stepped out of the alcove and began to walk, his night vision lighting the way. "Light the torches. It is a risk we have to

362

take. Torch light will be a sure indicator of where we are, but wolves are known to fear fire."

Marklus hurried after Crinte, leaving Legone, Alaireia and Starman to light the torches. "Crinte, something feels off about all of this."

"Yes," Crinte agreed. "There are many mysteries we don't understand, and as we grow closer to the source, they attempt to destroy us."

Marklus grew quiet as the chilling howls erupted again. "They are coming." His words sounded final as they drifted into the darkness.

Torchlight floated eerily, wanly illuminating the faces of Legone, Alaireia, and Starman as they jogged up to Marklus and Crinte. A flame flickered wearily, showing Starman's pale face. "I smell them." His words were bitten away by the darkness. "They smell of blood and wrath, fear and anger."

"Then you smell what I hear," Marklus said grimly. "They have lost something and believe our deaths can bring it back."

"Waste not your words," Legone said in frustration as they jogged together. "The air is not strong here. I fear we will not be able to breathe unless we begin to ascend."

A forced combination of stale air and rough, uncut stone, clinging to its mother, the body of the mountain, muffled their footsteps as they ran. The howling call of the gathering became muted in the distance, which was even more terrifying than the dripping, furious voices themselves. Marklus pricked his ears, listening for the bounding of padded, clawed feet, scratching against the unforgiving ground. He listened for the hot, heavy panting, coming hard and fast through sharp fanged teeth. Yet further sounds were drowned out as he began to hear the labored breathing of his companions.

Minutes, nay, hours later, the wide walls of the tunnels began to narrow, reaching like brothers forgiving each other after a long war. They returned to each other like lost lovers, their high arches swooping closer to the ground. Instead of a spacious drop of hundreds of feet, the tunnels closed in until the warriors could see the carved walls in the torchlight, standing only twenty feet away from each other. The air became thicker, a close denseness that forced the light from Starman's torch to snuff out, leaving nothing but a smoking, extinguished end.

"Re-light me," Starman called to Alaireia, who was not as far ahead as Legone. She turned, slowing her pace as she reached out her torch. The solid end clanged oddly against Starman's, and as the two flames combined Starman saw her beautiful face lit up for a moment. Her eyes were surprisingly bright and unclouded, yet wide open as she stared past Starman into the shadows. In one swift moment, she drew her sword, pointing it at whatever apparition hung behind, reaching to snatch the precious strings of life from him.

"Starman." Her voice sounded a mile away, even though she moved closer to him. "Draw your sword."

A guttural, deep-throated snarl cut through the air behind Starman. He involuntarily twitched in surprise as Alaireia moved past him, her sword ready to bite. Starman spun as his fingers closed firmly around the silver hilt of his sword. It rang out as he drew it, syncing with his will, the desire to protect his friends at all costs. As he held his light up he saw it.

A catlike creature hunched on all fours, its hind legs gathered in readiness to pounce. Squinty red eyes glared out of the darkness on the face of a giant panther. Matted, black fur blended into the shadows while tufts of abused hair stood out in the light. The panther hissed angrily at the sudden light in its eyes and reached out a paw to swipe at the torches, five-inch, razor sharp claws swinging close to Alaireia's relatively calm face. She swiped back with her sword, flashing it in front of the panther's face and taking a step forward, showing it she was willing to take on a fight if necessary. Snarling, the panther shot forward in a blur, its mouth open far enough for Starman to clearly see its lolling, pink tongue and jagged teeth. They were not the teeth of a normal predator of the sunlit lands; each one was a different shape, misshapen, as if the creature had gnawed on something it should not have. Starman was still reeling in surprise when he felt the furry tail of the creature around his neck, wrapping around twice before Starman could bring up his sword. Dropping his torch he choked, and in a panic reached a hand up to loose himself. It was already too late. The creature threw him, hauled him towards the wall, losing its hold as soon as Starman's body smacked into the stone and dropped to the ground, his sword clattering unhappily on stone floor. Unable to catch his breath, Starman's weak cry fell, unheard. But Alaireia's sword was gleaming brighter and she launched himself towards the panther that was already poised, ready to pounce again. It lunged towards her without hesitation, powerful claws reaching until it was upon her, and the two went down, biting, clawing, ripping. The light from Alaireia's sword danced bravely, fighting back against the aggressive, almost rabid creature of the night. It was anyone's battle until the light from Alaireia's blade disappeared, drowned out under the weight of the panther.

It was Crinte who reached Alaireia and the panther in the darkness, his night vision lighting the way for him as he drove his sword into the side of the panther and pushed it over. Seconds later Alaireia struggled out from underneath the panther, pulling her glowing sword out of its stomach. The panther shuddered once more in death and Alaireia placed her foot on its side as she wiped the murky blood from her sword. "Crinte," she said. Her voice shook, but she quickly regained control. "They are silent in this darkness. We did not know this one was here until it was almost too late."

Crinte turned his eyes on the path behind them. "It is too late," he replied.

Alaireia lifted her sword, turning to see what Crinte could already see with his waking vision. Behind her a sea of blackness stretched as far as her sword could show her. Sneaking towards her and Crinte were hundreds of black panthers, their eyes red, their jagged teeth poking out from their mouths. They moved stealthily and determinedly towards the five warriors, ready to pounce at any moment.

CHAPTER 44

TIME

Sarhorr crossed his arms in frustration. Time used to be on his side, yet now it seemed his enemy. The Five Warriors had succeeded in avoiding his Gims, even going so far as to kill one of them. But he had expected as much; they would not be the Five Warriors if they were not, at least, able to fight their way out of different scenarios. He knew they had, at last, entered the Slutan Tunnels, as he desired. The Tunnels, where they would be trapped, lost and disheartened, wandering in the dark. He was curious if they had run into his welcoming committee yet, and how they were faring. Fear. Terror. Those were all emotions the people groups responded to. Emotions which were foreign to himself. The fear was based on death and pain, two things which would never happen to him. His brother and sister were the only two who could, potentially, cause him fear and terror. But the fear of pain was all he would experience; life without death was what he had, and a life he would need to build for himself, now that he was free from the wishes of his siblings.

His time with the Green People danced before his endless memory. And the Tider, someone he did not expect. The Tider was different from all the other people groups and immortals. He had an uncaring, selfish attitude, and Sarhorr had assumed he could use it to his advantage. Yet, the Tider seemed to oppose him. In the last conversation they'd had, right before the banishment, the Tider had finally accused him outright, fear flickering behind his stubborn eyes, the color of a lake a midday.

"You are like me," he'd told the Tider as he walked around him. "You have the same desires I do."

"And what do you claim are your desires?" The Tider had been cold then, even behind his fear.

"To live and love forever. Aren't those all the desires of the peoples of the world? Life without loss. Love without regret. Passion without consequence. Only I have the ability to live a life such as the one you wish, but you have something I do not. Do you want to know what it is?"

"I'm listening." The Tider's words were clipped and hard.

"You have your people. The four people groups of The Four Worlds. You know them, and among them there is the desire for power, conquest, life, love, and passion. As one of them, you know this. But your time is short, riddled with death. Your minds are not equipped to live longer than a hundred years; your bodies fail and fade into the ground. You do not have time to fulfill your dreams of life. Time is what I have. Time is what I can give you, if you will do something for me." Sarhorr paused to look at the Tider. Behind his blue eyes a window of curiosity was open. His mind had been pricked. Sarhorr almost laughed with how easy it was. People groups were expendable. If he could not find one person willing to do his bidding, he could find another. Yet his similarities with this Tider made it devilishly fun. He wrapped his fingers around each other, clasping and unclasping them in glee. "I need

power, beyond what you have. Beyond what I have taken. And you can find it for me."

The confession of knowledge had come then. He could hear the anxiety behind the words that were spoken. The Tider was fighting with his mind, knowing attempts to flee would be futile. "You are a Changer, an all-powerful being. What could you possibly want that I have?"

Sarhorr laughed then, feeling the mirth bubble out of his body at the absurd question. "Find the Clyear of Power and bring it to me. I, in return, shall make you immortal, and spare the Green People from my poisonous death. The other people groups, well, they will not be as lucky."

"The Clyear of Power has been lost for decades; such a search is impossible."

Sarhorr shook his head like a disappointed teacher. "Excuses are for mortals. You shall have decades because you shall be immortal. Bring me the Clyear, and all other powerful beings you find along your journey. Do so, because you do not want me to do it my way; it will destroy your world."

The Tider gritted his teeth. "How do I know you will not destroy the world anyway, once you have the Clyear of Power?"

"A fair question." Sarhorr paused, a smug smile lighting his beautiful face. "I shall go to paradise. Now, be still."

Sarhorr reached out his hand to touch the Tider's head. As his impartation passed, the Tider screamed in pain as if all of his bones had been broken at once.

Now, Sarhorr still felt frustrated. The Five Warriors were coming, along with the Clyear of Power, but it wasn't what he wanted anymore. Since then he had learned, from conversations with stars, of a more powerful gem, with ten times the potency of the Clyear of Power. Now he knew what he truly desired. The Green Stone.

CHAPTER 45

A TASTE OF TROUBLE

"Starman, are you okay?" Marklus' voice called out to him, and a hand touched his shoulder. It was comforting, but not healing. The pain from being thrown into the wall remained.

"Yes," Starman replied, standing up with Marklus' help. "Is it dead?" The stinging numbness of pain receded as he squared his shoulders and picked up his sword.

"Yes." Marklus nodded as he reached for an arrow and gestured towards the wide expanse behind them. "But we have another problem."

Torchlight was unnecessary for what Starman turned to face. Alaireia stood with her sword held in one hand above her head. Its light glimmered and pushed against the darkness, driving it back to illuminate what it hid. Panthers hissed furiously, their crooked teeth bared, their red eyes blazing as they focused on Alaireia, and Crinte, who stood behind her. He had his hand out, as if mentally pushing them back, while his sword pointed towards them. Starman blinked as he looked at Crinte's sword, for the first time seeing ripples dashing past it. Starman swallowed hard as he looked back to Marklus, seeing Legone on the other side of him, an arrow ready to fly, yet they waited. They all waited, listening for unheard instructions.

"Go," Alaireia commanded, her voice sure and unwavering. "I can hold them. Run."

"Alaireia." There was a question in Crinte's voice, but he did not take his eyes off the panthers. "At least let me stand with you."

"I'm faster," Alaireia replied, knowing well what she was doing. "Go." She looked at him. "Why did you ask me to come if you won't let me do what I'm best at?"

"Run!" Crinte bellowed back to Starman, Marklus and Legone. Dropping his stance, he turned and fled, sword still in hand, powering down on the three. "Now!" he ordered them.

Seconds later, the ground began to rumble and quake, shaking under their feet as they ran, threatening to throw them off balance. Fissures began to open up, rippling across the stone ground.

Marklus felt the uncanny sense of deja vu as he ran against the quaking ground, and he realized what Alaireia had done. The next moment, a blast of light, golden hot, drove itself into the ground, widening the rift between the warriors and the panthers. Uncanny howls of anger bounced off the narrowing tunnel walls, driving themselves with a stinging force into the hearts of the warriors. They could feel it then, a taste of what the transformed felt, the helpless terror, the overwhelming pain, and finally, the furious desire for revenge and death.

The panthers leaped through the air, running across the uneven ground even as it crumbled under them. Reaching out with their claws, they pulled their bodies up, preventing themselves from falling completely into the void. Yet the ripples continued as Alaireia stood on the edge, the Clyear of Power in one hand, her sword in the other, a steady stream of light blazing from it. She lifted them together, her hands over her head, and brought them down in one, sweeping, final signal. A second bolt of white hot lightning shot across the ground the panthers lay on, scorching their fur and blasting bolts of fires into their midst. High pitched, whining cries could be heard as the panthers struggled, half of them retreating back into the darkness from whence they had come, the other half caught in the broken crumble of the heart of the mountain, scrambling to survive the fatal earthquake.

Alaireia brought the Clyear close to her mouth and whispered. The crystal horse lifted from her fingers and flew towards the path the warriors had disappeared down, a gentle light shooting through the air. Alaireia sheathed her sword, backing away from the edge. Summoning the last of her strength, she turned and ran—not a moment too soon as the ground crumbled beneath her fleet feet.

"Up the stairs!" Crinte called to Legone, who was in the lead. "We need to seek higher ground!"

The tunnels continued to crumble around them, but now the skull-crushing heaviness of the air had grown deeper and more intense. Each breath was a struggle, and the stale air burned their lungs as they breathed in. At first, Starman anxiously glanced around, hanging back, waiting for Alaireia to catch up even as Crinte urged him onward. Now, the struggle to breathe was final, causing him to focus on breathing alone. The deep rumbling of the tunnels continued as they threw themselves downwards in revolt, grief, and self-pity. The air closed around him, forbidding him further access to its putrid end, just as a hand on his back pushed him up the stairs. His feet obediently plodded up the wide, rail-less staircase, in reverse to what the black slide had done. Lights danced ahead of his eyes and he felt fresher air slide into his nostrils and the fog in his brain began to clear.

Ahead, Legone ran up the staircase, back towards the shallow regions of the tunnels, none too thankful to slip away from the panthers of the deep. At the top he could see the tunnel opening again, higher above him, and flicking flames hung above the doorway, welcoming him. It took only a second for him to realize someone had actually lit those torches, and chances were, someone had to constantly keep them burning. Legone froze, not a moment too soon as the edge of a battle axe floated past him, clipping off a strand of swinging hair. Legone ducked down, sliding an arrow into his bow and sending it back towards the top of the staircase in response. A strangled cry replied and Legone moved again, faster if possible, skipping up the stairs as a volley of angry axes and black arrows poured down on him. Axes clanged loudly against the stone, adding to the wrath of the crumbling tunnels behind him. Arrows tipped off the edge, diving uselessly into the deep. He saw an armed creature aim at him and duck out of view again, but Legone moved too fast for the creature. Turning to look behind he saw his company moving up the stairs at a much slower pace. "Watch out for the Gaslinks!" he shouted to them. He thought he heard Starman groan but wasn't sure as another axe hurled past his feet.

Legone reached for his daggers. With a few leaps, he was at the top of the staircase. Reaching out a hand, he grasped the first Gaslink he came into contact with. It dropped its bow in a surprised squeak at Legone's speed. Legone yanked it out of the niche it stood in and onto the staircase. "Leave my friends alone." His voice was grim as he stared into the glittering eyes, wondering if his message would reach The Ruler who had started it all. The Gaslink had no time to react as it was bodily lifted off the staircase and thrown into the pit. Legone turned to find another thirty Gaslinks lined up, staring at him calmly. A brief moment of hesitation passed over their seemingly emotionless faces. As one, they lifted their battle-axes and advanced.

Realizing his mistake, Legone momentarily cursed under his breath and threw his daggers into the necks of two of the approaching horde. They collapsed in a heap as he spun out of the way of two axes, backing down the staircase as he drew arrow after arrow. The Gaslinks advanced hungrily, boney fingers wrapped around their wicked weapons as they came onward, the pounding of their chainmail boots heavy against the stone. Legone felt like a gazelle being hunted as he backed away, on the defense. If he did not turn the tables soon, they would be on him like a lion devouring its prey, ripping him apart until there was nothing left but a bloody corpse. Legone stopped and whipped his long braid around his shoulder. He felt the air give way under his speed as he pushed all barriers aside. Bounding down the staircase, he picked up two battle-axes where they lay, unused. He twirled them lightly in his hands even though they felt off kilter and nothing like the way his bow nestled close to him, bending its strings to his will. His bow gave off comforting hushes of power, unlike the intense potion of the invincibility power of the Mermis or the electrifying waves the Clyear gave off. Something akin to love glowed in the heart of his bow and arrows, binding itself to his emotions, but the battle-axes he held were dead. Skill was what he needed in order to wield them, and in one move, further testing the invincibility potion, Legone leaped back up the stairs and dove into the midst of the Gaslinks.

Marklus, who was shoving a groggy Starman up the stairs ahead of him, looked up in time to see Legone the Swift moving in a blur into a swarm of Gaslinks. "Swift is overwhelmed, we have to fight!" he shouted. Dropping to his knees to get a better angle, Marklus reached for his arrows and took aim.

Starman drew his sword and took a deep breath. The clearer air washed through the windows of his brain and he ran. Blue tipped arrows slid past, almost as if they avoided him on their way to plunge into the skeletal bodies of the Gaslinks. The higher Starman climbed, the better his clarity became, until he was there with Legone. He raised his sword and roared as he dived into their midst, feeling the momentum of his blade as he swung. The amount of power behind him frightened him as he moved, and suddenly he was Starman the Warrior, flattening everything in his wake. He must have blacked out, for when he came to, panting, Legone, Marklus, Crinte, and Alaireia were all there, standing around him, and the Gaslinks were all dead.

CHAPTER 46

WHERE THE SORNS WORK

"They call it berserk," Alaireia told him later. "When a warrior becomes so enraged with bloodlust they kill everything in their wake. You seem to have more control over it though."

"I think it's the sword," Starman replied uncertainly. "I feel...different...when I hold it. Like I can defeat anything."

"You'll need it for whatever is ahead," Alaireia encouraged. She reached out and gently touched his shoulder.

They walked behind Crinte, Marklus and Legone, down the winding tunnels which appeared normal again, much like when they had first entered. Except now the warriors were even more guarded, expecting Sorns or Gaslinks around every twisted corner. The devilish panthers of the deep they attempted to forget, blocking the tormented howls from their memory. Hundreds of feet below them, amidst rock and stone, the incessant chipping of blade against rock continued.

Ahead, Crinte paused in front of the outline of a crudely carved door in the wall. "Mayhap we can rest here," Crinte suggested, reaching for the latch. "Marklus, what do you hear?"

Marklus leaned his ear against the door, scrunching up his face as he listened. "Nothing." He stepped away, confused. "The sound is muffled, or there is nothing to hear."

Crinte pushed down on the latch. "Ready?" He nodded at Legone's bow.

"Must we always open mysterious doors in the dark?" Legone muttered.

"It's that or sleeping on the road," Alaireia retorted.

The door swung open with an ear-splitting creak, bouncing uncertainty on unsteady, rusted hinges. The room was already lit up, as if someone had been there before them and forgot to turn the lights out. The five entered wide-eyed, staring up at the nine-foot-high ceiling, but the mountains of supplies were what threw them off. A narrow passageway snaked through the room, but on either side were mud-grey rocks and boulders. A pile of dirty shovels with splintered handles was tossed haphazardly on a slanting pile that looked as if it might crash if touched. Hundreds of blunted pickaxes had been tossed near a wide, round sharpening stone that lay on its side. Alaireia walked gingerly over to it, pulling out her daggers to test their sharpness. Starman gave her a disapproving look. "We shouldn't touch anything," he whispered.

"I know," she whispered back. "Better to have a sharp blade though."

Unfinished swords lay dull, propped up against the walls, their hilts more likely to wound the sword-bearer than the enemy. Shields, breastplates, helmets, mail, chains, and bows and arrows made of what looked like iron covered the floor, and had begun mixing with each other. It was clear that whoever had been responsible for keeping the inventory of weapons, armor, and tools had dumped them, sloppily, and left in an anxious rush.

"A supply room," Crinte said, understanding dawning on him as he stood in the middle of the room with Marklus, supplies rising as high as his waist. "This means the Sorns have to be nearby. This means the Tunnels are their base of some sort."

"Listen." Marklus held up his hand.

Clear and distinct, the echoes of metal rang through the supply room, and with each echo, each item in the room shifted a hair. Yet a second sound was added to it, one which made them freeze and listen, fingertips straying to their weapons, as if they could fight the intangible. Voices floated to them, lifted in song. They were thin and reedy, voices of the lost, vulnerable and hopeless in the depths. The rhythm of the song matched the consistent tones of digging but the words were muffled. Unconsciously, the five shifted closer, curious.

"They aren't afraid of who might hear them." Legone spoke questioningly. "If they know the turned creatures are in the tunnels, they are either in league with them, or..." he trailed off.

"They are following orders," Crinte replied as he walked towards the other end of the supply room. "After all, it's what we all do. Follow orders. Hastening the end. Even though we try to think for ourselves, there is always someone else two steps ahead of us." He turned for a moment, catching Legone's eyes.

Legone returned his gaze, level and calm, wondering how much Crinte the Wise knew. Legone knew it was time to set the plan in motion. It was time to talk to Alaireia. The mountains of supplies shivered, as if sensing his thoughts.

Alaireia stepped away from the sharpening stone, the wind in her movements upsetting the axes that lay near. One slid away from the pile and clattered near her feet, striking the ground in a deep, hollow clang. Sensing the fall of their leader, the rest of the axes gave way like a slow-motion waterfall, flowing off the pile to separation, each one clinging to the floor, blocking the way back. The balance in the room was thrown off as the swords dropped from where they had been propped against the wall, and one by one the weapons and tools and armor scattered and tumbled from their stations.

Crinte spun around, a perturbed look on his face as his hands flew to his sword hilt. "Hurry, this way!" he called to his warriors, running through the avalanche of supplies as they surged across the room like waves dancing in a current for the very first time. The hard face of the wall loomed before them, seemingly cutting off all exits from the room, but as Crinte looked down, he discovered a hole in the wall, lying a few feet off the ground. Hunkering down, he eased his way inside with Marklus right behind him. Crawling forward, he slid downwards for a moment. It was a roughly hewn tunnel, covered in dirt and grit, not likely made for travel back and forth. Crinte shook his head in frustration. The Slutan Tunnels were not at all what he was expecting, although he should not have been surprised. A quiet, underground tunnel that led directly to the Great Water Hole had to be teeming with life. At first, he'd thought the Sorns were hiding there. It seemed a brilliant way to escape from the Garcrats and Gaslinks who were constantly rounding up people groups and sending them to the Great Water Hole. But now, as he considered the story of Devine the Sorn, it seemed much more likely they were in service to Sarhorr the Ruler himself. Maybe warriors were needed to cross the sea and intimidate Mizine, but servants were needed to fulfill a purpose. After that, the mortals would be out of time. Crinte briefly recounted the days since the Mermis had given them the invincibility potion, The sixty-day warning; was that when the potion would end? Or when the purpose would be fulfilled? Either way, they were running out of time.

The voices of the Sorns rang out clearer as Crinte continued following closer. Words drifted to his ears. *Dig. Dig. Forever we must. Dig as long as we live. Morning to evening. Evening to morning. Never stopping to rest.* The sound droned on, words twisted inside out and repeated. It was a haunting song after all, the fear of running out of work lest they be dragged, kicking and screaming, to the Great Water Hole for transformation. The frantic dread could be heard beneath each strike of blade against stone. Crinte could almost see them, hunkered over their work stations, bulging eyes, round and large from staring into darkness. Fingers bloated, blackened, and stained from burrowing into the Esife Peaks. Their joints cried out in pain from the constant back-breaking work, but it was all that was left of them, their only revolt against transformation. Digging.

Crinte tumbled out of the rough tunnel, shaking sherds of dirt and rock off his tunic. Thick columns rose before him and he hid behind one as he took in his surroundings. He stood under a high archway and the road opened in front of, leading down into a wide cavern. Looking down into the basin, he could see an endless, vast expanse of stone. Torchlight twinkled below, spots of brightness in the darkness. He could see them clearly; dirty, scraggly Sorns. Some dug closer to the top, some further down below, while a spiraling road continued into the pit. Surrounding the cavern were other archways and passages, leading deeper into the Slutan Tunnels.

Crinte placed a finger on his lips as Marklus and Starman tumbled out of the tunnel and crept up behind him, shaking dirt from their shoulders. "The Sorns are here," Crinte whispered. "They are looking for something."

Alaireia and Legone joined them a moment later, both holding their daggers as if expecting the worst.

"What could they possibility want that they don't already have? And in the mountains of all places?" Starman asked.

Crinte sighed. "There are many jewels hidden underground, and one can only speculate on the price of them. It does not seem they would be worth much now, but I have not studied enough ancient texts about the underground to know. We should press on before they take note of us."

Marklus held out a hand, hushing Crinte as he listened. "There is an exit somewhere near here. I hear the air from outside filtering through."

"That could only mean one thing." Crinte hustled forward again. "More creatures are coming."

But before they could walk much further, ten bowlegged Sorns marched past the five with pickaxes slung over their emaciated shoulders. Their clothing hung in tattered rags, but they did not seem to notice as they weaved their way onto the spiraling road leading downwards.

"Aye!" one shouted to his comrades. "Need help down here?"

"Aye," another voice replied. "My passage goes all the way to Mizine. I need all the help I can get."

"Mine goes both ways," a whining voice called out. "It hooks up with the main passage to the Great Water Hole and it connects to the main passage to Mizine."

"Why are you here?" a voice spat out rudely. "If you've run out of work, you can begin your journey to the Great Water Hole. No need to put the rest of us out of work too."

"Nay." A flicker of doubt crept into the voice of a fourth Sorn. "Stay and work with us. Don't become one of those ugly, transformed mutts."

A scattering of hissing laughter bounced through the bowels of the mountain. Crinte turned to his warriors and motioned for them to follow him as he moved to hide behind another column.

"Have you heard the news?" a Sorn called out. "The hunt has begun."

"What hunt?" an ignorant Sorn chimed in.

"The hunt for the Five Warriors of course!" a Sorn replied, indignant. "Don't you know, they are coming to stop the Ruler. Remember Devine? That was his mission."

"They are here in the Tunnels?" a voice trembled out in both admiration and fear.

383

"Aye, maybe they were the ones who disrupted my sleep a few days ago," another added.

The clamor of voices began to rise as the Sorns talked, excited.

"Wait, what's the hunt for?"

"I heard the warriors breathe fire when they fight."

"Are the Gims coming for them?"

"I heard they have a light which can blast your body to pieces."

"Is that why the hunters of the deep awoke?"

"I heard the ground quakes when they walk."

"Didn't you hear that earthquake? That was them!"

"I heard they leave no survivors; they look at you and your head falls off."

"They won't survive the crossroads though, or the broken bridge."

"I heard their arrows are filled with poison; one touch and you fall to your death."

"But they are walking towards the trap, right?"

"How are we supposed to work if they could be right above us, destroying our work even as we dig?"

"I heard there is one who splits himself into five when he fights."

"I heard the immortals cursed them."

"Enough!" a voice roared, higher and louder than any of them. A whip cracked in the deep, silencing the voices. "No talking. Back to work!"

A painful wail was silenced as the whip cracked again and the Sorns grew quiet. The lash of the whip continued but the sounds of digging soon drowned it out.

Crinte peeked out from behind a column and turned to face Marklus, Starman, Legone, and Alaireia. "The hunt has begun and this is only the beginning. But I have faith in each of you to overcome all odds. It's time to run, and whatever you do, do not look back."

CHAPTER 47

THE CROSSROADS

Time drifted slowly in the unending tunnels, stretching into days—if there were days. The five continued to travel at intervals, stopping to rest for a few hours in wide halls before pushing onward. The uncanny feeling they were being followed turned into very real, eerie sounds; heavy boots marching in the deep, and wailing voices answering the crack of stinging, bloodied whips. Anticipation hung heavy on their minds, like an animal caught in a trap, waiting to be devoured. Finally, fourteen days after they had first entered the Slutan Tunnels, they reached a crossroads. Three lit torches were mounted on the wall between the two tunnels, one leading south, the other pointing north. Crinte paused as he led his warriors forward, drawing his sword as they walked out into the open, heading towards the northern tunnel.

"Crinte, according to your vision, both paths will ultimately lead us to the same destination?" Alaireia asked.

"Yes," Crinte confirmed. "Although the southern route will take longer. We should choose the route with the least potential of meeting the transformed creatures, but my mind's eye tells me nothing. Marklus, your ears?"

"The northern route," Legone interrupted as Marklus stepped forward, turning his head to listen to the tales each tunnel told. "Speed should be our aim."

"Wait." Marklus held up a hand, shushing Legone. "I hear heavy breathing on both the southern and northern routes."

"I can scout ahead," Alaireia offered, glancing at Crinte.

"No," he said quickly. "Our separation is exactly what they would want. To the north!" He moved forward with Marklus and Starman at his heels.

Alaireia froze as the torches flickered, disturbed by a breeze. As her eyes adjusted, she realized she was not staring at torches, but rather pitchforks materializing out of the shadows. Hot tongues of flames leaped around them, panting for more to burn. Black hands held them as not one but two hooded figures took form. One turned towards Starman, Marklus and Crinte, the other to Alaireia and Legone, effectively blocking them from each other.

Crinte turned quickly, pushing Starman and Marklus behind him to shield them from the force of the Gims' attack. The Gims moved between the north and south paths, and in one motion, dropped their pitchforks. They thudded to the ground with a snap, and flames shot into the air between the two tunnels as the Gims reached for their wide blades.

Alaireia blinked, her eyes darting to catch Starman's. He looked back at her, wide eyed in frustration as the Gims stood between them. Even as her hands automatically reached for her

sword, flashbacks of her attack on the Gim in the prairie overcame her memory. Before she could react, she heard the sounds
of marching as a stream of Gaslinks flowed into the crossroads.
There were hundreds of them, widening the gap between the
five warriors, swords drawn, ready to take them down. "Run!"
Alaireia vaguely heard Crinte's voice among the flames and
smoke that shot into the air, turning into a thick fog that hid
them from each other. A moment later, she felt her body hurled
roughly against the stone wall and Legone slammed into her
back. His mouth was close to her ear as he whispered softly,
"Lightfoot, I need a Boleck. An empty one. And I think you may
be the only one who can retrieve one for me."

She pushed him away in anger, coughing slightly as the fog
turned into smoke, filling her nostrils. "You tell me this now?"
she questioned him skeptically.

He grabbed her arm instead, pulling her towards the southern route. "I need to trap a spirit," he replied cryptically as
Gaslinks rushed towards them.

Alaireia tried to look at him, but the smoke was thickening
and she couldn't see his face. His words whispered around her
ears and she thought she saw a flash of blue as he dragged an
arrow into his bow. "I need it by the time we reach the Great
Water Hole. Don't fail us, Lightfoot."

She reached for her sword as his whispered words drifted
away like an afterthought, as if he were also speaking to someone invisible. Before she could reply, a battle-axe whirled
towards her shoulder, emerging out of the smoke like a taunting
arm. Lifting her glowing sword, she swung, her blade slamming
into it with a shrieking clang. She knocked it away and moved

forward, but her shining blade gave her a glimpse into hundreds of war-ready Gaslinks. They ran towards her, hands outstretched. In a split second, Alaireia weighed her options. The others were lost in the smoke, and while she could use the Clyear to clear the way, two Gims stood at the crossroads, and she wasn't sure she had the strength to fight both of them. Realizing the difficult position she had been placed in, Alaireia sheathed her sword, turned, and ran down the southern route into the darkness. Cold fingers of smoke reached for her, sliding through her hair, touching bare skin. She could almost hear icy words whispering through undead lips, "Run, run, and don't come back."

Already, the panic was mounting in her head. She knew what was happening: the intentional separation of the five warriors, allowing them to be hunted down one by one, drawn into the arms of the beast, playing into the hands of the Ruler. She swallowed hard in the blinding darkness; she would find them. She would meet them again when the roads met back up. They were invincible. They would survive.

But Alaireia was alone as she ran into the blinding smoke, as were the other warriors, stumbling, twisting, turning, and losing themselves as they disappeared, alone, into the labyrinth of the Slutan Tunnels.

CHAPTER 48

CRINTE THE WISE

Days later, Crinte paused in the bleakness pressing around him. Ahead of him, endless tunnels stretched onward, winding deeper into the mountainside. Each step forward began the descent, and although his head told him he was on the right path, his gut told him downhill was not what he wanted. An escape, a way to find sunlit lands again was what he desired. Mentally, he could feel the darkness growing on him, threatening to break his sanity. He wanted, nay, he needed to feel the warmth of the sunlight again, and taste the breeze ruffling his long blond hairs. Again, his thoughts flitted back to Legone's accusation: *"What have you possibly lost in all of this? You, our leader, who cannot relate to anything we have been through? What makes so you keen to save the world?"* Those words had hit home, but all the same, he had his reasoning for keeping quiet, for not explaining why he felt the desperation to save the Western World. The hollow memory of searing pain ripping his chest caused him to shudder, but even more so the deep memories he held close. The day Marklus had healed him in Zikeland, he had wanted to let the poison seep through his skin and take him to the other side.

Thirty years ago, he was born in Norc, a country deep in the west of Mizine, close to the coast. His mother and father were young and wild, loyal to no one and no country. Until he was five, he recalled living in the woods, sometimes in a cave, other times in a hollow tree where the lightning bugs entered at night and graced the darkness with a magical light show. His father had no trade, so each day, the three of them would leave to hunt and explore. Some days, they would not return to their make-shift home, and would build camps where they stood. But one year when the winter came, and the cold frost near Oceanic became too much, his father decided it was time to push on. His mother braided her long light hair and carried a basket full of supplies upon her back. When Crinte became too tired to walk, his father carried him on his broad shoulders, allowing him to use his slingshot to shoot at the birds they passed. Thus Crinte entered Cromomany and encountered the diverse people groups for the first time.

They traveled to the intimidating city full of tall males with great weapons, traders with unique treasures, and scholars with large books tucked under their arms. Crinte began to understand the way of the world, and he longed for the freedom of the woods, running and laughing with exhaustion from sunrise to sunset. His father grew distant, enthralled in books and the wonders of the world, and his mother grew quiet, no longer wild but calm. Instead of taking Crinte's small hands and dragging him outside, she would sit quietly by the fire, combing out her long hair and telling him stories of old. Confused at the change, he took to sneaking out and playing with the other children in the streets, causing dissension and disruption, upsetting his mother until his father decided to teach him how to ride. Young as he was, he understood the powerful beasts champing at the bit, aching to be let free to run. He learned to gain their trust, to command them to walk and run, and when at last he thought he had found his place in the land, his father grew restless and moved them again.

At ten years old, Crinte was furious when he found himself perched in an unending prairie in a sea of green stalks. His father had bragged on the great purchase he had made, a house at the edge of Zikeland. Crinte could not understand why his father could not see that every move away from Norc took more life from his mother; she grew thin and pale, listlessly watering the flowers that grew outside their door. Obsessed with knowledge, his father studied and explored the land around them, welcoming his wife and son to come with him, but they refused. Crinte still remembered that warm day; it had smelled like fresh cut grass as he walked through the prairie, frustrated with his new home and afraid he was going to lose his mother. He had crawled his way through a tunnel in the grass, mildly curious as to where it led. When he found himself gasping for breath on the ground, the searing pain paralyzing his body, he thought it might not be so bad to discover what was on the other side of death. It wasn't until the curly-headed boy with the blue aura touched him that he felt the beauty of life return. The air was fresh as he breathed it in, deep and pure. He felt as if he had been reborn. With his second chance, he knew what he would do with the rest of his life.

When the Zikes stood, bowing before Marklus, he realized what his father saw in his studies—the power of knowledge.

392

From that day forward, his vision was improved, and he found Marklus had transferred a gift to him when he had healed him. He began to study with his father, finding a love for the pursuit of wisdom, and he took his mother hunting until she began to sing like a young wild bird again. He spent long days with Marklus until at last the land faded under the sway of the Zikes, and again he found his life turned upside down. He continued east with his parents until his mother refused to travel again. She went back to Norc, while Crinte and his father pushed on, exploring the deep and dark secrets of the Western World.

Crinte understood what it was all people groups sought, and he understood his purpose at last: to ensure the freedom of the Western World. With his unsettled childhood, he knew they were all searching for some security to hold on to, a place to call home. Indeed, he could only call the Western World his home, a land he loved and would fight for. He had seen the doorway to death before, and knew the risk he took. After all, it would be much safer to stay in the south and wait for the war to arrive at their doorstep. But Crinte could feel the momentum growing with each step he took downwards into the darkness. He did not live for safety or love or power or peace. He lived for the risk, for the pursuit of purpose and the knowledge that he had done something honorable for the Western World with his second chance. He raised his head, and in that comfort, he knew the others had to be alive. They were moving forward, although he could not see them. He turned a corner and his path ended in a sharp drop off, and a vast bridge spread out before him.

CHAPTER 49

THE BROKEN BRIDGE

High archways soared skyward, opening up the narrow halls to a wide expanse. All roads led there, their entrances set high and low, far and wide from each other. Light glinted off the red-brown archways, betraying a glimmer of gold within, gifting the hope of discoverable jewels hidden far below. The path cut off sharply into a crater within the tunnel. Downward, there was naught but unending darkness, the path to the underworld should one seek to sink, never to rise again.

Legone stood nervously in an archway, looking ahead of him. Pulleys and strings hung over the pit, a complex system meant to usher one across to the other side. He could see where his path continued a hundred or more feet on the other side. There was only one route then, a wide path scurrying onward and away into the darkness. If he were to run and leap, the darkness would suck him in, pulling him down below. Yet he hesitated, waiting, listening for signs of life, the telltale chipping of hammers, the marching of Gaslinks, or the hiss of a fiery pitchfork. Nothing discouraged his path forward. Nothing told him to continue to stand still, so he walked forward, one foot stealthily in front of the other, ready for combat, expecting a surprise.

When he had lost the others, he thought he would be alarmed. After all, he was beginning to think of them like his family. They accepted him for who he was, cold and lonely, desperate and heartbroken. They listened to his opinions and offered their advice; they admired his speed and fighting technique without jealousy. Most importantly, they had entered the realm of the Green People and had passed through unhindered without blame or judgment. Paleidir's words had been a confirmation as she whispered to him when all the land was sound asleep. "Their hearts are pure, perhaps touched by betrayal but not enough to turn them. A sense of purpose surrounds your company. I see why you have returned, if only for retribution." She peered into his soul and found nothing lacking, and with every touch, power shifted through the atmosphere.

Shadows moved as he walked towards the pit. Stretching over it, he saw a bridge, flimsy with broken bits of wood between. Briefly, he considered whether it would hold his weight, but since there was no other choice, he continued forward. Side stepping a loose rock close to the bridge, he tentatively placed a foot on a thick piece of wood. The bridge swayed slightly, accommodating itself to his presence, but otherwise held. Barely daring to breathe, he placed his other foot much like a dancer and nimbly moved over the bridge. He was almost halfway when he smelled it. A rotten stench like a long dead animal, unburied, pecked over, filled the air. His pace quickened as he smelled it, knowing it was ahead, but turning back was no option at all. Keeping his movements fluid, he reached for an

395

arrow just in time to hear the thundering. The clattering of
hooves striking wood filled the air, and tumbling across the
bridge towards him was a two-headed boar. It stood three feet
high and was covered with long, coarse, reddish brown hairs.
Its back was shiny with a kind of fluid it seemed to secrete,
which had to be the cause of the terrible smell. Both heads had
two ivory carved tusks, gleaming clearly in the darkness. What
troubled Legone most was the size of its square teeth sticking
out from its mouth. As it ran towards him, pieces of wood
floated off the bridge and it opened its mouth, chopping vigorously at the air in its excitement to eat him. Wasting no time,
Legone lifted his bow and let an arrow fly, confident in his aim.
The beast lowered its head as the arrow flew towards it, and in
one motion shook its tusks, flinging the arrow out into space.
Legone swallowed hard; there was no time to attempt another
arrow. He flung his bow onto his back and ripped out his dagger, crouching, ready to take on the foul creature. It hurtled over
the bridge, teeth chomping, determined to trample Legone to his
death. At the moment of impact, Legone lunged, leaping up
over its head, attempting to reach the other side. The boar
leaped as well, one of its heads striking Legone's airborne leg. It
swung its head violently, knocking him to the left. Arms swinging wildly, attempting to catch hold of something, Legone
managed to throw a dagger before the arms of the darkness
reached out and swallowed him.

***

Alaireia breathed deeply, gasping in air as she attempted to catch her breath. A Gim had chased her to the bridge; she was sure of it as she stepped out of the tunnel into wide archways over a pit. Placing a hand on the wall, she leaned over, spitting and breathing in and out. It felt good to be away from the marching Gaslinks and the chasing Gim. Knowing she should attempt to steal its Boleck, instead she had turned away, giving herself more time to plan. The Clyear would help her, yet she had grown wary of using its power, determined to fight with the strength of her body. As of late, her feats tended to surprise herself.

When at last she felt able to breathe, she took a piece of mocholeach and chewed it thoughtfully while contemplating her next move. Calculating, she looked down at the bridge and back up at the ropes hanging from the ceiling. Moving closer to the pit, she studied the indentions she could see on the bridge. Cocking her head, she backed away until she was pressed against the unforgiving cold stone of the tunnels. She closed her eyes and breathed deeply, bundling all her energy within herself. Calmly, she counted down, numbering her breaths before springing forward. She set off in a dead run across the short space, and when she reached the pit, hurled herself into the air above the bridge. Her hands shot upwards, snatching at the ropes until they caught and she dangled hundreds of feet up over the blackness. Not pausing to celebrate her first success, she kicked her feet out, stirring up momentum as she moved forward, making her way from one rope to the next across the open space.

She was barely halfway when she heard something below her. Shifting, she moved faster, forcing herself not to look down but to listen instead. Something was below her on the bridge, stamping and leaping into the air, trying to catch one of her dangling feet. It made a jarring noise as its teeth ground back on each other, striking the air in a sickening rhythm. Alaireia shuddered as she moved, tempted to hop down from her precarious position and cleave some sense into the creature.

Out of the corner of her eye, she saw something four-legged leaping at her. A glimpse of white teeth told her enough. She increased her speed, swinging violently on the ropes as she neared the end of the ropes and the bridge. With one last heave, she caught the last rope. It swung out over the end of the bridge back onto solid ground. Alaireia let the rope go, tucking as she fell hard to the ground and rolled to a stop. Without stopped to examine her bruises, she leaped up and ran hard and fast, already hearing the pounding of hooves behind her.

***

Starman recalled Crinte's vision again as he snuck out of the quiet halls. The silence made him feel panicky, but each time he remembered the vision, it reminded him he was going the right way. In awe, he walked into the hall of arches and gazed around at their magnitude. It was unimaginable to him that the Sorns could have created such beauty out of mere rock and stone. Again, he was reminded of how little he knew of the world and how much his mind had been opened. As he stepped towards the rickety bridge, he wrinkled his nose at the smell of decay. Queasily, he took a step forward, holding his nose to keep from taking in too much of the smell and vomiting into the abyss. Here and there, he had to skip forward where pieces of the bridge were broken. It swayed gently as he walked, but he could see the other side before him, beckoning him to safer grounds, leading him away from the drop off. When he stepped off onto sure ground, he realized his heart was in this throat and he had been holding his breath. With a sigh of relief, he let go of the stress and walked forward, sure and steady, his head held high. Somewhere ahead, he thought he heard the echo of hooves striking pavement, but when he listened again, it was gone.

***

Marklus stood in the shadows, listening. Far below, he could hear the muffled sound of pickaxes striking stone, but even closer, he could hear the heavy breathing. There seemed to be no attempt to mask its presence. He looked out, assuming it was on the other side of the dark pit that spread before him. Above, thick pillars and high archways threw themselves downwards while bravely holding up the face of the rock. He grasped the spear he'd stolen firmly in his hand. His solo journey had continued along the route where the Sorns worked. Often he heard voices or saw them marching past, yet one day, as his supply of arrows grew low, he happened upon another supply room. An entrance had been roughly cut into the path and flames lit up the opening, displaying the square room full of pickaxes, buckets, rope, short swords, spears, and daggers. Quickly he had grabbed a few daggers, tucked a short sword into his belt, and last of all took hold of one of the long, shiny spears. It felt light in his hands, and he had wanted to throw it immediately to test its speed. Moving out of the room, he had continued forward, using it as a walking stick.

Now Marklus held the spear at eye level as he walked toward the broken bridge. It was hard to believe he was the only person in the hall of archways, but as he stepped cautiously onto the bridge, he heard the heavy breathing turn to short snorts. Marklus paused on the swinging bridge; the likelihood of fighting and falling to his death was far too risky out there. He backed away slowly and stood still. At the same time, the heavy breathing slowed again and he distinctly heard the sound of hooves as it relaxed.

Zikes, Marklus called.

O Marklus the Great, we hear, we obey.

How far away from me are you?

Three days from you and seven from the Great Water Hole.

Meet me where the tunnels end.

The Zikes scurried onwards and Marklus sighed with relief; they were only mere days away. He turned back to the task at hand, raised his spear and stepped boldly across the bridge. It wasn't until he was halfway across and there was no turning back that he heard violent pounding as the lumbering creature thudded across the bridge. A cloud of foulness hung dense in the air above him, and Marklus hesitated. A hairy creature leaped into view, almost as tall as himself had it been standing up on its hind legs. Four curved tusks were aimed at Marklus' chest. He planted one foot securely in front of him and the other behind, holding his weight. Lifting his arm, he attacked first, ripping his spear through one of the boar's large ears. The boar squealed and leaped, teeth chomping at Marklus. He stepped back and paused while the boar glared at him, dark eyes bulging out of its hairy head. One ear had started to droop and rivers of blood flowed out of it. Marklus took aim and jabbed again, this time taking out the right ear. The spear stuck in the creature's ear and it swung its head maddeningly. Furious at the onslaught, it drove forward again, stampeding towards Marklus in such a way he barely had time to draw his last arrow. The creature was inches from him as he aimed. There was a deafening roar as he loosened his arrow at the same time the creature bit down hard on his foot. Marklus roared, snatching his torn foot back even as he felt the bones snapping in half. Numbing pain rushed to his head and the world turned upside down. He could see the boar standing on the bridge, one head roaring, the other hanging lifeless with just the tail end of his arrow hanging from its throat. It took a moment before he realized the reason everything appeared upside down, but it was too late. His weightless body continued over the edge, down into the darkness.

***

Legone opened his eyes slowly, unsure of how long he had been passed out. Blinking in the shadows as his memory slowly came back to him, he sat up, touching his tender, aching head. A bump had swelled up to a pulsing knot from where he had struck his head during his fall. Miraculously, he had landed on a shelf in the rock, sticking out underneath the bridge. He looked up cautiously but could not tell whether or not the monstrous boar still lay in wait. He stood gingerly, walking forward in the darkness towards the cliff wall, shivering as he went. Placing a cold hand on the face of the cliff, he felt for a foothold and sure enough found one cut into the perfect shape and height for a Sorn. He reached for his dagger but recalled both of them were gone now; his trusty bow was all he had left to ward off the boar. Taking a deep breath, he began to climb.

***

Crinte was distracted as he walked forward. If his calculations were correct, the invincibility potion the Mermis had cast on him and his warriors would end in seven days. As of late. his visions were dark and he could not see beyond the tunnels anymore. Deep down, he knew the path led out, but the vagueness concerned him. He was no longer sure if his companions were on the right road. When he shut his eyes, he could see their shapes, but they were always the same, one hand on the wall walking slowly towards the light. The weight of the mountain was crushing down on his head, and he knew there was one option left he had not dared to consider previously. Crinte walked onto the broken bridge, watching his step as he moved from one slat of wood to the next, skipping over the stops where the bridge had been broken. It swayed gently under his body weight and he held his hands straight out for balance. Using the Horn for mind control was not his aim, yet it seemed necessary. He could not tell if the armies were marching as he hoped, or if his warriors would be with him at the end. Even as he stepped off the edge of the bridge, he felt uncertainty creeping in. A movement caught his eyes and he turned. A two-headed creature lay a few feet away from him, slumbering with a blue tipped arrow stuck out of one head. Crinte drew his sword and walked forward slowly.

***

Marklus came to in a panic, sitting up and reaching for his shattered foot. Bleak darkness surrounded him, yet as he reached for his foot, he realized he could no longer feel the pain. He wiggled his toes, surprised when the movement did not hurt him. Excitedly, he stared at his hands, waiting for the blue light to appear. A glimmer shot out, illuminating the ledge he lay on, warming his face as he gazed down. Placing his hands on his cheeks, he felt the warm glow surge through his body, healing every bone it touched. He stood at last, looking about the ledge he stood on. His bow lay beside him but the spear had disappeared. He bent to pick it up, noticing a pile of blue tipped arrows scattered nearby. "Swift!" he whispered as he picked them up, tucking them into his quiver until it was full. He turned towards the cliff wall, clenching and unclenching his fists. His companions were nearby; the Great Water Hole was seven days away. It was time to finish this once and for all.

The climb to the top of the cliff and back to the road was effortless. Marklus stood upright with his bow and arrow in hand, remembering the words of Tincire the Cron. *You cannot miss with these arrows; they are light, but will fly quickly and hit their mark strong and true every time.* The smell of decay grew overwhelming as he moved forward and he saw in front of him the boar's headless body. Someone had already slain it.

CHAPTER 50

THE HORN OF SHILMI

Power pulsed beneath his tunic, calling him, begging him to use it. Reminding him, if he did not use every means necessary to save the Western World when he could, he was unworthy of his quest. He touched it warily but it was clear the decision was no longer in his hands. Slowly, he opened the hidden pocket in his tunic and gently lifted out the Horn of Shilmi. He could see the power undulating under the surface of the bone, begging to be used, asking to be set free. He watched it slowly, letting it soothe his conflicted thoughts. There was a time when he thought blowing the Horn went against everything he believed in; free choice, the will to choose one's own destiny. Yet, as he looked at the Horn, he realized the fate of the world ultimately lay in his hands. He had chosen to take the fight to the Great Water Hole. He had selected four powerful warriors. He had started the Eka Fighting Camp to raise his army. The army he needed to complete his mission. Lost on the dark road with no warriors in sight, the signal of the Horn was precisely what he needed to complete his quest. He watched it, wondering if it was overcoming his mind with its power, if he was being held sway to what it desired. He wondered if the Horn wanted him to blow it; but of course it did. The hard bone was begging to be of use, begging him not to let its owner's death be in vain.

Crinte closed his eyes for a brief second and saw with his mind's eye the tough choices a leader had to make; the death of few to ensure the lives of many. He opened his eyes and glared at the Horn. It lay lightly in the palm of his hand, the bronze glinting slightly in the darkness. He drew his sword with one hand and held it out, as if to smash the Horn, watching the oracles slither through the blade, coming to rest as their powers glided near the Horn. There was a reason it had come to him. There was a reason all this was happening. Crinte opened his mouth and brought the Horn to his dry lips. He breathed in deeply, then blew with all his might. Air rushed from the base of the Horn to the opening, and a silvery twinkle began to sound. At first, it was small in the darkness, muted by the shadows, yet it continued to grow even as he stopped blowing. The silvery sound echoed through the shadows, growing larger and louder. He could hear the voices calling, beckoning, reaching out, persuading, changing minds. Small beings shot out of the air, almost quicker than he could see, shooting out in all directions, teleporting through the walls of the tunnels. They blew into the faces of those who were sleeping, waking them, pointing to the Great Water Hole. Crinte could hear those faint of heart become strong. They stood up everywhere and took up their weapons, marching forward with a song of triumph on their lips. They were coming from all over the Western World. The people of Mizine were rising up, the Zikes were coming, the Xctas were flying, the Sorns were marching with pickaxes on their backs, the Crons and Tiders with Ackhor's army. They were coming, the dam had broken lose, the river of warriors was on its way, and by dawn, the Great Water Hole would be swarming with them. Moved by the whirl of magic the Horn released, Crinte looked down at it. He no longer saw a Horn that gave him the power of mind control; he saw a Horn that allowed him to encourage those who heard it to be the best version of themselves. To march forward for a cause that would ultimately save their World. He felt a river of emotion overwhelm him, and Crinte sheathed his sword, tucked away the Horn, and began to run.

***

Something woke him. Perhaps a sound. Maybe a pebble falling in the endless enormity below. Likely a mouse, lost, looking for the light. Like him. Starman stirred slightly in his camouflage. The hole he had curled up in to sleep seemed like it might become his eternal shelter. When he closed his eyes, there was blackness. When he opened his eyes, there are more darkness, inky, pressing against him, hurting his head, crushing his heart, burying his soul. Day and night were no more, dreams of a distant life. He no longer remembered the faces of his friends or the feeling of wind on his face, or the sound of crickets humming him to sleep on a warm summer night. He could no longer taste the colorful foods of Trazamy City, nor remember the heady feeling the nutty ale gave him. He felt exhausted, as though each sleep drained more energy from him. He opened his eyes again and wondered why he should bother. His shoulders burned as he moved his neck, feeling the strain from the awkward position he'd lain in all night. It was the only reason he should rise, to stretch his muscles again, feed his hungry belly with mocholeach, and walk onward. Instead, he rested his head against the warm stone and blinked slowly.

That was when he heard it. He froze and sat up as best he could. There. He heard it again. The most delicate voice barely out of earshot. It was undeniable; the voice was meant for him, telling him something. He moved one foot, scooting forward towards the entrance of the hole. Pinpricks shot through his numb legs from where he had slept on them, but he ignored them. Again, he heard the voice calling him. It did not say his name, and it spoke no language he understood, but all the same, it was calling. He tumbled out of the hole, taking a moment to shake his legs out before moving towards the sound. The silvery voice filled his mind, reminding him of who he was. It assured him all was not lost. It was not the end after all. Starman felt the clouds of confusion swept from his mind, and although it was dark and the tunnels stretched onward, cold and bleak, he lifted his feet and began to run. The voices streamed around him, praising him, urging him on, faster and faster until he thought he could actually fly.

**

Where are you going? thoughts whispered in his head, attempting to dissuade him from his path. *Why do you think you*

408

will succeed when others more powerful than you have failed? Legone ignored them as he strode uphill, one hand on the hard, cold wall. The light was dim now, allowing him to see a few paces ahead; all the same, he was reluctant to fall again. The incessant humming of the voices told him he was too close. The Ruler, alerted to his presence, would be preparing. It had been apparent to him from their first meeting that their minds were at odds. Sarhorr, tall and irksomely handsome, was fierce and fast. His voice was smooth, compelling, intoxicating. A gentle spell lilted from his mouth, drifting through the ears of those who listened. The Green People had been rapt at his appearance, his words, his gifts. Those of a lesser order worshipped his very being. He walked among them un-forcefully, listening, suggesting, worming his way into their hearts. But Legone could see the shadow that followed him, and at first, he assumed it was his aura, just as the Green People gave off a pale light when they became emotional. One evening on his way to rendezvous with Paleidir, Lady of the Green People, he saw a dark form. Staying close to the castle walls, it snuck its way down the winding path leading to where the wind blows. Surprised, Legone watched it, barely making out the features of a diabolical being, dark and ancient. That evening, he climbed the intertwined vines of ivy to her hidden balcony where she rested on a chaise lounge. Waiting. She opened her arms to him as he lifted his legs over the ledge and sat down beside her. "Are there beings with the ability to shift forms?" he had asked, concerned, forgetting to even greet her.

She reached out a hand to caress his serious face and laughed. "Why would you ask me that?"

"Tell me, would I know if I saw one?"

"You are serious." She stood, letting the moonlight filter through her long hair. "Changers are old beings from the beginning of time, the last scraps of the creator's spark which formed this World. You would be unlikely to meet one, for they are above us, too distinguished to flirt with the people groups and too haughty to lower themselves to live with the immortals." Her long fingers rested on the balcony, gripping it tightly as she continued. "There is no place for them in this world. They are a mistake. If you ever met one, it would be unexplainable. They have two forms that make them indestructible. One is physical and one is spirit. We Green People call ourselves immortal because we never die, but we can be killed. Changers are truly immortal. If their physical form is killed, their spiritual form remains, and who can kill a spirit?"

"Would you know if you met a Changer?" he pressed. "Are they dangerous?"

She laughed lightly again, her voice rippling gently through the air like the tinkling of silver bills on a cold, crisp night. "Dangerous? There are no creatures in the World more powerful or dangerous."

"What if I met a Changer. What should I do?"

She turned back to him, bending to take his face in her hands. Her intense gaze met his questioning eyes. "Run as fast as you can, and never stop."

He paused, searching her eyes for more. "If need be, is there a way to stop a Changer?"

She looked at him, calculating. "There might be. What are you thinking, my love? What fears have sparked these questions?"

He averted his gaze from hers, lest she see into his mind by looking into his eyes. He pulled her warm body into his lap, nestling his face against the crook of her neck as he lightened his tone. "Just curiosity, nothing else."

But his curiosity deepened as he watched Sarhorr and wondered if he were immune to the spell of blindness cast upon the Green People. Indeed, it was not long after that Sarhorr had pulled him aside, backing him into a dark corner. "You do not trust me," he had whispered, his mouth close to Legone's ear, his voice whining, hurt with an undercurrent of spite.

"I do not trust everyone I meet," Legone had retorted.

Sarhorr backed away, his voice menacing as he leaned in again, like a snake playing with its prey before devouring it. "You are only a fly on my back, an oddity in the waves of fate. Do not try to stop me. It will be your end, and the end of your beloved Green People. I can sense when you are near, and if time passes and I find you on my trail, I will destroy you."

A chill passed through Legone as if the doors of death had opened and touched him gently. He felt the flow of his breathing halt as a malicious grin covered Sarhorr's face. He moved away, leaving Legone gasping in the shadows. It was only a few months later that Legone had taken Paleidir's advice and run as fast as he could. Now he wondered if he should have told Crinte the truth. Crinte simply thought Sarhorr the Ruler was a power-hungry immortal; a Changer required a completely different

411

mindset. A new set of rules applied, but maybe it was best he did not know, in case they failed altogether.

A signal disturbed his thought process and he lifted his head. The fog of evil whispers had left him, and a jeweled voice was calling, beckoning him. His heart leaped as he heard it, an unfamiliar voice, but as it grew louder, he realized one he had desperately wanted to hear his whole life. No longer were his movements cautious and fragmented. He began to run, speed lighting his feet, and he sped like a blur through the tunnels.

***

Alaireia held her ground as the Gim transformed. The heat from the pitchfork towering above her seared her face. She had tied her hair back, yet the tips felt crisp as they caught the ends of the flame. Every particle of her body begged her to run, screamed at her to save herself. Only her mind remained in her control, reminding her of the task at hand. In one hand she held her sword in front, shielding her body from the Gim's initial attack. The other hand held the Clyear as she whispered gently to it, telling it her desire. Bony white fingers appeared on the pitchfork despite the flames that licked at it. A sightless tall figure stood over four feet above her, its face hidden beneath a hooded cloak so black it blended into the darkness. It drew a long, wide sword and held it towards her, first moving its pitchfork towards her menacingly, then swinging its blade with a sure and steady hand. Alaireia lifted her sword to meet it and a resounding gong rang out. She ducked the next blow, and swung her sword upward, slamming it into the pitchfork. Sparks burned her skin, and flames leaped at her at the Gim lifted its sword to take off her head. Sensing her moment, she leaped up and blew into the Gim's face. Its sword came down heavy. Alaireia threw herself backwards and the Gim dropped its sword, using both hands to defend itself against the searching power she had thrown at it. A second later, the pitchfork crashed down as well. Alaireia rolled away from it, pulled herself upwards, and launched herself at the Gim. She struck it again and again with her sword, accomplishing nothing, as the outer shell of its temporary body was too thick. Relentlessly, she drove forward until a small object rolled out of the Gim's cloak. Alaireia dove with the Gim on top of her, reaching for it. The moment her fingers touched it, she felt a sickly quiver above her. With a scream, the Gim grew limp and disappeared. Alaireia stood up, holding the round object. It felt heavy in her hands but there was something else. Death was captured inside of it, and an odd feeling overcame her. She wanted to put it down and walk away; that kind of dark power was not meant for her. Shakily, she sheathed her sword and tucked the Clyear away. Again, she held the object at length, attempting to persuade herself to hold onto it.

Alaireia. She froze. *Alaireia,* it called again, louder. It was a voice she almost recognized. The sound of it filled her with hope, refreshing her spirit despite the evil object she held in her hand. *Alaireia! Come!* It was calling, beckoning. She could almost see two outstretched hands pulling her in, urging her to quicken her pace. She was needed. She was desired. Forgetting her dilemma, Alaireia took off down the lonely road towards the voice.

Marklus plodded down the sloping halls with weary feet. He could hear it, the tongues that belonged to the outside land. His desire for natural light increased with each step. He swore if he ever stepped out of the dark tunnel, he would never enter again. Life without the freedom to live and die on the land he loved was no life at all. He understood that now, even though he wanted to stop, to rest. He missed the banter of his companions. Just the thought of talking to anyone else besides himself and the Zikes would be comforting. Impatiently, he pushed curls off his forehead, reminding himself of how close he was. He hoped he was not alone. Suddenly, his heart leaped in anticipation as a sweet voice called out to him. Marklus could see a burst of light ahead of him; beings were begging him to hurry. Marklus wearily began to move forward, but the call intensified and came again. It picked up memories and danced them in front of him, reminding him of the reason he had decided to quest to the Great Water Hole in the first place. Now was the time. The day had come. It was the beginning of the end. Marklus picked up his feet and ran as fast as they would carry him.

***

Crinte stood at the bottom of the staircase, gazing at the light as if he would never look away. He had arrived. Five steps led upward, and on the other side, he was sure he'd see the Great Water Hole, dark and evil spread before him. For now, he stood calmly until he heard footsteps. He turned, a slow smile spreading across his face. "Marklus!" he called.

"Crinte!" Marklus ran forward, arms wide open. "You have no idea how happy I am to see you again."

Crinte laughed as he hugged Marklus roughly. "We made it, after all."

"Crinte? Marklus?" Starman's voice questioned as he jogged up, his eyes wide.

"Starman, you made it too!" In his excitement, Marklus reached for him as well. Crinte met Starman's eyes. "Well done," he said with a broad smile.

A shadow walked out of the hall. "I've been looking for you for days," Alaireia announced with a crooked grin as she walked up.

Starman folded her tightly into his arms before she could say another word. "I thought we'd never meet again," he said, his voice gentle as he leaned back to look at her.

Crinte nodded at her but Marklus joined Starman's hug.

A tall figure slipped up, and Legone's cold face was no longer a sore sight to see. "There you all are," he said solemnly.

For a moment, there was nothing but the sound of excited chatter as, all at once, they attempted to explain their own journey through the dark road. It was Crinte who pointed up the wide, rough staircase to the light above. "Shall we?"

THE GREAT WATER HOLE

Alaireia walked into the light, closing her eyes and holding her face to the breeze that blew back wisps of her shoulder length black hair. She could feel the hints of darkness leaving her eyes. The cobwebs of confusion drifted away and she breathed deeply. The air was filled with molecules of water, and a hint of iron stung her nostrils as she breathed in. Moisture gathered in her eyes as she opened them, and the view made her reach out for Starman, her fingers straying into his, entwining tightly as she stared. She gave a sharp meow of surprise at the landscape that spread before her. "It's beautiful," she whispered.

"I know," Starman replied in awe.

They stood on a ledge near the top of the canyon. Stretching as far as the eye could see were cliffs of rich, red rock, cutting through the land, opening up into yawning caverns with dangerous drops. Here and there, waterfalls poured out of the canyon walls, thundering down to meet the source of the rushing water. The sky above them was shades of pink and purple, a color barely seen in the light of a sunset. Clustering over the sky yet shining clearly, each on their own, were the stars, their white bodies glowing abnormally close to the world as if pulled by some magnetic force. Although there was no sign of the sun or moon, light shone as bright as daylight. The air was wet and chilly, and Alaireia's hand grew clammy as she clasped Starman's. She felt deceived. All along, she had been expecting to walk out of the Slutan Tunnels into the Great Water Hole, an evil land overflowing with transformed, dark creatures. In reality, it appeared she had caught a glimpse of paradise.

Starman continued to stand with his hand in hers, his mouth agape. Marklus' arms lay lax by his side, his face a mask of surprise. Crinte for once looked at a loss, but Legone stood a bit taller and tilted his chin in resolve. Using his bow, he pointed at the expanse around them. "This is exactly what he does." He glanced at the others. "We have come too far and fought too hard in the darkness to give in now. He wanted us dead, but if he can transform us, that is worse than death. A warm welcome and a glimpse of paradise is his way to take us down."

Crinte swallowed hard. "See the mist? That is where we want to go."

Marklus looked out. In the distance on the other side of the canyon, he could see a darkness hovering over the waters. Even as the breeze blew, he saw it, just as he had in his dream: a dark tower rising out of the canyon. Its glinting obsidian coloring stood out against the canyon as it rose, towering into the magenta sky, cutting off all hope. Suddenly the beautiful landscape felt lost in its shadow, and Marklus felt the chilly shadow of horror that quickened his breath, clutching at his throat. His hands were cold as he wrapped them around his bow. He could already hear the terrified screams below and the shrieks of the transformed. They had walked through halls of darkness, only to arrive at a bewitching graveyard with a decoy of peace resting upon it.

"Crinte," Marklus whispered. "Our orders?" He had imagined himself saying those words, but the moment had seemed much more epic, marching determinedly into the Great Water Hole with an army behind them, ready to take down Sarhorr the Ruler. In reality it was too quiet, too peaceful. At any moment, he expected the watchers in the tower to swoop out, whisking them away to an impenetrable prison.

"My friends," Crinte began, turning to face them on the rusted red ledge. "I have asked much of you. Your strength has been tested. Your minds have been exposed to what we truly face, a quest for power and an alternative paradise for immortals. In your hearts, you know the Western World belongs to the mortals, and our people deserve to keep this land, to live out our numbered days as we wish. That is why we are here, to put an end to this madness. That is why we find ourselves risking it all and walking straight into his domain, brave enough to face him head on. We have all lost something because of his selfish desires, our homes, our families, our loved ones. Today we end this once and for all. Today we stand together and face this demon from an alternate world. Today our power unites. This is our purpose, to trap this powerful being with what he desires most—power. Do not let your hearts grow weary, do not let them falter right here at the end. We have come too far to give in now. So I ask you, here at the beginning of the end, do you stand with me?"

Crinte raised his sword in the air, his eyes blazing as he looked at his warriors. Legone was the first to step forward. He pulled an arrow from his quiver and raised it in the air. "Aye!"

"Aye!" echoed Marklus, raising his arrow as well.

"Aye." Alaireia added her sword and a light began to shimmer within.

"Aye." Starman spoke clearly and surely. He joined his weapon with the others and a spark of light shot into the air as the blades struck against each other.

Crinte could feel the bloodlust surging through him, and his eyes turned gold as he looked at each of his warriors. "The armies of Mizine draw near," he told them. "We have little time before this region is thrown into chaos, and we need to make the most of it. Each of you needs to ensure your army is in place to fight off the guards. Our main goal is to confront him in the tower, and each of you have a unique mission to complete." He paused, letting his visions drift into their thoughts, showing each of them what they needed to do next. "Alaireia, the Clyear of Power is our bait. It is the one thing he does not have that will complete his ultimate dominion. Legone, the Boleck will be the trap. Once he becomes desperate enough to slip into spirit form, you must trap him in it. Starman, you and I must keep the path clear to the Great Water Hole. The Boleck with the spirit of Sarhorr must be cast into the waters of transformation to ensure his spirit death. Marklus, you stand between life and death. You will know when his demise is complete."

419

Marklus could hear the shadows from the other side whispering from the currents of the deathly waters. He remembered when he first set out for the Great Water Hole, foolish and alone, quickly tackled into prison. He recalled sitting in the grimy prison cell, waiting for something to happen, even if it were only the end. Here at last he found himself at the end, and adrenaline tingled through his body.

Alaireia pulled out her Clyear, whispering gently to it before blowing on it, cloaking them in shadow. They blended into the canyon walls as they began their last walk across the broad ledges to the other side of the canyon.

Starman held tight when Alaireia attempted to pull her hand away. "Don't let go," he said, looking at her with his deep brown eyes. "This is the end."

"You can't know that," Alaireia replied gently, turning back to stand face to face.

"But I do," Starman replied. "Remember what I once told you? If I am to die, I'd rather die surrounded by those I love. I thought I had to go home to be with those I love, but now I see that home is not a location. It's the people you love that make home worth it, and you are the one I love. You are my home. This is the end. So don't let go."

Alaireia felt a gentle smile touch her face. She shook her head in amazement as she gazed into Starman's calm, open and honest face. Yet as she looked into his eyes, she saw strength shining from them. "I always thought love was a weakness," she told him. "I thought it would be the downfall of all. Yes, I want you to live. I want to protect you. But I know you can do that yourself. I see strength in your love and it encourages me. This must be the unbreakable bond they speak of that makes the impossible happen."

Starman's face lit up in a smile for a moment. He squeezed her hand and walked forward, following the curving path inward.

Legone trod softly in the rear, an arrow nocked in his bowstring. He could see her again, standing in the wind, her sad, large eyes begging him to join her. Asking him to stay with her. If the world was ending, why not run away together and leave the ruin and destruction to others. He could hear himself answering: "Because it is our fault." She had lain beside him that night, holding him as if she would never let go. "You will lose your life if you fight this. You made a deal with a Changer, as did I. We have no power over him. You remember the exchange we made, so that he would leave us alone. We call it the banishment, giving him power so he would leave us alone. We alienated ourselves and he got exactly what he wanted. If you cross him, he will take everything." He had threaded his fingers helplessly through her long hair. "I know." She had taken his hand and pressed it to her heart. "You would leave me, your wife, once more? To live out her immortal days in sorrow?" He had felt his heart breaking again, afraid she would stray him from his fate. "I am here now." She kissed him gently, then more urgently, and the gloom of the world faded for moments as they were happy, as they had once been. Now the stark truth rose before him. He stood in front of the dark tower, gazing upwards. He only saw one path now; destroy Sarhorr at all costs. And he knew what that cost would be.

White streams of mist shot into the air from blowholes throughout the canyon, retaining the aura of mystery. Crinte led the way, watching shapes move back and forth. The further inland they went, the more the canyon came to life, echoes of what it really was screaming from each cranny and ledge. Booted feet struck against hard stone in every direction, and armies streamed by above them, chanting in sync. Far below, where rushing waters streamed into a deadly current, desperate voices cried out in terror as they were forcibly dropped into the transformative waters. The mist turned warm and grew thicker the further they walked into the beautiful nightmare, sticking close together, fingers impatiently tapping against their weapons. The tower loomed before them, but as they grew nearer, Crinte paused, watching it with narrow eyes. He turned to his warriors, motioning them to step back into the shadows of an overhanging ledge. Jagged points of the tower shot into the air while two horned creatures covered in gray armor guarded its massive doors. "I think the tower is a decoy," Crinte told them. "If we wanted to take over this land, our obvious focus would be the tower. Yet structures are built by mortals for shelter and safety. One with power needs none of those trifles. Legone, what do you think? Where would he be instead?"

"He will be proud of what he has accomplished here," Legone said. "He will survey the work of his hands, studying it, improving it."

Crinte looked up. "And for that, he will need a vantage point."

"He will sense us coming," Legone added. "We are an oddity in his land, a power source he will be prepared to meet."

Crinte nodded and stepped forward. "Wait," Alaireia said. She turned to Legone and held out her hand. "The Boleck."

"Ah." Legone's face relaxed as he gingerly took the round, bowl-like sphere. "Thank you." He held her eyes for a moment.

"I don't understand." Marklus spoke up. "The Ruler created Gims and Bolecks; how can you use his own creation against him?"

"We can, because this time we hold a greater power," Crinte confirmed.

"But what of his minions?" Starman asked. "They will protect him, keep us from reaching him."

Crinte's eyes glowed as he surveyed the land. "His armies are amassing in the southern valley. Yes, they may protect him, but they cannot stop us. If we must fight the transformed armies to reach him, so shall it be. Marklus, call the Zikes. The armies of Mizine must be close."

"Wait." Marklus held up a hand as he closed his eyes and strained his ears. "Listen."

"What do you hear?" Alaireia urged, her hands straying to her sword hilt.

"The armies are amassing, a barrier between us and him, but I hear the scurrying of the Zikes, the beating wings of the Xctas, and marching…it must be the armies of Mizine." He opened his eyes and looked at Crinte. "How did they get here so quickly?"

But it was Legone who responded. The light in his eyes was dull and bleak as he glanced at Marklus. "It's the power of the Horn of Shilmi. Crinte blew it back in the tunnels and it called all warriors, opening rifts in time and space to bring them here."

"I had to..." Crinte replied, trailing off at the enormity of what he had done.

"All armies?" Starman questioned. "What exactly does that mean?"

Alaireia stepped out from behind the ledge, her eyes seeing beyond the mist. Drawing her sword, she pointed. "Look. They have come."

Following the line of the blade of her sword, Crinte watched through the mist, his eyes gold as the armies of Sarhorr lined up in the distance, a glittering mass of mail, white bone, silver helmets, and black spears. They stretched away as far as his eye could see and onward, blocking the way up into the mountains. A vision captured Crinte's sight, this time displaying the past instead of the future. He was taken back to the very second he'd blown the Horn of Shilmi. From an aerial view, he saw people groups across Mizine leap to follow, but he also saw the Sorns marching out of the depths of the Slutan Tunnels and other people groups of Asspraineya begin to run towards the Great Water Hole. The massive army of Gaslinks working to cross the Dejewla Sea into Mizine turned as if answering the summons of their master. He could see them pouring from every corner of the World, the warriors coming to fight. They rippled through the air as if the distance were nothing, and as he stepped out of the Slutan Tunnels into the Great Water Hole, they did as well. Crinte drew his sword impatiently, his fingers quickening about it as he prepared in eager anticipation. It was his time at last. But it would not be a quick battle. His eyes were burning as he faced his warriors. "Come, let's show them what we're made of."

"As soon as there is an opportunity, I will go." Legone's voice was quiet as he followed Crinte. "He expects me. He will not kill me until he hears what I have to say."

"Legone." Crinte's voice rang with authority. "We will come with you. This is our quest. Let's finish it together." He moved out of the cove through the mists, walking towards a gray hilltop.

The smoking canyon lay on their left, while the dark tower rose in shadows to their right. Behind them stretched the country of Slutan, while ahead, some coming fresh out of the transformative waters, an army lay between them and the heights of the Great Water Hole.

"There are Xeros down there," Crinte warned. "Be wary of them."

At the crest of the hill, the warriors paused and looked down at the armies below them. Crinte turned to them, but as their eyes met each other's, they realized there was nothing left to say. Bubbling within them was the death defying determination, the realization they were about to leave everything they had at the battlefield. Comrades, clear in their quest, one by one they nodded in acknowledgement of all they had done for each other, and readied their weapons.

CHAPTER 52

BATTLE FOR THE WORLD

At the top of the hill, the Five Warriors stood. Marklus bent his elbow, reaching to pull a blue tipped arrow from his quiver. He could hear its voice even as he pulled his bowstring taut and lifted it, staring down in the valley, waiting. Legone the Swift stood to the right of Marklus, an arrow already in his bow. His face was grim but calm and resolute as he raised his bow, the muscles of his powerful arms straining. Crinte gazed down into the valley, watching every move as he raised his sword above his head, a symbol of victory that would be theirs in the end. On his left, Alaireia had planted herself, feet apart, her sword gripped in both hands. She watched the glowing line as it steadily moved with her breath, in and out. Beside her, Starman's eyes fell on his dangerously beautiful blade. He had a feeling deep in his gut that it was his last battle with it. As if sensing their arrival, a sudden breeze blew over them, and hints of the perfume from Spherical Land drifted past their noses as the invincibility spell lifted. But not one of them flinched.

In the valley, where the mists had cleared, the five could clearly see thousands of Gaslinks, Garcrats, and Xeros running towards them. Spears were raised high, dark flags fluttered in the occasional breeze, and the heavy thumping of thousands of footfalls in the canyon clambered through the wasted echoes. Sounds blended with the shrieks of the transformed, and a moment later the Slutan Army opened their mouths and roared a battle cry. *Grwahoo! Grwahoo! Grwahoo!* An abysmal thumping began, as if someone underground were playing the drums, thrumming against them in the deep. The creatures continued to run, eager for a taste of war, their only purpose left after their transformation. *Grwahoo! Grwahoo! Grwahoo!*

Marklus was the first to break rank, lowering his bow to shout out, "The Zikes are here!" Indeed, a river of green grass streamed over the barren rock of the canyon, surrounding them. In a flash, the Zikes transformed into their actual form, four feet tall with green electrified cones on their heads. They bowed wordlessly as they looked at Marklus with their large, terrifying eyes. The scent of fresh cut grass hung in the air as one stepped forward, holding a pinprick of poison.

"It would be our honor to lead the charge." Its voice was flat and grim.

Marklus raised his bow, standing firm as their leader. "Well then, lead on," he ordered.

In a blur of green, the Zikes surged down the hill towards the chanting Slutan Army, half of them transforming back into blades of grass while others kept their true form. Waves of them rolled down the hill, and there was a flash of green as the sharp points of the Zikes came into contact with the sharp mail of the

Gaslinks, who led the charge. Reeling in surprise, the Gaslinks raised their battle axes and continued forward, roaring. *Grwa-hoo! Grwahoo! Grwahoo!* A troop of Gaslinks dropped to their bony knees and raised their crossbows, aiming at the Zikes as they drew near. There was a beat before a command was shouted and the archers let loose their arrows. A stream of black hid the eerie light as the arrows arched above the Gaslinks. Sharpened arrowheads hurled downwards, aiming for the pointed Zikes' heads. All it took was the blink of an eye; one moment the Zikes were rushing towards the Gaslinks, in full form, the next they had vanished, transformed, and arrows hurled deep into the ground. The Zikes appeared once more in the midst of the Gaslinks, striking relentlessly with their poison, moving in rivers of glee through the Slutan Army as, at last, they had permission to do what they did best.

"The first wave," Marklus said. "They will take out the archers for us."

"Aye," Crinte agreed.

A sound made Alaireia whirl around, eyes narrowed. Behind her she saw a trail of light. It flicked back through the Great Water Hole, following a path that led south. Her breath caught as a division of the Mizine army appeared out of the mist, marching towards her. It was a small group of Crons, barely one hundred, but dressed in blue and carrying a flag with the crest of Mizine on it. They carried swords and spears with round shields of carved bronze on their arms. Their feet marched directly on the trail of light as they moved closer. Their dark eyes were set and determined, and when at last they stopped in front of Alaireia, one raised his hand to his helmet in salute. "We followed the light," he announced. "It led us here."

Alaireia walked towards them and raised her sword. Her face grew still and deadly as she felt the bloodlust rage up within her. "Are you ready to take back what they stole from us?" she demanded as she raised her sword.

"Aye!" the division of ex-prisoners shouted.

"Are you ready to fight with me?" she called.

"Aye!" the division of ex-prisoners replied.

She whipped around without hesitation, Starman by her side, and began to run. Her pace quickened as she gathered speed, racing downhill towards the armies of Sarhorr. Her army raised their voices as they followed her, seeking redemption as they ran.

As they entered the fray, Legone felt his eyes drawn into the air where black arrows still fought against the light. He could hear the beating of wings and the long, lonely cries of the creatures of the air. They soared above them, stretched wings, deadly talons and sharp breaks. "The Xctas have come," he whispered.

Crinte and Marklus looked up with him as the giant birds flew low overhead, disappearing and reappearing in the air as they flew towards the swarming valley. One swooped low and snatched up Legone in its sharp talons.

"Remember," Crinte shouted as the Xctas bore Legone into the battlefield, "we need to reach the ledges!"

An arrow shot out from Legone's bow, dancing as it spun its way into the battlefield, and he was gone. Airborne.

The sounds of battle intensified but the frenzy had only just begun as Crinte and Marklus stood alone in the gray mist of the hilltop. "It seems like a dream," Marklus remarked. "When I lay in the dark pit of prison, I never imagined I would escape, much less make it here to stand with you on this day. I have seen more of the world than I have ever known. I have met the wild things of the air and land. I have seen the havoc power can wreak. I am proud to stand with you on this day and see the dark days of the Western World come to an end."

"This, Marklus, is the final journey. But look!" Crinte turned around.

Marching towards them was the Mizine army from the Eka Fighting Camp, Ackhor and Tincire at the helm, covered head to toe in shining armor. They carried blue flags with the symbol of Mizine upon them, and each warrior was armed to the teeth with bows, arrows, swords, daggers, axes, spears, and more. They streamed over the Great Water Hole, thousands of Crons and Tiders, a sure force to be reckoned with. Crinte moved to greet them respectfully, almost in disbelief that they had actually come. He reached out his arm to clasp hands with Ackhor and Tincire.

Ackhor crossed his arms, glancing down into the valley at the war already in progress. "I see you have succeeded," he said, his deep voice offering a tone of admiration.

Crinte tilted his head in acknowledgement. "I see all the armies of Mizine stand united behind you."

Ackhor chuckled roughly. "We had some assistance, from a Simon the Brave, and Marklus," he reached out to clasp arms with Marklus, "your Zikes. And then that silvery call back

430

there…we found ourselves standing here," he finished curiously.

Crinte stepped back from the center of the hill, giving Ackhor full view. "Ackhor, your command?"

Ackhor shook his bearded head as he watched the abomination below him. "Only that you fight alongside me. It's time for payback."

"They need our backup down there." Tincire looked down the hill. "I will take the center division down."

"Crinte, you and Marklus take the left flank. I will take the right," Ackhor ordered. "Armies of Mizine," he called. "We have come to destroy the transformed creatures who seek to take over our land, once and for all. You have prepared, you have marched far, but now is the time to take your weapons in hand and show our enemy what you are made of. The battle is ours; you will need your strength and cunning but I have faith in you. I know you will fight this war and live to see the sunrise. Now lift your arms, people of Mizine, to war!"

In a thunder of voices and footfalls, the massive army of Mizine descended upon the transformed army. As they clashed into each other, shields rang, swords cried out, and warriors roared in glory and pain and death. The battle turned into a blur as the Slutan Armies and Mizine Armies further combined, neither gaining ground as they tore each other apart in the valley. Meanwhile, Sarhorr the Ruler watched from his perch, his mouth curling in a sneer as he waited for the one he knew would come.

***

Legone whirled on the back of one of the Xctas as they soared above the battle. The Xctas banked and turned, swooping back low to take out a group of Gaslinks, building some sort of contraption on a ledge close to the canyon. The air flowed over him, pulling back his long braid of hair, and Legone breathed deeply as he lifted his bow and aimed. His arrow, an extension of himself, spun through the air like a knife, burrowing in the neck of one of the Gaslinks below. It fell, gagging and grasping at its neck, bent fingers reaching to drag it out even as the life drained away. A second later, sharp talons ripped through ten Gaslinks, tearing at their armor and dragging them shrieking into the air. Giant wings beat below Legone as the Xctas thrust itself into the air, relentlessly tossing the writhing Gaslinks into the canyon. Legone slid another arrow into his bow, longing for the powerful wings to be his, but that gift he had given up in exchange for their help in battle. To some, it would not seem a fair exchange, yet the Xctas were skeptical and wary of the individual who could turn himself into one of them. Even as they let him enter their midst, they were not thrilled at his seemingly unnatural abilities and bade the heart of the mountain give it back. The odd sky rose before him as the Xctas gained height before it swooped back down into the fray. Although his eyesight was not keen like Crinte's, he saw the bizarre sky as if the entire universe had drawn closer to watch the beginning of the end. The face of a star moved in space; white, lidless eyes of a giantess anxiously flickered at him as she watched. He blinked in confusion, shaking his head at what he'd imagined he'd seen. Before he could get a second look to confirm his suspicions, the Xctas turned and dove back into the midst of the battle. Feathers burst from its wings as it fearlessly ripped through the transformed creatures. Legone pulled his feet up, away from the grasping reach of the creatures, and with arrow after arrow, shot them down. Shadows from the air wheeled about him as one by one the Xctas dipped and soared. But as soon as they drove a troop of Gaslinks back, twice the number would take their places.

***

Marklus had only walked midway down the hill, and now he stood, commanding the archers of Mizine. He was not sure how it had happened; they just flocked to him, eager to taste blood. They raised their bows as the army marched down the hill like an avalanche, incapable of stopping. Marklus raised his hand and bellowed, "Ready? Aim." Arrows pointed towards the sky. It was the long-range shoot, designed to thrust arrows high into the air and bury them in the hearts of the enemy, hundreds of feet away. "Fire!" His voice echoed through as other archers took up the cry. "Fire!" Blue tipped arrows covered the sky in an arching aura of cyan, almost turning the sky back to its original color. They dropped in slow motion like the first drizzle of raindrops before the tumult rush of a frenzied storm. Chainmail links of metal shattered beneath the force of the arrows, splintering apart as creatures fell, glittering eyes staring in relief at the magenta sky. "Again!" Marklus shouted, this time raising his bow as well.

Even as the arrows rained down, out of the corner of his eye he could see the black tower, floating ominously in his vision. It nagged at him, watching him, the eyes of the Great Water Hole. Even if Sarhorr the Ruler was not there now, it was a host for him and his transformations. Marklus shivered as he found his eyes drawn to the tower, watching the pointed spikes of its turrets drift in and out of view. His bow came down and he found himself walking towards it. The gray mist cleared before him, like a path, opening and closing behind him. If he had looked back, the archers would have been hidden from view, but he persisted. The mist hid his footfalls on the lifeless ground he crept over, until he could see the tower in full view. It glinted in the light like a polished stone, its angles drawing him deeper like a jewel of darkness, undulating colors changing beneath its surface. A slanted iron bridge led the way up into the tower, its coloring dusty beneath the shining tower. Realization dawned on Marklus and he stumbled backwards, his footing unsure. "Destroy it!" he found himself shouting. "Destroy it! Rip it down!"

O Marklus the Great, the voices of the Zikes hummed through his head. *We hear. We obey.*

Marklus felt his eyes grow wet as he swallowed hard, his mind already clouding, shutting down from the horror as he watched.

"Marklus!" a voice called out of the mist, and a shadow walked towards him.

Marklus turned, expecting to see Crinte, but instead found himself looking into the cocky, smug face of a lanky Cron. He furrowed his brow and pointed at him. "Simon the Brave? What are you doing here?"

Simon shrugged nonchalantly. "You said to call the army, and we are here."

Marklus grasped Simon's shoulder. "Good. Call your division of the army; tell them to destroy the tower. The Zikes will help."

Simon peered over Marklus' shoulder at the tower and looked back into Marklus' face.

"What do you see?" he asked curiously.

Marklus shuddered. "You may think it impossible, but the tower is made out of spirits, trapped between life and death. Destroying that tower will set them free."

Simon shivered and peered back over Marklus' shoulder, his eyes now wide. "But won't they destroy all of us?"

"That is entirely possible," Marklus conceded. "But whatever is going on in the tower is keeping the transformed alive. Go, I must find Crinte."

Marklus ran, leaving Simon the Brave standing stock still, staring at the tower. He did not see as the doors flung open and dozens of Xeros began to march towards the valley.

SARHORR THE RULER

It was dawn. Crinte could tell, although the light never changed. They had been fighting for almost a day, although the armies continued endlessly. Crinte could sense it was time; something had changed in the air, and soon the tide would turn one way or another. Crinte pulled back towards the hill, letting the armies of Mizine stream around him. It had been hours since he had last seen his warriors, and for a brief moment he wondered if Legone the Swift had taken to the ledges without him. A division of the army was at the black tower, being terribly beaten by the Xeros, although the Zikes were there. Zikes fought flesh, and the iron monsters were nothing of the sort. Tincire had brought some sort of explosives his division of the army was lighting and throwing into the midst of the Gaslinks. Most of the Garcrats were gone, the initiation round of the transformed doomed to death.

Crinte lifted his sword. Despite the death, it had seen it shone clearly, the oracles on it all pointing upwards. He swung it in a slow arc and they appeared before him, blinking off the end of his sword and hurling themselves into space. Visions danced before his eyes and he saw them clearly this time. He turned to the dark tower and pointed his sword at it, watching the spirits ebb and flow in their struggle. He saw beyond what Marklus had seen, and he knew what he must do. Lifting his sword in the air, he called them. "Marklus. Legone. Starman. Alaireia."

An Xctas flew overhead and Legone dropped out of the sky, landing on his feet in front of Crinte. He swung his bow into his back and pulled a dagger out of his belt. "It is time," he said, knowingly.

Marklus stumbled down the hill, out of breath, his curly hair wild. "If we don't take him down now," he said, "all of this will have been in vain. The Slutan Armies increase while the Mizine Armies fall."

Crinte placed a hand on his shoulder. "Drive a way to the ledges. We must ascend."

They ran forward just as a blast of golden light erupted in front of them, driving back a troop of Gaslinks racing towards them. They were lifted off their feet and hurled backwards, the force of their bodies creating shallow dents in the ground.

Alaireia walked out of the light with Starman beside her. Their eyes were narrow and red rimmed, their faces dirty and smudged. "You called," Alaireia said as she twirled a dagger, turning and throwing it at a Gaslink on her left.

"It's time to face him. Run!" Crinte shouted.

They dashed through the valley of armies, avoiding the river of death that lay between them and Sarhorr the Ruler himself. Bodies were piled like walls in the middle, black and blue arrows and flags, broken bows, bent swords, and cold eyes. Golden brown feathers dotted the landscape where the Xctas had fallen, bright red blood mixing with black, and the smell of flesh, bone, and marrow began to creep through the Great Water

Hole. The slaughter continued as the Mizine Army raged forward, bronze shields raised to the sky, avoiding the arrows that drifted lazily towards them. Spears were thrust in and out of bodies, while sparks from flame burst into the air. Cries of the wounded, the dying, the transformed, echoed eerily through the canyon and the battleground as the power struggle continued. The Xeros guarded the tower, striking down those who dared to fight against it, to bash in their walls. Yet the Five Warriors ran on, tearing through the Slutan Army, avoiding the Xeros that marched with them, ripping apart the Gaslinks who continued to chant. *Grwahoo! Grwahoo! Grwahoo!* The thrumming of drums rang in the deep like one great heartbeat, continuing to pulse and breathe. It was just when they reached the foot of the mountains, right when they were beginning to climb, when a group of bleary-eyed Sorns marched up to them, pickaxes on their backs.

Crinte paused, holding his sword in front of him and signaling for Legone and Marklus to hold their bows. "State your allegiance," he demanded of them.

A Sorn glanced up but his eyes appeared unseeing as he looked forward. His unwashed skin hung off his bones, his body nothing more than a waste. "We are going to die," he said, his voice barely heard above the cries from the battlefield.

"Then die with us," Crinte told them, stepping forward. "Die with us instead of in the canyon of transformed waters. Die with us fighting for freedom for this World. Die with us ending the domain of an uncaring power." The Sorns stood up straighter, raising their pickaxes as they heard the power and authority in Crinte's voice. "This is the war for the Western World." Crinte's voice rang out with iron certainly. "This is not the war to save

438

Mizine, or Asspraineya, or Slutan. This is the war to save our World, our homeland, the very ground on which we stand, and all the people groups. Crons, Tiders, Trazames, Ezincks, Sorns, and the immortal creatures of the air, the sea and the land. We are going to the last battle, and it is your choice. Come with us. Die with us fighting for freedom!"

"Freedom?" A Sorn spoke the word as if he had never heard it before, and turned to his comrades. "Freedom!" he repeated again, feeling the power as the word buzzed underneath his tongue. The Sorns raised their pickaxes in the air. "Freedom! Freedom! Freedom!" they chanted. "Aye, we will fight with you!"

"Clear a path to the ledges!" Crinte ordered, but the eager Sorns had already turned, running towards the heights, chanting as they went. Their thin bodies nimbly leaped through the air. Ledges above ledges, they ascended as the sky grew nearer and brighter. At times, they thought they could reach up and touch the silver stars, hanging low near the world. The intense heat from the canyon faded as they walked through the mists into a rough wind. The rock below them turned shades of white and gray with iridescent colors sparkling beneath the surface. Legone walked ahead, sure of his way, at ease among the heights. Before them the Sorns drifted and disappeared, leaving the beaten track, fighting the guards of the mountains. But the Five were sure in their path and followed it, clambering over rock and stone, leaping from ledge to ledge until finally their path ended against smooth rock with a sharp drop off on the other side. "I see him." Crinte's voice was breathless. "He is waiting for us. We stand on his doorstep." He turned, placing his hands on the smooth rock, rubbing them against it, searching.

"We are going in?" Starman's voice trembled slightly as he clutched his sword.

"Yes," Crinte replied as he pushed against the rock. A slight, inward move made the mountain tremble. "Ready?" Crinte asked his warriors.

Legone pulled an arrow taut in his bow and lifted it towards the crack in the rock. Starman drew his sword and squared his shoulders, feeling strength flood through his body, overwhelming the fear. Marklus raised his bow, but Alaireia lifted her Clyear. "Try to keep your footing," she told them.

Crinte slammed his weight against the rock and it slide open to reveal a shallow room with a staircase leading upwards to the top of the rock, back into the day-lit land. Two horned Xeros moved forward at their entrance, lifting their curved blades and advancing towards the warriors. Above them, an echoing cry began, shouting a warning over and over again. It sounded like a beast frantically flying back and forth. The Five Warriors hurled themselves forward, flying into action. Legone moved rapidly towards the staircase, ducking the Xero's blades and sending two arrows flying. They harmlessly bounded off their metal but Legone was on the staircase, headed upwards before they could stop him. Crinte and Starman stepped up, swords blocking the blows from the Xeros, and Alaireia lifted the Clyear and blew over it. The ground began to shake and she dived to the ground as a sword swiped near her neck. She, too, turned to the staircase and stumbled upwards as the first few steps crumbled. Marklus held his bow, calculating as the heavy monsters attempted to regain their balance on the shaking ground. He lifted his bow and let loose his first arrow. In surprise, he watched as the arrow sank into the Xero's armor. It collapsed with a crash, unsteadying the other monster who lunged for Marklus. Marklus leaped out of the doorway, sending the creature flying downward into the open space beyond the mountain. The stairs continued to crumble, kicking up clouds of black dust. Crinte coughed as he turned towards the staircase. "Let's go!" he shouted urgently. Keeping to the plan, Marklus and Starman followed at his heels.

***

Legone dashed up the stairs as they curved upwards, spiraling in circles until he walked out into the beautiful sky. A river of purple with stars floated above him, close enough he wanted to reach up and place his hands in the ripple. The air was calm, and looking down, he could see the Great Water Hole spread before him, but the sounds of death and battle had faded. Legone realized he was standing on a grassy knoll at the top of the Great Water Hole, a knoll which strangely reminded him of Shilmi.

"Legone, you have come at last," a gentle voice remarked.

Legone looked and saw him standing serenely at the edge of the mountain, looking over his transformed world. He wore a deep blue coat that looked as if it were made out of the midnight sky.

"You have come with your powerful friends, as I told you." He turned his head to look behind Legone and smiled as if joking. "Where are they?"

"Yes." Legone nodded and attempted to step forward, but his feet would not move. "I have come because none will stand up to you. I have come on behalf of the Western World. Do not do this!"

Sarhorr chuckled softly, spreading his hands. "Oh, but I have. Did you not see everything I have done to challenge you and your powerful friends as you journeyed here? You took far too long to find the Clyear of Power and the most powerful warriors in the land. You forced my hand. I had to do something to pull you out of your hiding place. The destruction of the Western World is your fault, after all. If you had kept to our deal, this would not have happened. But now, it is over. You stand before me, as you should."

"No!" Legone's voice was forceful and strong. "We made a deal. You will recall your armies and leave this World!"

"Or else?" Sarhorr prompted, a sinister grin covering his perfect face.

"I have come to propose another trade."

Sarhorr turned around. His body, swallowed in midnight, was pure and elegant. His eyes were round and dark with knowledge. His chiseled face was a masterpiece of perfection as he walked towards Legone, his sleek hair resting gently on his shoulders. "A trade? What could you possibly have that I would want? You, a mere mortal, would come to my kingdom and offer a trade? Now, I am curious."

442

Legone stepped forward. "I know you think little of mortals. We are nothing more than a blink in the eye in your lifetime. I know you are a Changer, searching for a home to call all the immortals to dwell with you. But I was told your secret. I know what can bring you down. If you had the Clyear of Power, well, it would be different for you. You truly know how to unlock its powers, to use it as it should be used."

Sarhorr's eyes narrowed. "Yes, and I demanded you bring it to me. But even if you have it, it is too late. I gave you immortality, and I can take it away. Our deal is off; I no longer need you or your powerful warriors. I no longer need the Clyear of Power, but if you have brought it, I will drain every drop of power from it." He moved closer to Legone. "But I have another use for you. We will see when I kill you and drop your body into the waters. You will enjoy your second life as a Gaslink, I think." He smiled coldly and reached out a hand for Legone's neck.

Legone attempted to move but his will slipped away. He felt fingers lifting him, crushing his windpipe while his feet wiggled futilely above the ground. His arms hung paralyzed by his side as he watched his own death.

"Drop him!" a voice commanded from where the staircase had been.

Sarhorr ripped his gaze from Legone's to deal with the new distraction. Standing in the stone archway stood a powerful female. An Ezinck. Her black hair mirrored his, her eyes were large, her skin dark, and she stood firmly, feet apart, a sword pointed at him in one hand while the other was balled up in a fist. Behind her, a Trazame stepped forward, his sword raised.

Two Crons stood behind them, their eyes dark and narrow, the bloodlust in their bodies rippling in the air. They were a walking pillar of death and power. Sarhorr could taste the intoxication as he stared at them, and a strong desire to consume their power almost overcame him. His eyes drifted back to the Ezinck; she had a stronger aura of ancient power he could almost taste. Throwing back his head, he laughed, lifting Legone higher in the air as he roared.

"The Five Warriors, come at last! I am happy to see each of you." He smiled while Legone twitched in his hand. "I was hoping to personally end you and let you enjoy your final transformation. See what I have created in a matter of years, and you have finally come to let me consume your power. Mortals are so predictable, so willing to make deals, and trade." He laughed again. He dropped Legone on the ground and moved forward, even as Alaireia drew back her arm.

"You." He pointed at her. "Give it to me."

"I will give you nothing but death," she spat back at him.

He turned his head, and out of the shadows stepped two Xeros. "Throw them into the pit," he commanded.

Crinte and Starman stepped in front of Alaireia, raising their swords as the ten-foot tall Xeros bore down on them. Alaireia dived out of the way, finding herself on the ground beside Legone. He had dropped his bow, and his quiver lay on the ground while he pressed a hand against his bruised neck. "Finish this!" Legone whispered, slipping an object into her hands, but a Xero grabbed Alaireia by the foot and dragged her up into the air. She sliced her sword in the air as she dangled, even from her upside down position seeing Crinte and Starman pushed back against the force of the Xeros.

Marklus, forgotten in the background, raised his bow and aimed his arrow at Sarhorr. It flew, straight and true, aiming for its mark, and slid right through his body. Sarhorr turned, his gaze locking on Marklus as he looked down at his unmarred body. "Think again, mortal one. You cannot harm me."

Sarhorr lifted his hand, and with a blast of power threw the warriors backwards, hurling them to the ground and rendering them weaponless. The Xeros stood above them, blades drawn, ready to strike the final blow. Starman coughed as he struggled to sit up, reaching for his sword just as the iron foot of a Xero smashed down on his fingers. Marklus felt a blade pushed into his side and he saw spots dance before him as his lifeblood was drained. Crinte shouted in fury, finding himself dragged upright by none other than Sarhorr the Ruler. Sarhorr considered him, warily. "I have always wanted to meet you, Crinte the Wise. But now that I have, I'm disappointed." He raised his hand and hurled Crinte's helpless body down the mountainside, laughing as Marklus cried out in horror.

Sarhorr turned his gaze on Marklus. "Torture. Then death. That is how I treat those who dare to defy me."

"Alaireia! Now!" Legone shouted, his dry voice barely croaking out of his wounded throat.

Faster than Sarhorr could turn his head, Alaireia, dangling from the hand of one of the Xeros, her sword on the ground below her fingers, pulled back her arm and threw the object through the air. Sarhorr ducked as the object flew over his head.

"You cannot kill me." His cold eyes bored into Alaireia's. "Keeper of the Clyear of Power. You cannot kill me."

"No." Alaireia locked eyes with Sarhorr. "I cannot kill you. But they can."

An aura of dark death swept over the grassy knoll, turning it black as the object Alaireia had thrown ripped open. Spirits poured out of it, the souls of Gims he had tortured into death. They reached for him, ripping his body, tearing away the mortal constraints. Pieces of flesh peeled from him like an outer shell, revealing his true identity. The mountain began to shake as Starman rolled out from under the Xero, sheltering his smashed hand as at last he reached for his sword.

"Run!" Marklus was shouting, holding his sword as he limped away, back towards the ledges.

The Xero dropped Alaireia in confusion and she stood, still staring at Sarhorr. "I have willed it to be so," she proclaimed, her voice layered with a power greater than his own.

Sarhorr felt his body stripped away, leaving his unprotected spirit. Darkness covered him, and bulky muscle and ligaments stood out as he felt his shadow wrap around him. Thick horns pointed out from his head and from his red eyes he saw Legone picking himself off the ground, red marks cruelly displaying on his bruised neck.

"Finish this!" Alaireia's voice rang in his ears as Legone saw his chance. He dived for the now empty Boleck as Sarhorr spread his spirit arms, and the waters began to thunder down as a waterfall erupted below him.

The undying eyes turned on Legone, and Sarhorr's now changed voice shouted, "You cannot kill me! I am immortal; this dominion of the Western World was only child's play. I warn you, this is the beginning of the end." He turned and leaped off the cliff, reaching for the waters to drag him down into the water hole.

"Legone!" Alaireia screamed. "Take this!" She lifted the crystal, winged horse and threw it into Legone's open hand.

Legone held her eyes for the briefest moment, lifted the Boleck, and ran towards the falls where Sarhorr had disappeared. Without hesitation, he took a deep breath and dove off the cliff into the streaming arms of the water.

CHAPTER 56

THE BEGINNING OF THE END

The ground shook beneath Alaireia's feet as she ran, leaping down the ledges, retracing her steps. The war was back, ringing in her brain, and ahead she saw Marklus, shooting at the creatures crawling out of the rocks. "Hurry!" a voice shouted, even as the ground behind her fell. Starman was also ahead of her, cradling one hand close to his body, the other holding his sword as he ran. They weren't going to make it; the ledges were already closing in on each other.

"Reach!" a voice called above her. She looked up to see Crinte, who should have been dead, riding on the back of one of the Xctas. He held a rope down to them as they ran through the mist. One by one they grabbed hold while the Xctas flew them back down, towards the battlefield.

It was mere moments before they stood on solid ground again, shaking as they huddled near, unsure of what had just happened. "It worked," Alaireia told them. "The spirits destroyed Sarhorr's physical form and forced him to transform. He jumped into the canyon and Legone went after him. And Crinte," she turned to Crinte, her voice breaking, "the vision I had at the house of Srackt happened just like you said. In the moment, it all seemed clear. I gave Legone the Clyear of Power."

"Then it is up to him now." Crinte nodded. "Well done," he told his warriors, turning his golden eyes on the battlefield. "Night falls; it is time for the tower to come down."

Turning, they stumbled back to the battlefield, ignoring their various wounds. Yet as Marklus walked, he felt the gap in his side close, as the door between life and death opened to him.

Just as Crinte said, night was falling; the lights in the sky were fading. There was a ripple in the sky and the stars glared white for a moment before they burst in a flash. The first star fell, shooting from the sky in a blur, creating a miniature crater as it struck the ground. Armies persisted dogged as the sheer heat threw them back and the mountain erupted in streaks of purple, blue, and pink. Warriors ran, dodging the fallen stars as they continued to crash into the terrain. But Crinte ran towards the tower, his sword out, as it began to shudder.

Marklus lost them in the chaos. He leaped up on a rock and drew an arrow. As he let it fly, the sky grew dark, and overhead he saw the mass of Xctas wheeling and circling, diving into the battlefield. From his post, he could hear shrieks and cries of agony as creatures around him crashed to the ground. Fingers of death reached up around him, welcoming the fallen, guiding them through the door to the other side. His mind reacted in a frenzy as he felt the death of the Zikes vibrate through him while their brothers and sisters mourned, then pushed forward in determination. He saw the archers shoot the great Xctas out of the air, their sharp eyes growing glassy as they plunged, beak first into the ground. Marklus reached for another arrow as the light faded and the stars lit up the battlefield in the ongoing struggle for survival.

At first, Alaireia could sense Starman was with her, wildly attacking, showing no mercy to his assailants. Their blows were even, stroke to stroke as they cut down skeletal Gaslinks standing in their way, pounded against the monstrous Xeros, unwilling to die, and cut open the voluptuous Garcrats. Arrows raced by them, daggers flew through the air, and battle axes cleaved open heads and hearts. The horrifying reality set in. Battles they had fought on their way to the Great Water Hole were no more than child's play; even as their comrades fell around them, Alaireia felt the horror with every blow. Precious life was stolen, heartbeats stopped cold—was it all worth it when the very one who started it all was nothing more than a drifting spirit?

A dark night consumed the Great Water Hole as it erupted in smoke, ash, fire, death, and blood. The Slutan Army pulled back, running towards the smoking canyon. The Mizine army followed them, pushing them back even as they fell amid the ruin. Crinte, at last reaching the tower, plunged his sword into it, setting the spirits free and watching the massive structure come crashing down, chunks and boulders of rock and stone crashing onto the battlefield. And when he looked, he realized the end of the world had, indeed, come.

***

Dawn drifted onto the Great Water Hole, scarcely noticed as they fought in the heat and mist. Alaireia felt her throat grow sore and rough, her nose hurt from breathing in the reeking fumes of death, and she found herself watching. Starman was gone, separated from her at some point during the night. The war raged around her in the valley, but her arms were weak without help from the Clyear. She could feel blood on her face and tasted it in her mouth as she continued to shatter bone. Mechanically she moved forward, until she saw the arrows pierce him.

Starman was in the middle of the battlefield, his sword raised again and again, each time just a hint slower than the last. He whirled around to face his assailants, driving into their hearts, whipping off heads, and an arrow pierced his side. He was too exhausted to be surprised, but because his momentum was already moving forward, he sliced off another head and tripped a Gaslink. A searing pain sliced into his already wounded body and he saw spots of light dancing in his eyes. A white light was shining and he could see a door opening; voices were calling, beckoning him to the other side. He opened his hands, his sword thudding to the ground, and reaching out his arms, he fell to the ground.

A heart wrenching scream echoed over the battlefield and when it ended, Alaireia realized it had been her voice. Tears of rage filled her eyes and she turned, coming face to face with a Xero. No longer afraid, she charged it. "This," she shouted at it,

451

"is for Starman!" The Xero reached out an iron arm and threw her across the battlefield.

Crinte held his blade as he watched, his face ashen, his body weary from the war. He lifted his face to the sky, watching it cry, and he realized that truly, Sarhorr the Ruler was gone. The intense heat from the stars began to burn away the gray mist, and as the air cleared, Crinte could see the armies of Mizine continue to overwhelm the dark armies, pushing them back over the edge. A weight lifted off his shoulders and he felt his heart come to peace. He turned to search for his companions but he could no longer see them, not even Marklus in the war stricken land. He watched, swallowing hard as he saw the destruction the war had wrought on the land.

Two days they had fought, and now helmets, metal, and iron lay shattered, digging into the rock. He could see white bone sticking up from broken bodies, and rivers of red blood joining the waterfalls that poured into the Great Water Hole. Blue flags fluttered in the breeze, pounded into the rock, signifying victory. Bodies were piled around them, and he could see where the people groups of Mizine took their last stand. He looked, realizing how few had survived. He placed a hand on his heart and lifted it to the sky, honoring those who had fought and died. Weariness wrecked his body as he turned towards the hill for a better vantage point even as the Xctas circled above, avoiding the falling stars. The war was over; he had to find his friends and assist the people of Mizine in recuperating.

***

452

Hot steam rose to meet Legone, forcing the threads of straight hair to curl up around his neck. He pulled his feet away from the lapping water. It seemed alive, determined to gather him in its heat, wrap its wet arms around him and pull him down to be transformed. His ears rang as he heard the Boleck he had trapped Sarhorr the Ruler in, shrieking in fear and anguish in the waters. The power of the Clyear had given him wings one last time, and Sarhorr's spirit form had been sucked into his own creation, effectively trapping him. Legone had then dropped the Boleck into the transformative waters. It was finished, and he might as well be. His legs threatened to give way, dropping into the churning waters, despite his mind forcing him away, against the protective rock. But the waters were rising; he did not have a choice. The dark creatures were very much alive, as if their minds were programmed for one purpose, even with the Ruler himself eliminated.

Legone sighed, feeling the first chills of death wash over him. His cold hands began to tremble; the numbness would soon set in and he would be finished. He eyed the brown, swirling waters. Dark mist stretched its long fingers towards him, welcoming him into the temptation of death. There was nothing left in life for him. The emptiness bothered him. There was no escape. Why not plunge in and have it over with? Why stand there waiting for the inevitable when it could be over in seconds? His foot slipped as the first waters reached the ledge, rushing over it. Despite the cold, a burning sensation ripped through his feet, forcing him to cry out in pain. A hollow ringing began in his brain; already his vision was failing him. He was going. He spread his arms and lifted his face to the sky where far above him the sunlight shone on paradise. *Paleidir*, he whispered. *My wings have been clipped. My destiny is complete. Farewell.*

He closed his eyes, and just as he leaned forward to give himself to the waters he saw, quite clearly, a way out. He was already in motion, falling forward, but the words of an elder tongue came to him. He spoke them as he fell on his back, arms spread out, and felt the Clyear catch him. He lay his hands on his heart, as if in death, and felt the crystal boat speed his way through the waters of the Great Water Hole. He did not have to open his eyes as they passed below the great falls, the boat spinning in circles as it headed towards the open current that led to the South World. Legone breathed one shuddering breath after the other as he drifted to sleep. He knew that when he woke next, he would be in the arms of his beloved.

***

The spirit sank in the Boleck, weary from fighting, exhausted from the pain that clipped it. He had been so close to utter domination. His rule had been sure, the demise of the Western World in his hands. Like a toy ball he had played with it, twirling it in his fingers, tossing it high, laughing at their blindness. But his desire for more had ultimately been his downfall. He had known Legone the Swift would come at last; he was one of a pure heart, able to see past the power games of the immortals. Those without eternal life appeared desperate for the one life they did have, and determined to let all people groups live the way they desired. Full lives of adventure and hope and love. It had been his ruin, and now he found his body destroyed, his paradise conquered, and his spirit broken. A shattering sound jolted him and he stretched in the nothingness. The Boleck had caught on a sharp rock pounded by waves, and he could hear it breaking apart. It was bound to happen sooner or later; his temporary prison slowly broke free. Too weak to resist, he let his spirit be carried along by the current towards the South World. It would take time, but he would regain his strength, he would rebuild, and next time, the mortals would not find a way to break him. He drifted and shrunk in Oceantic, dreaming of paradise, biding his time.

***

Alaireia lay in the melee of the war, her head propped up by one of the hideous creatures, her legs covered by another. Her fingers shook every time she tried to feel them, each time she tried to remind herself she was still alive. The pain from the arrow in her thigh had faded, but she could still feel the stab wounds in her side, and her mouth was filled with blood. At some point she had passed out from the pain, but now unwelcome consciousness had returned. She could feel the arid heat and smell the acrid smoke of burning flesh. She could still hear cries from those wounded and dying. Further away, the sound of war continued, the shouting, the frustrated grunts and the screams of pain. She closed her eyes, willing it all to go away;

455

here at the end she would rather be buried alive. The journey had taken every inch of her will, and now the tides of the battle had turned, and she was needed no more. Already her chest was tightening, and she gasped for the precious air she could breathe. She did not notice the shadow until it blocked out her view of the gray clouds. "Alaireia," an agonized voice whispered. She opened her eyes to look into the battle-weary face of Marklus. His brown curls were plastered to his dirty forehead; a combination of soot and blood covered his face. His tunic was ripped and torn in places and his bow and arrows were gone. He appeared unarmored as he knelt beside her, dragging the creatures off her legs. "Alaireia," he whispered. "Where are you going?"

She opened her mouth to tell him and blood dribbled out. "It's over," she whispered. "It's time."

Marklus shook his head as he attempted to wipe the blood from her face. "Alaireia, it's not time to give up."

"Marklus," she wheezed. "I am going. We won. Starman is gone. There is nothing left." She tried to move her fingers again, but they would not listen to her mind. "Tell the others…" Her voice was fading away. "I love them." She took one last shuddering breath and closed her eyes.

For some reason she could still hear Marklus and felt him place his hand on her heart. "Alaireia, don't talk like that. You know I hold the power of life and death."

Suddenly she was gone, her soul drifting away from her body, and for a moment she rose up and looked down. She could see Marklus at her side, she could see the blue light filling her empty body, and instantly she was no longer a spectator from above. She was clutching Marklus' arm and breathing wretched air that smelled sour but entered her body without pain and left it without collapsing her chest. Eyes wide in shock, she looked at Marklus, still gripping his arm. "Marklus," she whispered in wonder.

His eyes were wet as he snatched her in his arms and held her as life returned. She leaned into him in awe. After a minute, she pulled back, and tears of joy lit up her features. "Marklus, I was gone, I had left, but you brought me back."

Marklus looked at her. "I did more than that." He rose to his feet. "I healed Starman as well. Your hearts beat in sync; that was the only way I could."

Alaireia froze for a moment. "Starman."

"Come." Marklus reached out a hand to lift her up. "You will feel weak for a while as your strength returns. He is here, recovering.

Holding onto Marklus, Alaireia stumbled over the decaying bodies in the war zone. She could see Starman, wobbling on his feet, testing out his strength. He saw her and despite the mountain of bodies surrounding, him staggered over. "Alaireia! Marklus!" he called.

Alaireia paused and looked at Marklus, as if for the first time she understood, and she could not help the tears that threatened to overwhelm her. "Thank you," she said. "Thank you."

Starman slowly stumbled up to them. "I'm alive," he stated.

"I know." Alaireia reached for him with a sob.

Marklus let go as they flung their arms around each other, laughing in awe at the gift of a second life. It was Starman who touched Alaireia's face, leaned in, and kissed her. She responded by wrapping her arms tightly around him, gently kissing him back.

Marklus turned away from them to walk up the hill. As he did, he saw Crinte was waiting for him. "We won. It is over." Crinte reached out a hand to Marklus.

"It is done," Marklus replied. He turned one last time to look at the destruction of the Great Water Hole. Smoking bodies littered the ground, blue flags waved in the cleansing breeze that was beginning to blow, and two lovers brought back from the dead kissed in the desolation. The plan had always been to succeed, but as he surveyed the land, he realized he had never dreamed it was actually possible. A sad smile flashed across his grimy face for a moment, then Marklus turned and walked up the hill with Crinte.

THE BEGINNING OF...THE END

EPILOGUE

The Five Warriors. That is what they were called as Simon the Brave spread their tale throughout the Western World, personally supervising the statue that was erected in their honor. As those tales spread throughout the Four Worlds, those foolish enough told them to their children as a fairy tale, a legend of old, an impossible tale when the land was young and fraught with mysteries and power. There were some who believed, and some who did not, and some who missed the warning signs that the end was near.

Crinte the Wise journeyed back to Spherical Land, requesting again access to the kingdom above the clouds. He returned with The Healer who restored the Mermis as best he knew how, yet Mermis were never born out of clouds and mist again. Crinte the Wise eventually married Malaseya the Mermi, and so their bloodline extended, and eventually, a portion of them flew away on the Silver Herd, to the Eastern World.

Marklus the Healer left the Zikes at the Great Water Hole, leaving them in charge of ensuring no one dared live there again. He traveled with Crinte the Wise to Spherical Land, restoring the Mermis to their immortality once again. Finally, he returned to Zikeland and took up

459

his rule as the first Watcher, a Dunithair, ensuring the land was peaceful and blossomed once again. It was not long after the wind returned, and he asked of her what had happened to his brother.

Alaireia the Ezinck and Starman the Trazame spent most of their days between the fruitful land of Trazamy City and repairing the forests of the Ezinck. In a way, on perspective, he found his family again, for sometimes it is those who pull the best out of you who truly can stay with you throughout life. He and Alaireia shared the life anyone would dream of, a life full of love and passion and adventure.

No one in the Western World ever saw Legone the Swift again, but months later, the Clyear of Power washed his immortal body onto the shores of the South World. He woke again in the arms of his beloved, reunited with the Green People at last.

As for the spirit of Sarhorr the Changer? Now that is a tale for another World.

Dear Readers

Thank you for reading the story of The Five Warriors.

If you loved the book and have a minute to spare, I would truly appreciate a short review on the site where you bought the book. It can be short, so don't worry about trying to sound too eloquent.

Your help in spreading the word is greatly appreciated. Reviews from readers like you make a huge difference to helping new readers find stories like this.

TURN THE PAGE TO READ THE FIRST CHAPTER
OF THE BLENDED ONES

"No one can know the things he knows." The Mermi King twirled his golden scepter in his left hand as he perched on the edge of his throne. Snatching his dark eyes away from the globe undulating on the top of his scepter, he sighed as he turned weary eyes to his granddaughter. "Take him to a world where they will never believe him, even if he talks."

His barefoot granddaughter paced back and forth on the weightless surface below the King's throne. "You are asking us, the Blended Ones, to leave?" Her shoulder-length hair swished as she tilted her dark head and quirked a puzzled eyebrow, unafraid to test the King's authority. Her petite frame was just over five feet tall. She'd inherited her mother's midnight blue hair and her father's aura of authority and overwhelming desire for adventure. "You are asking us to go into exile?" Her voice faltered as she clenched and unclenched her fists, inadvertently brushing them against the silver feathers of her short tunic, created of feathers and mist. She paused to lift her eyes to the King's, blinking her thick, black lashes.

"I ask nothing of you that your heart does not already desire." King Vincsir's smooth voice reminded her of the lapping of waves after a violent storm. Leaning his scepter against his throne, he rose to his full height of six feet, his deep purple robe sweeping the dais. He wore a golden circlet on his head while his deep black hair hung to his shoulders. His build was just as slim and lithe as his granddaughter's, but his features were harder. His face was ageless, although his sharp, keen eyes looked tired. Underneath his purple robe, he wore a white tunic, allowing the delicate wings on his ankles to flutter back and forth as he floated off his dais.

His granddaughter paused as he stood in front of her, reaching out his long, smooth fingers to take her hands in his. "Indonesia." His words floated to her ears and danced around her head for mere seconds before they sunk into her mind, their meanings hazy like the morning fog. Further distracting her, he rubbed his thumbs across her palm as he spoke, his voice rising and falling like a lullaby sung to calm a fledging hatchling. "You and I both know you don't belong here. I've seen the shadows behind your eyes and the questions you've bitten back. You desire to leave and find your own place to belong, but you're afraid to ask. It makes sense; you were born here, and none of us were born here. We come from air and mist, at least until the curse. Our race is stagnant and will be until we find a way to procreate. But time is on our side as, although your father is a mortal, you are immortal. Our race must survive, and we must spread the blended across the Four Worlds. I know you desire to find your place and discover where you belong, so I'm releasing you. Since you cannot fly, take the Silver Herd and discover what lies beyond the Western World beyond Oceantic. All I ask is that you do me a favor and take Tharmaren the Wise to his exile to the Eastern World."

The silence after the hypnotic song jolted Indonesia out of her stupor. A sudden tingling behind her eyes forced her to blink away moisture, as if she'd just emerged from the land of sleep. She pinched her brows together as the rhythm of his words swarmed through her mind, yet clarity of meaning seemed lost and forgotten. He dropped her hands and stepped away a pace, his eyes narrowing as he watched her struggle to recall his words. He nodded as her face changed and the words he wished for her to remember marked themselves in her memory.

Indonesia smiled, her white teeth gleaming sharp and pointed as her mind latched onto the thoughts he'd implanted. Her heart began to race in anticipation. "I can leave? And take the Silver Herd?"

"Yes." The King's lips lifted, effectively removing the hostile demeanor from his stoic appearance. "Yes, Indonesia, and take the Blended Ones, your cousins—at least those who are willing. Fly to the ends of the World, find adventure, and find out where you belong." He stepped closer to her again, the smile fading from his face just as quickly as it had appeared.

Indonesia's brow furrowed, and the grin slid off her face. "What is it?" A twinge of anxiety forced her voice to bite the air much harder than she intended.

The King placed his hands on her shoulders, his height forcing her to look directly up at his sharp, golden eyes. "Your father is the last of the Order of the Wise, but he is not the One. Look for him."

"The One?" Indonesia swallowed hard, the hairs on her neck standing up as she moved her head to avoid her grandfather's hooded gaze. "I'm not sure why…" She attempted to pull away. "What do you mean? Isn't the world safe after all my father and his warriors did?"

"For now." The King's voice sank to a confidential whisper. "But I fear…" He trailed off, dropping his hands from her shoulders and turning away hastily in an attempt to hide his true thoughts.

"What do you mean?" Indonesia repeated the question, but her voice trembled with hints of fear.

King Vincsir turned back to her, flashes of regret hiding from her questioning gaze. "It is not to frighten you," he assured her gently. "You will see much in your life, but remember my words. And watch out for the Green People; they are up to something."

Read the entire story. Click here to grab a copy of The Blended Ones.

ALSO BY ANGELA J. FORD

The Five Warriors
The Blended Ones
Eliesmore and the Green Stone
Eliesmore and the Jeweled Sword

Tales of the Four Worlds

Myran

Join the email list for new releases and more. Go to
TheFourWorldsSeries.com

ACKNOWLEDGEMENTS

Special thanks goes to the amazing creatives I had the opportunity to work with.

To my sisters, Dorthea, Annie, Rebecca and Katrina for reading multiple rough drafts and burning the midnight oil providing comments, thoughts and suggestions for improvement.

Finally, thanks to my parents for encouraging books as the main source of entertainment. It still is to this day.

ABOUT THE AUTHOR

Brought up as a bookworm and musician, Angela J. Ford began writing *The Four Worlds Series*—a fantasy series—at the age of twelve. The storyline of those books was largely based off of the imaginative games she played with her sisters.

Angela originally finished the series when she was sixteen. After college, Angela began to rewrite *The Four Worlds Series*, bringing it from a child's daydream to an adventure young and old can enjoy. Since it is inspired by fairy tales, high magic, and epic fantasy, Angela knows you'll enjoy your adventures within the Four Worlds.

If you happen to be in Nashville, you'll most likely find her at a local coffee shop, enjoying a white chocolate mocha and furiously working on her next book. Make sure you say hello!

Stay in touch: TheFourWorldsSeries.com

Made in the USA
Lexington, KY
17 June 2018